## More from Lauren Baratz-Logsted

Johnny Smith Novels
*The Bro-Magnet*

Jane Taylor Novels
*The Thin Pink Line*
*Crossing the Line*

Diversion Books
A Division of Diversion Publishing Corp.
443 Park Avenue South, Suite 1008
New York, New York 10016
www.DiversionBooks.com

For more information, email info@diversionbooks.com

First Diversion Books edition February 2015.
Print ISBN: 978-1-62681-761-6
eBook ISBN: 978-1-62681-606-0

# isn't it bro-
## *mantic?*

**LAUREN BARATZ-LOGSTED**

**DIVERSIONBOOKS**

# My Wedding Day

I stand at the end of the aisle, trying to look calm.

Did I pick the right tux?

Of course I did.

I've been Best Man nine times before today, so you could say I'm something of an expert. I know all about the perils of a white-and-purple color scheme. I know the utter ridiculousness of going with turquoise and beige—who thinks these things up? Worse, who actually goes for it? Me, I went with your basic black and white. It was good fifty years ago, it'll be good fifty years from now, and hey, Frank Sinatra *rocked* this tux.

Naturally, when shopping for my tux I consulted Maury of *Maury the Magnificent! Your Place for Tuxedos and All Your Formal Wear!* After all, he'd helped me out once before when I needed a tux for the opera, even if it turned out that no one else was wearing a tux because the opera turned out to be in a barn.

"So you're getting married!" Maury said. "Well, well, well."

Since all the tuxes Maury sells are named for famous people, we reviewed my options together.

"How about this?" I suggested.

The tux in question was all black, including the shirt, which was shiny. OK, it was the first thing I saw.

"The Martin Scorsese?" Maury shook his head. "That one's only good if you're going to the Oscars and you also happen to be Martin Scorsese."

I was tempted to ask him why he kept it in stock, since I doubted anyone in Danbury went to the Oscars and I was sure no one in town was named Martin Scorsese. But it's been my experience that when you are relying on someone else to help you out, it's preferable not to insult them or question their competence before they have.

"What about this then?" I asked.

This time I'd selected something that looked like your basic tux.

"The Jean Dujardin?" Maury shook his head again. "I reserve that for my French customers."

Since when did Danbury have a big French population?

"Besides," Maury continued, "it's like with that Italian guy, that Robert Benigno. It's just a flash in the American pan. Give it another year and people will be saying, 'Jean Du-who?'"

We went through some more tuxes and I learned that, at least according to Maury, I don't have what it takes to pull off The Johnny Depp.

"What's that still doing there?" Maury wondered aloud.

"What is it?" I said.

"The Joaquin Phoenix. Huh. It's got to go back to the shop."

"Hey, what's up with this one?" I said. "How come there's no shirt?"

"Oh, that's The Taylor Lautner," Maury said. "It's really more of a novelty item."

There are novelty items in tux stores? Who knew?

So, yeah, anyway, I ended up with The Frank Sinatra tux. Corny as it may sound, I want my love with Helen to be timeless so I went with the most timeless of tuxes, named after the most timeless of singers.

That's why I'm not really worrying about what I'm wearing. What I'm really worried about, as the clock inches toward four P.M.—3:56, 3:57, 3:58—is this: *Will she show?*

Because I'm thinking, maybe if I was her, I'm cutting out and hitting Atlantic City instead?

"Don't worry," the voice at my side says. "She'll *be* here, Johnny."

I look down at *my* Best Man, Big John, sitting in his wheelchair in his black-and-white Frank Sinatra tux.

"There's no *way* she's not showing up for this," Big John says, briefly grabbing my hand and giving it a squeeze.

Wait a second. If he's reassuring me because he's worried

I might be worried, then does that mean that secretly *he's* worried too?

That can't be good.

Have you noticed, this is my wedding day?

And then the bell in the church tower chimes and some music starts and I'm thinking, *What's that called again? What music did we settle on?* And then I remember, oh, right, it's called Pachelbel's *Canon*. And then there she is, at the top of the aisle, Helen, with her auburn hair and her china skin and her blue-green eyes. She's wearing a long, slim white satin dress and some veil thing she told me was called a Juliet cap that has this sparkly circle thing on top and a veil coming down the back, like what Jackie O wore when she got married for the first time; Helen, her hand in the crook of her father's arm, and I think, it's the only thought in my head:

I have never seen anything more insanely beautiful in my entire life.

Helen and me, we debated back and forth for months: Small wedding v. big wedding? Because we figured, both of us already being in our thirties, maybe we shouldn't go for the big show? Maybe we should go small, conservative, casual, tasteful. But then we thought: screw that! Neither of us has ever been married before, neither of us plans on ever doing this again, we are each other's one and only, so let's make this the greatest day of our lives until now.

This is how I ended up with the Frank Sinatra tux – the best, most classic, most expensive tux the market can bear. This is how we ended up with attendants – I can't even believe I'm even thinking that word: *attendants*? What kind of world am I living in now?

But there's my dad, Big John, who as you already know is my Best Man. There's Sam, right next to him, wearing a tux. Sam, in case you're new to this story, is my best friend and she's also a lesbian. When Helen and I told her we wanted her in the wedding party, she said, "That's great. And I'll love you forever,

Helen, for making Johnny happy. But I swing for Johnny's team so I think I'm wearing a tux."

On the other side of Sam is Billy Keller, who's regarded me as his best friend like forever.

And then there's Helen's side.

Her Matron of Honor is Aunt Alfresca which is downright weird. Ever since Aunt Alfresca married Big John five months ago, back in January, I don't even know what to call her. Do I still call her Aunt Alfresca? Is she expecting me to call her—I can barely even say the word—*Mom*? The mind reels.

And so I move past Aunt Alfresca to Helen's next in command, another bridesmaid, Carla, Helen's friend from that prophetic Yankees game way back when.

That's an easy one.

But now we move onto Helen's next attendant, who is… Alice? Tell me what kind of world does that make sense in?

Really, though, there's something about this attendants stuff that has never made sense. But maybe that's because between Helen and me, all we have in terms of prospects for female attendants is my aunt who's always been convinced I'm responsible for the death of her sister due to the accident of my birth, a friend of hers who to this day remains suspicious of me, and a woman who for a long time I thought I was in love with and who never thought I was good enough for her.

Yeah, that sounds about right.

But none of that matters right now, because the preacher man is winding down—yakkety-yakkety-yak—and I'm guessing it's time to make our vows.

"I met you as John," Helen says clearly, "but I've come to know that you are Johnny. I've never known anyone like you. You make me feel—what's the word?—unselfconscious. You make me feel—what's the word?—accepted. And I can only hope that, however long we both shall live, I will do the same for you."

Without thinking, without thinking that every one of a hundred and fifty people are watching us closely, I reach out and adjust her veil a bit so I can better see her whole face. She's *so* pretty and as my fingers make contact with her cheek, her skin is just *so* soft. In that moment, we are the only people in the entire world.

But then she looks up at me, expectantly, and I realize: Holy shit—am I on?


"Her face and name launched a thousand ships," I start, "but this was never about that. I could quote or paraphrase movie taglines: 'I'm just a boy, standing before a girl,' or 'You had me at hello.' But the truth is, you had me when you didn't judge me for what I appear to be on the surface. You didn't judge me when I took you to that barn opera, which, may I just say, was one of the oddest evenings of my life. You didn't judge me when I turned out to have a ridiculous cat named Fluffy—that I only got to impress you. No, you never judged me. Instead, you accepted me—the person I was pretending to be and the person I really am. Honestly, Helen, can anyone really be surprised that I love you as I do?"

I reach out, wipe one glistening tear from her beautiful eye.

It's good for a man to know what his job is in this world and this I can do:

I can wipe the tear, whether happy or sad, from her eye.

And then we're doing the vows thing and I *love* this part. I can *do* this part. It's like playing baseball in high school. My team's down by three, it's the bottom of the ninth, two outs, bases loaded and I'm at bat. The pitcher's got great stuff, I've seen his stuff, but I know *my* stuff is better and as the fast ball crosses the plate right in the middle of the strike zone, my bat cracks against it and I know that baby's sailing right out of the ballpark. This is exactly like that. It's like I've been waiting for this moment my whole life.

That stuff about honoring and cherishing—honoring and cherishing Helen? I can *so* do that. In sickness and in health—are you kidding me? I can't wait to be tested. Well, it's not like I'm hoping for something really bad to happen to her. But, like, if she gets a cold or something? I can and will make her homemade chicken soup. Hey, I own a cookbook! And that thing about "til death do you part"? I think of my old friend Leo, who died last fall of a broken heart after his own wife of a gazillion years, The Little Lady, died. It's like Leo's right there in the church with me as I take that final vow, promising that:

Yes, I will love this one woman as long as we both shall live.

I'm not exactly a kiss-the-girl-in-front-of-a-hundred-and-fifty-people kind of guy, but when the moment comes, I put my hands on the sides of her face and as I lower my lips to hers and make contact, I will the rest of the room to disappear and I only hope and pray that in that kiss, she feels how very much I love her, how determined I am to keep her this happy forever.

And then before I know it, we're riding in a horse-drawn carriage down Deer Hill Avenue with all its stately mansions – stately mansions by Danbury standards – heading toward Tarrywile Mansion for our reception. Did I really just do something that's going to result in something called a *reception*?

And then there's Helen tilting her head up toward me, and I'm leaning down toward her, and this is so much different than that kiss in the church, that kiss that was just for show, just for other people. Even though it felt wonderful when everyone else cheered and clapped at that kiss, there's no one here now but us and the carriage driver, and this kiss is so much better than anything I've ever imagined in my life.

And that's when it hits me. Oh, my God—is Helen really my…*wife*?

# My Reception

We did the whole receiving line thing back on the steps outside at the church, which was good, gave us a chance to greet everybody.

When people'd come through the line who were newish to me—some of Helen's business acquaintances, stuff like that—after being introduced to them, I'd turn and say, "This is my dad, Big John, and this is his wife Alfresca, my aunt." The looks I'd get after that, the double takes like we were some kind of hillbilly inbreeders—I realized then it was never going to get old.

"Even on your wedding day," my best friend said, "still playing games with people's heads. You're never going to grow up, are you?"

"Nah, Sam," I told her, "probably not."

Then I turned to the next person in line, Mary Agnes, the woman who married Helen's oldest brother Frankie last October and at whose wedding I was Best Man for the last time prior to my own wedding.

"I can't believe you two did it!" Mary Agnes said, opening her arms wide to embrace both of us at once. "And to think," she said to me, "this all started with you asking Helen to marry you at my wedding!"

"Yeah," I said, feeling embarrassed, "I've been meaning to apologize to you about that for a long time now, but I could never find the right time or words."

"Apologize?" Mary Agnes said. "What in the world do you have to apologize for?"

"Well," I said, "that was kind of a jerky thing I pulled. There I was, I was supposed to be giving the toast at *your* wedding, it was supposed to be all about you and Frankie, and instead I turned around and made it all about me. I'm sorry. Sometimes I

11

can be such a jerk."

"You're kidding me, right?" Mary Agnes looked incredulous. "How can you think that I minded? I delayed my own wedding several hours so everyone including me could watch the Mets play in the World Series, which, I might add, was worth it since they won. But can you imagine if they'd lost and then we had to go ahead and have a big party? It'd've been more like a funeral. And even with them winning, by the time I walked down the aisle, my dress was all pitted out from all the jumping and shouting I did during the game. After all that, do you honestly think I minded that when the time came for you to toast me and Frankie, you were so overcome by your own love for his sister— whom I love and regard as my own sister, I might add—do you honestly think I minded that you were inspired to ask her to marry you right then and there?"

And I realized in that moment that however much I may have been…*fretting* over the inappropriateness of my own jerkiness for months now, Mary Agnes was never the kind of woman to hold a grudge about it or even mind in the first place.

Right then, I was absolved.

I turned to the next guest in line.

"Can you believe the Mets this year?" I said.

"I know, right?" Frankie said. "Ever since Niese got his nose fixed, he looks better, he breathes better, he even throws better."

"I know, right?" I said. "And you know who paid for him to get it done, don't you?"

At the same time, we both shouted, "Beltran!"

And now we're on the lawn outside of Tarrywile, the whole Wedding Party getting our pictures taken while the guests hit the open bar inside. Helen's talking to her parents, the photographer's waiting for them to stop talking so he can take a picture of just Helen with her parents, when I notice the bottom of her gown is all twisted funny, so I lean down and straighten it out, make sure it lays just right on the grass, study my work.

"I can't believe you, Johnny," Sam says.

"What'd I do now?" I say.

"Look at you, all straightening out the dress and everything, making sure the gown looks perfect. That was just so…" Sam says, and I wait for her to fill in the rest of that sentence so the result will be something more along the lines of: "That was so… *girly*." But Sam surprises me when she finally says, "…*nice*."

"Thanks," I say, but my eyes are all on Helen as the photographer finally snaps the pic of her with her parents. "She's beautiful, isn't she?" I ask Sam, even though I already know the answer.

And Sam, my friend who is almost always acerbic, surprises me a second time by answering in all seriousness:

"Yeah, Johnny, she really is."

"Mr. and Mrs. Billy Keller," the wedding singer announces.

"Sam and Carla," the wedding singer announces.

What? I think. They don't get last names?

"Mr. and Mrs. Big John Smith," the wedding singer announces.

There's a louder fanfare now and Helen looks up at me. "We're up next," she says. "Are you ready for this?"

Am I ready for this? I nod fiercely. I was made for this.

"And the moment we've all been waiting for," the wedding singer announces, "your bride and groom and mine…Mr. and Mrs. Johnny Smith!"

The room explodes into applause as Helen and I enter and I think to myself, *Mrs. Johnny Smith. She gave up a cool last name like Troy to become Mrs. Johnny Smith. How cool is that?*

But there's no time for me to revel in the coolness of that or in the oddness of the wedding singer referring to us as "your bride and groom and mine," because suddenly I'm terrified. And the reason I'm terrified is because I know what comes next: the first dance.

I am not known for my dancing.

Months ago, I suggested to Helen—scratch that, I *begged* her to take dancing lessons with me. Drew and Stacy, Billy and

Alice—they all took dancing lessons before their weddings and the results, if unexotic, were at least passably not embarrassing.

But Helen said: no. Helen said, and I quote, "Don't worry, I've got this one covered."

Did I mention that I'm not known for my dancing?

If it's a slow dance, I look like a stick figure; if it's a fast dance, I look like a yahoo—that's how that song goes. I've never really minded this about myself before—OK, I've never really cared, at all—but I've also never been the center of attention like this before either; never been one of the only two people dancing in front of a crowd of over a hundred. So as I walk with Helen on my arm toward the dance floor, faking a confidence I don't feel, all I can think is: This cannot end well.

We hit the inside edge of the parquet floor, I hear the beginning strains of some music that sounds vaguely familiar but that in my state of abject terror I can't place, and Helen stops me. "Stay right there," she whispers, and, "don't worry, I've got this covered."

Why does she keep saying that? Now I'm really worried. What does she have covered?

She extracts her hand from my arm, strides across the dance floor, meets up with her Matron of Honor, Aunt Alfresca, who produces two Mets caps from I don't even know where.

Helen studies the two caps and, deciding something, tosses the larger of the two across the dance floor. I may still be terrified, add to that confused, but if someone throws even remotely well and gets the flying object at least in my vicinity, I can catch it, which I do. I shag that Mets cap one handed and raise a quizzical brow in Helen's general direction.

She mimes putting a cap on her head and I think: Seriously? We're gonna get our hair messed up? But, didn't we like pay extra to look good today? Still, if that's what she wants…

I slap the cap on my head, wait to see what she's got planned for me next.

The band's getting louder, the music jazzy like something you'd hear in a strip club as Helen slaps a Mets cap on her own head, right over the Juliet cap so the veil's flowing out from under the Mets cap now. Then she bends her knees, snapping her fingers and jiggling her shoulders as she—there's no other word for it—*shimmies* across the dance floor toward me. When she's halfway across, I realize where I know this song from because I know the words to this part: *Buy me some peanuts and Cracker Jacks, I don't care if…*

Oh. My. God. She's doing an erotic shimmy dance in my direction to the tune of "Take Me Out to the Ballgame." I *love* this woman!

As she reaches me, she gives one last raunchy shimmy before falling into my arms—it can't have been easy dancing like that in those delicate high-heeled satin wedding shoes—and as I hold her close, I think that I don't care if I look like a stick figure or a yahoo at all because the song has it exactly right:

*I don't care if I never get back.*

So, yeah, we decided on the chicken.

Last year, when we met, I was a pescatarian. It was for philosophical reasons but somewhere along the line I realized I was being hypocritical, so I'm back to eating everything. But who knows? That could change again at some point. People do change, in this life, if only occasionally.

When it came time to pick out the wedding meal, we were thinking: Shrimp? Prime rib? But one of Helen's brothers is deathly allergic to shellfish, Big John's cholesterol is high and yet he can never resist meat if it's an option, so. Anyway, like Helen said, if people are coming for the food, they're coming for the wrong reason, right?

So we went with the chicken.

"Good chicken," she says to me now, forking another bite into her mouth. How sexy is that?

"I know, right?" I say.

"I heard the Mets won earlier today," she says.

"You heard that too?" This is shaping up to be some great day.

Then there's the tinkling of silverware against glass and on the other side of Helen, I see Big John forcing himself to his feet. Sometimes he can still stand for brief periods of time but it's never easy. I told him no one'd care if he gave his toast sitting down but when Big John gets something into his head…

I've given so many toasts at other people's weddings—ten, to be exact, including Big John's—and I've always wondered what it would be like when it was my turn to be toasted, not ever really believing that that day would come.

And yet now, here we are.

"What a day," Big John says with a shake of the head like he can't quite believe it—him and me both. "What a day." Another head shake. "Hey, how about those Mets?"

The crowd laughs, most people clap but a few don't. What—do we have some Yankees and Red Sox fans in here? The mind reels.

"In all seriousness," Big John goes on, "you have no idea how happy I am to be here because I never thought I'd live to see this day. Johnny was always such a great kid and then he grew up to be—well, really—the finest man I know. Still, I never thought he'd…" Big John pauses, let's the silence sit. "Still, here we are. And if Johnny'd been a girl, I couldn't ask for no better daughter than for him to've been just like Helen."

OK, so that part where he supposes me being a daughter is a little odd, but I can't expect everyone to give the kinds of toasts I give—and at least he didn't hijack my toast to propose to someone else like I did at Frankie and Mary Agnes's wedding, so there is that. Plus, that tear in his eye is killing me.

Big John raises his glass and chokes out the words, "To Helen and Johnny."

Everyone drinks, but as Big John resumes his seat, I hear a rustle to the left of me and I see Aunt Alfresca rise from her seat, glass in hand.

Oh geez. As Dorothy Parker used to say: What fresh hell is this?

I know that sometimes in addition to the Best Man, the Maid or Matron of Honor also makes a toast—hey, I've been to a lot of weddings! Plus, before my own, Alice made me read a wedding etiquette guide. Still, I didn't anticipate this. What can Aunt Alfresca possibly be planning to say? Let me see if I can imagine it…"Dear Dearly Assembled, we are gathered here today and I am here to inform you, that on the day of his birth, my nephew—who's also now my stepson—killed his mother, aka my sister."

Yeah, that oughta do it. That oughta put everyone in the mood to do "The Chicken Dance." How does that go again? *I don't wanna be a chicken, I don't wanna be a duck, but what the fuck?* Story of my life, even on my wedding day.

"Helen." Aunt Alfresca raises her glass in Helen's direction. "My husband's right: You'd make a fine daughter and you will make one." She waves the glass around until she has me in its sights. "And Johnny."

Oh, great. Now she's going to say how my mother really wanted a daughter and how that's what killed her: my maleness. Maybe she'll even start throwing the word penis around—wouldn't be the first time.

"Johnny."

Wait a second. Are those *tears* spilling over the lower lids of Aunt Alfresca's eyes?

"Your mother," she says in a husky voice, "would be so proud of you." She pauses before adding fiercely, "*I* am so proud of you."

Well, crap.

Now I got tears spilling out of my eyes too.

If Aunt Alfresca and me have ever hugged before I sure don't remember it. But we hug now, hard.


The troops've all been fed, Helen and her dad did the father-and-daughter dance—so beautiful—and now the floor's open for dancing and everyone's going at it. Well, except for Big John, who kind of cha-cha-chas from his wheelchair. In fact, the whole bridal party is doing a kind of cross-pollinated dance at this point: Big John dancing with Carla, Sam with Aunt Alfresca, and Billy with Helen. That leaves me with…

"So," Alice says wryly, "I guess it's us?"

"Well, yeah, I guess," I say. "Or we could, you know, just sit or find something else to eat, if you'd rather."

"I think I'd like to dance," Alice says, holding her arms out to me.

As I assume the position, I think of the last time we danced, at her wedding, and how she got mad at me later on for hooking up with her cousin without knowing her cousin had any name other than Three Sheets, as in three sheets to the wind. Geez, I hope this ends better than that.

"Look at them," Alice says with a chin nod in the direction of Helen and Billy. "If this was their wedding day, Helen would now be Helen Keller."

"Hey, that's pretty funny," I say.

Then I wonder if it really is funny and if Alice will give me grief for saying it is. The famous Helen Keller was deaf, dumb and blind. Did I really just make a Helen Keller joke at my own wedding? Am I really that un-PC? But wait, it was Alice who said it. Oh, crap. Now I'm confusing myself here.

"And," Alice goes on, apparently oblivious to my quandary, "if you and I had gotten married today, I'd be Alice Smith now."

It's a good thing I didn't just drink something because if I had it'd be flying out of my nose as I snort.

"As if," I say on the other side of the snort. "You'd never accept Smith as a last name. You'd say Alice Smith sounds too common."

"Maybe so, maybe so. Still, did you ever wonder…"

I'm looking at Helen, dancing with Billy, and I'm wondering: Is that woman really my *wife*?

"I'm sorry, Alice," I say, "did you say something?"

"I was just wondering if you ever wondered…" She stops, clearly irritated, which with Alice is something of a perpetual state, at least when it comes to me. "Never mind. You know you dance like a stick?"

Yeah, well.

Wait a second. Did I miss something here?

• • •

So Helen and me are working the room.

That's what you do when you get married: you dance, you eat, you dance some more, and you make sure to talk to each and every one of your guests.

See? Etiquette, right?

We're at the table with some of my old friends and their plus-ones: Drew, Matt—those kind of people.

"Hey, Johnny," Drew says, "we're doing shots. Have a round with us."

"Thanks." I hold up my hand. "I think I'll pass."

"What?" Drew says. "You saving yourself for the wedding night?"

The truth is, I am. Helen and I stopped having sex about three months ago because we wanted our first night as man and wife to feel like a big deal and I don't want to show up with nothing to contribute. Hey, I read my Shakespeare in college. I know all about wine and its relationship to desire and performance. As a matter of fact, other than a few sips of Champagne to go along with the toasts, I've kept dry all night. I figure, hey, I can always get tanked on the honeymoon. But tonight is for us. Still, I sure don't want to explain all that to these mooks. It'd be indelicate. So instead I just shrug.

"Maybe later," I say.

"He's smarter than you are," Stacy says, punching Drew in the shoulder. "Remember how bad off you were on our wedding night?"

"Yeah," Drew says, "well, at least I wasn't the one who spent the whole honeymoon in the crapper."

Ah, love.

"Catch you guys later," I say.

Helen and I move on to the next table, which is all her work cronies. Steve Miller could be at my friends' table but since he's a lawyer he and his wife are here. I recognize JJ Trey and Monte Carlo. I was at a Yankees game with them the day I met Helen—long story; and was even jealous of Monte Carlo for a time—even longer story. Most of the table turns in our direction with big smiles as we approach because that's what happens at weddings: the bride and groom get treated like royalty. So I do the Old Home Week thing with JJ and Monte, get introduced to a few others I've never met before. But there's one guy—blond hair, kind of...*Gatsby*-ish, like in that old movie with Robert Redford—who's sucking on an e-cigarette and who doesn't even acknowledge me until I hold out my hand to him and say, "I'm Johnny Smith, Helen's new husband. And you are...?"

I kind of expect him to be thrilled to meet me because, well, like Sam's always pointing out, other guys just love me.

But he barely shakes my hand as he says, "Ah yes, the housepainter. Daniel Rathbone here."

"Nice to know you, Dan," I say.

"Actually," he says, "I believe I did just say it's Daniel."

"Tomato, tomahto," I say with a what's-the-difference smile.

The smile I get in return is distinctly chilly. Or maybe I'm just seeing things that aren't there? Maybe I should give this guy the benefit of the doubt?

"Nice tux," he says.

"Thanks," I say, fingering my Frank Sinatra lapel. It *is* a nice tux.

"Although," he adds, "I half expected to see you wearing painter's pants."

I laugh. "Painter's pants? At my own wedding?" This guy is joking, right?

"Well," he says evenly, and there's that smile again, "you have to admit, you would be more comfortable, wouldn't you?"

Wait a second here. Did this guy just *diss* me? At my own *wedding?*

No, that can't be.

"See you later...*Johnny*," he says, like he's dismissing me.

"Um, OK...*Dan*."

More dancing, garter removed and tossed, bouquet tossed (Go, Sam!) and yet more dancing.

And then time speeds up, rapidly, as time sometimes has the unfortunate tendency to do.

Every wedding reception I've ever been to, the bridal couple leave before everyone else. But Helen and I decided in advance: We did not want to miss a single second of our own wedding celebration.

So as the clock ticks the last minutes toward eleven P.M., our witching hour, only ten of us remain, slow dancing: Carla with some guy from the office who's stayed behind, Sam with Lily, Billy with Alice, and Aunt Alfresca who's sitting in Big John's lap, her arms around his neck as he describes a box step with his wheelchair. I may not know the names of any other dances in relation to what they look like—and what exactly is a Lindy?—but I can tell he's moving his chair in a box shape.

And then there's me and Helen. I look down at her, thinking how right it feels to have her in my arms, and wonder for maybe the millionth time in the past few hours:

Is this woman really my *wife*?

# My Wedding Night

If you think I'm going to divulge intimate details here, you are sorely mistaken.

Suffice it to say that after our official driver, Sam, drops us off at our hotel—Helen: "You want to come up for a drink?"; Sam: "Thanks, I'm good"; Me: "And you won't forget to take care of Fluffy?"; Sam: "Do I *look* like I'm going to starve your cat?"—we head up to our room.

Suffice it to say, Helen needs help with the back of her dress, it's almost painfully sweet, then about an hour later it becomes incredibly raunchy, and finally it is the nicest feeling I have ever had in my life. Who knew that nice could feel so nice?

After all that, we're keyed up—about the day and night we've had, about the day and days to come—but eventually Helen drifts off.

And as I look at her head resting against my shoulder, even though the arm I have underneath her starts to tingle and fall asleep, I don't try to shift her to give that arm relief.

Instead, I tuck a stray hair behind her ear that's tickling her nose and think to myself with utter satisfaction:

This woman is my *wife*.

# My All Aboard

Kidding. *Kidding!*

What—you think I've become so self-absorbed that I think everything is about me, my, mine?

Of course I know it's simply "all aboard" as in—*honk, honk!*—all aboard the cruise ship, baby!

That's right. We're going on a cruise.

Back when Helen and me were talking about possible honeymoon destinations, we went through all the possibilities: the cultured, like Europe; the exotic, like Africa; the staycation, a word I abhor, as in staying home and just going to Mets games all week. But we rejected them all. The first two because they seemed like they'd require a lot of planning when we were already planning the wedding, the last because it turned out the Mets were going to be out of town for most of the week we'd set aside for our honeymoon—how inconvenient. So we opted instead for a cruise to tropical climates. Sure, it was cliché and kitschy, but if you can't be clichéd and kitschy on your honeymoon, when can you be those two words I'm not about to repeat for a third time? Plus, we figured it'd be great. Neither of us has been on any vacation in so long, we thought it'd be just nice to laze around by the ship's pool and later the beach, with no pressure on our time whatsoever to do anything but bask in the sun and each other. We'd have plenty of time later on in our married life to become cultured and exotic.

Has anyone else noticed how suddenly everything in my life has become "us" and "we"?

And here *we* are:

Cruising, *baby!*

At the top of the gangplank, a photographer snaps our pic

as I hold Helen around the waist from behind. The photographer says we can purchase it later, a lovely memento of our time at sea. How cool is that?

Even though the ship doesn't leave until four P.M., we're on board by two and checked into our mini-suite with balcony. It cost a little more but it's still less than we would've spent on Europe and Africa, plus I need those windows. I can't stand the idea of being too fenced in. It'll be good to be able to see the ocean.

"You were right," I say, testing the bounce of the queen-sized bed as Helen checks out the bathroom situation. "Our luggage isn't here yet."

Helen did all this online research first and discovered that sometimes it takes hours before your luggage makes it to the stateroom on the first day. But who wants to wait hours to hit the pool? So, being the smart egg that she is, she took our bathing suits and shoved them in this beachy carryall thing she got for the trip.

When she emerges from the bathroom…

"Whoa!" is all I can say.

Sure I've seen Helen in her undie things before, but never in a bathing suit, and she is just truly *whoa*. There are a couple of triangles and strings involved but not much of either and the color, well, if I were going to paint a room in it, I'd say the closest match at the paint store would be Cerulean Sky.

"You are the hottest thing I've ever seen," I say. "But wait a second. Are other people going to see you like that?"

She laughs and throws something at me, which I catch.

My bathing suit? A little less skimpy than hers. Actually, they're those jammy things. About twenty years ago, it was all Speedos. Guys'd be walking around like, "ooh, here's all my junk" and "see how big my junk is"; now we wear stuff that says, "ah, I got no junk, and besides, I've been eating too many French fries lately." The fickle world of men's fashion. Go figure.

"Of course they will," she says, "but does it matter? After all, you're my husband."

*Husband.* I'm a husband! Was there ever a greater word in

the history of the world?

"And you're hot," she adds, as she pulls me close and unbuckles my belt, the better to help me change into my swim trunks.

And now I can think of a few other pretty great words.

We hit the deck and find a couple of vacant lounge chairs by the pool. Not everyone was as prescient as us—bringing our bathing suits on board in a carryall—so there aren't as many people around the pool as you'd think. Mostly, people are walking around in their shorts and jeans, drinking fruity drinks and hanging over the railing and waiting for the ship to set sail.

Even though I'm more of a beer guy, I figure "When on a cruise ship…" So I flag a passing waitress and order two of the day's specials—Papaya-Pineapple Paradise—for me and the little Mrs.

Wow, that's sweet.

I look at my wife, lying on her stomach, and I wonder when thinking of her that way—*my wife*—will start to get old. I'm thinking never.

"Hey," I say, "did you pack any suntan lotion in that carryall thing?"

She reaches in, tosses me a plastic bottle of something, which I catch backhanded. I love it when she throws stuff at me. She's got such a good arm.

"Are you worried about getting burned?" she says, one eye closed against the mid-afternoon sun.

"Nah," I say, "I spend so much time outdoors, and being half Italian, I don't worry about it so much. I was thinking more about you. That red hair, that fair skin…"

"Oh my gosh," she says. "How could I have forgotten? I'll turn into a lobster." She pulls her hair to one side. "Could you do my back for me?"

"I don't know, lady," I say, like I can't believe she's asking me to do something so hard, as I squirt some lotion onto my hands and rub my palms together. "I don't remember there being anything in the vows to cover anything so difficult as this."

"Well, if it's too much trouble…" She starts to lever herself up from the chair.

"Shh," I say, putting my hands on her shoulders and rubbing the suntan lotion into her naked skin.

I could do this kind of trouble all day long.

Our sunbathing is interrupted by the lifeboat test, which feels kind of like being in a sardine can what with all the people jammed close together on the deck, life preservers around our necks. But when I feel Helen's hand take mine and give it a squeeze, and I look down at her—my own little sardine—it's not so bad.

I also vow to myself to never tell Sam that I just referred to Helen, even if only in the quiet of my own mind, as "my little sardine"; I'd never hear the end of it.

About a half hour before we set sail, Helen reaches into her carryall and pulls out her cell phone.

"I thought you can't get reception on a cruise ship," I say.

"You can't once you're out at sea," she says, "but you can when you're still in port. I researched it."

She researched it. How cute is my wife?

"Cool," I say, pulling my own cell out of my pocket as she starts punching in a number. "Maybe I'll give Sam a call, make sure she's all set for work tomorrow."

Sam picks up on the second ring.

"Hey," she says, "aren't you supposed to be on your honeymoon?"

"I am," I say, "but I won't get reception again until we pull into port in the Bahamas and I want to make sure you're all set for the jobs this week."

Sam's a would-be novelist but until that takes, she paints interiors and exteriors with me.

"Of course I'm all set," she says. "First up tomorrow is the

Ryan job. I'll get the paint on the way: Blue Lagoon."

"No, no, no, no, no," I say, perhaps a bit too vehemently. "Sheila Ryan only *thinks* she wants Blue Lagoon, but what she really needs is Hidden Lagoon."

"What if she complains it's not the color she picked out?"

"Trust me on this. She'll be thanking you."

"OK, you're the boss...*Boss*."

I hate it when she calls me that.

We go over the jobs and the required paint for the rest of the week.

"Hey, your dad called," she says. "I figured we wouldn't be playing poker this week, what with you being away, but he invited everyone over to his house for Friday. He said your aunt was going to make some kind of quiche."

The weekly poker games have always been at my place with me, Big John, Sam, Billy, Drew and, for the last year or so, Steve Miller in attendance. Normally I'd hate to miss a week, but I look over at Helen, her pretty mouth moving fast as she talks on the phone, and I don't feel like I'm going to be missing anything. And, you know, quiche.

"That's great," I say. "Have a good time. And hey, keep an eye on GH for me."

*General Hospital* has really been heating up lately. I originally started watching it as a way to be more likable to women because Alice told me all women love GH, which, as it turned out, was false—Helen didn't love it and she still doesn't completely love it—but now I'm hooked.

"Do you think I'd miss it?" she says.

"I know, right?" I say. "That soap magazine they have at the supermarket said something about Sonny revealing some kind of huge secret to Johnny Zacchara."

"That can't be good."

"Whatever it is, Johnny Z'll probably freak. Sonny can be such a tool sometimes. Hey, do you think something really bad is going to happen to Robin?"

"Well, that's what the magazine said."

"So, how's the cat doing?"

"It's only been twenty-four hours."

"I know, but I've never left him alone for this long before."

"I think he misses you. He's eating and using the litter box and everything but whenever I go in there, he zooms around the place like he's on cocaine or something. I think he's trying to find you."

That is so unlike him. Usually, Fluffy moves so little, people think he's dead. As a matter of fact, I don't think I've *ever* seen him "zoom" around the place.

"Poor little guy," I say.

"Yeah, well. That's what you get for getting a cat to impress a girl and then running off with the girl."

"Yeah, well. See you a week from Monday."

"OK, Boss. Travel safe."

I put my phone away but Helen's still talking on hers.

I stretch out my legs, lean back, cradle my fingers behind my neck.

Now there's a funny word: *cradle*.

But ah, paradise.

In the pool, there are already little kids frolicking. Kids always know the good stuff. The adults may forget to pack their own bathing suits into carryalls, they may be more worried about getting more fruity drinks than about frolicking. But any kid who's ever been on vacation knows that the very first thing you do, as soon as possible, is you throw on your bathing suit and you jump in that pool.

Yes, paradise.

Yesterday was nearly perfect, easily the best day of my life. Sure, there were a few off moments, like that dance with Alice where I didn't know what she was talking about and then she went all Alice-crazy on me and that brief interlude with that Dan *Rath*bone character—what was his problem?—but other than that, it was a perfect day. And this is shaping up to be another one and all I can see is a string of nearly perfect days stretching out for the rest of my life.

"Sounds good, Daniel," I hear Helen say. "I'll check in again when I get to port."

She drops her phone back into her carryall.

"Who was that?" I say.

"Daniel," she says. "From the office."

"On Sunday?"

"We needed to go over a case that's coming up." She shrugs. "You called Sam, didn't you?"

"Well, yeah, but…Was that Daniel *Rath*bone?"

"*Rath*bone?" She laughs. "You say his name like you're trying to hawk up some phlegm."

Yeah, well.

"I do?" I make my 'what are you—crazy?' face. "I don't do that. Why would I do that? I only met the guy for the first time yesterday. I never even heard of him before yesterday. Come to think of it, what was he doing at our wedding?"

"He works in the office."

"But I never heard of him before," I say again.

I don't know why I'm making an issue of this. There's no big deal, right? But I sound like I'm making an issue of it, which I don't want to be doing, but I can't stop saying things and asking questions because it would just look strange if I just stopped.

It's kind of like the time Jon Stewart was on David Letterman's show and for some insane reason Stewart started talking about underwear and then out of the blue said that Letterman's such a big star he probably doesn't even need to wear underwear anymore, he probably has staff members to reach around him and just hold up his junk. Even though everyone, including Stewart after a while, realized that Stewart had inadvertently ventured into the territory of That Which Should Never Be Mentioned (In Terms of Dave's Staff), Stewart could no longer stop at that point. He just had to keep on making stupid awkward jokes.

This is exactly like that.

Almost.

"Maybe you never heard of him because he's new," she says.

"Well, if he's so new," I counter, "why did you invite him to our wedding?"

See what I mean about this being like the Stewart thing?

Once you start on one of these paths, it's almost impossible to get off again.

Poor Jon Stewart.

"It's a fairly small office and I'd already invited everyone else there." She shrugs. "You know how that sort of thing is."

Actually, in my world it's just me and Sam at the office, so, really, I don't.

"Why?" she presses when I don't say anything else. "Did you not like him when you met him at the wedding?"

What can I say? That in the brief time I spent with him, Daniel *Rath*bone made me feel like my shoulders were up somewhere around the tips of my ears? That he made me feel *dissed* on my own wedding day?

I can't say that. And anyway, I don't *want* to say that. This is so stupid. Why did I even start this? And I'm probably wrong about whatever I was feeling around him anyway.

"He was fine," I say. "He seemed like a fine…*chap*." And as I'm speaking, I manage to convince myself that this is true.

"Seriously?" She studies me closely.

"Absolutely," I say. "As a matter of fact, I think we should have him over for dinner sometime so I can get to know him better—you know, once we get back to Danbury."

"That'd be great," she says. "You know, I never really noticed it before, but whenever we do stuff, it's almost always with your friends, with your family."

Huh. I never noticed that before either.

"It'll be good to do something with one of my friends for a change. And I'm sure you'll like Daniel once you get to know him. He's really very nice."

"Oh, I can already tell from the brief time I spent with him, Daniel is one prince of a guy."

Hey, I can afford to be magnanimous. Daniel may be the nice new guy in the office, but Helen is my *wife* and I'm the husband here.

"You know, though," I can't help but add, "it is kind of fun to say Rathbone like you're trying to hawk up some phlegm: *Rath*bone. *Rath*bone. *Rath*—"

*Honk! Honk!*

And there's the ship's whistle blow!

Helen and I rush to join the other passengers at the railing as the ship reverses out of its slot. Since we didn't plan ahead for this and others did, there are several rows of people between us and the actual railing. So as the ship swings around and we head out through the harbor, I hoist Helen onto my shoulders so that she can get a good look at Lady Liberty—the ultimate symbol of freedom—as we sail on past.

Feeling the weight of her on my shoulders, her naked legs hanging down around my neck, holding her up and making sure she doesn't fall:

I am so made for this husband shit.

We hit the mini-suite for a little R&R before dinner and it actually turns into no R or R, but rather, just a lot of acrobatic sex.

A guy could get used to married life.

Afterward, we change for dinner. The ship leaves daily programs in the staterooms to tell you what to expect, and the programs also say what the dress code is for that night's dinner. Tonight says "Casual," I guess because it's our first night out and there's that thing of maybe not everyone having had their suitcases delivered yet. But ours have been delivered and apparently the wife feels like dressing up.

I know this because when she comes out of the bathroom, she has on a form-fitting red dress that ends somewhere above her mid-thigh and sky-high red heels. I've always known her to be a conservative dresser—you know, her being a D.A. and all that—but I guess she figured she'd take the opportunity of the cruise to bust out of her buttoned-down look a bit. A red-haired woman in all of that red? Va-va-va-voom.

And, just so she knows what I'm thinking, "Va-va-va-voom," I say.

Then I change out of my jeans and T-shirt and put on chinos and a white button-down shirt instead so I don't look completely out of place with her.

• • •

On the ship, passengers are assigned tables in the more formal dining rooms for meals although there are other dining options. I'm fast learning that on a cruise, the one thing there's never a shortage of is food or photographers snapping your picture, but that's OK; I love having my picture taken with Helen—it's like a tangible proof of our love. How corny is it that I just said that? And what's worse? I don't even care! Of course, I haven't eaten at an assigned table with specified others since I was in grade school, but I figure this could be fun, a chance to really get to know some new people. Who was the last new friend I made? Steve Miller? That hardly qualifies.

Our table is located near the back of the ship with a wide-open view of the wake we're cutting through the sea behind us—this is cool; I like a good view—and our four tablemates are already seated, two other couples. The couple to our left, based on the lines in their faces, is a lot older—I'm guessing early seventies, at least—but they both have hair so black, it looks like it was shellacked on. The woman is wearing some kind of a housedress thing while the husband has on a cheap brown suit.

I introduce myself and my bride and I suppose I mention that we're on our honeymoon.

"Boris," the man says gruffly in a strong accent. He jerks his head at his wife. "Natasha."

I laugh. "That's funny," I say.

"Why is that funny?" he says in the same tone of voice.

Shit. I guess he's never seen *The Rocky and Bullwinkle Show*.

"No reason," I say. "So, where you all from?"

"Cleveland," he says.

"I meant before that." I wave my butter knife before buttering a roll. "You know, the accent."

"Ru-*SHA*!" he says, and there's a salute in his voice now.

I'm guessing he means Russia.

"Well, that's cool," I say. "On my father's side, one of my grandparents came from Russia. I don't remember the town, but maybe if you say which town you're from…"

He leans close so he's practically in my face.

"Why you ask so many questions?" he says.

Ouch.

The woman half of the other couple comes to my rescue.

"I'm Daisy," she says. "That's my husband—he's Tom."

Daisy and Tom look like they're barely rocking fifty. Daisy has on a pretty dress—not sexy like Helen's, but pretty enough compared to what some other people have on this first night at sea—while Tom is sporting the prep-school chino look although his button-down shirt is light blue and he's added a navy blazer to the mix. His thinning hair looks like it's thinking about taking a permanent hike but Daisy's is blond and incredibly expensive looking.

"Congratulations on your wedding," Daisy says with a look that's a little difficult to decipher. "How lovely for you both."

"*Thank* you," I say with perhaps more enthusiastic appreciation than the situation warrants, but I'm still getting over whatever just happened with Boris and I'm grateful for her kind words.

"Tom and I are here because he thought we should go on a cruise to mark our twenty-fifth wedding anniversary."

"Twenty-five years! Why that's—"

Daisy snorts. "Like a cruise is going to fix anything after twenty-five years of pure hell." Then she knocks back the entire contents of her glass which—sniffing the air—I'm guessing is pure Scotch.

Wow. This is going to be a fun table.

After surviving the rest of dinner—I think I had some kind of meat—we consult the daily cruise planner to decide what to do next. Sure, we could go back to the mini-suite for some more...*you know*, but we did that most of last night, again when we got up this morning and right before dinner, and, you know, you can't spend your whole life doing *you know*, tempting as that might be. Plus, there's so much to do on a ship.

"You want to go dancing?" I offer, magnanimously, I think.

"There are a lot of various dancing options on the ship." I look. "There's ballroom and a disco…" Sure, I know I'm either a stick figure or yahoo dancer, but my wife is all dressed up—that outfit shouts, *I want to dance!*—and anyway, no one knows me on this ship.

"*Karaoke!*" my bride screams. "They have karaoke—I *love* karaoke!" She grabs my hand and tugs me in a direction. "Let's do that."

So, I guess we're doing karaoke.

The room where they have the karaoke is done up in black and a dark red that clashes with all the red Helen has on. The room kind of looks like a rundown strip joint, not that I have that much experience with that kind of thing.

I look around for a free table and spot one right in the front row. As we make our way over there, Helen reaches out and grabs a thick black leather-covered book, a few small scraps of paper and a stubby pencil from I guess you'd call it a captain's stand.

We sit there and listen to a woman in the performance area belting out an Adele song. You can't swing a dead cat these days without hitting someone singing an Adele song, but at least this woman has a good voice. I mean, it's really good.

Speaking of cats, I wonder how Fluffy's making out? Maybe I should have asked Sam to sleep over with him instead of just checking in twice a day.

I order some drinks from the waitress and she gives me a huge smile. It occurs to me that I've been getting that a lot since we've been on the ship—waitresses smiling at me big. This is an unusual experience for me because usually I don't have that kind of an effect on women. But maybe they just treat all the passengers that way? You know, hoping for bigger tips?

Helen's studying the contents of that black leather-bound book like she's going to find the Holy Grail in there or something.

What is that thing—a menu?

"Are you hungry again already?"

I don't say this in any kind of judgy voice. Sure, I've heard of women getting married and then packing on a hundred pounds right away. But I'd never care about something like that—even a hundred pounds heavier, Helen'd still be Helen. Still, we did just have a pretty big meal and I am curious.

"No," she says, eyes glued to the page. "This is just a list of all the songs they have."

A list...

"*You're* going to sing?" I'm shocked. I've never heard her sing before. We always listen to the sports station, The Wave, when we're in the car together.

I wonder how the Mets made out today...

"Of course," she says. "Why else do people go to karaoke?"

How would I know? I never go to karaoke.

"I've got it!" she says. Then she scribbles something on one of the little scraps of paper and brings it over to some D.J. type of person, who adds it to some other scraps in front of him.

We wait and wait through a few more singers—some good, some OK, some truly sucky—Helen swinging a red-heeled toe impatiently all the while.

At last, the D.J. calls out, "Helen Smith!"

Helen Smith? I do like the sound of that.

Helen practically bounds out of the chair and as she does so, she grabs onto my hand, yanking on it.

"Come on," she says.

"Oh no," I say, digging my heels in. "This is your thing—you sing."

"But it won't be half as fun without you." She makes a little pouty face I've never seen before. "I want to do a duet—this is our honeymoon."

There are a lot worse things than your new wife wanting to do couple-type things with you—like, say, being Tom and Daisy, and hating each other's guts after twenty-five years of marriage.

So I make a decision. Even though it strikes me as a horrifically embarrassing thing to do, I will sing a karaoke duet with my wife in front of all these strangers. After all, how bad can it be? She probably picked out some really cool song—maybe a little Green Day—plus, I used to sing in the church choir. Aunt Alfresca made me and then they made me a soloist. I'm told I actually have a very fine tenor.

So really, this won't be bad at all. In fact, I suddenly think, this will be excellent, a dream come true!

And the reason I think *that* is because like all Americans, I've seen those movies where friends spontaneously burst into song – you know those movies, like *The Deer Hunter* or *My Best Friend's Wedding*—and everyone sounds really great, leaving everyone in the audience to wish that they had great-sounding friends they could spontaneously burst into song with.

This is going to be exactly like that.

This is going to be so cool.


This is nothing like that.

I realize that as soon as my wife starts singing "*Friday night and the lights are low...*" and it hits me: She picked out *ABBA*? There must have been thousands of song choices in that book and the one she chose with that Eureka! look on her face was *ABBA*? And seriously, "Dancing Queen"? Then something else hits me: She's painfully off-key. And then a third thing hits me, which would be her fist in my shoulder, followed by a muttered, "Your turn to sing."

Oh, no. How can I sing this awful song in front of all these people? But how could I ever just walk off the floor and desert my bride?

So I open my mouth and start to sing.

"*You are the dancing queen...*"

Kill me now.

Somehow, I get through it. There's even a fair amount of applause when we're done, which is better than the rotten tomatoes I was expecting. Maybe people are just being polite? Of course everyone does love a pretty woman in a red dress and then too, I do have that great tenor.

When we return to our seats, Helen is all exhilaration.

"*Yes!*" She holds her hand up for a high five.

What choice do I have but to high-five her back?

"Yes," I say, trying to sound like I mean it. At least my smile is genuine. After all, she really is cute.

And at least that's over with.

"Well, that was fun," I say.

"Fun? *Fun?* That was *amazing!*"

"Absolutely. Now maybe we should…"

But she's back to avidly studying her song bible again.

She can't possibly be thinking…

"Perfect!" she says and then proceeds to scribble something on another piece of scrap paper.

She can't seriously be planning on doing that again, can she?

I say as much, but a bit more diplomatically.

Or maybe not so diplomatically. What comes out of my mouth is: "You want to do that *again*?"

"Of course," she says, looking at me like I'm crazy. "Who can possibly stop after just one?"

Who indeed?

"Don't you like music?" she asks me.

Of course I do. I'm a guy, so I love music, great music, but this?

Without waiting for my answer, she goes up to give her song selection to the D.J. person and a few minutes later, when her name is called, she tries to grab my hand again to drag me with her. But this time I dig my heels in more firmly.

"I really wish I could," I say, "but I think I threw my voice out on that last chorus—you know, diggin' the dancing queen and all." I can't believe I'm lying to my new wife. "And anyway," I go on, "I'd really much rather sit here and listen to you."

"Really?" She smiles. "You think I'm that good?"

"Let's just say that you are…something."

"Aw." She tilts her head to one side, a misty smile on her face as she reaches out to caress my cheek. And then she's off to sing another song.

I tell myself that maybe it won't be as bad as last time. Who knows—maybe somehow my singing was throwing her off? I tell myself that maybe this time she'll pick something more suitable to her lack of any vocal talents, like maybe a Taylor

Swift song. I'm not exactly a big Taylor Swift fan—all that girly teenage angst, Romeo and Juliet, yadda yadda—but those kinds of songs can be talked as much as sung and Helen's got a fine speaking voice; she's like the reverse of Madonna who can sing great but sounds like long red fingernails on a chalkboard whenever she just talks.

I can't believe I'm sitting here praying for a Taylor Swift song. But I don't even get that.

*"Well, you can tell by the way I use my walk, I'm a woman's man…"*

Oh, sweet everything that is holy, no.

She's singing a *Bee Gees* song?

The love of my life can't sing for shit *and* she has sucky taste in music? How did I not know this about her?

I'm sure this song was considered hot a few years before I was born—in fact, I know it was and that John Travolta was considered to be really cool—but some things don't stand the test of time and this song is one of them. I try to think of movie songs that have stood the test of time. Maybe that one from *Titanic*? At least within the context of the timeless sadness of the movie and the story, it still works.

And then I panic.

Holy crap. She's not going to sing Celine Dion next, is she? I start rifling through that black leather-bound book like a madman. Is Celine Dion in here?

Just then I feel that thing where someone's eyes are drilling into your head and I look up, only to see my singing Helen staring at me with a quizzical look on her face. So I hastily close the book, push it away from me, and give a smile and little wave like the one Max the Dog gives when he's caught riding on the back of the sleigh by the Grinch.

Not that Helen's a Grinch!

Or that I'm a dog. Not really. Although I do feel bad for thinking that my wife sucks at this thing she's doing, which she does—suck at it, that is, royally.

But it's fine. Isn't it? After all, this is just one evening. It's not like she's going to be singing a soundtrack to our lives for the rest of our marriage. After tonight, I'll be able to forget all about this. And, you know, maybe these are the only two awful songs she loves.

Somewhere around Helen wondering *"whether you're a brother or whether you're a mother,"* two women approach—two very hot women, I might add, which may sound like an obnoxious observation to make since I just got married but their hotness is an objectively verifiable fact. It's not like I'd ever want to do them or anything.

"Do you mind if we sit with you?" one of them says. And, I don't know, I could be crazy, but is she coming on to me? I have so little experience with such things. Practically none, really.

The other one starts to slither in next to me and I hold up a restraining hand.

"No!" I practically shout. "No," I say in a more reasonable voice. I point at the stage. "I'm with her."

The one who's half sitting slithers back out again, a disappointed look on her face.

"Well, if you change your mind and want to hang out later," she says, "we're staying in 913."

"Um, thanks but, I think I'm good."

What is going on here? 913? I could use some 911!

Mercifully, my wife finishes singing. Even more mercifully, the D.J. announces that's it for karaoke for the night.

*Thank* you.

As Helen exits the stage, there's more applause—maybe not as much as for the girl who could actually sing Adele, but still a respectable smattering and at least there are no boos, which, if she weren't my wife, would not be uncalled for. In fact, there's a group of about ten guys in the back, standing on their feet, hooting in some kind of foreign language and whistling. My wife, apparently, has admirers.

As she makes her way back to me, I think maybe it would have been better if everyone booed. Then she would never even consider doing this again. And then I think about what an awful thing that is to think. How could I wish such a thing on my wife? She would be hurt, crushed. So instead I decide that I am grateful to all the people who clapped, whatever their motivation, grateful that they didn't break my wife's heart.

"So," she asks me, eyes bright with triumph and expectation and hope, "how was I?"

"You were…" I take her hands, searching for a true thing I can say, finally settling on: "You *are* beautiful."

And that, at least, will always be true.

We hit the late-night show in the big room at the end of the ship and it turns out that, this being the first night out, there's no comedian or magician or anything cool like that. There's just something that's billed as "An All-Star Tribute to America," which really just means a bunch of the staff from the cruise ship singing mash-ups of patriotic standards with popular tunes of the day. "The Star-Spangled Banner" mashed up with Bruno Mars' "Grenade"? "*And the rockets' red glare/I'd catch a grenade for you/the bombs bursting in air/throw my head on a plate for you*"—I think not.

Plus, the singing sucks.

At least this time, though, it's not my wife doing the sucky singing.

The next mash-up, "America the Beautiful" and Coldplay's "Viva La Vida," fares no better—"*Oh beautiful for spacious skies/feel the fear in my enemies' eyes*"—but at least it rhymes.

"Isn't this great?" Helen whispers to me at one point. "Isn't this everything you dreamed the cruise would be?"

I can't say that it is, not necessarily, but I can say that being on a honeymoon with Helen, having her be my wife, knowing that we will spend the rest of our lives together is even better than anything I ever dreamed.

So "Yes," I say. "Yes, it is."

Back in the mini-suite it turns out that—what do you know?—we still have enough energy left over for one more *you know*.

And so another nearly perfect day, in what will undoubtedly be an endless stream of them, ends.

# Smooth Sailing

And the second day, our first full day at sea, is just as nearly perfect.

Well, actually, there are two minor problems.

Apparently on cruise ships, people who know what they're doing go to the pool area very early in the morning and leave the towels from their staterooms on lounge chairs, even if they're not planning on actually using those chairs for several hours, to reserve spaces for later before all the chairs get taken. Apparently Helen read about this selfish practice when she did her pre-trip research. Apparently Helen asked me to do this when I went down to grab an early-morning coffee, while she stayed behind sleeping in, but I have no recollection of this request and when we circle the deck repeatedly looking for two empty chairs together after emerging from our cabin around eleven A.M., Helen looks miffed that the only two adjoining chairs are in the undesirable section in an upper deck far removed from the action around the pool. Apparently, although no words are spoken to this effect, that miffed look is directly my fault.

But the miffed moment passes.

Even though it is caught on camera by one of the roving photographers; maybe we won't purchase that one.

The only other less-than-perfect thing that day? More karaoke at night.

Oy.

But other than that?

Nearly perfect.

I could get used to this.

# Uh-oh

The next morning, although we are due to dock at our first port of call at eleven A.M., I wake early with the intention of not making the same towel mistake twice, even if we don't get to the pool before exiting the ship. But you know what they say about the best laid plans, right? You wake with the aim of being your wife's wet dream Cabana Boy but the cramp in your gut sends you rushing to the toilet instead.

Oh, gosh. What is that? I can't remember the last time I felt like...

And there it goes again.

This. Is. Not. Good.

And it gets worse when Helen starts pounding on the door. "Johnny, can I get in there? I have to go...*now!*"

Oh, shit. And in more ways than one.

Maybe in a few minutes I'll feel better? Maybe this is just something I ate that has to work its way out of my system and it will do so, like, really soon?

"Can you wait a few minutes?" I call out hopefully.

"No, I really can't," she says, sounding desperate. "I have to go *now.*"

What to do...what to do...

If I stay here, I'm selfish. But if I get off this seat now, this could get ugly.

Still, I am the husband, the man, and Helen is my wife. So it's my duty to flush, disinfect, squeeze my butt cheeks together as tight as I can in the hopes that no accidents occur, vacate the premises and hope it doesn't smell as bad in there as I fear it does.

Because, you know, bad smells can be a turnoff and destroy

any prospects of morning *you know*.

But Helen doesn't seem to notice any smells at all as she hurls herself past me, slamming the door in my face. A little rude and harsh, I must say, but considering the threatening roils in my own gut, I can't say that I blame her.

About five minutes into her occupation, I'm not sure I can hold things together much longer and I tap a knuckle against the door.

"Honey? Do you think maybe I can get in there for a few minutes?"

"Just give me one more minute," she says in a strained voice.

A minute? I start thinking, strategically, about where the nearest public men's room might be, but when it hits me how far away it is, I doubt I'd make it.

When she comes out, I take her place, and so we continue switching places at fairly regular intervals.

At one point, it's her turn and I hear a little voice say, "I'm not sure how much more of this I can take." I don't know if she's talking to me or deliriously talking to herself, but I fully understand how she feels.

"Honey?" I call. "I'm going to get help."

"How?" she says. "You're sick too."

I know that. How am I going to get help?

"I don't know," I say. "I'll call the Infirmary."

"But what good will that do? They can't give you medication through the phone and I'm sure they don't make house calls or just deliver."

"Then I'll go down there," I say firmly. "I'll get help."

"You'd do that for me?"

"Of course. Also, do you think I could maybe get in there for a few minutes before I go?"

"Please be careful," a pale-faced Helen urges me as she heads back into the bathroom and I turn to exit the mini-suite.

Why would I need to be careful?

But then I realize why as a cramp seizes me.

Go back or go forward?

Never since Hamlet has such a momentous debate raged.

Eventually, though, I decide to go forward. After all, how embarrassing would it be to return to Helen now and tell her that after promising to get help, I don't have it in me? Or at least not that. Plus, I'm already on the other side of the door, the hallway side so, like a National Football League quarterback who's already begun his motion, I'm committed to completing the play.

This leaves me no choice but to tighten my sphincter by squeezing my butt cheeks together ever tighter, which causes me to walk like a bowlegged, swaybacked nine-months-pregnant lady as I lurch my way down the hallway, around corners, down stairs and stairs and more stairs, around another corner and then another hallway until I get to the Infirmary, only to discover:

There's a line.

Well, of course there's a line.

And it is excruciating to wait in it as it moves at a snail's pace—I won't even detail the contortions I go through to keep things together—but at last I make it to the end and as I once was at godawful Yankee Stadium, I'm in the *front row*!

I go into the small office that is the Infirmary and there's the doctor: a shrimpy old guy with glasses and a bowtie. I don't know what I was expecting: Dr. Patrick Drake from *General Hospital*, maybe? Whatever it was, it wasn't this.

"So," I say, trying to be genial, "this is some sweet deal you've got here. Cruise-ship doctor? Must be great."

And *why* am I making small talk when I have more, um, pressing needs?

Oh, right. Because, as Sam endlessly points out to me, I'm the idiot that does things like this, only to wind up with every single guy in the world wanting me to be his Best Man.

But apparently my usual charms are wasted on this guy because he just stares at me with a sour expression as he says, "On call twenty-four hours a day and crammed into this shoebox—do I *look* like I'm having a luxury cruise-ship experience here?"

"Well, when you put it like that…"

"What seems to be the problem?"

"I guess you'd say my problem is, um, scatological."

"Come again?"

Seriously? I'm an educated guy, he's an educated guy, or at least I hope he is—do I really have to spell this out for him?

He just keeps staring at me and I realize that, yes, apparently I do.

"I got a bad case of the shits, doc."

"Well, doesn't everybody," he says dryly.

"Oh," I say, hooking a thumb over my shoulder to indicate the line I just waited through, "is that what they have too? What do you think it is, some kind of food poisoning?"

"No."

Well, there's a hard and firm diagnosis.

"But my wife's got it too," I say.

He regards me over the tops of his glasses. "And did you and your wife eat the same things for dinner last night?"

I think about this. "Well, no," I say. "She had the shrimp, I had the steak. She got a side salad, I went for the potato."

Geez, all this talk of food isn't helping my stomach any.

I try to go on. "She had—" But the doctor cuts me off.

"Did you both have even one item that was the same?" he presses.

I think about this too. "No," I finally conclude. "We didn't even both have bread and I had the cheesecake while she had the—"

"It's not food poisoning," he says, cutting me off again, and I'm thankful for this because it saves me from saying and hence thinking about "chocolate mousse."

Oh, crap. I just did. Think about it, that is.

"Well," I say, "even if we had different stuff, maybe it was prepared in the same contaminated water or something?"

"How many times do I have to keep telling you? It's not food poisoning."

"OK, then what is it?"

"You're suffering from a norovirus."

"What's that?"

"Oh, please. Like you could distinguish a norovirus from a rotavirus if I explained it to you."

Ouch.

"Let's just say it's highly contagious," he says. "One person on a ship gets it? Half the people on the ship get it. But it won't kill you. Why, in about twenty-four to sixty hours, the situation should resolve itself all on its own."

"Twenty-four to sixty hours? But this is supposed to be my honeymoon!"

"Yes, well, and these are supposed to be my Golden Years. We can't all get what we want. Just be sure to keep hydrated. Take plenty of fluids, preferably containing sugar and electrolytes."

"But isn't there something I can take? This is brutal."

"I can give you something."

He goes to a cabinet, takes out a bottle, shakes something into a cup and hands it to me.

I look down. There's just one pill there.

"Just one?"

"I can't give you more than that," he says. "In cases of severe abdominal pain—which you obviously have—it can be dangerous to take even over-the-counter remedies, plus they can prolong the pain. Being as you're in obvious distress, however, one pill won't kill you and it may alleviate the worst of the symptoms for a few hours so you can at least get some rest."

"But what about my wife?" I say. "She's really sick too."

"You expect me to give you a pill for your wife without examining her? But that would be unethical! No, I'm afraid she'll have to come here on her own if she wants a pill. Now, take it."

I go to put the pill in my mouth but then I think, wait a second. How will Helen, in her condition, ever make it down here under her own steam? It'll never happen. And she's suffering.

Then I do put the pill in my mouth, but instead of swallowing it, I only pretend to swallow it for the doctor's benefit and then tuck it under my tongue.

"You're a Yankees fan, aren't you?" I say, but it comes out all lisped and garbled since I'm holding that pill down with my tongue.

"Come again?"

"Never mind," I lisp/garble some more. "Thanks a pantload for all your help."

Then I exit the Infirmary, doing my bowlegged, swaybacked pregnant-woman routine all the way back to the room.

When I get there, I find Helen sitting gingerly on the edge of the bed, looking positively drained. I put my hand behind her neck and lower my face toward hers.

"Johnny," she says weakly, "I don't think this is the time… I'm not really up for…"

I press my lips to her half-opened ones and drop the pill I've been concealing onto her tongue—thank goodness I'm so dehydrated from being sick because otherwise, no doubt it would have dissolved already—then I pull back.

If one of us is going to feel better sooner rather than later, let it be Helen.

"Swallow," I say.

After she does so, I hurry to the bathroom and shut the door behind me.

I do remember saying those vows about "in sickness and in health" just two days ago, but I never thought they'd come around to bite me on the ass so quickly like this.

# Stuck in Port

A wide balcony view seems like a fantastic idea until you wake in the morning, after twenty-four hours of being sick and taking care of someone else who is sick, and you look out at all that moving blue-green water.

"What a gorgeous day!" Helen cries with glee.

Well, at least one of us is enjoying it.

Yesterday, after getting back to the room and giving Helen the pill, I hurried things along in the bathroom in case she might need to use it again. But when I came out, she was fast asleep on the bed. I doubt the pill could have done anything so quickly—I think she was just worn out from being so sick—but sleeping did work some magic, particularly since between bouts of my own sickness, I kept her supplied with cool towels for her forehead. I even woke her every few hours and made her drink things so she'd stay hydrated.

And now it's a new day, the ship has docked in a new port, and Helen looks as though she was never sick in the first place, while I'm still feeling...

You know, I'm not feeling as bad as yesterday, but I'm still not feeling anything remotely resembling good.

"So what do you want to do today?" Helen says. She's wearing the Cerulean Sky bikini she wore on the first day and she's got some brochures in front of her and I'm guessing that while I was still sleeping, she went down to the shore-excursions desk and picked them up.

I explain about the not-feeling-as-bad-but-still-not-feeling-good thing and Helen drops the brochures and comes over to the bed, lays a cool hand on my forehead.

"Poor baby," she says. "I wish I could do something for

you. I still can't believe what you did for me yesterday, giving me the one pill so I'd get better quicker."

I guess I am a pretty great guy.

"I know," she says. "Why don't I go down to the Infirmary? I can pretend I'm still ill and get the doctor to give me a pill and then I'll do the tongue-hiding thing like you did so I can bring it back to you."

"That's a sweet offer," I say, grabbing onto her hand and kissing it. "But I think the worst has passed. I think if I just stay here and rest today, I'll be good as new by tomorrow and then we can at least enjoy the last port stop together before the ship turns for home."

"That sounds great," Helen says, but her smile is a bit off. It's not like she's not trying—I can tell she's trying to look genuine—but that smile is still off. "I'll just stay here today, in case you need anything."

"You know what?" I say. "Don't do that. Instead, why don't you go to shore, take in the sights, spend the day doing whatever you want to do."

"Really, but—"

"I'll be fine here. Hell, I'll probably just sleep the whole time. You'd only be bored."

"I'd never be—"

"Go, Helen. I'll be fine."

"Really?" And now her smile is genuine, it's so wide, and I can tell she's just itching to get out there and meet the day full on.

"I love you."

"Oh, I love you too," she says exuberantly. She puts her hands on either side of my face, kisses me square on the mouth, before adding, "So much."

And then she grabs her carryall and she's gone.

I spend most of the day alternately sleeping and drinking fluids and going to the bathroom. It's finally mid-afternoon and I feel like I'm pretty much done with all three of those activities, at least for the time being, so I click on the TV. I start flicking through channels until I come across some talk show I recognize. I recognize it because it's whatever that crapfest is that comes on right before *General Hospital*.

Over a year ago, ABC began replacing its existing soaps with talk shows because, *supposedly*, the audience for daytime soaps is going down. Also, because talk shows are a lot cheaper to produce. So far, two long-running soaps have met their premature demise that way and there's ongoing rumors that GH will go the same sorry route and that Katie Couric will take over its spot. I've got nothing personally against Katie Couric—for an older woman, she's got a nice set of wheels, and she's even a pretty good journalist—but I *need* my Carly Jacks fix in the afternoon. Carly Jacks is one crazy chick. And now that she's kind of with Johnny Zacchara? Their chemistry is off the charts!

But wait a second. If this crapfest is on the TV now, then maybe that means...

I look at the clock and when I hear a familiar voice, I turn back to the TV.

Ooh, there's Patrick Drake—I was just thinking about him yesterday!

I settle in to watch, as happy as I can be at the serendipitous events—the bathroom bouts notwithstanding—that have conspired to bring it about that I am able to watch GH for the first time since last Thursday. I didn't get to see it last Friday because I was too busy doing pre-wedding shit and I've been on this boat since Sunday without even realizing I could watch this here and now it's Wednesday, so I've missed three episodes.

But wait a second. They're talking about something and I don't understand this. They're saying that Robin—Robin Scorpio, Patrick Drake's wife; Robin Scorpio, who's been on the soap like forever—is dead. How is such a thing even possible?

"How is such a thing possible?" I scream at the TV, rising up to my knees and clutching my hair. "Robin is *dead*?"

This information is so shocking, I don't know what to do with it. The soap mag said something bad was going to happen to her, but *this*?

Then, as the show cuts to commercial, I remember we're in port now and that maybe my cell phone works. Quickly, I call the one person I know who will care about this as much as I do.

"Sam," I say when she picks up, "what the fuck is going on? How can Robin possibly be dead?"

"She's been dead since last Friday," Sam says in a bored tone of voice, like this is old news.

"You mean you knew about this and you didn't tell me?"

"What—and spoil your wedding? I do know how you feel about Robin."

This is true.

"So how'd she die?" I ask, not sure I really want to know. But, you know, I *have* to know.

"Explosion." There's some chomping so I know Sam is eating. She's probably in my place, eating my food and drinking my beer and watching my TV. Well, my old place. After next week, and the closings on my condo and Helen's house, that place will be someone else's and I'll be moving into the house I bought with Helen on the other side of town.

I hope that if Sam's consuming all my consumables, she's at least taking care of Fluffy while she's doing so.

"Robin was working on that serum to save Jason's life," Sam goes on. "You know, from that brain thing he's got? But then some toxic chemicals spilled, she insisted on going back into the lab for the serum even though Patrick begged her not to, then the emergency door locked shut behind her to protect the rest of the hospital from the spillage, she had enough time to get the vial to save Jason into some little slot in the door and Patrick was able to get it on the other side, but then, well, with all those toxic things spilling in that small closed space—kaboom!—she was vaporized."

"Vaporized?"

"Well, all the rescue worker gave Patrick afterward was her wedding ring, so I guess you'd call that vaporized. There was no indication of there being any other remains left."

"It sounds awful."

"I know, right? And poor Patrick, he was watching through

the window in the doorway, so he saw his wife die right before his very eyes."

"I can't believe I'm hearing this."

"See now why I didn't tell you earlier? I knew you'd react this way."

She's right. I'm absolutely devastated. It's like I've lost a member of my family.

"Of course now," Sam continues, "naturally, Patrick's on a rampage, refusing to save Jason's life with the serum because saving the stupid serum cost Robin her life. It's a big fucking mess. Oh, shh, show's back on."

I settle back down to watch, with Sam still on the other end of the line, and we continue to talk during commercials.

"So how's Fluffy doing?" I ask after they cut to the break following Police Commissioner Mac Scorpio receiving the news that the niece he raised as his own daughter has died trying to save a hit man.

"He's good," Sam says. "He's settled down a bit now that he's gotten used to you being gone, plus I've been spending more time over here."

I knew it. Still, ouch on the cat. I wouldn't have thought I could be replaced so easily, even with just a feline.

"I'm sure he misses you, though. He keeps looking at me like, 'Hey, what happened to The Man? Did he do something bad like I did that time when I got sent to the basement?'"

"Poor guy."

"I know, right? And poor me too. It's not the same not having you right next door."

"Well, I haven't officially moved out yet."

"No, but you will be moving straight into your new home as soon as you get back, so."

Show's back. Poor Sonny. He totally breaks down when he learns about Robin. Well, who can blame the guy?

"Things good with Lily?"

"Never better," she says.

"Everything going OK with the jobs so far this week?"

"Good enough. Oh, by the way, you were right about

the Ryan job and Hidden Lagoon. That was totally what the customer wanted, even if she didn't know it herself."

Of course I was right. Paint is the one thing I know. Paint: It never lets you down, and I never let it down.

More GH and now it's Carly talking to Shawn. I used to have high hopes for Carly and Shawn, but now that I've seen her with Johnny Z, I just hope the writers let this one ride for a while. And now Patrick's talking to Jason's wife, Patrick's refusing to save Jason's life and then it's fifty-five past the hour. End of show.

I click off the TV.

"Robin was vaporized," I say, "so there was no body. You don't think that somehow Franco's still alive?" Franco is a recurring psychopathic character named Franco who also happens to be played by the Hollywood actor James Franco. It's all very meta. "I mean, I know we saw Jason kill Franco and all, but maybe that's just what we're supposed to think? Maybe in reality Franco is really still alive and he just orchestrated all this to get to Jason like he's always doing?"

"Never mind that now," Sam says. "You're supposed to be on your honeymoon and yet you're watching GH while yakking on the phone to me. What gives?"

So I explain about the norovirus.

"Oh, I've heard about those things," Sam says. "Harsh. That's why I never take vacations. Too much shit can happen. So you're both sick with this thing?"

I explain about how we were both sick and about the pill and giving it to Helen and her feeling better this morning.

"Aw, so now she's nursing you after you made the big sacrifice and then nursed her?" Sam's not usually an "Aw, that's so sweet" kind of girl but that's exactly what she says to me now.

"Not exactly," I explain. And then I further explain about the beautiful day, me not wanting Helen to miss it and me urging Helen to get out there and enjoy herself.

"And she just went?" Sam says.

"Well, no," I say. "I really had to talk her into it."

"But still, she went."

"Yes, but—"

"But nothing. *You* wouldn't have gone off and left her behind."

I try to object to this. "Maybe I—" But Sam's on a roll.

"You wouldn't have. You're Mr. I'll Carry This Pill In My Mouth That Could Save Me And I Won't Swallow It And Instead I'll Bring It Back To You And Transfer It To Your Mouth— which, I might add, is kind of gross—So You Can Feel Better Quicker. *That* guy would never have left his sick wife behind."

"But I was starting to feel better. It wasn't like I was going to *die* or anything."

"I don't care," Sam says. "You never would have done that to her and she should never have done that to you. Fucking women."

I keep trying but no matter what I say, I can't convince Sam that what Helen did was OK and by the time we hang up the phone, I'm starting to have my doubts too.

*Was* what Helen did OK?

But as soon as the doubts enter my mind, I shrug them off, push them aside.

So what if maybe Helen does a few things differently than I would.

Aren't differences between people what make the world go around?


An hour later, I'm still lying there, digesting the death of Robin and what Sam said, when I hear the cabin door click open.

My wife bounces into the room, still in her bikini, her hair slicked back with water. Now there's a face.

"I had the most *amazing* day!" she says, all exhilaration. Then she must see something in my expression, because her own changes. "What's wrong?" she says, coming right over to me. "Are you still feeling poorly?" Looking sympathetic, she places a hand on my forehead.

"That too," I say. "But also, Robin died."

"Oh no!" She takes one of my hands in both of hers.

"What happened?"

"She blew up in the lab, trying to save Jason. One minute she's there and the next—poof!—vaporized."

The image is still fresh in my mind because even though I never saw it when it first happened, they reran that part near the end of today's episode. Soaps'll do that.

"How awful!" She pauses, looks confused. "But who's Robin? I never heard you mention any friends named Robin before. And you say she worked in a lab?"

"On *General Hospital*," I say.

"Oh," Helen says. And just like that, the comforting hands are removed from mine and she moves away from the bed, starts unpacking a wet towel and things from her carryall. "That's too bad."

Sam and me've tried getting Helen interested in GH, and she even watched it with us occasionally in the beginning, but she's really never taken to it in the way that we have.

"It really is," I say. "Too bad, I mean. Even though I've only been watching the show for a little over a year, I've seen flashbacks to when she was just a little kid on the show. She's been on, like, forever. How can they do that to a legacy character like that?" I'm still in shock. "The mind reels."

"I can only imagine," Helen says.

And just like that I realize that Helen can't imagine, nor does she particularly care.

"So, how was your day?" I ask.

She brightens. "It was *amazing*!" she says again. "I met a really great bunch of people—German tourists—and we played volleyball on the beach all day."

"That sounds like fun," I say. "Did you remember to put suntan lotion on? I'd hate to see you get burned."

"Oh, it was fine. One of my new friends took care of it for me. So, do you want to get ready for dinner?"

I think of the idea of food. It's been over twenty-four hours since I've had anything other than liquids, but after what my body's been through, I'm still not ready for food.

I explain as much.

"So I guess, then, I don't know," she says, "I'll go find something and eat it back here in the room?"

When she puts it like that…

"Why don't you get changed and go to dinner?" I say. "Really, just because I'm not up for it, that's no reason for you to be cooped up here."

"You sure?" she says.

I assure her that I am.

And once again, after a quick clothing change, my wife is gone.

A few hours later, maybe around nine P.M., she returns.

The two nights I ate with her, we were in and out of the dining room in less than an hour.

"Wow," I say, "you were gone a long time. Did Boris and Natasha and Tom and Daisy suddenly get more interesting?"

"No," she says. "I didn't eat with them. I ran into those German tourists I told you about and we decided to exercise one of the other dining options."

"Oh," I say. "That's great."

And it is, right? I mean, I do want her to have a good time on our honeymoon, don't I? Still, it's inescapable that I'm starting to feel a little bit put out.

"You up for getting out?" she says.

I think of how tired I'm feeling. I know I didn't do anything all day but being sick takes a lot out of a person, sometimes in more ways than one. Plus, there's still that whole thing about the loss of Robin.

"I don't think so," I say. "I'm sure by tomorrow I'll be good as new again."

"You sure?" she presses. "There's a lot going on tonight. I'd love you to meet my new friends."

"I'm sure," I say. "But why don't you—"

Do I even need to say what happens next?

• • •

The red numbers on the digital clock switch over to 1:05 A.M. as I feel someone slide into bed next to me.

I yawn, half asleep as Helen turns her back on me but scooches backward until she's nestled into me so I can spoon her from behind.

"Nice night?" I say.

"It was great," she says. "We finished off by having drinks in the casino after the late show. But before that, we went to karaoke. They all got up with me and we did 'Fernando.' In Spanish."

"Wow, I'm sorry to've missed that."

This is both true and not.

I love seeing my wife have a good time, but listening to a bunch of German accents sing one of an awful Swedish band's worst songs in Spanish?

"Oh, and between karaoke and the late show," she says, "we went bowling."

"In that dress?"

Obviously, she's not wearing it now, but when she left earlier for dinner she was wearing a green version of the red dress she'd worn on the first night out.

"I took my heels off," she says, as if that would be the problem with bowling in that super-tight mini-dress. She snuggles closer. "You'll be well enough to do things tomorrow, won't you?"

"I'm sure of it."

# On the Beach

The next morning, when I open my eyes, I see that my wife is up bright and early again, already in her bikini. This one's cut just like the skimpy Cerulean Sky one, but if it was paint I'd be forced to conclude that the color is Canary Yellow. I've never actually been a fan of Canary Yellow—I've seen too many kitchens ruined with that clichéd color—but anything looks good on Helen.

"Are you going to finally get out of the room today?" Helen says. "This is our last stop before heading home."

When she says it, it hits me that it's true. We were at sea the first two days and then I missed the next two days when we were in the Bahamas and then Tortola because I was too sick. If I don't get off today, I will have spent my entire honeymoon on the boat.

"Of course," I say. "I'm feeling terrific."

But the truth is, I am not feeling terrific.

As we hit the beach, a private island owned by the cruise line, I am not feeling terrific at all. It's paradise here—the sand is practically pink, the blue-green ocean clear with the vista only broken by the cruise ship anchored in the distance, the temperature a perfect eighty-five degrees with no humidity—but the kind of sick I've been is worse than anything since I was a kid and I'm still feeling weak.

So Helen and I find two lounge chairs under an umbrella down by the water and after I put suntan lotion on her—wow, whoever did this for her yesterday did a great job, I think, as I notice there aren't even any tan lines as I shift the strings of her bikini to make sure I've got her covered—we settle in to read.

She's got some work she brought along while I'm reading a literary novel by one of those Jonathans from Brooklyn. It's actually not half bad. It's about this family and then some stuff happens.

About an hour into the sunbathing, Helen puts aside her work.

"I think I'm going to go see if anyone's up for volleyball," she says. "Want to come?"

"Nah, I'm good here," I say. Really, I'm not up for volleyball. Normally I'd love to play—I love any competitive sport, including tackle bowling—but in my weakened condition, with what little food I've consumed in the past few days, I'd probably go up for a spike and just pass out.

"You going to be OK here with your book?"

"Absolutely. It's just getting to the good part. The patriarch, The Uckoy—he's known as The Used Car King of Yonkers, right, like in the title of the book? He let his descendants take charge of his fleet of dealerships but it turns out he hates retirement and now he wants it all back. Everyone's so mad, I'm thinking a lot of people will die before this is all over with."

Turns out I was right about that. An hour later and both the oldest daughter's husband and the trusted accountant of The Uckoy have bit the dust in a spectacular fashion. For a literary work, there's a lot of graphic death going around, but I suppose so long as the author keeps throwing around words like ineluctable, termagant and enisled, no one will label it a mystery.

Truth to tell, I'm feeling pretty enisled on my lounge chair, but that state will not hold for long because apparently I have a visitor.

"Would you care for a drink?" The voice is very young but given the question, I'm expecting the questioner to be an island waitress, so I'm half surprised when I look up.

• • •

Standing before me is either a little girl or a midget. She's only about three feet tall but it's hard to tell how old she is because she's all covered up, wearing a pink terrycloth robe that comes down to her ankles, a matching towel wrapped turban style around her head and big sunglasses that cover most of her face. They're so big, they slide down her nose and she pushes them back into position with an annoyed forefinger. On her feet, she has bunny slippers, so I'm going to go with the theory that this is a little girl and not a midget.

Geez, she looks a little young to be hustling drink orders.

"My mother says that when you're out in the sun," she continues before I have a chance to answer, "you should drink something every hour. I've been watching you for an hour. You haven't had anything to drink."

Her sunglasses slide again. Clearly, this is a source of ongoing annoyance because this time, after she shoves them back into position she just holds her forefinger there. Insurance.

"You know, you're right," I say, feeling a little lightheaded as I rise to a more sitting position. "Maybe I should—"

"I'm Willow," she says, cutting me off. Now she thrusts out the hand that's not attached to the finger that's holding the sunglasses in place. "Just give me your keycard and I'll get us some drinks."

"I don't know if I should—"

"Do I really look like a thief to you? What do you think, I'm going to find some kind of wizard who will take your card and then magically find a counterfeiter who will make a copy of your keycard for me out of the generosity of his heart so that late at night I can sneak into you and your wife's cabin while you're sleeping and take all your stuff? Puh-lease."

I seize on the only thing I can make sense of in that nonsensical mess.

"How do you know I have a wife?" I say.

"You're wearing a wedding ring, duh. I suppose that could mean you're gay—I *am* from Connecticut—but I saw you with that woman before. Tallish—or at least taller than me. Red hair. Lousy taste in bikinis."

I agree that that is an accurate assessment of my wife. While I resent having to admit to the last part, particularly since Helen's taste in bikinis is only bad in terms of the Canary Yellow one, saying yes is easier than trying to explain why the answer is both yes and no.

When you've been sick for a few days, you need to forsake qualifying things.

"I knew it," Willow said. "I saw her with you before and I see her with them now."

"Them? Who's them?"

"*Them.*" Willow gives a chin jut, causing me to look over my shoulder. "The volleyballers."

And there's my wife, in her Canary Yellow bikini, spiking the volleyball and then leaping around in triumph. The people she's playing volleyball with are all tall, all blond, all men.

And they're all wearing Speedos.

What the...?

"Keycard," comes Willow's impatient voice. "If I'm going to get us those drinks, I'll need that keycard."


Helen's still celebrating her spike, jumping around in circles as her teammates high-five her and clap her on the back. Did one of those guys just pat her on the butt? I'm sure that didn't happen. She's jumping and circling and as she circles in my direction, she catches me looking.

"Johnny!" she calls, waving her arms. "Come on over here!"

I rise from my lounge chair and do as I'm directed.

"I want you to meet my new friends," she says. "This is Dirk, Felix, Jurgen, Klaus, Maximilian, Sven, Swen, Uwe and Wolfgang."

I feel numb as I shake hands, the handshakes I get in return all hearty, and I am unable to tell a Sven from a Swen. Really, in those Speedos, they all look alike. They're all sporting their junk proudly in those tight suits and I vow to look anywhere but down. If I do, I know I'll only feel insecure.

It occurs to me that when Helen told me she made new

friends, she never said anything about them all being guys.

"And this is Johnny," Helen says to them.

What, not even *This is Johnny, my husband*?

I try not to look as offended as I feel.

"Do you want to join us?" Helen says. "The teams'd be uneven but the other side isn't as good as mine. They could use the help."

"Thanks," I say, feeling unaccountably further miffed, "but I also made a new friend."

"Oh?" Helen raises her eyebrows, questioningly. And now it's her turn to look a little miffed.

"Yes. Her name is Willow. She went to get us drinks."

"Hey!" a small voice behind me yells. "Where do you want me to put your keycard?" I turn, and there's Willow, holding a drink and my keycard in one hand, a second drink in the other hand which is also holding up her sunglasses, different than the ones she had before; these are harlequins.

"So yeah," I say to Helen. "I guess I'll go have that drink now."


"What's with the new sunglasses?" I ask Willow.

"I thought they'd work better than the others, but they don't," she says. "I charged them to your card along with the drinks. I hope you don't mind. If you'd like, we can set up a plan for me to pay you back. What kind of APR do you accept?"

"What kind of…How *old* are you anyway?"

"I'm eight, if it matters. Do you think it matters?"

"I guess it doesn't really. And, um, don't worry about paying me back for the sunglasses."

"I wasn't," Willow assures me. "What's your name?"

"Johnny."

"Johnny what?"

"Johnny Smith."

"OK, Mr. Smith."

"I'm not Mr. Smith. No one calls me that. Mr. Smith is my dad. Come to think of it, no one calls him that either. We're not really a Mister kind of family."

"My mother says you should always use Mr. or Mrs. or Ms. when speaking to your elders, unless of course they're family members. My mother says it's a damn shame that kids these days are brought up with no manners."

"And that's how she puts it? A 'damn' shame?"

"Not exactly. I edited that part in."

"So what are we drinking?" I ask, tilting my plastic cup toward her in a toast.

"Virgin Pina Coladas. You don't think they'd give me anything with hooch in it, do you?"

We sit in silence for a bit, watching my wife cavort with the German volleyballers.

"If she was my wife, Mr. Smith," Willow says, sipping on her virgin Pina Colada, "I wouldn't let her do that."

"Marriage isn't about letting or not letting your partner do stuff," I say, like I'm some kind of expert. Really, this is only my sixth day as a married person, and already I'm feeling confused by it all.

"I'm just saying," Willow says. More sipping. "What do you think the odds are that they're all gay?"

At her voicing my secret hope, I choke on my own drink. Then I do the math.

It is estimated that one-tenth of the world's population is gay. If that's true, and I see no reason to doubt scientific fact, then if there are nine guys in Speedos playing beach volleyball with my wife, chances are, rather than all of them being gay, chances are that they're all straight and their one gay friend stayed back home in Germany.

"Not good, I'm afraid," I admit.

"That's what I thought," Willow says. "But I was kind of hoping. You know, for your sake."

"There's nothing wrong with what they're doing," I say. "They're just playing volleyball."

"Maybe so," Willow says, "maybe so. But when is a volleyball *just* a volleyball?"

"Thank you, Sigmund Freud," I say.

"Who?" For the first time since I met her, Willow looks puzzled. Historically speaking, usually I have that effect on females much more quickly than this.

"It doesn't matter," I say. "Let's just say, you make a good point."

Back in the mini-suite at the end of the day, Helen is once again aglow with excitement while I am feeling somewhat less than. And not because I've been sick. And not because Robin is dead, although that still hurts.

"You seem a little quiet," Helen says. "Didn't you have a good day today?"

"Oh, it was great," I say. "And, you know, I finally got to meet your *friends*."

"Why'd you say that like that?"

"Say what like what?"

"*Friends*. I've heard you use that tone of voice only once before, when you said the name of that guy from my office: Daniel *Rath*bone."

"I don't think I say those things in any particular way."

Do I?

"Didn't you like them?" Helen persists. "I was so sure you would. I wanted you to."

And suddenly I can tell that she did.

"What's not to like?" I say. "They're good at volleyball, they had solid handshakes—I told you what Aunt Alfresca always said about handshakes, right?"

"That they shouldn't be limp like a cod."

"*Exactly*."

"Every time you tell me that, you use the Italian word for cod, but I can never remember what that is."

Wait a second. Is she trying to tell me that sometimes I repeat myself?

"Anyway," I say, "their handshakes were solid." I can't help adding, "Like their bodies." And further can't help adding, "In those Speedos."

"I know, right?" She strips off her bathing suit and heads for the bathroom. "I didn't think anyone still wore those."

You and me both, kiddo.

We're all dressed for dinner. I'm wearing my chinos and another white button-down shirt plus a tie that Helen helps me with, because it's one of those formal dinner nights, and Helen's got a dress on, same cut as the red and the green, only this one's black. With her deepening tan, she looks amazing in it, insanely sexy too.

We're almost to the open doors of the dining room when I hear a stampede of thundering feet.

Oh, shit. I hope the ship didn't hit anything.

But when I turn to see what the commotion is, I see Helen's new friends running toward us.

Soon, they're surrounding us, or really the Germans are just surrounding Helen. Me, they're wedging off to one side.

Since I can't keep their names straight and I know I never will, I'll just assign random names to various speakers.

"Helen, don't eat in the dining room," Dirk says.

"Come with us, Hel," Uwe says.

Wait. Someone else calls her Hel? I thought only her family and I did that.

"We're going on deck," says Wolfgang.

"We're going to get pizza," Sven says.

"And beer," Swen says, "lots of beer."

"We're going to eat pizza and drink lots of beer and watch the sun sink into the ocean," says Felix.

Chatty bastard, isn't he?

"But Johnny and I were going to—" Helen starts to say, but Maximilian cuts her off.

"Oh, Johnny! We did not see you there! Of course, you will come too."

Gee, thanks.

"What do you think?" Helen says. She poses it as a question, like it's up to me, but I see the hopeful look in her eyes. I can tell this is what she wants to do. It's not really what I want to do, but...

"Well, I guess it's preferable to having Boris tell me I ask too many questions or watching Tom and Daisy head for divorce court, right?"

"I know." Helen throws her arms around me, which reminds me that while these German guys may be her new friends, I'm still her new husband. "It'll be fun, right?"

As I hug her back, I think:

*Sure, it'll be fun. Won't it?*

Oktoberfest is probably overrated, I'm thinking as Uwe approaches the table. On cruise ships you can get these buckets of ice in them with a half-dozen beer bottles shoved in among the ice and Uwe's got buckets of beer balanced on each arm like some kind of drunken milkmaid.

I twist off a top and chug down most of the bottle as I listen to them recount, blow by blow, the last two days of beach volleyball. Apparently, the first day in port—when Helen and I were both sick in our cabin—the Germans also played volleyball on the beach, but apparently that pales in comparison to the time spent playing with Helen, which they continue to recount.

Did I mention that they're doing this blow by blow?

After the pizza and the beer and the sunset—and getting our pic snapped by a roving photographer who positions us with Helen in the center, her constellation of Germans surrounding her with me off to one side like some lonely star—the decision is made to go bowling. I say "the decision is made" because I had no part in making it.

At bowling, I get to see what the Germans already discovered the night before: what my wife's backside looks like when she bends over to bowl while wearing a skintight mini-dress.

Well, at least as promised, she does take off her sky-high heels to bowl.

There is that.

. . .

And then we're at karaoke again.

I really don't feel like singing, so Helen goes up herself. The song she picks? "The Winner Takes it All," by ABBA. When she opens her mouth and the first notes come out, it's really just…*not good*. But then before it can get even worse, I hear that thundering sound again, and there's Dirk, Felix, Jurgen, Klaus, Maximilian, Sven, Swen, Uwe and Wolfgang, surrounding my wife to help her with her song.

"The Winner Takes it All," as music trivia experts can tell you, was originally called "The Story of My Life"—even music trivia experts who hate ABBA can tell you this—and as the ten sing their song about the humane obliteration of a heart, I hope it will not be the story of mine.

"*The gods may throw the dice/their minds as cold as ice*," the Germans sing, *loudly*, I might add. In fact, their singing drowns out Helen. I listen to their voices and must grudgingly admit that they sing very well, even this crappy song. And as I watch them sing, arms around each other's shoulders, crowded in around the mic, it hits me: They're *saving* Helen, saving her from being exposed yet again as being a truly awful singer.

Then I look around at the crowd and people are actually enjoying themselves and sure, the song still sucks, painfully so, but the crowd is enjoying it because the ten singers are enjoying *themselves* so much, just like the singing actors in *The Deer Hunter* and *My Best Friend's Wedding*.

And that's when it further hits me that:

Shit. The Germans are having my movie moment with Helen.

The decision is made, after karaoke closes for the night, to skip the show and head straight for the disco.

In the real world, in this day and age, no one would ever be caught dead saying, "Let's go to the disco." But there can be no arguing that this gaudy room on the ship, with its mirrored balls and strobing lights, is exactly that.

Geez, I hope they don't play Bee Gees music all night.

Thankfully, they do not, just some other awful crap. I can't stand the idea of dancing to this but suddenly my wife is Ginger Rogers with nine Fred Astaires.

Which is how I wind up sitting by myself, watching them form a conga line, Uwe or Dirk or Felix's hands on my wife's swaying hips as they snake through the other dancers. *Ce-le-brate good times—come on!* I think not.

There's a TV behind the bar, the Mets are on, the Mets are winning 10 to zip, and I don't even feel like celebrating that.

I'm still sitting there, observing the dancers, when a woman comes up to me. She's OK-enough looking, as far as non-Helen women go, with clean brown hair and she's wearing some gowny type of purple dress.

"I was wondering if I could impose on you to dance…" she starts to say, and I don't hear the rest because I'm already half out of my chair, thinking this could be good, I'll show Helen, she'll see what it feels like to watch me dancing with someone else.

But then the woman finishes her sentence, and what she finishes it with is, "…my daughter Willow? You made such a strong impression on her today and she does love to dance."

A head pops around the corner of the woman's gown. The head no longer has a turban, there's no annoying sunglasses anymore so I can see her eyes are blue, and her hair is somewhat carroty.

"Hi, Mr. Smith!" she says. Then she comes all the way around and I can see she's all spiffed out in a pink lace dress, white ankle socks and shiny black shoes. On her wrist is a rhinestone bracelet.

I did not know kids dressed like that anymore.

"How ya doin, Willow?" I say.

"I'll be fine if you'll dance with me," Willow says. "It's been my lifelong dream to dance with a man other than my father on a cruise ship."

It must be nice to have such exact dreams, so easily fulfilled by one single thing.

I look at the mother and she's got this "please" look on her face as in "please do this thing so my daughter will stop talking about it" or maybe it's simply "please don't break my little girl's heart."

So what choice do I have?

I extend the crook of my arm in Willow's direction—"Miss Willow, if you will, please," I say—and she latches onto it with both hands.

Once we're out on the dance floor, since "Celebration" is still playing, I launch into my yahoo dance but Willow starts yelling at me over the music.

"Mr. Smith! Mr. Smith, I can't dance like that! I prefer the box step! Do you know the box step?"

"I think you better lead, kid," I say.

So she does, holding out her hands and forcing me into position.

We're silent for a time, and then:

"Mr. Smith, did you know you dance like a stick figure?"

"Women have been known to make that observation before," I allow.

Willow looks tickled at being lumped in with *women*.

"Mr. Smith? Do you think it's working yet?"

"Is what working yet?"

"Making Mrs. Smith jealous."

"Making…"

"That's why I asked my mother to ask you to dance with me. You looked like you needed help."

That's what this is? A *pity* dance? And here I was thinking the kid maybe had a cute little crush on me when all the while it was just *pity*?

"So is it working, Mr. Smith?" Willow prods eagerly. "Does she look jealous yet?"

I look over at my wife, still conga-ing with the Germans, all of them oblivious to me.

The Germans, the Germans, the Germans. I don't know why I keep saying that. It makes it sound like I'm obsessing about the fact that they're German. But it's not like I'd be ecstatic if a bunch of Italian guys or Russian guys or Swedish guys were constantly crowding around my wife. The nationality is not the point.

"Nah," I say, "I'm sorry to disappoint you, but I don't think so, kid."

When Willow's mom comes to collect her after the dance, Willow thanks me, I thank her, and as Willow starts to walk away, her mom leans back and, with a lascivious smile, says, "You are *hot*, Mr. Smith."

After the night I've had, I must admit, that is mildly gratifying, but still.

What the fuck?

There's more of drinking and singing and dancing and everything, including eating, but none of it matters.

None of it matters except that when we finally do get back to our cabin, even though we haven't *you know* in three days, since before I got sick, I am not in the mood, and I'm not in the mood because, quite frankly, I'm starting to get a little pissed.

So I just roll over and, without thinking of what Helen might want, I go to sleep.

# Stormy Weather

Who knew that if you booked a cruise to the Bahamas in June, there's a chance you'll run into a hurricane on the voyage back? I guess there's a good reason it's called Hurricane Season.

And now, on our last full day at sea, there's a good reason why Helen and I don't leave our mini-suite, which should be a good thing—you know, all that alone time. The boat is rocking like crazy and it's all we can do not to fall over the side of the bed.

So instead of going anywhere, we stay there and do something we've never done before. We fight.

Well, maybe *fight* is too strong a word for it. I mean, no voices are raised and even though I'm thinking the word *selfish* and from the look on her face it's a safe bet she's thinking the phrase *big baby* or maybe even *dickwad*, nothing like that comes out of our mouths. Instead, other things come out of our mouths, and it all starts with me saying:

"So how come, when you told me you made a bunch of new *friends*, you never mentioned they all happen to be guys?"

"I didn't realize that was a salient feature of who they are."

"Not a—"

"They're just people, Johnny, good, fun people. What does their gender matter?"

Can she really not know?

And why is it that I'm suddenly feeling in the wrong here?

"Would it have been better," she continues, "if I'd hooked up with a bunch of women instead?"

"Well, now that you mention——"

"Because that was never going to happen. Have you not noticed, that I don't make friends with women easily?"

Have I not—

"My only real girlfriend is Carla, Johnny. I grew up in a household of guys. Well, except for my mother. I've always been more comfortable with guys than with girls. They *like* the things I like. I'm more *like* them."

I think about this and I realize that this is true.

This must be why she had to fill out her side of the wedding party with Aunt Alfresca and Alice. Having no other real female friends besides Carla, she had no one else to ask.

And now that I think about it, I can see why she'd have trouble getting along with other women. Helen is so smart and beautiful, other women probably feel threatened being around her.

Still, is this what our life together is going to be like, Helen hanging out with a bunch of guys while I'm relegated to an observer's role, feeling left out, when I'm usually the one at the center of any group of guys?

When I mention feeling left out around the Germans, Helen gets a little heated.

"And whose fault is that?" she says, clearly frustrated. "You were so...*not yourself* around them. Usually you're so engaging. All guys love you—you know that. But it's like you couldn't be bothered to try. You wouldn't play volleyball during the day—"

"I'd been sick!"

"—and then at night, all night long, you wouldn't sing, you wouldn't dance, you wouldn't talk to anybody."

"I'd been sick!"

"So, what—the whole world's supposed to stop and take care of you?"

And that's when I hear the words *big baby* and possibly *dickwad* coming off of her.

"*No*," I say, frustrated myself now. "The whole world doesn't have to take care of me." And this is when that insidious word *selfish* enters my own brain, as I add, "But it would be nice if my own *wife* did!"

"You're the one who told me to go off and have a good time. You said there was no point in us both staying cooped up and being miserable."

Did I say that? Were those the exact words I used?

Funny, now, I don't remember. Still, I don't think I said *exactly* that. Would I have ever referred to us being in a cabin together, even if one or both of us was sick, as being cooped up and miserable? Not after just a few days of marriage. But would Helen have really felt that way if she'd stayed behind with me?

And now I am feeling cooped up and miserable because that stupid storm is keeping us cooped up and I'm miserable because we're stuck in this stupid vortex of a sort-of fight—how did we get here? and so quickly? I don't want us to be a couple that fights, not even a little bit—and I don't know what else to do to get out of it, so I do the first thing I can think of which is to kiss the girl.

I kiss my wife, and I can't believe this is the reason for it, to shut her up. I kiss her because I don't want to hear her say or imply anymore that I'm being unreasonable for being upset that she spent so much time hanging out with a six-pack and a half of blond Teutonic gods in tight Speedos when I was still sick, especially since I was only still sick because I'd given *her* the only magic pill we had between the two of us so *she* could get better quicker.

I kiss her to shut her up. Oh, it sounds so awful when I say it like that. But when she kisses me back, and her kiss is immediate and fierce, I remember all the reasons I do love her, why I fell in love with her in the first place, because she's smart and she's beautiful and she's funny and she loves me and she's just so *Helen*, and as kissing turns into the first love-making session we've had since Monday—can it really have been four days? how did we let so much time pass? Oh, right. I was in the bathroom. Anyway, as one thing leads to another, before I stop thinking at all, I think: Maybe this really was all my fault. Things will be fine once we're home, as if none of this ever happened. Well, except for the good things.

From there on, everything is just sensation and wonder.

. . .

About fifteen minutes after we're done, I realize what time it is and fiddling around on the nightstand, I find the remote, click on the TV.

"You're going to watch TV?" Helen says. "Right now?"

"GH is on now," I say. "It's Friday. They may have flashbacks to when Robin was younger. I love those flashbacks. Some of them go back so long ago, it's practically historic, like before Sonny had two big dimples and only had one."

"I'm fairly certain it's not possible to grow a second dimple."

"I know but still."

"And you're really going to watch this now?"

Now I start second guessing myself. "Well," I say, "only if you don't mind."

She shakes something off. "Oh. No. It's fine," she says. "I'll just get some work done while you watch."

And that's what she does and it is fine, I can see that whenever I look at her during commercial breaks.

And it's fine later on, when the storm clears and we at last emerge for our final dinner and we get thundered by the Germans who want to whisk Helen away but after looking at me, instead of saying yes, she says, "No, thanks. It's Johnny's and my last night together here. I want to spend it with my husband."

# All Ashore

I am so glad to be back.

# Over the Threshold

We stop off at my condo first because I want to pick up Fluffy before heading over to the new house.

Carla was supposed to take care of things on Helen's end, letting the movers into her place, and Sam was supposed to handle everything on this end, both letting the movers into my place and letting them into the new house so they could move all our stuff in.

This means that when I walk into my condo, the last time I'll ever be here except for the walk-through with the new owners later on in the week, the place is entirely empty except for the cat and his things, which Sam has left all waiting for me in the middle of the living room: litter box, litter, food and water bowl, bag of food, basket of toys, kitty-transport thingy.

And there's the gray-and-white puffball cat, who starts racing toward me as I step through the door, Helen behind me. I drop to my knees to greet him, but when he's just inches away from me, Fluffy skids to a sharp stop and does a one-eighty, settling down on his haunches. Even though his back is to me, his head is slightly tilted to one side, so I can see his upturned nose and it's almost like I can hear the wheels of his furry brain spinning. It's like his brain is saying, *Just act all nonchalant. There's nothing to see here. Be cool.*

"Oh no," I say. "You're giving me the back?"

"What's that?" Helen says. "What are you talking about?"

"Can't you see?" I explain. "The cat is giving me the back. It means he's offended and his feelings are hurt. This manifests itself as anger. But then he doesn't want to show that either because that would prove he cares so now he's pretending like I don't exist. He's all mad at me because I went away and left him, so now he's trying to pretend he doesn't care that *I* exist."

"Wow," she says. "You're really getting a lot out of that turned back."

"I've been reading up." I turn my attention back to Fluffy. "Aw, don't be like that," I say. "It's not like I had a choice. I *had* to go away. It was my honeymoon!"

"Hey!" Helen says. There's an "I resent that" tone to her voice but I figure she must be kidding. I mean, after all, she's gotta be more mature than the cat, right? She must know I'm just saying that to make Fluffy feel better.

I inch over on my knees in Fluffy's direction and when I'm right behind him, I snake my hand around until it's right under his chin—one of his sweet spots—and start scratching him like crazy.

"Aw, who's a good cat," I say in my talking-to-the-cat voice, which is a voice that is a bit lower than me speaking naturally and which also tends to go more quickly, running words slightly together.

At first, Fluffy resists, but it's not too many scratches before he gives in and his purr box starts motoring.

"That's better," I say. "You're a good cat. Yes, you are. Yes, you are." He turns to face me and we rub noses.

"I don't remember you talking to the cat so much before," Helen says. "Did you always do this?"

"It's something I read about." I scoop Fluffy up in my arms, prepare to put him in his kitty-transport thingy. "Hey, Helen," I say, "can you grab his other stuff?"

Home sweet home.

We pull up in front of the new house. Could I *be* any more excited? Sure, I'll miss being next-door neighbors with Sam. Where was she when I picked up Fluffy, by the way? Oh, right. Sam being Sam, which is not a whole lot different from Fluffy being Fluffy, not being there was probably her version of giving me the back, meaning she's offended at me for moving out of the condo and leaving her behind. That's cool. I'll catch up with her at work on Monday or maybe tomorrow she can come by and watch the game, one or the other. So anyway, back to…

Home sweet home.

I've never been a homeowner before. I mean, sure, I owned the condo, but that wasn't a house. Now, *this*, on the other hand…

The house isn't a wimpy color, you know, like a beige or anything, but it's not something ridiculously bold like purple which has a tendency to piss off the neighbors. It's not modern, like a McMansion, but it's not super-old like an original Colonial. It's not like the yard is practically nonexistent, but it's not so sprawling as to qualify as a selfish use of natural resources. The house is neither too small nor too big, kind of like the Three Little Bears' house, and the porch—

"Are we going to go inside today, Johnny?" Helen cuts into my reverie.

"Oops, sorry," I say, "of course."

But then I have trouble figuring out the logistics of the thing. The thing is, I want to carry Helen over the threshold but when I got out of the car I immediately reached for the kitty-transport thingy with Fluffy in it, so now I've got the key in the door and the kitty-transport thingy in my other hand and…

"Here." I try to get Helen to take the kitty-transport thingy but she just holds up her hands.

"No, really, that's OK," she says.

"But I have to carry you over the threshold," I say.

"No, really. I'm good."

"Just take it."

"OK, fine."

So she takes it in one hand and then I scoop her up into my arms while she's still holding it. I look deep into her eyes, she looks back into mine, we share a solid kiss and then I step us over the threshold, symbolically embarking on our new life together in our new home.

"Wow," I say, "the inside of this place is so…*white*. Crowded too."

"Can you let go of me so I can put the cat down now?" Helen says.

I bring the rest of Fluffy's stuff in.

Here's the thing: Yes, I knew this place was all white inside when we bought it. I mean, obviously we did look around inside the place. But we liked the exterior and the neighborhood and we did like the interior layout. Now sometimes you'll see condos that are all white on the inside, like the owners just leave it the way it was when they first bought it, kind of like my place was until I painted it all in the hopes of impressing Helen. And sometimes you'll even see expensive houses in magazines where everything is a pure white, which I think is supposed to look all classy and arty and shit, but which I always think just looks sterile; and no, that single red apple on the table in such houses does not make a fashion statement. But I guess I didn't think before we moved in here about what all this vast whiteness was going to look like. We're going to have to do something about this.

And here's another thing: There're tons of gift-wrapped boxes, wedding presents we never got a chance to open, including an enormous one that nearly reaches the ceiling.

"I'll bet that's the grandfather clock I asked my parents for," Helen says happily.

Wait a second. Grandfather clock? I'm not crazy about those things, all that *bong, bong, bong* all the time. But I guess I can worry about that later.

Because here's the last thing: When we hired the movers and simply told them to bring everything from both our places over here, I guess we weren't planning ahead. In the living room beyond the foyer, there are two of everything: sofas, armchairs, ottomans, coffee tables, even TVs. And none of the things match each other. Something's going to have to be done about this too. Of course, the two big-screen TVs are not necessarily a bad thing.

And at least the hardwood floors that run throughout the house look good.

Helen heads for the staircase to the upstairs as I pick up the litter box, which is kind of full and not just with litter. Geez, you'd think Sam, knowing we were coming back today, could have cleaned it out one last time.

"What are you doing?" Helen says.

I look over and see she's stopped at the base of the stairs.

"Trying to figure out where to put Fluffy's litter box and other things," I say.

"In the basement, of course."

"OK."

I head for the door to the basement.

"Wait," she says.

I stop.

"You're going to do that now?" she says.

I turn. "Well, yeah," I say. "I kind of have to. Being plunked into a new environment can be very unsettling for a cat. Fluffy may even get confused and reject his litter box altogether because it's not exactly what he's used to. I don't think that's something either of us really want, so I'm just trying to give him the best chance to acclimate himself."

"I see," Helen says. She drops down to sit on the bottom step. "I guess I'll wait then."

I hit the lights and decide that the landing six steps down is the right place for the litter box, so I leave it there. Then I set up the food and water bowls in the kitchen. Man, this room is white. Finally, I open up the spring-lock metal door on Fluffy's kitty-transport thingy.

"Come on out, guy," I say.

But he just stays there.

"I think he looks freaked," I say. "He does this same thing sometimes when I take him to the vet. Does he look freaked to you?"

"I'm not sure I'd go so far as to say that."

"Come on, guy." I go to the toy basket, grab something, come back with it. "Look what I've got. It's Blue Bunny."

Blue Bunny is Fluffy's favorite toy. I'm not really sure it's a bunny—sometimes, I think it looks more like a mouse—but it is definitely blue, vividly so. It's small and plush, it's got a rattle inside that makes noise when you shake it, and there's an elastic string extending from between its ears. At the other end of the string is a little plastic hoop and when I hold onto that hoop and make the whole thing jiggle, Fluffy goes crazy chasing after it, which is very cool to see because Fluffy's usually such a super-mellow cat it's hard to get him excited about anything. In fact, Blue Bunny excites Fluffy so much, I've had to repair that elastic string several times after Fluffy's batted right through it, which means that string is starting to get a little short.

Oh no. What will happen when Blue Bunny can no longer be made to leap?

But I don't have to worry about that just now because Blue Bunny is doing his job, luring Fluffy out of the kitty-transport thingy, and Blue Bunny continues to do his job as Welcome Ambassador as I bounce him to the kitchen to show Fluffy where his food and water will be from now on. Fluffy stops to take a drink which is a good sign. If he were really freaked out, he might not be able to eat or drink at all. But then, come to think of it, it is a hot day, so maybe he's just really thirsty.

Then I bounce Blue Bunny some more—now he's kind of reminding me of those bouncing balls in karaoke machines that tell the singer when to sing each syllable—right to the basement door and then down to the landing.

Fluffy sniffs the edges of the box, looks at it, looks up at me.

"Really," I say, "it's the same. It's just a new location. Kind of like when they move your favorite TV show around in the schedule. The show itself doesn't change."

I guess maybe he doesn't understand that part.

"Really," I say again in my most encouraging voice.

Fluffy puts one tentative paw into the box and then searches for somewhere safe to put a second paw. Fucking Sam. This part of the process could have gone so much smoother if she'd just put a little more thought into things.

But then, eventually, all four paws are in and…

"Success!" I scream up the staircase. "He peed!"

"That is…marvelous," I hear my wife say in a voice that does not quite match mine in enthusiasm.

Well, I shrug to myself. She hasn't been living with Fluffy every day for the last year like I have. I suppose it would be unfair of me to expect her to match my level of excitement at Fluffy's every feline accomplishment.

Back upstairs on the main level, Fluffy sniffs the air and starts walking around the edges of the room.

"Look!" I say. "He's walking the perimeter!"

"Is that some kind of technical term for what he's doing?" Helen wants to know.

"I don't know," I say. "If it's not, it should be. But anyway, I think what he's doing is figuring out just what exactly are the dimensions of his new space."

"You don't think maybe he just feels like stretching his legs after peeing?"

"Oh, look! Now he's jumping onto the window ledge."

Whether he was figuring out the dimensions of his new space or whether he was simply stretching his legs post-pee may be open to debate—although I do know which side I come down on—but he definitely did just jump up onto the low-lying ledge of one of the long Victorian windows in the living room.

"Here," I say, going over and turning the gold latch at the top of the window, "let me open that for you. You know, you're right? It is a little stuffy in here."

"Do you think we could look at the upstairs now?"

And upstairs turns out to be just as white as downstairs.

"So we'll do some painting," I say, "and sooner rather than later."

It's just as crowded too.

"And we'll have to get rid of a few things," Helen says.

I can't say I blame her. The master bedroom in the new house is a generous size, but I don't think it was ever meant to hold two beds like this.

Still, I wonder which things will go?

"You know what?" Helen says. "I'm hungry. Are you hungry?"

I shrug. "I could eat."

Come to think of it, we got off the boat at a little after eight this morning, it's after one in the afternoon now—I'm thinking I could eat a lot.

"What do you think?" I say. "Do you want to go for a second breakfast, maybe grab a burger somewhere?"

"I know," she says and for the first time since I carried her over the threshold, she looks truly excited. "Let's go...*to the grocery store.*"

I take her hands in mine.

"You mean like two married people?" I say.

She squinches her eyes with glee and smiles wide. "That's *exactly* what I mean."

Wow, our first real married-couple type of act as a married couple.

I kiss her and even though we're both starving, that kiss turns into us doing another married-couple type of thing before leaving for Super Stop & Shop. Deciding whose bed to do that thing in does slow us down—hers—but not by much.

Ah, married life.


The problem with going to Super Stop & Shop—where we walk through the aisles, arms linked as we push the cart together, just like any other married couple—is that when we come back, someone has to actually make the lunch.

I never realized how not-big-on-cooking we both were before. But tuna sandwiches seem manageable once we locate the boxes that contain kitchen items and fish the can opener out of the last box we look through, plus there's the added bonus that Fluffy gets to lick the can. We can't decide which set of dishes will be our primary ones, though, hers or mine, so we leave those in the boxes for now and just eat off of paper towels instead.

Once lunch is over, there's the question of what to do next.

"Want to watch some TV?" I suggest.

I don't think the Mets're playing until later, but there must be some sports thing on—probably a lot of sports things—and I wouldn't mind stretching out on one of the sofas with a nice cold beer.

"Right now?" Helen says.

If Sam asked me a question like that, I'd probably answer with something sarcastic like, "No, of course not. I meant a week from Tuesday at 8:23 in the evening." But this is Helen, so instead I say, "Well, yeah."

"But shouldn't we unpack first?"

I think, *Unpack?* But out loud, I say, "You mean right now?"

"No," she says. "I meant maybe a week from now."

I look at her blankly.

"Of course I mean now," she says.

"But that seems so...*sudden.*"

"So what do you propose we do? Wait a year?"

"Well, no, not that long. I mean, that would be ridiculous."

She just looks at me.

"So," I say, "I guess we're unpacking now?"

We're working on the bedroom, because in a way that is easiest. See, even though our dressers don't match each other in style, we do each need a dresser so we don't have to decide which one to get rid of. We're also unpacking books.

"It's so quiet in here," Helen says. "Mind if I turn on some music?"

She's found her CD player and set it up on one side of one of the beds, her bed, but that's OK because after what we did in it earlier, I'm feeling very fond of that bed.

Maybe I'm feeling too fond of it and that fondness is distracting me, because without thinking first, I say, "Sure. Whatever you want."

It's only as she's slipping a CD into the player that I begin to wonder what she'll be putting on and it's only as I hear those four annoying blondes from Sweden start to sing "Waterloo" that I realize, *Holy crap—ABBA again*.

How did I not anticipate this moment?

Oh, right. I thought when we left the cruise ship behind us, and karaoke along with it, that that would put an end to ABBA. But now it's followed us back, it's here, it's *in my home*, and what the hell am I going to do? My wife loves this, she's singing along with it for crying out loud. How am I going to ever tell her that her taste in music sucks?

I *can't* tell her *that*.

Can I?

No, no, of course I can't.

So what do I do? I suffer through *the entire disc*, right up to the very last song, which is also "Waterloo," because it's not enough that they sing it in Swedish as the first song of the album, oh no, they also have to close out the album with the English version.

Please, shoot me now.

But not before I make sure that we don't have to listen to anything like *that* again.

"Honey?" I suggest. "Maybe we could just listen to whatever's on the radio for a while?"

She thinks about it for a moment but then shrugs and switches the CD to radio.

Phew. I can go back to unpacking my books in peace.

"Hey," I say, "my cat book!"

"Your what?"

"This is the book I was telling you about," I say. "It's what's been helping me figure out what goes on in Fluffy's mind. See the title: *What's Going on in Your Cat's Mind*. Where do you think I should put it?"

"On your side of the bed?"

And that is…?

I look around, realize we definitely are going to be using her bed, so I find her second night table and put my book on it.

After I put my book in its place, I realize my wife is singing. The song on the radio is one I like, "Lonely No More" by Rob Thomas, only I've never heard it sung before quite like Helen is doing now and then she commits a cardinal sin. She sings, "*Open up to me, and let me do your girlfriends.*"

No, no, no, no, no! How can someone garble a line of a well-known song like that? And what kind of sense would that make? *Open up to me, and let me do your girlfriends.* Dude! If you're doing your girl's girlfriends, there's a good chance you'll be lonely forever, even I know that.

So of course the line isn't that absurd thing Helen just said. The line is *Open up to me, like you do your girlfriends.*

Big difference. Are we all agreed on this?

Oh my god, my wife is a song garbler.

But wait. I can just tell her this, can't I? I can gently tell her that the lyrics she just sang were wrong, and further explain chapter and verse on why they're so wrong. We'll laugh about it together, right?

Then I realize, no, I can't tell her. She'd probably be hurt— who likes to have it pointed out to them that they're foolishly wrong?—or worse, angry at me. No, I better just keep quiet on this one.

But really. Crap. A wife who can't sing is not great. A wife who garbles lyrics is not great. But does she have to be both?

Maybe she doesn't do the garbling thing all the time?

By the time we finish unpacking I will know:

She does it: All. The. Time.

# Sunday Bloody Sunday

I'm jolted out of sleep by a sound I hope to never hear again in my life, that of my wife letting out a bloodcurdling scream.

"What?" I shout, my eyes snapping open just in time to see her body jackknife. Holy shit. Did she just become possessed by the devil? Is she having a heart attack?

But no. As her arms and legs settle down into a more natural position, I see Fluffy sitting on her pelvis.

I know it's wrong but, yeah, I laugh.

It's probably just relief, relief that neither her soul nor her body are in imminent peril, but I do laugh.

Which is obviously a mistake.

"It's not funny," she says.

"I know but—" I laugh again.

"Just get your cat off of me," she says.

*My* cat? But now that we're married, shouldn't Fluffy be *our* cat?

Still, judging from the stormy expression on her face, perhaps now is not the time to argue semantics with her.

"What the hell was that?" she says after I scoop Fluffy off of her. "Why would he do that?"

"Aw, he wasn't trying to hurt you," I say. I look over her body at the alarm clock and just as I suspect: It's six A.M. "He's just being a feline alarm clock."

"He's doing what?"

"It's a habit he's gotten into." It's true. It's something he started doing during the past three months before we got married, the period when Helen and I stopped sleeping together. "He knows what time I get up in the morning on weekdays, so sometimes he jumps on me around this time to make sure I get up and fill his kibble bowl, maybe play a little."

"But it's Sunday. He does this on Sunday too?"

"Well, yeah. I mean, he's a cat. He doesn't know what day of the week it is."

"I don't think it's a good idea for him to sleep in here anymore," Helen says. "I think we're going to have to start closing the bedroom door when we go to sleep at night."

Close the...?

"I just can't have it, Johnny," she says. "It *hurt*. And did you see how scared I was? I thought I was going to have a heart attack."

Well, when she puts it like that, but...

Seriously? I'm going to have to give up sleeping with Fluffy?

I close the door with Fluffy on the other side. I wonder what's going through his furry little brain. "Did Fluffy do something wrong?" "Why you do Fluffy like this?" Whenever I picture Fluffy's thoughts, it's always with him thinking of himself in the third person because I don't think "I" is in his vocabulary. He must be so confused by all this.

But as Helen spoons her back into me, that feels good; and when we fall asleep together for another few hours, that's also good; and when we take our first shower together in our new home, that's even better.

Working out what we're going to have for breakfast is more of a chore, but somehow we manage. And Fluffy doesn't look *too* hurt.

Later, Helen comes to me with a list she's made.

"Even though it's a Sunday," she says, "I called the movers. They're going to come back today and take away everything we don't want."

I look over the list. Apparently everything we don't want includes everything of mine with two exceptions: my pool table and the second big-screen TV.

"I guess this is OK," I say. "Maybe at some point you and me can go shopping? You know, pick out furniture we both like?"

"Sure," she says, "that could happen. We might do that at some point. OK, can you let the movers in? I'm going out for a bit."

"Out?" Without me? "Where are you going?"

"To pick up paint charts. I want to start looking for colors to paint this place."

Paint? But isn't paint *my* job?

# Can't Trust That Day

Monday arrives and with it a return to work. Helen left a half hour ago and I'm watching the morning shows with Fluffy when the doorbell rings, so I hit the mute buttons before answering it.

"Sam!" I say when I see who's on the other side.

Sam and me aren't much for hugging but we indulge now because it's rare for us to go a whole week without seeing each other. We actually talked on the phone yesterday; in fact, I called everyone to let them know that Helen and I were back. While I was on the phone with Sam, I started to invite her over to watch some sports but Helen shook her head so I never finished the invitation, which was actually kind of awkward. If memory serves, I believe it went something like, "Hey, you want to come over and…go to work with me tomorrow as planned?" When I got off the phone, Helen said it was simply that it was our first weekend in the house and she thought it would be nicer with just us two, plus we had a lot to do, which was understandable.

And anyway, none of that matters now because Sam's here.

"Ooh, I like what you've done to the place," Sam says, snaking by me into the foyer and beyond.

"You do?" I say, unaccountably pleased. Hey, I know what I'm feeling—I'm feeling house-proud!

"Not really," Sam says, turning in a circle to take in the living room and the dining area that's through an arched doorway. "It's just what you say when you walk into someone's new home." She shakes her head. "I don't get it."

"What don't you get?" I'm still reeling from the revelation that maybe she doesn't really like what we've done with the place.

"I let the movers in for you. I know they brought your stuff in. I saw it with my own eyes. So, where'd it all go?"

I explain.

"Let me get this straight," Sam says. "Helen made you get rid of all your stuff but kept all of hers?"

I guess that pretty much sums it up but those are not the words I would have chosen.

It doesn't help that just then, the grandfather clock Helen's parents gave us bongs eight times—loudly—to mark the hour.

"Well," I say after the eight bongs are finished, "I did get to keep my pool table and the big-screen TV." I give a chin nod to the far corner of the living room where both TVs are set up perpendicular to one another in front of the sectional and ottoman. The movers had left them side by side but Helen and I decided this arrangement would work better.

"Now that is cool," Sam says.

"I know, right? Check this out." I pick up the remotes and unmute the two TVs. "I can watch *Morning Joe* and one of the stupid network morning shows at the same time. No longer will I have to choose between politics and finding out what Brangelina are up to."

"It's like the ultimate in luxury."

"I know, right? I do worry about Angelina, though. Do you think she eats enough? I don't think she eats enough."

"She's spraying to mark her territory."

"Angelina?" I say. I'm confused.

"Your wife," Sam clarifies, "the little lady."

"Don't call her that, Sam. Leo's wife was The Little Lady and she's gone."

"OK, then, Mrs. Smith. Mrs. Smith is spraying to mark her territory, just like a cat. That's why there's only her stuff here except for the extra TV."

I narrow my eyes at her. "Were you reading my cat psychology book while I was gone?"

"Maybe."

"And do you have to call her Mrs. Smith? You make it sound like she should be baking pies."

"Yeah, but didn't Angelina play Mrs. Smith in that movie she and Brad fell in love with each other while filming—you know, *Mr. and Mrs. Smith*?"

"Do you think we could go to work now?"

We stop by the paint-supply store first and then Leo's to pick up coffee. Even though Leo's been dead since the fall, the coffee shop is still called Leo's, only now a young husband-and-wife team own it and nothing is the same. It's got, like, a couch in the middle of it now. On the whiteboard, all the breakfast and lunch specials are listed in various scripts, each with a different-colored Magic Marker, and it's all just too bright and perky for first thing in the morning. The coffee doesn't even taste the same. And the husband part of the ownership? Not a big sports fan.

I'd find another place to get coffee in the morning, but, you know: force of habit. And the owner isn't really a douche or anything, so long as we don't talk about sports.

Guy's name is Bailey.

Him: What can I get you?

Me: Two large coffees to go—one black, the other practically white and sweet—and the largest sugary thing you've got.

Him (two minutes later): Here you go.

Me (paying): Thanks.

Him: No. Thank *you*! Have a good one!

Definitely not the same.

I leave Leo's, juggling two cups of coffee and a bag with some large sugary thing in it for Sam and there's Sam in the passenger side of my truck. She's got the windows down because the day is already shaping up to be a scorcher but she likes to put off turning on the AC for as long as possible. She's got on a T-shirt and super-short shorts—summertime work uniform for her—and her insanely long legs are propped on my dashboard as she bops to some music she's got coming from the radio.

I get in the car, switch the station to The Wave, hand over her sugar injection, and tell her to get her feet off my dash as I key the ignition.

Pull into traffic, her legs are still on the dash.

"If we get in a really bad accident," I say, "your legs'll

get broken."

"If we get in a really bad accident," she says, "I'll probably be dead anyway so I doubt I'll notice."

Fucking Sam.

She slugs back some coffee. "So, how's married life treating you? The Wife getting on your nerves yet?"

I'm not sure that "The Wife," said like that with capital letters, is an improvement over Mrs. Smith.

"It's great," I say. "And no, why would she be getting on my nerves?"

"I don't know." Sam shrugs. "I always figured that's what happens after two people get married."

"Says the woman who knows so much about marriage."

"You never know. I might do it someday. It's legal in Connecticut now. So tell me more about your honeymoon."

I start by telling her the good things—like how it constantly amazed me and still amazes me that Helen is my wife—but before long, for some inexplicable reason, I find myself telling her about karaoke and Helen's singing.

"Your wife, that gorgeous creature, can't carry a note?"

"Not a single one," I say. "On top of that, she garbles lyrics." I tell her about the Rob Thomas song.

"Who does that?" she says. "If you don't know the lyrics, why would you make crap up?"

"I know, right? Isn't it better to just hum? You know, *dee-dee-dee-dee-dee*?"

"Exactly," she says.

We ride in silence for a few minutes, feeling complete satisfaction in our agreement on this issue. But then I start to feel bad. Should I be talking about my wife like this, out loud, even if it is only with Sam?

The guys on The Wave are talking about the Ike Davis situation.

"Could only happen to the Mets," one of them says. "Whoever heard of Valley Fever before this? And did you hear about that guy who lost nearly a whole year's playing time when he had it? OK, we're taking calls. Caller, you're up. Who've we got on the line?"

"Never mind that," says a voice I know and love well, a voice that just last year I used to think of as Sexy Caller until I discovered it was Helen. "The media does this all the time. You people find one guy—one guy!—who was out for nearly a year with it, but that's not a typical case. It's really not a big deal. Davis'll be fine. So untwist your panties and just let the team play ball."

*Click.*

God, I love that woman.

"Well," Sam says, "at least she didn't sing her call in. So, are you getting on her nerves yet?"

"No," I answer immediately. "Of course not."

But wait a second.

Am I?

We pull up in front of the job, the McMillan place.

"What're we doing today, Boss?" Sam asks.

"Living room," I say, "Chartreuse Chamber's the color they picked out."

Sam makes a face. "That sounds purely awful."

"I know, right?"

"We're going to have to stop doing that," Sam says.

"Doing what?"

"Saying 'I know, right?'"

"But we always say that. We've been saying that, like, forever."

"I know and that's why we have to stop. We need something new, fresh, *different*."

Huh.

"Um, I'll get right on that," I say. "Now where were we?"

"You were telling me the McMillans want a Chartreuse Chamber living room, I was saying it sounded awful, then you said that thing we're not going to say anymore, so it's my turn to pick up with: And we're going to do it anyway?"

"Yup."

"You're not going to try to talk the customer out of it, like you had me do with the Ryan job?"

"Nope."

"How come?"

"Because sometimes you have to just let other people do whatever they want."

"That sounds so Zen. Stupid too. You do know that living room's going to look like shit, right?"

"Yeah, well."

On the plus side, the man of the house is home and sometime after we bond over the Mets but before the job is finished, he offers me free use of his ski lodge in Vermont for a week next winter. I'm supposed to call ahead.

Sam rolls her eyes at me as I tuck his business card into my pocket.

Hey, at least I've still got it.


Nice thing about being your own boss, you can set your own hours. This means that by three in the afternoon, Sam and I are stretched out on opposite ends of the sofa in my new home, feet meeting somewhere in the middle, each with a bottle of Sierra Nevada Pale Ale as GH starts.

On both TVs.

"Oh my gosh," Sam says, "this stuff with Robin Scorpio is killing me."

"It's brutal," I agree. "People finding out one at a time, having to relive it each time someone new gets told—it's like water torture, but you know, not."

The nice thing about having a best friend you've had for years is that you can say anything, even bust each other's chops, or just say nothing at all, simply living your lives side by side as Sam and I do for the next half hour while watching GH.

Well, it's not *just* the two of us. Fluffy, who's grown a taste for music, wanders in at the theme song, plopping himself on the coffee table and staring at the screen.

Is it just me, or is this cat acquiring more personality? And here I thought cats were supposed to become boring once they were no longer kittens.

We're at the halfway mark in the show, which you can always tell because there's a longer commercial break, when I hear the front door open.

"Hi, honey," my wife, who can't sing, does a surprisingly impressive Ricky Ricardo imitation, "I'm home!"

I hear the sound of things being dropped on the table in the foyer, high heels being dropped on the hardwood floor, and then my wife rushes into the living room, arms outstretched. The show's just come back on. Still, I'm about to rise anyway when Helen skids to a stop in her bare feet.

"Oh," she says. "Hey, Sam."

"Hey, Mrs.," Sam says. "I heard your honeymoon was good." She tilts her beer in Helen's direction. "Get you a beer?"

Sam's long been in the habit of offering me beverages in my own home. It can be occasionally annoying, but mostly I've gotten used to it.

"Hey, honey," I say, "you're home early. How was your day?" When I say this, I feel very much a married man but in a good way. There's nothing wrong with clichés when they work for you.

"It was annoying," Helen says. "People kept asking me if I was pregnant yet. I guess that's what happens when you get married."

"Seriously? Huh, no one asked me that today."

"Probably because the only person you see is Sam. For years, people asked me when I was going to get married, like everyone has to live the same cookie-cutter lives. Now I'm married for about five minutes and everyone wants to know when I'm going to have a baby. Even the guy from the courier service asked."

"The guy from the courier service? What'd you tell him?"

"I told him to shut up and leave my package."

Ouch.

"At least I got out early," Helen says. "There was an unexpected continuance in one of my cases."

"Cool." I'd really like to hear more about her day, but I hear the voice of Carly Benson Quartermaine Corinthos Jacks coming from the television and my attention is torn. I love Carly. "Hey, you wanna watch with us?"

"What're you watching?" Pause. "Oh, GH." Pause. "You're watching GH on both televisions?"

"I know, cool, right?"

Sam gives me a dirty look, like she's been doing all day whenever I slip up and say "I know, right?" like we used to. But this time, I give her one right back. Hey, I interjected a "cool" into it, giving it a different spin. And anyway, change is hard!

"I don't know," Helen says after a long pause, during which her gaze has ping-ponged between me and Sam, apparently trying to decipher our dirty looks but then giving up. "It seems like it may be a gross misuse of the dual-TV system."

I hear feet padding away and look up to see my wife walking out of the room.

"Hey, where're you going?"

"Dining room. I think I'll look over those paint charts."

I shrug and turn my attention back to Carly.

Show's over and, swear to God, there are tears in my eyes.

I look over at Sam and she's blinking. "Damn stupid allergies."

"Oh, come on," I say, "that was a killer, wasn't it? When they told Robert Scorpio, I thought I was going to lose it. No parent should ever have to hear about his only child getting vaporized."

"Would it be any better if he had a dozen other children?"

I think about that. "OK, you got me there."

Into my line of vision comes a furry paw and I see Fluffy, stretching himself before he returns to what has come to be one of my favorite of his positions. His back legs are extended behind him and a bit to the side, but his front paws are curled inward under his chest, head erect, very Sphinx-like—you know, if the Sphinx were a furry gray-and-white puffball.

"I love it when he does that," I tell Sam. "Doesn't he look like a lion?" I think how Fluffy looks exactly like one of those stone lions that guard the front of the New York Public Library as I scratch him under the chin and transition into my talking-to-the-cat voice: "Who's a proud lion? Who's a proud lion? Yes, you are. Yes, you are."

I stop, suddenly horrified at what I'm doing, what I hear myself saying.

"Oh no," I say, turning to consult Sam. "When I call him a proud lion, do you think that confuses him? I mean, do you really think he *thinks* he's a lion?"

Before Sam can answer, though, a voice comes from the dining room.

"No, I don't think the cat thinks he's a lion. In fact, I'm fairly certain of that." Then: "I'm going upstairs to take a shower. When you get a chance, you might want to look at these colors I've picked out."

I hear my wife's tread going upstairs, the bathroom door closing and the shower being turned on.

"It's that Alanis Morissette song all over again," Sam says with a sigh, "except that this really *is* ironic."

"What're you talking about?"

"Last year you got a cat to impress the girl and you started watching GH to impress the girl. Well, it turns out the girl doesn't like either. In fact, I think it's safe to say she hates them both."

"Wait. What? What are you talking about? Helen doesn't *hate* Fluffy. How could anyone hate Fluffy?"

"So maybe hate's too strong of a word, but she's certainly not in love with him. Not like you are."

"I am not *in love* with my cat."

"'Who's a proud lion?' Seriously, Johnny?"

Before I can object any further, my best friend has one more thing to say.

"And, since this is Me Giving Advice Away For Free Day, even though you didn't ask: Yup, you're definitely getting on her nerves."

# A Problem with Paint

*Paint: It Never Lets You Down.* That's the motto of the business my dad, Big John, originally started; the business I then worked side by side with him on for years; the business I now carry on with on my own, keeping his name and legacy alive even though, you know, he's not dead.

So the idea that paint, that substance that I love, should somehow turn around and bite me on the ass is beyond belief. And yet that is exactly what has happened, spectacularly so.

Not really knowing what to say after Sam informed me that I get on my new wife's nerves—or at least that some of the things I do have that unfortunate effect; which, I'm positive she's just wrong, wrong, wrong about, particularly the part about Helen disliking Fluffy—I head into the dining room to look at the paint charts Helen mentioned; Sam's right behind me, but she may just be going to the kitchen to grab herself another beer.

What I see when I get to the dining room, the chosen colors circled in heavy black marker...

I'm not even sure I can say.

"This is just so...*wrong*," Sam says.

"It's gotta be a joke, right?" I say.

"Absolutely. Must be. I mean, no one in their right mind would..."

We mull. And we're still mulling fifteen minutes later when Helen comes into the room, hair slicked back and wet from the shower, work makeup scrubbed off, shorts and Mets T-shirt on. I smile. I love when my wife looks like this. Hell, I love all of her looks: buttoned-down for work, casual like this, fancy, stark naked—really, it's all good.

"So," she asks, excited, expectant, "what do you think of

the colors I picked out?"

Unless she's an amazingly good actress who's also pulling my leg, the thought occurs to me that the colors she circled are no joke to her.

"It's been a long day," Sam says, "so, yeah, I think I'm just going to go now. Same time tomorrow, Boss?"

I nod my head and she's gone.

Helen jams her hands into her pockets and does a slight bouncing thing, like she can barely contain herself. "Well?" she prompts.

"Well, um, yeah, these are…different."

"But good different, right?"

"Well, I guess they're not all different. I mean, Canary Yellow. Which room is that for, by the way?

"The kitchen."

"Ah. Canary Yellow for the kitchen—that's pretty conventional."

"Conventional?"

"It's"—the word is out of my mouth before I think about it—"cliché."

"Cliché." The dead sound to her voice clues me in to the fact that I have made a verbal faux pas. And yet I can't stop myself.

"Everybody does it," I say. "You can't swing a dead cat in Fairfield County without hitting a Canary Yellow kitchen."

I at least exercise the restraint needed to keep from saying that Canary Yellow kitchens are anathema to me.

"What about the other colors I picked out?" she asks.

I regard the two colors in question: Pink Panties and Paint It Black.

"Which rooms were you thinking of these for?" I ask. I'm thinking: Maybe guestroom for one, garage for the other?

"The master bedroom. Both of them. I was thinking two walls of each."

"That's, um, radical."

"Is that better or worse than cliché?"

How best to answer this…Neither? Both? Certainly, I shouldn't answer it truthfully.

I decide on a different tack.

"I guess I'm just a little surprised, that's all," I say.

"Surprised?"

"Well, yeah. I mean, I figured we'd be picking out colors together. And, you know, paint: it's what I do."

"So that means I shouldn't have any say in my environment here?"

"Well, no, but—"

"Since you're the expert, you should get to decide everything and I just have to live with it?"

"Let's put it a different way. Your expertise is the law, and I respect that. I certainly would never presume to interfere with one of your cases."

"Oh no? Hel-*lo*! Loopholes? Does that ring any bells with you?"

*Loopholes.*

Crap.

Before I met Helen, Steve Miller, one of my clients who's now my friend and who happens to be a defense attorney, asked me for help finding a loophole for one of his clients, because legal loopholes are kind of a hobby with me. It turned out that Helen was the losing D.A. on the other end of that case, which I found out only after meeting her, which eventually led me to trying to throw her off the track by telling her that I don't like loopholes at all; but rather, I favor ice holes, sinkholes, peepholes, and blowholes. I don't think I've left anything out, other than the fact that I wound up looking like a real asshole. Also, apparently I wasn't as smooth with the talking as I thought because, apparently again, Helen has clearly known it was me behind that loophole all along.

"That was before I met you," I say. "I would never interfere with one of your cases now."

"Gee, thanks."

I look at my wife. She doesn't look happy.

Wait a second. Are we having an argument here? No, of course not. That can't be it. Still, she doesn't look happy.

"If we try with these, er, colors," I say, "will that make

you happy?"

She considers. "Yes," she says simply.

"OK, then." Really, how bad can it be? Besides, it's just paint. (I can't believe I just said that. *Just* paint? It's never *just* paint nor is paint ever necessarily just.) Still, we can always paint over it if it doesn't work.

Then something occurs to me.

"Hey, Hel," I say, "back when I first met you, those colors you had me paint all the rooms in your old place—how'd you arrive at those? I mean, those were so different than these."

And they were. Those colors were all so…tasteful, if noneventful. But these? Canary Yellow, Pink Panties and Paint It Black? It's like a Benjamin Moore horror show.

"Oh, that," she says. "I consulted an interior designer."

She con—

Shoot me now. I *hate* those people. Sure, sometimes they're right about things—I mean, I don't want to malign a whole group of people who aren't Ponzi scheme artists or anything—but so often they're just so wrong. And the results of the wrong ones? They never really say anything real about who their clients are.

But wait another minute.

Does this mean that my wife's real self is Canary Yellow, Pink Panties and Paint It Black?

To console myself, I drink lots of beer. And then, I start dinner.

It's only our third day here, so Helen and I are still figuring out the who-cooks-what-things-when logistics, but it seems fair that whoever gets home first should make dinner, which today would be me, even though she was also home well before four.

We have steaks, which is good. Any man can make a decent steak. It's almost embarrassing if he can't. After a quick call to Aunt Alfresca, I know how long to nuke the potatoes in the microwave. Considering what the plates will look like—dark-colored meat, at least on the outside; light-colored potato, at least on the inside—I think we're going to need some vivid color for an accent. Consulting the freezer, I settle on frozen spinach, read directions on the back of the package, and voila.

We eat in the dining room, even use candles instead of electric light. And it's…nice.

It occurs to me that for the first time in my life, I went to work this morning, came home from work in the afternoon, and my wife came through the door not long afterward. Being married to Helen—it is just one constant stream of firsts.

Between the beers and my thoughts, I'm feeling all rosy and warm, and when Helen laughs at something I say and I see a piece of green spinach caught in one of her dogteeth, I think: How cute is that?

And later on, when Helen and I snuggle on the couch watching some new-to-us TV show, *Shipping Wars*—that one trucker Roy really cracks me up, the way he leans out the window and shouts at another driver, "Why, yes, I do own the road!"—and Sam buzzes my cell to ask how things went with the paint chart, I extricate myself from the snuggle and take the call in the kitchen, where I tell Sam that the paint situation is fine and about how cute my wife looks with spinach in her teeth.

"I'm just going to say this once," Sam says. "Beware how the spinach turns."

What the hell is she talking about? I stare at the phone in my hand. Is that the name of some new soap opera?

# TGI-Poker-F

Between the rehearsal dinner two Fridays ago and being still on the cruise ship last Friday, it's been three weeks since we've had our regular poker game so by the time the end of the week rolls around, I'm itching to play.

Of course Sam's already in the building before the others arrive. She's been here since we knocked off work early to watch GH. What an episode. There's a lot of crazy shit going on. Kate Howard, highbrow fashion mogul, who was born Connie Falconeri, now has a split personality. You can tell when her alter ego, trashy Connie, is about to take over, because it happens whenever Kate puts on this dark red lipstick. Now Connie wants Johnny Zacchara to sleep with her and if he says yes, Sonny Corinthos will go absolutely nuts. Like I say, crazy shit.

Sometimes the guys arrive for the game one at a time at two-minute intervals, almost like they arranged it with each other in advance, meaning I might as well just stay there standing at the door until they're all in.

The first to arrive is Big John. Even though he uses the wheelchair most of the time these days, he uses double canes when he knows there will be steps, like my front porch, and that's what he's doing now. I'd offer to help but he's got his fierce leave-me-alone-I-can-do-it-myself scowl on and it's only a few steps so I let him.

"Johnny! How's married life treating you?" he asks when he reaches the top.

Now there's a question I'll never tire of hearing.

Maybe it makes me some kind of sap, but I don't care. I spent over three decades on the outside looking in, thinking I'd never have this thing, marriage, and now—poof!—I have this thing. I'm so grateful to have it, I will *never* get tired of hearing people ask me how it's going.

"Great," I answer. "How's things going with Aunt Alfresca?"

"Well, you know your aunt."

I do indeed.

Next up is Billy.

"It hasn't been the same without the game the last few weeks," he says.

"I know,—?" I feel Sam's glare and stop myself mid-word, switching gears to "I hear what you're saying." I look to her for approval but she rolls her eyes. Crap.

"So how's married life treating you?" Billy asks.

"Couldn't be better."

And here's Drew with a case of reinforcement beer. It's the cheap stuff but you gotta admire Drew's insistence on economizing even though the recession hasn't hurt him any. Plus, Stacy doesn't like him to spend too much on beer unless she's there to drink it.

"How's married life treating you?" he says, shoving the case into my arms.

"Terrific," I say.

Finally, there's Steve Miller.

"Sorry I'm late," he says. "I had trouble getting out of the office."

"You're not late." I do the math. "The first one only arrived six minutes ago. Well, unless you count Sam. She's been here for about four hours."

"So, how's married life treating you?"

What is it with these people and the constant questioning? It's like everyone's trying to take my marital temperature or something.

"Supercalifragilisticexpialodocious," I say.

"Come again?"

"It's dynamite."

I shut the door.

• • •

I'd clap my hands together to show it's time to get down to business, but I'm still holding Drew's case of crappy beer.

"I'll take that," Sam offers.

As she goes into the kitchen, I clap my hands. "So, who's ready to play?"

People grab beers, Sam pours a spare bowl of chips, and we all head for the basement. Big John makes it down the first short flight, but then we get to the landing, which is crowded with Fluffy's stuff, and he sees the longer flight extending downward.

"Whoa," he says. "I don't remember your old place having so many stairs."

"It's OK," I say. "I got it, Pop."

I scoop him up.

It's not the easiest scoop in the world. I mean, there's a good reason he's called Big John, although he is smaller than he used to be.

"You know," he says, "a third of a century ago, it was *me* carrying *you* around."

"Yeah, well," I say, "just returning the favor."

Downstairs, the others are already seated, having reserved two chairs side by side for us. The setup here is pretty much the same as it was in the old place. After GH, Sam and I positioned a huge piece of plywood over the pool table and arranged folding chairs around one half of it. It's not exactly an ideal way to play poker—the way the chairs are, it'd be way too easy to cheat from the corners or the end position—but it's how we do things and the only one we have to watch out for cheating is Drew. Really, the only major difference with this setup is that I no longer have a hula-girl chandelier hanging over the table, but I got rid of that shortly after Helen came on the scene.

"That's some kitchen you got up there," Billy says as I start to shuffle.

"It's very yellow," Drew says.

"Yeah," I say.

We painted the kitchen on Wednesday. We're supposed to do the master bedroom this weekend. I don't really want to think about it.

I'm almost done dealing when there's a thunder of light-footed steps coming down the stairs and there's Helen coming through the doorway. She's got on white shorts, a black T-shirt, and a green visor on her head.

There's a flurry of "Hey, it's the bride!" and a lot of hugging and kissing ensues. Helen grabs a folding chair from the small stack left against the wall and sets it up on the other side of Steve.

"Did I miss anything?" she says, scooching her chair closer to the table.

"Um, what're you doing?" Drew asks.

"What do you mean what am I doing? I'm going to play."

"*You* play poker?" I don't mean to sound so shocked but I kind of am. Helen's never mentioned an interest in poker before.

"I grew up with brothers. So sure, I've played a few times before. Why? Is my playing a problem?"

"Just don't tell the other wives," Drew says. "We've never had a woman in the game before."

Helen does a chin jut at Sam. "What about her?"

"That's just Sam." Drew does a dismissive wave. "The wives know she doesn't count."

This'll be good, I think. As much as I've been looking forward to getting back to my weekly poker game, part of me has been dreading it too. What with having to work all day during the week, it already feels like too much time apart. Now that we're married, it seems like we should be spending every free second together, so it'll be good to have her sit in on the game this one night.

Helen's chin juts out at me this time. "You going to deal or what?"

God, she's cute.

Turns out my wife can play cards, which we learn when she takes us to the cleaners on the very first hand.

"Well, this is fun," Billy says. "Anyone need another beer?"

He's handing beers around from the mini-fridge in the

corner when there's more thumping on the stairs.

*Thump. Thump, thump, thump, thump, thump.*

I look around the table, counting heads. Since no one's left to go to the bathroom, that can only be…

"Hey, Johnny," Big John says, "what's that thing your cat's got in his mouth?"

We all look at the cat, who's entering the room, dragging a doll by the hair. The doll is shaped like a Barbie, meaning she's stacked but has an absurdly tiny waist. And yet she's not like any Barbie I've ever seen so I don't think she can really be one, except for the hourglass shape. She's got slightly blue-tinged skin, a blue fairy dress on, plastic wings coming out of her back, and her hair—all ratty from Fluffy dragging her everywhere by it—is a vivid dark blue. No, I don't think she really is a legitimate Barbie, unless she goes by the name of Slutty Blue-Haired Fairy Barbie, which can't be right.

"We found her on the side of the street," I say. "I always take Fluffy around the neighborhood for a walk on his leash after work. One day, we saw the doll lying there. Fluffy was interested but I figured some little girl would come back for it. By the third day, I figured she was just abandoned so when Fluffy was still interested, we brought her home with us."

We all look at the cat some more.

Since we're such a mixed group, I refrain from going into the thing where I imitate what I imagine to be Fluffy's voice growling, "I *loooove* her."

"I think he thinks she's his girlfriend," I say. "I think he might be in love with her."

Fluffy's lying on his side now with the doll's hair in his mouth, pawing at her midsection like crazy with his back feet.

"That's kind of sick," Drew says.

"He's just a cat," I say.

Big John deals the cards this time. Helen wins again.

We do the thing where everyone talks about what's been going on at work.

When it's my turn, it goes like this:

"Not bad, but one of the jobs was a bit much. It was too crowded."

"Too crowded?" Steve says.

"New construction," I say, figuring that explains everything.

Apparently, though, Sam doesn't think anyone other than Big John and her and me will understand this, because she expounds, "What Johnny means is, there were a lot of other people still doing work there: Paul the Mason, Everett the Window Washer, Bob the Builder."

I'm half surprised when no one laughs at the last person she names. Well, I thought it was funny.

"It's not like they get in our way so much," Sam goes on. "It's just that they're always asking Johnny to do stuff with them. 'Johnny, do you want to go for a drink?' 'Johnny, you want to grab a bite to eat after this?' 'Johnny, why don't you come back to the house with me to watch the game?'"

"It's just too hard when they're all there at once." I shrug. "I don't want to hurt anybody's feelings and I can only be one place at a time."

"I had a great day at work," Helen says. "Daniel took a case off my hands that I've been hoping to dump on someone else."

"Daniel Rathbone?" Steve says.

Helen nods.

"Great guy."

"I know, right?"

Drew deals. Helen wins.

"Do you think it's too late to change the cat's name?" I wonder aloud. "It's just that, I've been thinking. His personality's been changing so much lately—Doesn't he look more like a Yoyo to you now?"

We regard the cat, our heads tilted to one side. He's curled up with his girlfriend now, asleep.

"Nah," Drew concludes. "He's still a Fluffy."

Billy deals. Helen wins.

● ● ●

At nine o'clock, cell phones begin going off with a few *pings* signifying text messages thrown in: first Billy's, then Drew's, then Steve's, then Big John's.

Well, that last one's new.

Soon, the room is filled with the sound of four people talking on phones and texting, some more loudly than others.

I know I'm a guy and everything—duh—so I'm supposed to be into every tech gadget that comes along, but I've never really gotten into the whole texting thing and neither has Sam. We talked about it once and we agreed we *like* hearing the sounds of other people's voices. We especially like hearing other people laugh out loud—literally—and we further made a pact: we're each responsible for killing the other if one of us ever, *ever* types out LOL.

Helen looks across the table at me. "What're they doing?"

"It's the wives," I explain.

"And this happens every week?"

I shrug. "Pretty much."

"It's kind of annoying, all that talking and texting. Don't they know we're trying to play a game here?"

"Hey, I don't do it," Sam says. Then she fishes her cell out of her pocket. "They'll probably be a while. Might as well give Lily a call."

"So, how've you been?" I ask my wife across the table and over the chatter of the others.

"I've been good," she says. "I married this great guy and today I had a turkey sandwich for lunch."

"White or whole wheat?"

"Rye."

"Ah, Rye. I've painted more than one house in Rye. You come here often?"

"First time, but I'm liking it. There's this one guy in the game who is hot-hot-hot."

"Is that a visor on your head or are you just happy to see me?"

And that's what we do: We make silly as-if-I-just-ran-into-you flirty small talk while the others jabber.

At last, conversations begin to end, cell phones get put away. Now the only one left on the phone is Billy, which means it's impossible not to hear when he half shouts, "I *said*, I'll be home whenever I *get* home!"

And then he's off the phone too.

"Problems with Alice?" I ask. I don't really want to, but it almost feels like it'd be rude if I didn't, like if you overheard someone saying they've got cancer and the next thing out of your mouth is, "Hey, anyone want some more chips?" I mean, how can you not ask?

"We've been fighting a lot lately," he says. "No biggie."

Isn't it, though? Alice has always been something of a prickly pear, but I don't remember ever hearing her and Billy fight before and certainly I never heard him raise his voice in exasperation to her like that. Come to think of it, Billy never gets exasperated. For as long as I've known him, he's been so mellow, like the human equivalent of the way Fluffy used to be before we moved into this house.

"Stacy and me are fighting too," Drew says.

Well, that really is no biggie. Drew and Stacy fight all the time. They fight so much, sometimes I picture them fighting with each other even before they met.

"Katie's not in the best mood," Steve says.

"Your aunt's a little quiet tonight," Big John says.

"What?" I say. "Is everyone fighting with their wives?"

"Not me," Steve says. "I just always do what she wants."

"Your aunt and me don't fight," Big John says.

"Never?" I say.

"Not so you'd recognize. She gets mad about stuff but when she does, she expresses it by coming into the living room and switching the station from sports to something she wants to watch."

"But doesn't that piss you off?" Drew says. "That'd piss me off."

"Not really," Big John says. "It's a small price to pay for

peace in the house. And HGTV isn't such a bad channel. Hey, did you know you can get a mansion in Nebraska for what you'd pay for a shack around here? Why didn't I ever think of moving to Nebraska?" He doesn't wait for an answer. "But you know what's really weird?" Again with the no waiting. "It's supposed to be House *and* Garden TV. But it's always all houses and never any gardens. Where did all the fucking gardens go?"

I deal again. Helen wins. Yeah, that's right. She wins and wins and wins.

The game breaks up around ten because no one except Helen has any money left.

We see people out at the door.

"See everybody next week," Helen says.

"Oh," Drew says. "Will you be here next week? Playing again, I mean."

"I was planning on it," Helen says.

"That's great," Drew says. "I'll bring more money."

"Now that you guys are back," says Billy, the last to go, "we should get together and do something—you know, the two couples."

"That sounds great," I say, and I think it does. Now that I'm married, what could be more fun than getting together with another couple and doing married-couple shit?

"Fantastic," Helen says. "Why don't you and Alice come over here tomorrow night?"

Wait. So soon?

"We'll make dinner," Helen offers.

*We* will???

"I'll tell Alice," Billy says. "She'll be thrilled."

And he's gone too.

"That was so much *fun!*" Helen says, throwing her arms around my neck and laying a loud kiss on my lips.

"It was," I say, "it really was. But were you serious? You'll be playing in the game every week?"

"That's what I was thinking." She pulls away a bit. "Don't you want me to?"

I pull her in tight again. "Of course I do."

Don't I?

Of *course* I do. The way she beat everyone—I'm proud of her, aren't I? I mean, I should think about taking this woman to Vegas!

Still…

"Do you always win like that?" I ask.

"Off and on." She shrugs. "But pretty much."

"Well, you might want to try more off than on, at least occasionally, because if you keep winning like that, I don't think people're going to want to come here. They'll think we've got a racket going."

My wife caresses the back of my neck with her hands. I'm thinking: She wants me.

"You know your hair's getting kind of long?" she says. "Maybe you should get a trim tomorrow."

# Eek, There's a Hair in My *Zuppa*

Barbers, in my experience, are not selected for their proficiency with comb and scissors. Rather, they are selected based on their ability to give good banter.

This is why I've been patronizing *Stavros of Greece* for years.

The first time I met Stavros, I was six years old. Big John brought me for a haircut because he said the bowl Aunt Alfresca'd been using to cut my hair wasn't doing my looks justice. To tell the truth, I was pretty scared. Even back then, Stavros's hand shook while holding the scissors. But then Stavros started filling me in on the content of his days—"about noon every day, I break to go bang my mistress"—and my fears disappeared amidst his storytelling. Twenty-eight years later, he keeps the same schedule; same mistress, even. The only things that have changed is his hair—once jet black, his thick curls are now almost all white—and now he's got a lot of lines on his face.

"Johnny!" Stavros shouts when he sees me. When Stavros keeps just looking at me, the patron in his chair starts to look nervous, probably because Stavros's hands are still flying around his head like a blind Edward Scissorhands. "What do you think? You think Favre'll make a comeback this year? I think he'll make a comeback this year."

"God, I hope not," I say.

"What do you mean? The guy cracks me up. Remember that time he sent that lady a picture of his junk using his cell phone? What a buffoon! Everyone knows a cell phone makes anything you take a picture of look small!" He shifts the comb to his scissors hand and demonstrates, holding two fingers about a half inch apart.

And welcome to the world of Stavros.

Here, the problem isn't that an ageing and overpaid quarterback sent an unsolicited picture of the lower part of his naked body to some unsuspecting woman. It's that he was using the wrong photographic tool to snap the pic of his junk.

"I just hope the Jets don't go for Peyton," I say. "I like Sanchez. He just needs confidence."

With anyone else, I'd mostly be talking baseball this time of year, but Stavros will only talk about football. He says that baseball is for sissies and that in basketball they show too much leg, which makes me think he probably hasn't seen a basketball game since the '70s. Stavros says football is the only manly sport. Stavros is big on things being manly. That and junk.

Stavros finishes up with the other customer, who pays, and then it's my turn to assume the chair. Stavros fingers the hair at the back of my neck.

"I'm not trying to turn away business," he says, "but your hair doesn't seem too long to me."

"Yeah, well, my wife says I need a trim."

"Your *wife*? When did you go out and get yourself a *wife*?"

What's he talking about?

"What're you talking about?" I say. "We've been talking about this for months. I got married two weeks ago. I told you about that."

"You most certainly did not."

Is he pulling my leg? Once I asked Helen to marry me and she said yes, I started talking nonstop about the wedding to anyone who would listen, meaning I've been discussing it with Stavros every time I've come in here for the last eight months.

"If my favorite customer had told me he was getting married," he goes on, "I would think I would remember such a thing."

I look at him and his face is a combination of confusion and—what's the word for what I'm seeing?—anger. I've never seen him look like this. Stavros may be excitable on everything from politics to Brett Favre's junk, but nothing ever gets him *mad*.

And that's when it hits me: He's not kidding. He truly has no recollection of the many, many times we've discussed my wedding. Could Stavros be getting Alzheimer's?

What should I do here? Do I insist on the facts, which I know to be true, or do I let it go? And then I think, what good will I do him if I insist?

"What was I thinking?" I say, hitting myself in the side of the head and giving Stavros a how-stupid-am-I look, which I guess I am—stupid, that is—since I just hit myself in the head. "It was the coffee shop where I couldn't stop talking about it. You're absolutely right. This is the first I've mentioned it here."

"That's what I thought." The anger has mostly gone away, leaving just a trace of self-righteousness which soon dissipates as well into his typical good nature. "So, you got yourself a wife."

"That I did."

"And what's her name? She pretty?"

"She's beautiful," I say, something I've told him many times before. "Her name is Helen," I say, which I've mentioned many times too.

"That's great, Johnny. I never married, but that doesn't mean it's not right for other people."

It feels funny talking to him about Helen, now that I've realized what's going on, so I change the subject.

"How about you?" I say. "What's going on with you?"

"Oh, me, well." He starts to cut my hair. "Soon's we're done here I'm going to close up shop for a few hours to go bang the mistress."

Well, I think, at least Stavros hasn't forgotten everything.

After the haircut, I head over to Big John's for a cooking lesson with Aunt Alfresca. I want tonight to be special—our first couple over for dinner—but have no idea what to make, so I called her and she said to just come on over.

I come into the kitchen through the back door and find Aunt Alfresca standing at the counter with a rolling pin.

"Where's Dad?" I say.

She jerks her head toward the living room. "Asleep on the couch in front of the TV with his hand in the waistband of his pants. Where else would your father be?"

That question doesn't appear to be expecting a legitimate answer so I just shrug.

"Let's get down to business," she says, "before someone wakes up and starts demanding his lunch."

I try to picture Big John demanding anything from Aunt Alfresca but it doesn't fly. More likely, she demands he eat lunch at a certain time whether he's hungry or not.

"Since it's friends and not family you're cooking for," she says, "you'd do better to build a meal around what you know they like rather than just serving whatever the hell you feel like giving them. So? What do they like?"

"Well, Billy's like me. He likes pizza. He likes steak. When it comes to food, we're basically into your basics."

"And what about his wife, Alice? What does she like to eat?"

Hmm…now that one's more difficult…

What *does* Alice like to eat?

I think back, trying to remember. Given that I've known Alice for over a quarter of a century, I had a crush on her for most of it and now she's married to my best male friend, you'd think I'd have a ready answer, but I got nothing. Except for weddings and cafeteria food back when we were in school, I'm not sure I've ever seen Alice eat anything. It's amazing she's not anorexic. Then I remember something, the one clue I have to the kind of food Alice likes.

"Amusing boots!" I say with a triumphant snap of the fingers.

Aunt Alfresca scrunches her face into a disgruntled configuration. "What the hell are you talking about, Johnny?" The rolling pin is raised threateningly.

I raise my hands in defensive posture. "Don't hit me!"

"Sorry. Involuntary reflex." She lowers the pin. "But really. Amusing *boots*?"

In my excitement over having remembered what Alice likes, I forget the threat of being hit. "You know," I say enthusiastically, "amusing boots." I hold my hand out with the tips of my thumb and forefinger touching to demonstrate. "Those little hors d'oeuvres thingies. You know—those classy things you make just a couple of each and they're supposed to whet the appetite for something not so little? "

"Ah, I get you." The dawn of recognition lights Aunt Alfresca's eyes. "*Those* boots."

"Exactly!" I say. "I knew you'd know what I was talking about. This one time I was invited to Billy and Alice's house for dinner, she served them. The thing was, I didn't know what they were at the time—"

"And now you do?"

"Well yeah. But at the time. I thought there'd be a lot of them, like regular hors d'oeuvres. So, like, I ate them all before anyone else got a chance to have any."

"*Marone*," she says, "I raised a *gavone*."

It's never a good thing when Aunt Alfresca talks Italian at me, particularly if it rhymes.

"Here's what we're going to do," she says with a sigh. "We're going to come up with a menu that'll be pleasing to both of your guests and that will also manage to atone for your previous... *boots* sins. Now, then, to make your crust..." More sighing. "Scratch that, Boots. No point in trying to bite off more than you can chew at your first dinner party. OK, in the freezer case of Super Stop & Shop..."

In the freezer case at Super Stop & Shop, I find the brand of dough Aunt Alfresca recommended and then I proceed to shop for everything else on the list she's given me.

Oh, and what has Helen been doing while I've been getting my hair cut, absorbing cooking advice, and doing the hunting and gathering? Painting. She said a friend was coming over to help her with our bedroom. It's kind of tough to picture Carla with a paintbrush in her hand, but anything that keeps me from having to paint my own bedroom pink and black with my own hands, I'm all for it.

• • •

*Thump. Thump-thump-thump-thump-thump.*

What's that sound?

I drop the groceries on the kitchen counter and head for the staircase. As I climb, the thumps get louder. When I reach the second floor, I see Fluffy hurling himself against the closed door to the master bedroom. Oh, I get it now. Helen and Carla must have closed the door to keep the cat from running through the metal trays of paint and then tracking little pink and black paw prints all over the floor. It's a smart move on their part but the poor guy's freaking out. Fluffy has always had issues with closed doors and Helen's recent policy of closing our bedroom door when we go to bed at night has not helped. Whenever I go to the bathroom and Helen's not around, it's easier to simply leave the door open. Otherwise, he'll hurl his little body repeatedly against the door as if to say, "Let me in! I know you're doing exciting things in there!"

I put my hand on the doorknob but then stop shy of turning it.

"Sorry, Fluffy," I say, scooping him up and bringing him to the bathroom. The thing is, if I don't put him there, he'll just run into the bedroom as soon as I open that door and then he'll do that running-through-the-paint-trays thing that Helen and Carla have wisely been avoiding.

"Look," I tell the cat, pointing at the toilet bowl, "fresh water if you get thirsty. This'll only be for a short while."

As I close the bathroom door behind me, careful not to catch it on Fluffy's reaching paw, I hear a slow ticking sound. What is that? Has the shower got a leak?

Back in the hall once again, this time I do turn the knob on the bedroom door all the way, pushing the door open, only to be greeted with…

"Johnny! Paint any good houses lately?"

As the speaker reaches out for a handshake and I numbly pump back, I wonder:

Daniel *Rath*bone? What the hell is *Dan* Rathbone doing in

my bedroom?

He's got an e-cigarette propped above his ear and he pulls it out now, drawing on it hard and blowing e-smoke in my direction. I notice some specks of hot-pink paint freckle his cheeks.

"Isn't Daniel great?" Helen says. "When he heard me say in the office that I was going to be doing some painting myself this weekend, he offered to help."

Great is not the first word that comes to mind when I think of Daniel.

"Hey," that great guy says to me now with a self-deprecating shrug that strikes me as all self and very little deprecating, "I couldn't let her do it all herself. And I was kind of surprised you weren't going to be helping her, considering what you do for a living and all. It's kind of funny, isn't it? You not painting your own house—it's like the cobbler's children going barefoot."

Oh, it's so funny, it's a real scream.

The only good thing about finding Daniel Rathbone in my bedroom? At least I don't notice the paint on the walls.

But I don't have time to think about any of that because soon Daniel's gone, the cat's out of the bathroom, and it's time for me to think about getting started on dinner preparations.

*Ding-dong!*

Helen and I go to answer the door together and find Billy and Alice on our porch, as expected. What isn't expected is the physical distance between them. They're standing so far apart, their bodies are like #6 and #10 bowling pins left standing, just waiting for someone to come and knock them down with a hard spare. Seriously, I had no idea our porch was so wide.

"Come in, come in," we say.

As Billy walks past us, ahead of Alice, he hands me the six-pack he's been holding.

I look at it: Sierra Nevada Pale Ale. "Nice," I say with an appreciative nod.

Alice rolls her eyes and turns to Helen to inform her, "They always do this. They always bring the same exact beer to each other's homes and they always make appreciative noises like it's something special."

"Well, it's a good beer," I point out.

More eye-rolling on Alice's part. But what does she expect me to say? 'Oh, this crap again?' Why would I ever say that? It is a good beer!

Alice hands Helen the bottle she's holding.

"Ooh, nice wine," Helen says.

"Thanks," Alice says with a big smile.

Seriously? Like what Helen said was any better than what I said?

We show our guests into the living room.

"Nice tunes," Billy says.

Queen's "We Will Rock You/We Are the Champions" is playing. I took charge of the sound system before our guests got here, telling Helen I'd take care of that in addition to the food so she wouldn't have to worry about anything, given the hard day she put in painting. But really, I was just worried about what she'd play.

"That song." More eye-rolling from Alice. Sometimes, I worry she's going to roll those eyes right out of her head, which wouldn't be as funny as it sounds. "It reminds me of being in the gym at basketball games during high school, watching the guys play."

What's wrong with things that remind you of high school?

"I imagine Johnny was good at sports in high school," Helen says.

"Oh yeah," Alice concedes. "There was nothing he couldn't play well."

"Here," Helen says, taking the six-pack from me, "let me get us some drinks."

"Let me help," Alice says, following after her to the kitchen.

Soon, Billy and I hear the sound of our wives bonding.

"What did you do today?" Helen asks.

"I went to the gynecologist. He is *such* a Chatty Cathy. Does that ever happen to you?"

"Oh my god, yes," Helen says with enthusiasm, as if she's been waiting forever to talk about this very subject to another woman. "The last few years, he just goes on and on and on. I keep wondering: Is he lonely?"

"I know, right? I keep wanting to say, 'At least let me put my clothes on first!'"

Helen laughs. "I know, right?"

Apparently, neither Helen nor Alice received the memo from Sam about how we all need to find something new to say in place of 'I know, right?'

Billy and I do our version of bonding.

"Work going good lately?" I ask.

"The same. You?"

"Couldn't be better." I regard Fluffy. Since the initial flurry of excitement inherent in having people in his new space, he's sacked out on the ottoman. "Doesn't he look like a proud lion to you?"

"Absolutely," Billy agrees as the ladies return with drinks for everybody.

Just then the oven timer dings.

Helen starts to head back to the kitchen but I wave her to a seat.

"Don't worry, honey," I say. "I've got this."

Alice raises her eyebrows in an I'm-impressed look. "He's got this," she says. "Impressive." Then to Billy: "How come you've never *got* anything?"

Gee, I'd love to stay and watch them argue, but I don't want my mini quiches to burn.


On the platter I extend toward our guests, in addition to the four mini quiches—Lorraine because Aunt Alfresca encouraged me not to overcomplicate things—there's a small glass bowl with a cloudy yellow liquid in it and there are four avocado and goat cheese crostini with balsamic tomatoes, four bacon-wrapped king prawns on rosemary skewers and four of your basic stuffed mushrooms; the mushrooms I tacked on at the last minute for symmetry's sake, figuring that if there were four of us there should be four each of four items.

And now I've said the word four so many times I'm going to call a moratorium on that word for the rest of the night.

Screw four.

Since Billy and Alice are our guests and Alice is the female portion of their marriage, I offer the plate to her first.

"What's all this?" she says.

"I wanted to make something you'd like," I say, "and I know how much you like amusing boots."

"Amu...*what?*"

"Amusing boots. You know, those things you made that time I came for dinner but then I ate them all because I didn't realize that was all there was."

Oh, crap. Now I'm worried she'll be offended. After all, she only served one set of four amusing boots when I was at her house while I'm serving them four sets of four. She'll probably think I'm trying to "outdo" her in the hostessing department.

And double crap, I'm back to saying four again. This is worse than 'I know, right?'

Funny, though, Alice doesn't get pissed at me like I expect her to. Instead, she smiles, takes a bacon-wrapped king prawn on a rosemary skewer and says, "Actually, I think the term you're looking for is *amuse bouche.*"

And this is the worst kind of crap of all. *Amuse bouche?* Not 'amusing boots'? Did Aunt Alfresca know this? Of course she did. These days, Aunt Alfresca watches the Food Network like it's the Mets, the Jets and the Knicks combined. Yet she didn't correct me. Instead, she called me Boots at one point which perplexed me at the time. And now I realize my nickname from her will probably be Boots for the rest of my life.

Alice goes to put the prawn in her mouth but I stop her.

"No, no, no, no, no," I say. "You dip it in that." Then I give a chin nod toward the glass bowl with the cloudy yellow liquid. "Lemon olive-oil dip," I explain.

She dips, tastes, and her face goes all orgasmic. "Oh my God, that is pure heaven."

"Thank you," I say, moving on to offer the plate to Billy, who takes a mushroom; and Helen, who goes for the crostini. Me, I grab a mini quiche not because it's the most tempting, but because no one else has grabbed one yet and they just look so unloved sitting there like that.

"I can't believe you did this for me," Alice says, taking another bacon-wrapped prawn; I could point out to her that what she is doing is *not* proper *amuse bouche* behavior, that there is one each of everything for each of us. But I can't really blame her. The prawns *are* the most impressive. They're what I'd be going for myself if I weren't stuck eating these quiches.

"Billy never does anything like this for me," Alice says, her mood visibly turning. "If he cooks at all, it's a steak."

"Yeah, well," I say in a light tone of voice. Just then I'm saved by the oven timer going off again, which is a good thing because in terms of breaking Alice's sudden bad mood, I got nothing.

"I hope people are still hungry," I say, popping another mini quiche in my mouth.

I'll tell you one thing. Mini quiches got nothing on the best party hors d'oeuvre of all time:

Chips In A Bowl.

In the kitchen, the ridiculously yellow kitchen, my wife gives me a slap on the bottom as I'm bending over the open oven door. Not wanting to get knocked into the oven like Hansel—or is it Gretel? Nah, it's the witch—I straighten up.

Helen whispers in my ear from behind, presumably so our guests can't hear her, "Did you really make all that for Alice?"

"Not just for her," I say. Hey, those *bouches* were for all of us.

"Were you trying to impress her?"

Impress…

Of course I wasn't!

Was I?

"No," I say. "But in case you haven't noticed, she can be a little prickly. I just wanted to start the night out by serving something I knew she'd like." A thought occurs to me. If Helen's asking all these questions, does that mean she's...jealous?

"I swear," I reassure what I think needs reassuring, "I was just trying to be a good host. You didn't mind, did you?"

"Are you kidding?" she says. "I think it's incredibly sweet." Then she snakes a hand around the front of me and caresses a part of my anatomy you should *not* touch when a man is trying to get dinner on the table. "And sexy, very sexy."

I serve dinner in the dining room. For the main course, I went with a simple pizza—buffalo mozzarella, crushed tomatoes and garlic, tiny strips of fresh basil. The crust is only store-bought but what can you do? Aunt Alfresca said making your own homemade can be a little dicey for a first-timer. There's also a big salad and I make sure everyone's got enough beer and wine before I sit down at the head of the table, across from my wife.

*My wife.*

Never gets old.

Billy helps himself to a slice of pizza and his eyes widen with pleasure as he takes the first bite.

If the *amuse bouches* were for Alice, the pizza is for Billy.

There's a thump and Fluffy lands on the table.

Alice looks a little startled, probably from that big thump, but then goes back to serving herself some salad. I'm about to gently remove Fluffy when Billy reaches across the table to give Fluffy a rub under the chin.

I start settling back in my chair, thinking maybe this is OK. After all, Alice and Billy have a cat, so they get this. They know that so long as Fluffy's not making a full-frontal attack on our food—and he's not; he knows if he waits patiently, he'll get something when we're done—it's no big deal. This is simply Fluffy trying to socialize, trying to be part of the group. But then:

"Do you think you could put him in the basement until we're done eating?" Helen suggests.

She's smiling when she says it, so I'm tempted to point

out—again—that I've read that having a cat on the table while eating is not unsanitary in any way. But then I think, hey, this is her preference, it's a dinner party with friends, the idea is for everyone to have a good time—well, obviously it's not Helen's idea for the cat to have a good time, but still—so I figure what's the big deal.

"C'mon, guy," I say, scooping the cat up, taking him to the basement stairs, setting him down on the landing and adding a whispered, "you'll be out again before you know it," before shutting the door on him and returning to my place at the table.

For a while, everyone just eats and I'm fine with that. It's never occurred to me before but there's a peculiar satisfaction to preparing food for people you love and watching them enjoy it.

OK, it's too fucking quiet in here.

"How's work going, Alice?" I say.

Geez, I hope it's OK to ask her about her work. If anyone died a grisly death recently, that could put a damper on things.

Alice is a nurse which has always struck me as a bizarre job for her to have. After all, she can be a little…harsh at times, so how does that work? Does she just *scare* people into getting better?

But apparently no one's died lately, or at least not in any disturbing fashion, because all Alice says is, "The hospital switched me to third shift for a while but that's cool. Billy and I don't see too much of each other but at least I don't have to DVR GH. I can watch it right when it airs."

"It's been so good lately!" I say. "Well, except for that stuff with Kristina."

Kristina, Sonny Corinthos's daughter, dropped out of Yale and returned home with a film crew in tow to shoot a reality series called *Mob Princess*, starring her family.

"I'm pretty sure that's not possible," I say. "She doesn't even own the house and yet she can sign a release for them to shoot inside there? It's crazy. Her mom's a lawyer—doesn't she know this?"

"I know, right?" Alice nods vehemently. "That storyline is driving me absolutely up the wall. I understand that in the summer the writers increase the storylines involving younger characters because kids are out of school and watching, but do the storylines have to be so lame?"

"I know—" I stop myself in time. "Yes, I agree completely."

"So, obviously, you're still watching," she says.

It was Alice who first advised me to watch GH in order to make myself more appealing to women.

"Wouldn't miss it," I say. "As a matter of fact, Sam and me make it a habit to knock off work in time each day so we can come back here and watch together on the two TVs."

I think she'll comment on the two TVs—after all, Helen has pointed out to me that it's an eccentric use of the TVs for Sam and me to watch the same program on both—but apparently, for Alice, this is not the salient feature in what I've just said.

"You have someone to watch with?" she says wistfully. "That just seems so...*nice*."

"Yeah," I say, "but even if you and Billy have different schedules right now, he still DVRs it so you can discuss it together later, right?"

"Nah, I stopped watching," Billy says.

Why would he do that?

"I guess I just lost interest," he says.

"He lost interest in a *lot* of things," Alice adds.

I don't even want to know what she means by that, so, "More pizza, anyone?" I offer.

I get no takers.

Instead, Billy says, "It just started to seem, I don't know, what's the word?" He consults the dining room ceiling as if he might find what he's looking for, then he levels his gaze dead on Alice. "Stupid," he says. "It started to seem stupid."

Alice knocks back about half of her glass of wine and turns away from her husband, her eyes resting instead on me. "Like I said, it sounds like it must be nice, having someone to watch with."

"Hey," I say, "come by anytime. We're here most weekdays at three P.M."

She considers. "Maybe I'll do that," she says.

But of course I know she won't. I was just saying the polite thing, because I needed to find something polite to say, and Alice was simply saying the polite thing in return. But Alice and I have never been *friends*. Alice has never even *liked* me.

I'm in the kitchen getting dessert—it's just ice cream, and no, I didn't make it myself, but it is the expensive stuff—and Helen has followed me in to help, when we hear the muffled sounds of my best male friend and his wife fighting in the other room. From the insult of his not watching GH anymore, they'd proceeded to the injuries of all the other things he no longer does that he used to do, and believe me, I was right: some of them, I did *not* want to know about.

"I don't remember them ever being like this before," I whisper.

"It's awful," Helen says, putting her arms around my waist and pulling me close.

"Maybe they're just having an off night?" I suggest.

"He's so insensitive," she says.

"He is?"

"Didn't you see the way he helped himself to the pizza before offering it to her first?"

That seems like a minor offense to hang a guy for. But then I think of other little things, like him deriding GH when he knows she loves the show. It occurs to me, then: Alice may be something of a shrew—although she did seem better than usual tonight until Billy provoked her—but my old friend Billy can be something of an insensitive jerk.

"You would never do something like that," Helen says of Billy's pizza behavior. "He obviously doesn't care about what she wants or needs anymore."

"Well, I wouldn't go that far," I say. "Like I said, maybe they're just having a rough night? Besides, I've been told once or twice that I can be pretty insensitive myself."

"So?" Helen says. "It's not like you try to be. Instead, you try so hard to do everything right for everybody. Even when you screw up, anyone can see how hard you try."

"I guess…"

"Promise me." She leans back far enough that she can place a palm on the side of my face as she gives a head jerk toward the fighting in the other room. "Promise me we will *never* be like that."

It is an easy promise to make.

I can't stand to look at all that pink and black.

The battling guests are gone, the cat's been let out of the basement but frustratingly locked out of the master bedroom. Helen and me, reveling in our "we will never be like that" vehemence, began ripping each other's clothes off on the way up the stairs, determined to reaffirm our relative perfection as a couple.

But in the bedroom, there is all that pink, all that black, and it's all together.

So, for the first time, I keep my eyes closed while making love to my wife.

Afterward, I'm in the bathroom brushing my teeth when I hear that ticking sound again, that sound I heard in the afternoon. What the hell is that?

I check the shower knob but there's nothing leaking in the shower, press my ear to the tiled wall—still nothing. I'm looking all around me, trying to figure out what it is, and then I realize it's coming from above. At last, I look up, look all around the upward perimeters of the room, and that's when I see:

Over the doorway, just a smidge off center so as to make its placement slightly maddening to those of us who are partial to perfect symmetry, is a clock. The frame is some kind of black filigreed metal surrounding an antique-white face with old-fashioned black hands. This is the source of the ticking.

"Hey, Helen?" I call out. "What's this thing doing here?"

"What's what thing doing where?"

"This thing over the bathroom door."

"Oh, you mean the clock?"

"Yeah. That."

"I bought it when I went out to get the paint this morning. It makes me crazy when I'm in the bathroom and I don't know what time it is."

I suppose that makes sense. I mean, we've all got our own quirks, our own likes, our dislikes—our tics, if you will. Still, couldn't she just put her wristwatch on the bathroom counter like normal people if she wants to know what time it is? Plus, shouldn't she—I don't know—*consult* me before making purchases that result in permanent alterations to our environment?

The clock continues to tick. Loudly.

# Sunday Dinner

When the phone rings the following morning, it spells disaster. Well, if a phone could spell.

"Hello?" I answer the phone on the bedside table.

Some of my friends have given up on having real phones in their homes completely, preferring to rely on their cells. But just like I don't like texting, I'm old-fashioned about my phone usage. Cell phones are fine for their convenience when I'm out and about, but when at home, I prefer something sturdier, something that fills my hand.

When Helen and me first talked about setting up house here and she found out I intended to keep my old phone number, and I further explained why, she laughed. "You'd probably like one of those old black jobs with a finger dial like on *I Love Lucy*," she said.

"I would," I admitted.

"Or better than that, go back even further in time, get one of those things where you hold one piece to your ear and talk into the other."

"That," I agreed, "would be ideal."

And now I've said all I'm going to say on the subject of phones.

"You coming over today?" the voice on the other end of the line says. It's Big John.

"Are we coming over today?" I echo out loud. Helen looks up at me drowsily, a question in her eyes. It's eleven o'clock and we've slept in after our late evening the night before. *It's Big John*, I mouth.

I'm thinking I should tell him yes. I've kind of missed him, even if I did just see him for poker on Friday. But we were surrounded by lots of other people then, so it wasn't like real quality time. As I'm about to accept, though, Helen makes a guillotine gesture, running her finger across her throat. I'm guessing that means no.

"I don't think we—" I start to say but Big John cuts me off.

"It's your aunt's birthday," he says. "You gotta come."

"Shit," I say. "It's her birthday again? Already?"

"Once a year," he says, "like clockwork, whether we like it or not."

Crap, how did I forget? I remember what Leo from the coffee shop once taught me, about the importance of remembering significant dates, and I hope I never forget Helen's birthday.

*It's Aunt Alfresca's birthday*, I mouth to Helen.

She closes her eyes and gives a wincing *damn* look, but then opens them again, sighs, nods.

"Of course we'll be there," I say to Big John. "What time do you want us?"

"An hour?" he says.

"An hour?" I think frantically of all we still have to do: shower, feed Fluffy, get a present. "But—"

"Your aunt said noon," he says. "She said noon is the perfect time to start the celebration of her birth." Pause. "You know your aunt."

Yes, I know my aunt. Crap.

Twenty minutes later, we're showered, the cat's been fed, our teeth are even brushed. Now, what to do about a present…

"We got so much for our wedding," Helen says. "A lot of it we don't even need. We could give her one of those."

"No, we really can't," I say. "Aunt Alfresca is vehemently against regifting."

The problem is, with the clock ticking, we don't have time to go to the mall, what with all that going from store to store, trying to find the perfect thing…

But wait: ticking—that's it!

"We could give her that new clock you just bought for the

upstairs bathroom!" I say, excited. Am I killing two birds with one stone or what here?

The answer turns out to be the latter. Apparently, I'm doing what here, as Helen points out when she says, "*What?*"

"I just figured—"

"I just bought that clock."

"I know but—"

"It was the only one they had just like it at Home Goods. So why in the world would you want to give it away?"

I imagine if I alternatively suggest we give Aunt Alfresca the grandfather clock her parents gave us—*bong, bong, bong!*—that would be the wrong thing to say too? And right, I realize resignedly, that would be regifting.

"No, of course, you're right," I say. "What was I thinking?" I do that thing where I hit myself on the side of the head to indicate my awareness of my own idiocy. "We'll get her a present at Super Stop & Shop."

She looks at me like I'm an idiot. "You're going to get your aunt her birthday present from Super Stop & Shop?"

Here's the thing, though: I do know what I'm doing.

As we wander the specialty aisle of Super Stop & Shop, I'm almost sure of it.

"So how old is Aunt Alfresca anyway?" Helen asks as I pick up and reject fuzzy slippers—too impersonal.

"Now, that is a good question," I muse, my eyes scanning, scanning, "that I do not know the answer to. But I'm thinking, not nearly as old as you'd think. Big John and my mother were pretty young when they had me, Aunt Alfresca was my mom's sister, so. I don't know. I'm going with *timeless*."

"I like that." Helen links her arm through mine. "I hope some day you look at me as timeless."

"I already do." I kiss her nose.

But since my eyes are still open, I see…

"Perfect!" I say, snatching up the big box before any other savvy shoppers grab it out from under me; it's the only one left.

Helen raises a skeptical brow. "Fuzzy slippers were wrong and that thing's...*right?*"

"Absolutely," I confirm. Then I see something else. The package is small but you can push the button through it and when I do, a little red dot appears on the ground at my feet. I wave the package around and the little red dot dances. "Let's get this too," I say.

"You're going to get your aunt a laser dot?"

"No. It's for Fluffy. See on the side here, it says: *For cats.* But hey, if Aunt Alfresca doesn't like her main present..." I press the button again. "OK, let's go pay."

"Shouldn't we gift wrap it?"

She has a good point. Aunt Alfresca is as hard on unwrapped presents as she is on regifted ones.

"You're right," I say, "but I don't think they do gift wrapping here."

We go to the appropriate aisle and I select wrap, scissors and tape.

"We can wrap it in the car," I say.

"Smooth," she says. "Card?"

"I am so lucky to have you," I say, kissing her on the mouth.

Seriously, if I'd shown up without a card, it wouldn't matter how good the present was, Aunt Alfresca would crucify me.

We look at cards, quickly, since we're running out of time.

Helen keeps suggesting things, but they're all joke cards, so finally I have to tell her, "Aunt Alfresca hates funny cards."

"Who hates funny cards?"

"Aunt Alfresca." Didn't I just tell her that? "She says humor is too subjective. She says every time someone else tells a joke, it's a crapshoot."

I look at the serious nephew cards, which I've always given her in the past, but I want something Helen can sign too. Finally, I find a serious card that goes on and on, in bad poetry, about what a wonderful human being the recipient is. Perfect, and hopefully, Aunt Alfresca won't get the irony.

And what's even more perfect?

On the front of the card, it says: *From Both of Us.*

I am now, officially, part of both of us. I *love* this marriage shit.

"OK," I say, "I think that's finally everything: present, potential backup present, wrapping and wrapping utensils, card."

I start heading toward the checkout lines. Since it's Sunday, they're really long. Crap, will we make it on time?

"Wait," Helen says.

I turn and see her gather a bunch of thin, long, flat rectangular items. She waves them at me.

"I don't think that's necessary—" I start to say.

"It's just a little something," she says.

"But we've already got this," I say, indicating the big box in my hands with my chin.

"I know," she says, "but I want to give her something just from me."

"Really, that's a lovely gesture but—"

"Every woman loves chocolate," she says, "unless of course they're allergic."

"Yes, but not—"

"C'mon, Johnny." She tugs me toward a previously unopened register aisle that's miraculously opened up just for us like one of those retail mirages a person is fortunate enough to stumble upon every now and then. "We don't want to be late."

As we're paying, it occurs to Helen to ask me if I have a pen—"I don't have a pen. Do you have a pen?"; "I don't have a pen"—so we wind up having to borrow the one from the cashier so we can sign Aunt Alfresca's card.

We stand on the doorstep, our now-misshapen presents in hand. Turns out, it's not so easy to wrap presents inside a motor vehicle. I've got my hand on the knob, ready to open the door, when Helen presses on the buzzer. I guess she doesn't feel comfortable yet just walking in. So I take my hand back and we wait for someone to come open the door.

That person turns out to be Big John, who's in his wheelchair. Must be a bad day.

"Come in, come in!" he says. "You're practically," he consults his watch, "on time. Just two minutes late." He gives a nervous shrug. "Well, what's two minutes? Maybe she won't notice."

We follow him into the kitchen. I look around.

"Where's the birthday girl?" I ask.

"Oh God." He rolls his eyes. "She's on Twatter."

"*What?*"

"Twatter. You know: Twatter! That thing everyone uses now."

"No, I don't know that thing."

"*Twatter.*" Now he's getting exasperated. He holds his hands up, starts wiggling his fingers like crazy. "One-hundred-and-forty-character limit. People saying crap to other people in short bursts on that Internet thing."

"You mean *Twitter!*" Helen says triumphantly.

Now Big John looks wounded. "What'd I say?"

I could correct him but I'm just relieved to realize he was making sense, even if we didn't know what he was talking about for a while there. When he was waving his fingers around in empty space like that, I thought he was having a fit.

But wait a second here…

"Aunt Alfresca *tweets*?" I hate using that word. I'm a grown man. If I use the word 'tweets' it should only be in relation to birds.

"So you *do* know what I'm talking about," he says.

"I know what Twitter is," I admit, "but I've never used it."

Which is true. I never bother with any of that tuff. I did have a Facebook account, for about five minutes, but then all these obscure people from high school I hadn't talked to in over a dozen years started friending me and I canceled it. Hey, if I wanted to keep in touch with any of them, I'd have picked up my phone and given the old rotary dial a spin. I wonder if Helen has a Facebook account—funny, I've never thought to ask.

"Well," Big John says, "your aunt does. And she uses it… and uses it…and uses it. Your aunt, I'm afraid, has discovered social media. I can't get her off the damn thing!" He looks at Helen. "She's in the den, honey. Maybe you can get her to come out?"

Helen graciously complies, first setting down her small package on the kitchen table.

"Here." Big John chin nods at the large package I'm still holding. "You put that down too and help me with lunch. Your aunt was going to cook but she got caught up in her tweeting."

I put the package down as he rolls over to the fridge and opens the door.

"What're we having?" I ask.

"We're grilling," he says, handing me a platter with hamburger patties on it. I take whatever else he hands me and follow him outside.

"So what does Aunt Alfresca," I resent having to say this word more than once in a single day, "*tweet* about?"

"I don't know," he says in a regular voice. Then he makes a come-closer gesture with his hand, and when I do, he whispers, "One time, I snuck up behind her while she was so absorbed she didn't notice I was there, which isn't easy to do. And get this: I'm pretty sure she's mostly tweeting about us."

My eyebrows shoot up so high, I think I just injured my hairline.

"*Us?* What could she possibly say about *us?*"

"You don't want to know, but it almost always rhymes. Mostly, it looks like all kinds of funny shit."

"But I thought Aunt Alfresca hated humor. She always says it's too subjective."

"Oh, that's just other people's senses of humor. Her, she thinks she's very funny."

I digest this as he fires up the grill.

"She thinks she's going to get a book deal out of all this," he says.

"A book deal?" There is, literally, no longer anywhere further for my eyebrows to rise.

"Yeah, you know, like that stupid-shit guy. You know that guy?"

"I have no clue."

"Oh, come on. Everyone knows that guy. You know, the

stupid-shit guy! He tweeted about obnoxious stuff his dad said, people thought it was funny, he got a book deal, then they made a TV show with William Shatner only I don't think that lasted very long." He looks at me closely. "None of this ringing any bells?"

I shrug, shake my head. "I can tell you what's going on on GH."

He waves a dismissive hand at me. "Anyway," he says, "your aunt says that guy's a loser. She says he wasn't even using his own material—he was using his dad's! She says that her way is much better because hers is all authentically shit *she* says."

"Sounds like she's been saying a lot."

"Don't I know it." He tosses some patties on the grill. "I forgot the barbecue sauce," he says. "Can you go back inside and get that, and grab the salad from the fridge while you're at it? It's in a big bowl, lots of green stuff and shit inside—you'll know it when you see it."

By the time I return, Big John is through with Twitter for the time being and on to something else.

"So, how's married life treating you?" he asks.

He just asked me this two days ago, at the Friday night poker game, but I guess he feels the need to take my marital temperature again already, like maybe something's changed in that amount of time.

"Good," I say, "fantastic. But what about you? After all, you and Aunt Alfresca are still newlyweds too."

"Oh, you know," he says, "*marriage.*"

But I don't know.

"What does that mean?" I ask.

"It's just that, your mother and me were married so long ago. And really, we were only married for a fairly short time before you were born. And well, you know what happened after that."

Right. She died.

As is our custom, we share a moment of silence for my dead mother.

"I guess I'd forgotten about all the compromises that go

into a marriage," Big John says after we lift our heads.

Now I really don't know what he's talking about.

"Compromises?" I echo.

"Yes, compromises," he re-echoes. "You know, all the little…*accommodations* that go into making a marriage work. She does things one way, you do things another way…And don't get me started on toilet paper!"

"Toilet paper?"

He sighs. "It's like this. If I'm in the toilet and I use the last sheet, I make sure to change the roll so she doesn't get stranded. That's considerate, right? But then, she always gets mad anyway. She says I don't put it on the right way. She says the paper should come out in a certain way for it to be right. Over? Under? Who cares? It's toilet paper!"

Well, actually, the over-under debate is not to be taken lightly and as far as I'm concerned there is a clear winner, but from the look on his face, I realize that this is not the time to offer my two Charmin cents.

He sighs again. "I guess I'd just forgotten how it's the little things that can trip you up. Gotta stay on top of that stuff," he says as he flips burgers onto buns, "gotta stay on top."

"What are we staying on top of now?" Aunt Alfresca says as she and Helen enter. But before we can answer—or, you know, come up with a good lie—Aunt Alfresca looks at me with a big smile and goes, "Boots! Boots is here! Hey, how did those amusing boots work out for you last night?"

I narrow my eyes at her suspiciously. "You knew what they were really called all along, didn't you?"

"Pish-tosh." She waves a dismissive hand. "They loved it on Twitter."

Wait a second. She really has been *tweeting* about me?

The food is spread out on the table on the back deck and we're all gathered around. The wine has been poured. We drink a toast to the birthday girl before digging in.

"Ah, grappa," Big John says, smacking his lips together.

"Get a load of your father." Aunt Alfresca waves her salad fork. "You'd think he's an Italian, he acts like such a goombah sometimes, but I'm the Italian here!"

"So I like *Jersey Shore*," he says, a peculiar mix of embarrassed and defensive.

"He likes that Snooki," Aunt Alfresca informs me and Helen with a knowing smirk.

"Hey," Big John says, and now it's pure defensive, "Snooki's just misunderstood!"

Maybe this is another little something else they bicker about, like the toilet paper, so I seek to change the subject.

"So, Aunt Alfresca, I hear you have a Twitter—" I'm about to say *obsession*, but even I know enough to stop in time because that would be a mistake, so I finish with: "-ing?"

"I don't have a *twittering*." Aunt Alfresca rolls her eyes. "I have a Twitter account," she recites, "on which I tweet to the Twitterverse and that activity is called tweeting. There is no twittering or at least not like that. If you're going to try to sound cool, you should at least get the terminology down first." Then she smiles. "Hey, Johnny said twittering—I think I can find a tweet in that!"

I shudder to think what the Twitterverse will be saying about me next.

"So how's that Twitter thing working out for you?" I ask.

"It's great," she says. "I've got over a hundred thousand followers."

A hundred thou...

I feel the grappa go up my nose as I choke.

Helen pats me on the back, which is helpful; she's been so quiet, I forgot she was here.

"You know what pisses me off, though?" Aunt Alfresca says. Without waiting for an answer she goes on. "*Big shots*," she says. "I follow Nick Mangold from the Jets, I follow Sylvester Stallone. I advise Nick on wines because everyone knows he's a fan of wine, I tell Sly he still looks good, but do they ever tweet back? No! They won't even follow back!"

Can you imagine that?

"But don't worry," she says, "I'll get them."

Wait, is she threatening a three-hundred-pound NFL center and *Rambo*?

"I'm very funny," she says with a sly smile, "hysterically so. Eventually, *everyone* will be following me. Hey, did your father tell you about my plans to overtake that stupid-shit guy?"

Lunch has been eaten, wine has been drunk, cake has been had. I wish I'd thought to count the candles because Big John knowing Aunt Alfresca's penchant for exactness like he does, he probably put the right number on plus one to grow on. And, you know, the top of that cake was crowded.

Now, it's time for presents.

"I already gave her mine," Big John says.

"What'd you get her?" I ask.

"My own laptop," she says. "Now I don't have to sit in front of the computer all day and hurt my back. I can carry my laptop from room to room when I tweet. So thoughtful."

Big John blushes and waves a hand as she kisses him on the cheek.

*Enabler*, I think. If Nick Mangold eventually learns all our family secrets, it's on Big John's head.

I retrieve our presents from the kitchen, set them down on the table. Helen chin nods that I should give Aunt Alfresca mine first.

"This is from, uh, me," I say as I nervously finger the red laser in my pocket, just in case.

Aunt Alfresca rips through the crumpled paper and then just stares at the picture on the box.

More nervous fingering of the red laser. Then:

"A *Snuggie*!" Aunt Alfresca clasps her hands together. "I've always wanted one, but I never thought to buy one for myself!"

I smile at Helen. Do I know what women want or what?

"Quick, someone hand me a knife," Aunt Alfresca says.

Big John wipes off the cake knife, hands it to her, and she slices through the sides of that box like some kind of a professional, I don't know, *knife person*.

She removes the garment from its packaging and slides her arms into the blue fleece.

"Look!" she says excitedly. "It fits!"

Well, not exactly.

Aunt Alfresca, for all her loud energy, is a fairly diminutive person so she is swamped by that giant body blanket.

"I'm going to use it right away," she says happily, sitting back down in her chair.

I am inordinately pleased with myself. This is the most excitement she's shown about any present from me ever.

"But won't you be hot in that thing?" Helen says. "It must be nearly a hundred degrees out today, Aunt A."

"Aunt *A*?" My aunt no longer looks happy. Rather, she looks fairly pissed off. "Please, dear," she says, "don't ever call me that again. I do not want my name reduced to an initial like that old Auntie Em from that stupid *Wizard of Oz* thing with all those flying monkeys."

I'm tempted to point out, in my wife's defense, that it's Auntie *Em*, not Auntie *M*, so it's hardly the same thing, but I can see that already Helen is taking this outburst in stride.

"Gotcha," she says calmly, "no more initials for you. How about a present from me instead?" She pushes the wrapped collection of rectangular-shaped chocolate bars across the table as an offering.

Aunt Alfresca eagerly tears through the paper but when she sees what's inside, her expression darkens.

"*Lindt*? You brought me *Lindt*? Swiss chocolate. Feh. Feh." She makes a spitting sound. Then she gets up from the table. She nearly trips over the Snuggie as she starts to walk but catches herself in time and pulls up the hem. Then she heads off to the kitchen with her offending chocolate present, probably intending to smash it into little bits with a hammer before throwing it all away.

"She doesn't like Swiss chocolate?" Helen asks bewilderedly after the blue Snuggie has completely disappeared from view. "But I thought she knew food."

"Yes," I say, "but she's completely unreasonable on the subject of the Swiss. I tried to warn you back at Super Stop & Shop. She hates them. *Hates* them."

She's even more bewildered now. "What kind of person hates the Swiss?"

"Aunt Alfresca. She can't stand that they're neutral. She thinks they should take sides, just make up their minds already."

"That's crazy."

"Maybe. Whatever you do, though, just don't get her started on Roger Federer." Something suddenly occurs to me and I smile. "But this is great."

"How is this great? Your aunt hates my present. She thinks I'm some kind of stupid…*Swiss-sympathizer*."

"Maybe so. But she's finally treating you like crap. You're one of the family now!"

Five minutes later, we're still sitting there—"I'm pretty sure those Lindt bars were manufactured in New Hampshire," Helen says; "I know, Stratham, to be exact," I say, "and I've tried explaining that to her before, but trust me, it's a nonstarter"— when Aunt Alfresca returns to the table and sits down as if nothing's happened.

"Well, this has been pleasant," she says, taking Big John's hand.

"It really has," he says. The sun is starting to lower over his shoulder and a wistful expression tinges his face. "You know, I've always dreamed of this. When I was growing up, we always went to my grandparents' house—my father's parents— every Sunday for dinner. Then, when your mother and me got married, we went every Sunday to my parents' house for dinner. I always dreamed that someday *I'd* be the father hosting dinner every Sunday."

He's never told me this before.

"You've never told me this before," I say. "How come you never said anything?"

"You were single," he says. "A single guy, going to his

dad's house for dinner every Sunday—how loserish is that? But now…"

He leaves the sentence open but his meaning, his desire is clear: He would like Helen and me to come to this house every Sunday for dinner.

I look at him sitting in his wheelchair, looking a little smaller than he did even just two days ago. He won't come straight out and ask for what he wants, but he wants it.

We can give him that, can't we?

"Sure," I say without asking Helen first, "we can do that."

It's after midnight when the phone rings and both Helen and I are asleep; we've got work the next day.

"Hello?" I say groggily into the mouthpiece.

"I was tweeting while watching the *Masterpiece Theatre* I DVRed and when I got up to go to the bathroom, I tripped," comes Aunt Alfresca's voice at me at full volume. "This present you gave me is a *death trap*!"

# Next Time, On GH

It's Monday morning, I'm hurrying to get off to work, I've said goodbye to the wife already, I'm at the front door ready to head out, and suddenly the cat starts weaving in and out of my legs nearly causing me to trip over him.

"What?" I say, regaining my balance.

Fluffy starts trotting toward the kitchen, stops, looks over his shoulder to see if I'm following.

"What?" I say again. "I filled your food and water this morning already. I know I did."

Again with the trot, stop, look.

"I'm going to be late for Sam," I tell the cat. "You know how she hates that."

Fluffy doesn't seem to care about that as he trots again, stops, looks.

So, what choice do I have?

I follow the cat.

Fluffy leads me into the kitchen, where he trots over to the refrigerator, and then he settles down into a sitting position on his back haunches, just staring at the door.

"*What?*" I rarely let myself get exasperated with the cat, but honestly. "What is it you want?" Does he not realize I'm on some loose semblance of a schedule here? Still, when he keeps staring at the refrigerator, if only to appease him, I fling open the door.

"I get it," I say, finally getting it. "You want a treat. But it's not time for a treat." Still, I grab the canister labeled "Indoor Adventures" and wave it at him. "Is this what you wanted?"

I expect him to get all excited like he does whenever I shake that canister, preparing to chase after the tasty chicken-flavored morsel, but instead, he just keeps sitting there and gives me this look like, "No. It's not time for a treat, you idiot."

"What then?" I say, replacing the canister on the top shelf in the fridge.

And that's when I see it.

On the bottom of the mostly empty refrigerator—mostly empty except for lots of beer, a half-drunk bottle of leftover wine, the canister of Indoor Adventures, eggs and a tomato; what am I going to cook for dinner tonight?—is the gallon jug of water that I filled up last night and put in there.

Even though a large portion of the work Sam and I do is interiors, you never know what might come up. Plus, it's shaping up to be a brutally hot summer. Driving around with the sun beating through the windows, going out to get stuff from the vehicle, just generally working too hard—it's a real challenge for a painter to stay hydrated enough in a summer like this.

And Fluffy *knew*.

I grab the jug by the handle, give the cat a good scratch under the chin.

"Thanks, guy," I say. Then, "Hey, Helen!" I call out to the wife, who I left doing some last-minute stuff on her laptop before she heads off to work. "You're not going to believe what the cat just did!"

Silence.

I shrug. "He literally stopped me from leaving the house without my water jug. I guess he's memorized my morning routine and, I don't know, he must have been worried I'd get dehydrated. Isn't Fluffy amazing?"

Silence. Then: "Yeah. The cat's a real brain surgeon."

Huh. She doesn't sound impressed like I thought she would be. Maybe she's still, I don't know, *miffed* at the conversation we were having earlier?

Oh, well. Nothing I can do about that now, I realize, glancing at my watch—shit, I'm late!

• • • •

I get a 50-50 luck-out with Sam. The lucky 50 is she doesn't give me a hard time about being late, plus she is duly impressed by the tale of the cat's concern with my hydration. The unlucky 50 is that she does give me crap about the Martin kitchen, which is the job we're starting with first thing this morning.

"Let me get this straight," she says, chomping on the sugar thing I bought her at Leo's. "You're now living with a Canary Yellow kitchen at home, a kitchen color you *hate*, but when Mrs. Martin told you that's the color she was determined we paint her kitchen, you talked her out of it no problem and now she's going with the far more soothing and tasteful Hampton Haze, which may be a little dull but at least not clichéd?"

The temptation to say *I know, right?* is so strong in me right now, I literally have to bite my own tongue.

I'm careful not to bite hard enough to draw blood so that's not nearly as idiotic as it sounds.

"How come," Sam presses, "you couldn't work that same magic with your own wife?"

And there's that temptation again.

We pull up in front of the Martin job, start unloading the vehicle: stepladders, paint, tarps, that kind of stuff. Next, we knock on the door, schmooze the customer ("No one has taste in color like you!"), mix the paint and get down to work.

A couple of brushstrokes in...

"Hey, Sam," I say, "do you ever think I'm, I don't know ...*selfish*?"

"Are you selfish?" she muses. "Hmm..."

She stops painting as she considers this which, I must confess, bugs me a bit. A professional painter should be able to hold down a conversation while working. Plus, she is on the clock here. Plus, if we take too long at our jobs, we could miss the beginning of GH.

"I mean," she continues to muse, "how are we defining selfish here? You're generous with your beer." This is true. "Your house is my house, your chips are my chips." Also true. "And I'd like to think that, if there were just one slice of pizza left in the box, you would at least make a half-assed attempt at offering it to me first before grabbing it for yourself." Yes! That is so me! "So no," she concludes, "I'm not seeing selfish there."

I know,—

I mean, me neither!

"On the contrary," she says, "I'd say that based on the man I just described, you're generous to a fault."

"*Thank* you."

"So," she says, finally taking up her brush again, although I do notice, she doesn't do anything with it, "what brought this on?"

"Me and Helen were having a discussion this morning," I start.

"Oh, you mean a fight?" she helpfully interjects.

"*No*," I say annoyed, "it wasn't a *fight*." I don't know why I'm feeling so bugged. The word she said, it's just a word, right? But I'm still bugged as I clarify, "It was a discussion."

"OK," she says, "gotcha. So, what were you and The Wife discussing?"

"She said we only ever do things with what she refers to as 'my people.' Well, actually, she says 'your people,' but if I said that, it would sound like I was saying 'your people' meaning 'Sam's people' which would make no sense —Helen doesn't even know your people! Who are your people, by the way?" Sam just stares at me, not unlike the look Fluffy gave me earlier while standing in front of the fridge, and I shake my head at myself. "Anyway, Helen says we always do stuff with my people."

"*Always*? That seems a bit strong. How long have you two kids been married—about two minutes?"

I think about it. "More like a little over two weeks."

"Is that it?" She's clearly shocked.

And, when I think about it, so am I.

So much has happened: the wedding, the honeymoon, getting used to the new house, painting rooms the wrong colors, having her join the poker game, having friends over, visiting relatives, getting *clocks*. When I put it like that, it sounds like a lifetime. Can it really be just a little over two weeks? But that's so short. And in that time, things feel so...*different?*

"What did you guys do this weekend?" Sam asks.

"Well, you already know about Friday," I say, "the weekly poker game at my place. Then, yesterday, we went to Big John's for Aunt Alfresca's birthday. He says he wants us to come every Sunday and I agreed. Oh, and on Saturday, Billy and Alice came to dinner."

"That is a lot of your people," Sam says.

I guess I can see where that might be true.

"But that doesn't make you selfish," she says.

"You know, Helen never actually used that word," I point out.

"OK, maybe there was just an *inference* then and when you asked me before if I thought you were selfish, when you further started talking about this, I simply *inferred* that she had."

"Wait a minute," I say, finally hearing what she said thirty seconds ago; sometimes, I operate on tape delay. "Doing stuff with my people all weekend doesn't make me selfish?"

"Of course not. Hasn't Helen ever been in a relationship before? Doesn't she understand The Principle Of The Unequal Balance Of Power In Two People Doing Stuff?"

"Wait a minute," I say again. "There's a whole *principle*?"

"No *duh*! It states that in any relationship, be it romantic or friendship, the overwhelming power over what the two do socially lies primarily with one of the parties. You always wind up doing more at one person's house than the other person's, stuff like that. It's just like my friendship with Maureen O'Hanrahan in junior high school."

"Who had more power?"

"Her."

"So what happened?"

"It turned out what I wanted to do was kiss her while what she wanted to do was kiss guys, so that was that."

Huh.

"You know," Sam goes on, "when you think about it, your relationship with Helen, it's not really so different than your relationship with me."

"I would beg to differ on that."

149

"No, really, think about it," she says. "When's the last time we hung out at my place?"

I try to think but can't remember a time and that includes when I lived right next door to her for over seven years.

"Um, never?"

"And when's the last time you did anything with me and Lily?" she presses, referring to her steady girlfriend of nearly a year now.

"Well, I have *met* her," I say defensively, adding in a grumble, "and I did invite her to the wedding."

"Hey, I'm not complaining. I'm just making a point. We always hang out at *your* place. We always do stuff with *your* friends."

"So I am selfish."

"*No.* I *like* your place better than my place. I *like* doing stuff with your friends."

"Doesn't Lily mind?"

"Not so much. She likes her alone time, likes having me to herself when we are together, and she doesn't really like your friends."

"She doesn't like me?"

"Your *friends*. She likes you just fine. It's just some of your *friends*. You gotta admit, Drew's a douche."

"True."

"Stacy's a bitch."

"No argument there."

"Alice ditto."

"But she has her moments."

"Billy can be a bit annoying."

"Ah, you've always just been competitively jealous of him."

"Steve Miller's an idiot."

"Oh my God, how did that guy ever get to be an attorney? And a *successful* one!"

"Aunt Alfresca—no one can talk to her without going crazy."

"Did I tell you she *tweets* now?"

"No, and please don't."

"You're not going to say anything bad about Big John,

are you?"

"Of course not! Everyone loves Big John!"

"I know, right?"

She glares at me, then shrugs. "I gotta give you that one."

"So, basically, we're saying every one of my people, with the exception of Big John, is annoying or a bitch or a douche or just generally impossible."

"Except me? Pretty much."

"And Lily's not crazy about them."

"But *I am*. I love those crazy douches! And you do too!"

This is undeniably true.

"But to someone who's maybe still a bit of an outsider—Lily, even Helen—they can be a bit much in large doses and you did say you and Helen spent the entire weekend with your people."

I'd been kind of hoping we were done for the day with the phrase *your people* but, apparently, no such luck.

"What do you propose I do?" I ask.

"Well," she says, "obviously, we're not giving up the Friday night poker game."

"Obviously," I agree.

"Plus, Helen's kind of a part of that now. She *likes* playing poker with the guys, I could tell, even though I can't say any of us loved getting cleaned out by her."

I ignore that last, instead proceeding with: "And I can't renege on going to Big John's every Sunday. I can't break his heart that way—I just promised him we would!"

"Of course you can't. What about Saturday?"

"Saturday?" I stop and think. "I think we're free. What'd you want to do?"

"Not us, you idiot." She rolls her eyes. "You and Helen and *her people*. You've got fixed things to do every Friday and Sunday but having Billy and Alice over last Saturday was just a one-off. Why don't you suggest to Helen that she arrange something to do this coming Saturday with *her people*?"

Huh. Why didn't I think of that? Come to think of it, why didn't Helen just come out and say that since obviously, as I see now, that's what she wanted?

"If you're the one to suggest it," Sam goes on, "there's no way for anyone to accuse you of being selfish, inferred or otherwise."

OK, then. OK then!

"Thanks," I say sincerely, "now maybe we can get back to work? These walls aren't going to paint themselves, you know."

"I hate it when you say that." She goes back to painting. *Brush, brush, brush.* Then: "So how come you never ask me about my writing or how my brother's doing? Kidding. Kidding! I don't have a brother."

The doorbell rings.

It's five minutes to three, I'm in the kitchen rushing to get everything together before the show starts.

"Hey, Sam, you want to get that?" I shout as I pour chips in a bowl. "I'm kind of busy here."

"Sure thing."

Soon, there are voices coming from the direction of the front door but I don't pay attention because I'm busy getting two beers from the fridge, setting them down on the counter, and soon after that Sam's in the kitchen with me.

"Who was at the door?" I ask, handing her the bowl.

"Alice," she hiss-whispers as she takes it.

"What'd she want?" I ask, picking up the two beers.

"I don't know," she whispers again, "but she's sitting on your sectional, in the living room." She looks at the two beers in my hands. "I think you're going to need another beer."

Sam precedes me with the bowl of chips as I follow behind with the three beers.

"Hey, Alice!" I say genially enough when I see Alice sitting there, ramrod straight, in the dead center of one side of the sectional. She's so centered, it's like she measured the distance from both sides. "What are you doing here?"

"You invited me," she says, "the other night. You said to come by sometime to watch GH with you and Sam." As she talks, she has an insecure look on her face like she's unsure of herself. I've known Alice since we were in elementary school and I've seen her look that way how many times? Oh, right: *never*. "Did I misunderstand you?" she says. "Because if so, I could just—" She starts to rise.

"No, stay, stay." I wave her back down, hand her a beer.

"Show's starting," Sam announces and she settles down on one side of Alice while I settle down on the other.

We sit like that—eat, drink, watch—for the next few minutes until the first set of scenes are over, the opening theme song rolls and the show breaks for commercials.

"So," Alice says, still awkward, "did everyone have a nice rest of the weekend?"

"Yes," Sam and I say at the same time. Then I turn to Sam, "You know, I know we're supposed to hate what Johnny Z. did and all, offing his grandfather like that, but I've felt sorry for him ever since the revelation regarding his sister/mother."

Claudia was supposed to be Johnny's slightly older sister before she got murdered, but then it was revealed that she was really his mother. Looking at the actors, this seems an obstetrical impossibility.

"What an absurd storyline," Sam agrees. "Do the writers think we're idiots?"

"I know, right?" Alice says, looking more like her usual self in her excitement to be contributing. "I googled. The actress who played Claudia is only four years older than the actor who plays Johnny Z."

Sam and I exchange a look and Alice catches it.

"What?" she says, awkward again. "Is that too weird that I googled something like that?"

"Not at all," I say. "Sam and me did too—googled, that is. It's just that"—how do I put this so it's both delicate *and* I don't sound insane?—"we're not doing that anymore. That whole *I know, right?* thing—it's over."

"*I know, right?* is *over*?" Alice is shocked and, really, who can blame her?

"Show's back," Sam says.

"I'll explain during the next commercial," I whisper across to Alice.

But at the next break, Alice tries to make small talk again. She asks, "So how was Aunt Alfresca's birthday?"

"How did you know we went to Big John's to celebrate Aunt Alfresca's birthday?" I ask.

"I didn't know that was what you did to celebrate," Alice says, defensive. "How would I know that? What do I look like to you, a stalker? But I did know it was her birthday—doesn't everyone know that?"

Well, actually, I myself had forgotten until Big John called…

It occurs to me that Alice, who I really have known for so long, knows a lot about my life, my family. Really, the only people who've known me longer than Alice are Big John, Aunt Alfresca and Billy. Well, Drew too, but he hardly counts.

"Plus," Alice adds, "Aunt Alfresca tweeted about it."

"Never mind all that right now," Sam says, turning to Alice and thus drawing Alice's attention. "How do you feel about all this *One Life to Live* shit?"

"You mean the migration of characters to GH?" Alice wants to know.

"What else would I be talking about?" Sam says, which is very rude but also perversely nice at the same time. Like Aunt Alfresca giving Helen shit about Switzerland, it's like Sam's welcoming Alice into our GH flock.

"I think it's very presumptuous," Alice says. "Just because ABC cancelled *All My Children* and *One Life to Live*, we've got to make room for other actors? And that Starr Manning chick— so annoying. On the other hand, McBain is out-hotting Jason Morgan, even if his hair's a joke. And Todd Manning? Don't get me started. He's putting the sexy back in sociopathic killer."

"Agreed on all counts," Sam says. "Get you another beer?"

Next set of commercials, Alice has already learned that she doesn't have to do make-nice conversation, asking about our weekends. Instead, she says, "I *love* the two-TV approach to watching!" Pause. "And I can't believe you guys talk about the show all during commercials—it makes it so much more fun."

"Yeah, well, what else would a person talk about during the show?" Sam says, knocking back some beer.

I look at Fluffy, who may be stretched out on the ottoman but his eyes are half open. I think of what he did just that morning, saving me from dehydration.

"See his face?" I say, studying him more closely. "Look at how he's concentrating. It's like he's trying to figure things out, studying everything. He always looks like he doesn't quite get it, *not quite*, and yet he keeps trying."

"Or," Sam says to Alice, indicating me with her beer bottle, "instead of discussing the show, you could do that. But why would you want to?" Then, more loudly, to me: "I think you're reading too much into the cat. Maybe he just has to poop?"

Soon, they're both giving me crap about what an idiot I am. But, I don't know. It's some kind of OK.


Show's over and we're high on what we've seen.

"Can you believe Heather still has Luke hostage?" Sam says.

"Can you believe that thing with Todd showing up with that mask and chainsaw to feed Luke pineapple chunks?" I say.

"I wonder what Luke's doing about his toilet needs?" Alice, ever practical, says.

We're not just high on the show. We're also high on all the beer we've been drinking while watching the show. How many empties are littering the coffee table?

"Oops," I say, "time for another round."

"So." When I return, Alice leans her elbow against the back of the sofa, leans her cheek against her palm, and studies me closely. "You were going to explain to me, you know, why we're ditching *I know, right?* after all these years?"

So I do. I explain. I explain how it was all Sam's idea, how she said we'd been doing it for too long, how we needed something new.

Really, as far as explanations go, it's not much of

an explanation.

"Sometimes," Alice says when I finish, "it's like you're still a boy."

Despite the beer, which usually embarrassment-proofs me, I am embarrassed by this.

Alice must sense this because her hand reaches out and grabs on to mine.

"No, I really like that about you." She pauses. "Don't ever lose that," she says before releasing my hand.

I don't need to look at Sam to know: the eyebrows are up.

Then, perhaps to cover for the awkwardness of what just happened, we all begin talking at once. We try to solve the dilemma of finding a replacement for *I know, right?* And while we don't manage to do that, we do get off on a tangent concerning phrases that make us crazy.

"Too much of a good thing," Alice offers. "How can there be too much? If a thing is good, I'm almost always going to want more."

"The definition of insanity," Sam says, "is doing the same thing over and over again while hoping for a different result. But that's not insanity, is it? Isn't it just stupidity? Like, dude, learn a lesson!"

"An eye for an eye makes everybody blind," I contribute. "I mean, I don't want to diss Gandhi but how does *that* make sense? No, see, for that to be accurate, it'd have to be two eyes for two eyes. Otherwise, in most cases, everyone's still got one eye."

"I can't *stand*," Alice says, "when people tell me *Don't go there*. I feel like I'm being told to: Just. Shut. Up."

We howl.

"Or *It's complicated*," Sam says. "Almost nothing is ever that complicated, it can't be explained. No, when you say that to me, what you're really saying is, 'Bitch, I just don't feel like telling you.'"

More howling.

"*It's all good*," I contribute. "No, it's not. The only reason you're telling me it's all good is because you know there's something in whatever the thing is that's supposed to be all good that is bugging the crap out of me!"

Howl, howl, howl.

In fact, so much howling, that when someone says, "What's going on here?" it takes a full round of us looking at each other to realize none of us said this.

On the contrary, it was Helen.

"You're home!" I say.

"Apparently," she says.

Didn't someone ask a question a minute ago?

Then I remember that it was her and I also remember what she asked. Since she's used to coming home to Sam and me watching GH, or sometimes just the aftermath, I realize she can't mean that. So she must mean...

"Oh," I say. "Oh! Yeah, the other night when Billy and Alice came for dinner? I said Alice should come by and watch GH with us sometime. So."

"Thanks again for dinner the other night," Alice says.

"You're welcome," Helen says, warming up a bit.

"So," Alice says, reverting to small talk, "really hot day out there today, huh?"

"I know, right?" Helen says.

"Wait." Alice looks puzzled. "Didn't anyone tell you—"

I give Alice a please-shut-up look.

She looks back at me blankly.

If it were permissible for me to do so—permissible in more ways than one—I would tell her right now: "It's complicated." I would tell her that because, even in my beerish state, I can see what this is like for Helen right now: the three of us sitting close together on the couch over here, her standing alone over there. If Alice further tells Helen that the three of us—*us*—have decided to retire the group catchphrase and replace it with something else, there is only one way that can make Helen feel and that is left out, like we are conspiring, like there is an us and a her; I mean, of course there's an us and a her—that's simply the grammar of the current situation. Still. Yes, even I can see all of this.

But I can't say any of that, not here, not now.

Fuck, it's complicated.

And yet somehow, even though Alice can't possibly understand all that has just rapid-fire gone through my head, she knows enough on her own as a human being to finally go back to her previous question and rephrase it as the rhetorical, "Didn't anyone tell you how beautiful you look today? When it's hot like this, it's all I can do not to look like a rag. But *you*!"

"Thank you," Helen says, but she looks leery. Well, who can blame her? My wife is not a stupid woman, never that, and she must know something's off here even if she has no way of knowing what it is. Still…

Thank you, Alice.

"I think I'm going to change out of these clothes," Helen says to me, "maybe check out Facebook before dinner." Then, to the room at large: "Nice seeing everybody."

"This was really great," Alice says when I walk her to the door a minute later.

What do people usually say to that?

"Hey, come by anytime," I say.

And she does.

Tuesday, five minutes before GH, Sam and I are positioned on the couch waiting for the show to start, there's a knock on the door: Alice. Wednesday, we're late getting out of the last job, so it's twenty after three when we pull up in front of the house, and there, waiting for us in her car: Alice.

I begin thinking this is like an idea I once had for a great story. You know how TV talk-show hosts like Jon Stewart are always saying to guests at the end of the show, "Come back anytime"? Well, what if one day a guest did? What if, the day after his guest appearance, the guest shows up at the studio because he was told to "come back anytime" and he's a slightly twisted person who doesn't feel like he has anywhere else to go? When he shows up the day after, the people on the show are all like, "What are you doing here?" and he's like, "Jon Stewart said to come back anytime." They think it's funny at first, a gag, but he does it the next day and the next and the next. Suddenly, no one thinks it's funny anymore nor are they friendly to him. Eventually, he gets thrown out and the studio puts him on a Don't Allow In list. And then, of course, he gets *mad*.

I figure it could be a short story, a dark comedic horror thing along the lines of Peter Abrahams' novel *The Fan*, only instead of a baseball fan and a baseball star, it would involve a guest and Jon Stewart.

This thing with Alice, while by no means exactly the same, reminds me a little bit of that, as she continues to come back again anytime on Thursday.

And, yes, she comes back on Friday.

# Weekend Worriers: Friday

On Friday, Sam and I are a little late getting home from work so when we get there, Alice is waiting on the stoop.

"Sorry we're late," I say, hurrying to let everybody in. It's five after three. We've already missed the first set of scenes.

"No problem," Alice says, coming into the kitchen with me to help get the beer and chips while Sam heads to the living room to turn on the TV. Alice started doing this—helping me get provisions—sometime earlier in the week. Wednesday, maybe? I don't mean she started helping me for today on Wednesday— that would mean we'd spent the last forty-eight hours in the kitchen, getting beer and chips! Which, obviously, we have not. I mean she started the habit then.

"Still," I say. "I only have your home phone. Why don't you give me your cell too so I can call you next time we're running late so you'll know what's going on."

I pull my cell out of my back pocket and stand there, waiting for her to give me the number so I can program it in.

But it's suddenly silent in the kitchen—one of those strange *too* silent moments you sometimes stumble across in life—and I glance up from the phone to see Alice staring at me.

"That's just so…*considerate*," Alice finally says softly, an expression on her face that's surprised and—I don't know —wistful?

I'm not sure I get either of those things. Surprise? But aren't I known to be a considerate person? And wistful—what's that all about?

I wait, finger poised over the cell, and at last Alice says,

"Oh, right!" and gives me her number.

As I'm putting the phone back in my pocket, I hear Sam shriek from the living room, "Johnny!"

"What?" I say, running in to see what's wrong, only to find her standing in the middle of the room, remotes in each hand, aimed at the two TVs like a gunslinger. She's pushing buttons like mad but nothing's happening.

"I can't get them to turn on," she says. "What's wrong with the TVs?"

I put my hands on my hips. "*Fluffy*." I'm so disappointed in him. He knows I don't like this, but he just stares back at me from where he's sprawled out on the ottoman.

"The *cat* did this?" Sam says.

"Yes," I say, getting down on my stomach on the floor and snaking my hands behind the sofa so I can adjust the plugs in the powerboard. "It's his new *thing*," I say, giving Fluffy another glare after slithering back out. "Try the remotes again," I tell Sam.

She does and now the power lights are on but still no picture anywhere.

"Sometimes you have to fiddle a bit," I say. "Here, let me have those."

"The cat's new 'thing' is to turn off both TVs?" Sam says as I fiddle.

"Actually, he's never done both at once before. This is new. Usually, he just gets the one. Sometimes, for good measure, he'll unplug a computer or Helen's laptop when she's charging it."

Now there's still no picture but in the middle of the screen there's a notice saying to call the cable company if there's a problem.

"Don't worry," I say, "that'll go away in a few minutes.'

"But why would Fluffy *do* that?" Sam wants to know.

"Obviously he's acting out," I say with a shrug.

"Acting out? But he's a cat!"

"Apparently." I regard his furriness. "But that doesn't mean he doesn't have feelings."

"So what's he so upset about?"

"Search me. If I knew what the problem was, I would fix it."

The picture's finally back, but it's on MSNBC from this morning, so I switch it over to GH before handing Sam back the remotes. Then I head over to the basement door, which is always propped open so Fluffy can get at the litter box, and grab his leash off the coat rack.

Sam and Alice are already on the couch, beers in hand and staring at the screen, when I return.

"You've got to stop this," I tell the cat as I attach the leash to his collar. "I'm worried that, one of these days, you'll fry your furry little self."

"What are you doing?" Sam says, briefly tearing her eyes away from a TV.

"Taking Fluffy for his daily walk." I pick the cat up, set him on the ground. "C'mon, boy."

"But GH is on."

"I know. You can fill me in on what I missed when we get back."

"But GH is practically half over already and Todd Manning's on."

I look at the screen.

"You love Todd Manning."

Well, love may be an extreme term, although it is hard to tear my eyes away. Still...

"Yeah, but if Fluffy's upset enough he's unplugging both TVs now, I think I really should take him for his daily walk. I don't want him getting so upset he goes after the plug on the fridge next. It's summer—all the beer will get warm. And anyway, I just don't want him upset."

I'm at the front door, leashed cat by my side, when I hear Sam say, "He's crazy. Don't you think he's crazy?"

I'm about to respond to this aspersion on my character when I hear Alice, who's been strangely silent ever since Sam's first shriek, say, "Maybe. But he's also kind of wonderful."

I try not to hurry the cat along in the walk—I mean, I get why he's intrigued by that squirrel, although I'm also glad he's on a leash because otherwise that squirrel would be toast—but I would at least like to catch the tail end of my show.

"Yeah, I know I said I liked Carly and Johnny Z. together," I tell the cat as we near the front door on our return, "but now that Todd's on the scene, I don't know. Her chemistry with Johnny Z. is hot, but her and Todd just sizzle. It is a lot to consider. Yeah, I know you're not as into it as I am. Maybe you would be if there was a soap starring cats? Hmm, I wonder what that would be like…"

I'm so wrapped up discussing things with the cat that I don't notice there's now a fourth vehicle in the driveway but I definitely notice there's another person in the house after Fluff and I enter, I release him from the leash, rush into the living room to catch the last few minutes of GH and see…

"Helen! You're home!"

Sam and Alice are right where I left them on the couch, side by side, but now Helen's on the ottoman, high heels off. All three are sitting ramrod straight. It's so weird. Is this some kind of proper-sitting contest? Maybe it's a girl thing?

"Yes," Helen says, "I am."

"That's great. You haven't been home early since…" I try to think.

"Monday," Helen supplies. "The last time I came home early, it was Monday. Every other day this week, I've had to work late, or at least regular hours."

"Right, right," I say, stealing a glance at the screen. At least it's a commercial. I look at Sam and Alice: still with the ramrod posture. What gives?

I notice there are only two beers on the table.

"Can I get anyone a beer?" I offer.

Sam and Alice, eyes forward: "No, thanks."

"Helen?"

She shakes her head.

"Well, if no one else…" I head to the kitchen to grab a quick beer for myself.

Open the refrigerator door, snag a cold one, pop off the cap, turn around and…

I give a little jump, startled.

"Helen!"

Apparently, she followed me in, because she's standing two inches in front of me.

"So," she says in a low voice, "Alice has been coming by every day this week?"

"Well, yeah. I didn't mention? I could've sworn…"

"No, you didn't. Which is odd, I think. I'm not sure which is odder, you not mentioning it or her coming by every day."

"Well, I probably didn't mention it because by the time you get home, I'm just so happy to see you that nothing else matters." I move to hug her. "As for—"

"Oh my *god*!" Sam and Alice shout from the other room.

I race to the living room, only sloshing the beer a little as I race.

Is it just me, or does it seem like I'm doing a lot of hurrying and racing today?

"What is it?" I demand, a little breathless.

Sam and Alice are dumbstruck, pointing at the screens.

I follow the pointing fingers. "Robin Scorpio is *alive*?"

We talk excitedly all through the brief *Next time on General Hospital* promo that follows the end of the show—"But Robin was vaporized!"; "How can she still be alive?"—and while the credits roll. We're still talking when Helen comes through on her way to the stairs, laptop case in one hand, a beer in the other. Apparently, she changed her mind about the beer.

We stop talking.

"Looks like something exciting happened," she observes. "I think I'll go up and get a little work done, maybe take a shower"—she pauses, looks straight at Alice as she finishes with, "so I'll be fresh for the poker game tonight."

Oh, shit.

Last Friday, we told Helen that she wasn't supposed to let on to the other wives about playing poker with us. Why would Helen do this? She's not usually forgetful about things. And how's Alice going to react to this?

"I thought Sam was the only woman allowed in the game,"

Alice says carefully. "But you play too?"

"I do live here." Helen shrugs. "What else am I going to do, sit around knitting while there's a party going on in my own basement every Friday night?"

I would've expected Alice to be mad about this revelation, because I'm aware that women can get mad about this kind of stuff. Plus, she's Alice, and mad has mostly been her natural state in life, that and bitchy. But instead, there's that wistful thing again.

"Must be nice," Alice says, "being one of the guys, or one of the guys and Sam anyway."

"It is." Helen gives a tight smile, one I don't think I've ever seen on her before, and a brisk nod of the head. "It definitely is."

Then she turns and we watch her walk the rest of the way up.

Well, this is awkward.

I swivel to Sam and Alice—"So, who's ready for a beer now?"—but both of them are rising to their feet.

"I think I'm just going to go," Alice says, adjusting her shirt.

"What? No! But we haven't even discussed the show yet."

She's already heading for the door, though. "I really should go now." And she's gone.

"Me too," Sam says.

"But it's Friday. You always stay straight through until it's time for poker."

"I know. And I'll be back later. But right now I just think you could use some, I don't know, *alone* time." When she says this last, she casts her eyes up at the ceiling, toward the faint sound of the shower running.

Somehow, I don't think she's talking about me communing with God.

Happiness, conflict, happiness, conflict—is anyone else sensing a pattern here?

When I get to the bedroom—the bedroom which is still pink, still black—the sound of the shower is louder and I sit down on the bed, waiting for Helen to come out. Beside me on the bed is her laptop, which just happens to be open. I suppose that while I'm waiting, I could knock off another chapter of *What's Going on in Your Cat's Mind*—which I obviously do need to figure out—but my eyes stray to that open laptop where I notice that her Facebook page is open.

Huh. I've never actually seen Helen's Facebook page before. But that makes perfect sense since I'm not even on Facebook.

Still, a strange feeling of curiosity overwhelms me as I look closer at the page, like maybe I'll get a glimpse of a side of my wife I wasn't aware of. I love discovering new things about her. But wait a second. When I discovered that she loves crappy music and garbled lyrics, did I love that? Still…

Feeling a little more hesitant, I look. On the left, I see most of her contacts are listed under family, with just five under friends, which strikes me as a bit sad for some reason, even though I have zero friends on Facebook. My wife's five friends are Carla (obviously), Steve Miller, Monte Carlo, JJ Trey and Daniel Rathbone. In Daniel Rathbone's photo, he's standing on the deck of a boat with a fishing rod propped up in his hands, a big marlin hanging from the rod, an e-cigarette poking out of his mouth—out of Daniel's mouth, not the marlin's—and that's when I realize that same picture is all over her page.

I look at the timeline. Apparently, she and Daniel were communicating right before she got in the shower. Maybe they were discussing a case? But they wouldn't do that in public like that, would they?

I peer more closely at what was said:

Daniel Rathbone: You really kicked prosecutorial butt today!!!

Helen Troy: I know!!!

Lawyers talk in overabundant exclamation points???

Daniel Rathbone: See you soon!!! Well, relatively.

Helen Troy: Can't wait!!!

See you soon? I guess Daniel must mean Monday at work. I'm not really crazy about that "Can't wait!!!" from Helen. Maybe she means it ironically? I'm still mulling that when she walks into the bedroom, towel-drying her hair.

She looks surprised to see me there, her eyes moving back and forth between me and the laptop. Then she cocks her head as though listening for something.

The house is silent.

"No TV?" she asks with more surprise.

"They left," I say.

"Sam too?" And yet more surprise.

I nod. Then, because I have to know, I ask, "Why'd you do that downstairs? Telling Alice you're in the poker game now."

She shrugs. "Well, I'm not going to lie about it."

"No one expects you to lie. But it's not like Alice asked you about it. You offered the information."

Again with the shrug. "I guess I just didn't see what the big deal is."

"It's not a big deal." I'm feeling defensive now, although I don't know why I should. "It's that"—I'm about to say that it seemed to me that Alice looked hurt, instead of her usual angry, like she felt left out, but for some reason I stop myself. I start again with "It's that," finishing with, "what if Alice tells Stacy and Aunt Alfresca? How will that make them feel?"

I'm thinking *I* know how that'll make them feel. After years of being kept out of the game, they'll be pissed. Stacy will peck at Drew until he caves and brings her with him. And Aunt Alfresca? She'll probably tweet about it!

"I hadn't thought about that," Helen says, and I can tell she hadn't. "Do you really think Alice would do that—tell the others?"

I think about it and shrug. "I don't honestly know. Alice—"

"I actually did want to talk to you about Alice," Helen cuts me off.

"What about Alice?"

"I can't believe she's been coming here every day—every day!—and I only found out about it because I came home early today. If I'd never come home early again in my life, were you never going to tell me?"

"What are you talking about? You make it sound like there

was a plan not to tell you. There was no plan. Why would there be a plan?"

"I never said there was a plan. Did you hear me say that? Why, as you say, would there be a plan?"

Sometimes I forget my wife is a prosecutor but right now I am totally remembering and oh is she good. She's so good, I don't remember what the question was. So what else can I do? I just start talking.

"Alice came by on Monday. You know that. When she and Billy came to dinner last Saturday night and she found out Sam and I watch GH together every day, she said that sounded nice, so, being polite, I said she should come by anytime. It's just what you say in those situations. I never thought she'd actually do it. But then, like I say and like you already know, she came by Monday."

"And she came again on Tuesday."

"Well, I guess she must have had a good time on Monday."

"But you never mentioned she came on Tuesday."

"I did not."

"So she had a good time on Tuesday and came back again on Wednesday, had a good time on Wednesday and came back on Thursday, had—"

"I'm familiar with the pattern."

"Right. And at no time, in the middle of that her-having-a-good-time-and-coming-again-and-again, did it ever occur to you to tell me?"

"Why *would* it?" I could be wrong, but I think my voice just went up a notch. God, I'm feeling defensive. Why am I feeling defensive? "It was no big deal."

"No big deal?" she echoes.

Let me interject here for a minute. Back when Helen and I first became a couple, one night we were drinking and we got on the topic of people we'd been involved with previously—my list was actually very short, minuscule really, while hers was shockingly short too—going all the way back to childhood. So we, like, told each other everything. You would think two adults in their thirties would be smart enough to know that indulging in the "Ooh, this is a shiny new relationship! Let's find out *everything* about each other, including every little sexual blip!" was not a good idea. But, apparently, with our relative lack of experience, we did not know this. This means that Helen knows all about my previous feelings for Alice and while she's never seemed to be bothered by this in the past at all and has in fact seemed to like Alice, now that conversation is coming back to bite me on the ass with…

"Alice is the woman who was once the girl you had a thing for, for most of your life, and you don't think it worth mentioning when, out of the blue, she suddenly starts stopping by every day when I'm not home?"

"It's not like that!" I say, my voice doing that slight-rising thing again. What is going on? I never raise my voice when talking to anybody. Suddenly, it's like I feel an invisible rein, like I've been pulled up short. "Wait a second," I say. "Are we having a…fight?"

"Are we?" And just as quickly, Helen looks the way I feel. "No, of course not. God no. It's just…"

"Just what?" I reach a hand out toward her, a hand she grabs onto.

"It's just I know the history between you two and—"

"What history? When I was a boy, I liked her. But I'm a man and I love you."

"I know that, but." She leans into me. "I think she's got a thing for you."

"*Alice?*"

"Why else would she be here all the time?"

I don't answer her question. Instead, I roar with laughter as once again I say, "*Alice?*" More roaring. "You have *got* to be kidding me." At last, I control myself. "No woman, in the history of the world, has had more distaste for a man than Alice has had for me. Really, the woman barely tolerates me. In fact, the only reason she's put up with me all these years is because of Billy."

"Then why has she been—"

I put my finger to her lips. "Shh," I say. "I don't know why Alice has been coming here every day—maybe something's going on with her; maybe she just really hates to watch TV alone—but whatever the reason, I can assure you it has nothing to do with her having a thing for me. The very idea."

Helen presses her body into mine and I am instantly aroused.

"Maybe she wants a piece of that," Helen says, pressing harder.

The idea is so laughable, I nearly lose my hard on, but I'm not so easily deflated.

"The only person who gets a piece of that is you, Mrs. Smith," I say, pressing right back at her.

Now we're both laughing and we're still laughing as she tackles me onto the bed, next to the laptop.

I'm kissing her, she's kissing me back, when suddenly it hits me:

"You were jealous," I say.

"Was not," she says.

"Were too."

"Was not," she insists.

"Does that mature technique work for you in court?"

"All the time," she says, straddling me and lowering her face to mine.

Something about the words "jealousy" and "court" being bandied about in a short period of time, even if the bandying is all initiated by me, starts a thought niggling in my head and that thought has to do with that open laptop and her Facebook page and Daniel Rathbone—why do they need to chat online together when they were just at work a short time ago?—but before I can properly phrase a question that doesn't sound entirely assholeish, my wife pushes my T-shirt up. Then she reaches out a hand and, while kissing down my front in a southerly direction, folds the lid down on the laptop.

What was I going to say to her again?

I have no idea.

"We're good?" I say when we're both finished.

My wife smiles, lays another kiss on me. "We are so good."

• • •

Seven o'clock, the doorbell starts ringing and so begins the weekly influx of troops at regular five-minute intervals. A part of me expects to see the wives come with their mates: Alice with Billy, Stacy with Drew, Aunt Alfresca with Big John, Katie Miller with Steve, although why Alice would ever call up Katie— who she only just barely knows—is beyond me. But that doesn't happen, so apparently Alice kept her newfound knowledge to herself.

This is a good thing and Helen looks at me with a sigh of relief; no doubt, she's been feeling a bit guilty about possibly causing disgruntlement among the troop mates. But if none of the wives are here, except for Helen, there's another woman who's not here either, and that is a bad thing.

"Where's Sam?" asks Big John, the last to arrive and the last to ask this question although it's already been asked by all the others.

"I don't know," I say.

"But Sam's always here," he says.

"I know. She left right after GH, said she'd be back."

"On Fridays, she always stays after GH, right on through until it's time to play cards."

"I know that too."

"So why would she do that—leave in between, I mean?"

I look over at Helen. What am I supposed to say—that my wife made Sam and Alice feel uncomfortable somehow, and the both of them scampered right out of here? I can't say that. Besides, it's not really true. Is it?

"Maybe she had to do something," I say. "What am I, Sam's keeper?"

"Yes. But in the meantime, let's go play cards."

We do that and we start playing, we play for a half hour, but it's really not the same, and then…

*Ding-dong!*

"I'll get it," Helen says, jumping up from behind the stack of her winnings. Well, one thing's the same, at least the same as last week.

She goes toward the stairs in her shorts and as I hear her pound-pound-pound up the stairs, I picture those sexy legs of hers.

"Who could that be?" Drew says. "Did someone order pizza? I could go for pizza."

Billy taps him on the shoulder.

"What?" Drew says

"It's probably not pizza," Billy says.

"No?"

"No, it's probably Sam."

"Oh. Oh!"

If it is Sam, then why aren't they coming down right away, I wonder? So, while we wait, we discuss...

"How about those Mets?" Steve asks.

"Ah, they're not going anywhere," Big John says, "but Dickey's having a helluva season."

Whenever I think of the season R.A. Dickey's been having, and I think of it often, I can't help but think of Leo from the coffee shop too and wish he'd stayed alive to see it. A knuckleballer on track for the all-star team, a knuckleballer on track to win at least twenty games and maybe even the Cy Young award...and he actually plays for the Mets! Leo loved the Mets. Every morning on the way to work, I'd stop for coffee and giant sugar things for Sam, and Leo and I'd talk sports. Now it's just that new owner guy Bailey there. Bailey doesn't know sports, not in any way that counts. I hate change.

What's keeping Sam so long? If it even is Sam at the door. Maybe it really is pizza?

"So," Big John says, "the Knicks traded Jeremy Lin."

I used to be a Lakers fan for the longest time because Kareem Abdul-Jabbar was my favorite player, even though he retired when I was just a little guy, before I practically even knew what basketball was. Sometime last year it occurred to me how absurd it was to keep following the Lakers, so now I'm on to the Knicks.

"No more Linsanity," Drew says.

"Or stupid puns," I say.

"So now what've we got left," Billy says, "Chandleranity?"

"Anthonyanity?" Steve tries.

"Stoudemireanity?" Drew manages to garble out.

"None of the above," I say, "and thank God for the end of inanity."

"Huh?" Drew says.

Pound-pound-pound down the stairs, but this time there are twin pounds, plus the sound of women laughing, and a second later Helen and Sam tumble into the room. I don't know what they were laughing about, but clearly they've been having a good time together, and Helen shoots me a smile and a wink. Whatever they've been talking about, they're obviously cool together again.

"Sorry I'm late," Sam says, pulling up a chair. "What'd I miss?"

"Just the usual inanities," I say. "Where've you been?"

"The new guy finally moved into your old place next door."

"Really? What's he like?"

"Young, from Massachusetts. He likes hawkey."

"Did you say hawkey?"

"Yes. That would be hockey to you, but he pronounces it hawkey. I don't even understand what he's saying half the time—it's like he's from another country. I swear, it's going to be like living next door to Ted Kennedy if he were still alive, really young and drank cheap beer."

"What kind of beer?"

"Budweiser." Sam snorts.

There's an awkward silence as we all glance at Drew who's staring at the table. Drew always brings a case of Budweiser.

"Sorry, Drew," Sam says, a rare contrite look on her face. "I didn't mean—"

"It's fine." Drew gives a magnanimous wave. "But it is the King of Beers, you know. I think people forget that sometimes."

What can you say to that?

We don't even try.

"So you've been with the new neighbor this whole time?" I ask Sam. For some reason, I feel unaccountably hurt by this, like

I'm being replaced.

A new guy in my old place? More change. This is so not good. And how small am I?

"Well, yeah," Sam says. "I mean, I had to break the guy in, didn't I? When I left, I told him I already have the spare key to his place, but that he was going to need to stock the fridge with better beer if he expected me to be stopping by on any kind of regular basis."

Fucking Sam.

"What did he say?"

"What do you think he said?" Sam shrugs. "He promised to get better beer."

The table laughs.

While the others are still laughing, Sam looks at me, shakes her head. "Don't worry, Johnny. He can buy all the Sierra Nevada Pale Ale he wants to—and I will drink it on him—but he'll never be you."

Fucking Sam—she is a thing of beauty. But wait. Am I really that transparent?

She shakes her head at me again.

"So," she says, grabbing the deck of cards, "is everyone ready to shut up so I can deal?"

A few hours and several dozen inanities later, everyone's heading back out the door as Helen and I bid them all goodnight. The guys and I do the playful punch-each-other-on-the-shoulder guy thing and—what am I seeing here?—Helen and Sam hug. This is both strange and awkward, since neither Helen nor Sam are exactly your huggy types. I still don't know what they said to each other while the rest of us waited down in the basement for them—maybe I'll never know—but at least my best friend and my wife are cool with each other; from the looks of things, cooler than they've ever been.

What more can a guy want?

"We're good?" my wife asks after we shut the front door.

I take her in my arms, lay a kiss on her. "We are so good."

# Weekend Worriers: Saturday

My wife looks so beautiful sleeping, the midmorning sun through the blinds making diagonal stripes across her face, I hate to wake her. Instead, I write a note, leave it on the empty pillow beside her. But as I'm tiptoeing toward the bedroom door, she stirs, opens one eye, aims it at the alarm clock and then at me.

"Where are you off to so early?"

"I figured I'd hit Stop & Shop, pick up some things for tonight."

Taking Sam's advice, I told Helen to ask some of her people to dinner this weekend and she took me up on it, said she would invite two.

"That's great," she says. "What are we having?"

Now that I think about it, she never said who the two are, so: "I don't know. I guess I'll wing it."

"Sounds industrious." The one eye that's been open closes and she tucks her hands under the pillow beneath her cheek, a contented smile on her face.

A thought occurs to me. "I think I might be a little while. I think I'll stop off and see Stavros."

The eye opens again. "Didn't you just get your hair cut last week?"

"Yeah, but Stavros wasn't himself. Actually, I'm a bit worried about him, so I thought I'd just pop in, see how he's doing."

The eye closes again. "My husband." The contented smile returns. "Such an incredibly sweet man."

• • •

175

"Johnny!"

Stavros looks as surprised as Helen was that I'm going to get my hair cut two weeks in a row, although that's not what I'm here for, but soon I realize that's not what's surprising him.

"It's been so long," Stavros says. "I thought I'd never see you again."

Apparently, unless he's pulling my leg, Stavros doesn't even remember me being here just last week.

"Uh, yeah," I say. "How long has it been?"

He goes back to trimming the hair of the customer in the chair. "Months, at least," he says after a moment's thought.

What am I going to do about him?

Stavros looks up at me and narrows his eyes, waving his scissors in a menacing manner. "You been going to one of my competitors? One of those fancy-schmancy super-cutting places?"

I hold out my hands in protest. "What? No! Of course not! I would never go to anyone but you."

"Well, OK then." Mollified, Stavros goes back to work. "Still, all this time way, your hair must be getting long. Just a sec and I'll do you after I'm done with this guy."

"Actually, I didn't come in for—"

I stop myself as Stavros stops cutting hair, gives me a quizzical look. If I finish the sentence out in the way I originally intended, what we'll wind up with is 'Actually, I didn't come in for a haircut,' then Stavros will say, 'Then what did you come in for?'—since I've never just stopped by just to chat before—and then what will I come back with: 'Because I'm worried you're losing some of your little gray cells?' No, I can't say that. So:

I hold out my open palms, roll my eyes at my own idiocy and say, "I forget what I was going to say."

At this, Stavros laughs. "You too? That happens to me sometimes, but you're too young for that, Johnny."

He finishes with the customer, they settle up and soon I'm in the chair for a trim I don't need.

Stavros drapes the cape around my neck. "So," he says, "what are you up to today?"

"After this, I'm going to hit Stop & Shop, get some things for the dinner party my wife and I are having this weekend."

"Your *wife*?" In the mirror, I see the look of deep shock on his face. "How come you never told me you went and got yourself a *wife*?"

Since I reminded him of it last week, after having discussed Helen with him many times in the past year, I don't know what to say to this.

"I guess it slipped my mind?" I shrug.

He laughs appreciatively, like he could see how this could happen, a man forgetting about his own wife.

"Hey," I say, "how you been feeling?"

"How else would I be feeling?" He pounds himself on the chest. "I'm strong as an ox." And I can see that he is. Stavros's mind may be failing him on some levels, but he looks like he could take me. OK, so maybe that's a slight exaggeration, but still.

"How about those Jets?" I ask.

"Oh my God," he says. "Did you hear Peyton's not coming? We're getting Tebow instead!"

This is good. Word of the Tebow acquisition just hit the news on Thursday, so even though Stavros doesn't remember that I was here just last Saturday, at least he remembers this.

"I know, right?" I say enthusiastically—not enthusiastic about Tebow, but rather because Stavros at least has some short-term memory. But wait a second. Did I just slip and say 'I know, right?' Ah, fuck it. Sam'll never know. She's not here and I can say whatever I want to. "It's crazy times," I go on, more enthusiasm. "I think they're just fucking with Sanchez's head. Do you think they're fucking with Sanchez's head?"

"Oh, I *definitely* think they're fucking with Sanchez's head." In the mirror, Stavros waves the scissors at me, a reminder. "So what are we doing today?"

I regard my own image, the image that doesn't need a trim at all. "Oh, I don't know," I say. "Really, I think just a half inch off'll do it."

"A *half inch*?" Stavros looks disgusted as he shakes his head.

"That can't be right." He tilts my head forward, runs a comb through the back. "It's been so long since you've been here, it's *got* to be more than *that*."

Even if his mind is going, his eyes still work. Can't he *see* my hair doesn't need much of a cut?

My head's still tilted forward but I crane it just enough so I can see Stavros's reflection in the mirror. And what does that reflection tell me? He's smiling devilishly and—oh, shit—he's got the buzz razor out. Is he going to try to get even with me, because he thinks I've been two-timing him with another barber, by giving me some kind of radical cut?

T-bone or London broil?

"Mr. Smith?"

I'm in the meat section of Super Stop & Shop, trying to figure what to get.

"Mr. Smith?"

Helen never said who exactly she invited over, but I'm figuring it's got to be one of the brothers and a spouse. Maybe it's Frankie. and Mary Agnes? I wouldn't mind seeing them. I'll bet Frankie loves a good steak.

"*Mr. Smith!*"

I feel a tiny finger jab me in the side and turn around but there's no one there. I feel another jab and realize it's coming from below, so I look down. Carroty hair. Blue eyes. Oh. Oh!

"Willow!" It's the little girl from the cruise ship. "What are you doing here?"

"It *is* you," she says. "I wasn't sure at first. Your hair's different. All of them."

I reach a hand up, feeling my newly and completely naked neck. Making up for what he thought was a lot of lost time, Stavros went a little crazy with the scissors.

"It doesn't look bad, does it?" I ask.

Willow tilts her head to one side, considers. "That depends on what kind of look you're trying to achieve."

I could ask for clarification, but I'm not sure I'd like the answer. So, instead: "What are you doing here?" I ask again.

"I told you I live in Connecticut."

"You don't live in Danbury, do you?"

"No. We're visiting relatives. We're going to have a picnic and my mom said we should stop and shop so we'd have something to bring. This looks like a good place for that and it works out very well."

"How so?"

"Well, it *is* called Stop & Shop."

"Actually, I meant the other part."

"Oh. That. You've been on my mind a lot lately."

I feel my eyebrows shoot up. Unfortunately, there's not much of a hairline for them to hit anymore. "I *have*?" Aw, this is cute. Maybe she's got a crush on me?

"Definitely. So, how's married life treating you?"

"It's, um, great." What a bizarre question for a little kid to ask!

"It *is*?" She sounds skeptical. "Are you completely *sure* about that, Mr. Smith?"

"Of course. Why wouldn't I be?"

"You do know what Shakespeare says about marriage, don't you?"

"I'm not sure what you're getting at." I fold my arms across my chest. "Maybe you should enlighten me. What does he say?"

She frowns. "Well, maybe *says* was the wrong word. But a survey of Shakespeare's complete plays shows that comedy always ends in marriage in Act V. I think there's only one obvious conclusion we can draw from this."

"And that is?"

"Shakespeare ended his comedies with marriage in Act V, because he knew that there's no good in showing an Act VI. *That's* when all the bad stuff happens."

"Actually, I think he ended them in Act V because he wrote five-act plays."

Why am I defending Shakespeare's artistic choices to this kid? Next, she'll be lecturing me on what a great guy Macbeth was and how Richard III was simply misunderstood!

"Yes, I know that." Willow rolls her eyes. "But then why don't they get married earlier in the play? It's always at the very end, in the last scene, like he didn't want people to see what happens next."

She makes that sound so ominous.

"How old are you again?" I ask.

"Everyone does that." Willow sighs, like she expected better from me. "But it's not a valid argument."

"I just, I don't know what it is you're trying to say here, Willow."

"I just—"

"Willow!" a woman's voice calls.

"I just worry about you a lot," Willow says hurriedly. "That's all, Mr. Smith."

"There's nothing to worry about," I reassure her. "I'm fine."

"*Willow!*" The voice is more stern now and around the aisle corner comes Willow's mom from the cruise ship. "*There* you are." She looks at Willow, her eyes as stern as her voice—I imagine it could get a parent rattled, losing sight of a kid in a big grocery store—but then she catches sight of me and it's all smiles. "Mr. Smith!"

"Hey there, Mrs.—" I realize I've never known Willow's last name and thus I finish lamely with: "Willow's Mom."

"Actually, it's Miss or Ms.," she says.

"When my parents were thinking about getting married a few years back," Willow cuts in, "I talked them out of it."

"Willow!" Ms. Willow's Mom says, scandalized. She shakes her head. "It's probably easier if you just call me Diana."

"I practice what I preach," Willow says. "If Act V never ends, you never have to deal with Act VI."

Diana shakes her head but I can tell: the scandalized looks, the head shaking—she still thinks her daughter's the greatest kid in the world.

"Care to go to a picnic with us, Mr. Smith?" Diana offers.

"He has other plans," Willow says. "He's married."

"Ah, well." Diana sighs. "I'm going to get in line, Willow. Meet me at the front of the store."

"I don't know if you can tell," Willow says after she's gone, "but things didn't work out with my parents. They broke up."

"I'm sorry to hear that. So…keeping them from getting together didn't keep them from splitting up?"

"Good one, Mr. Smith. I have to go now."

"OK, but hey, Willow. Try not to worry about stuff so much."

"I'll try. And get the London broil instead of the T-bone. The T-bone is a more impressive cut of meat but London broil is a great cut if done right, so long as you know what you're trying to achieve with it. You know, unlike with your hair."

I'm still thinking of Willow—or, more accurately, trying *not* to think about her bizarre worries concerning my married life—as I arrive home with my sack of groceries, round the entry into the kitchen and see…

My wife on all fours down on the kitchen floor.

Now, I wouldn't exactly characterize myself as a sexist pig, although some might, and in the years I spent in the unmarried wasteland hoping to break in I never once fantasized about having a wife be barefoot and pregnant on my behalf, but the sight of my wife on her knees in short-shorts scrubbing the kitchen floor…Well, it is hot.

"Hey, someone looks good," I say.

Her hair's pulled back in a ponytail but some strands have come loose and as she glances up at me, she blows them out of her face.

"Hey, where'd most of your hair go?"

"Why? Does it look bad?"

"No, not bad," she muses, her head tilted to one side, "just very different. It all depends what you're going for."

Grateful that she's not horrified—I've always feared that underneath my thick hair I might have one of those misshapen heads—I don't ask for further clarification.

"Don't walk on the floor yet," she says when I attempt to place a foot over the threshold.

181

"I wouldn't dream of it." I take the foot back.

"Give it a few minutes after I'm finished, then you can come in."

I am more than content to stand there for as long as she wants me to, grocery bag in hand, watching her do what she's doing.

"I've been cleaning," she says, still scrubbing away.

"I can see that."

"No, I mean the whole place."

It is a hardship, tearing my eyes away from this vision of my wife, but I do so long enough to glance around the kitchen—everything sparkles—then turn and crane my neck to see the dining and living rooms; the whole place is spotless.

"You didn't have to do all this," I say.

"Of course I did. We've got people coming in a few hours and the place was a mess."

This is true. In the short time we've been living here, we've fallen into a pattern of, well, general messiness. It's just so hard during the week to find time to get everything done, particularly when there's so much I'd rather do with my wife than, you know, wipe down a counter or swish a toilet bowl.

"I mean you could have waited for me," I say. "I'd have been happy to help."

"But you were getting the groceries and later on you'll make dinner. I figured it was only fair."

"My, that's…very democratic of you."

She blows the annoying stray hairs out of her face again as she backs the last few inches out of the room. Rising to her feet, she turns to face me. "You know what we need?"

I look a question at her because honestly, right now, I don't feel like there's another thing in this world that I need. I just love this woman so much.

"We could use a wife," she says.

"A wife?" I laugh. "I thought I already had one."

"You know," she says, "a wife for both of us—someone to do all this day-to-day stuff like cooking and cleaning so we don't have to."

Shifting the groceries to one side, I put a hand on her hip and pull her in close to me. "Whatever you want," I say, "whatever makes you happy."

I lower my head, kiss her, press my hips into hers enough that she takes a step backward into the kitchen.

"Hey." She pulls away from me. "I know where you're going with this. *Not* on my clean kitchen floor."

Rats.

She snakes around me, heads for the stairs, doesn't even turn around as she instructs, "Put the groceries away first and then meet me in the bedroom."

OK, so maybe I'm not going to get laid on the kitchen floor, at least not right this minute, but it's Saturday afternoon and if I'm not mistaken my wife just informed me that we're about to have sex in our bedroom.

My life is not bad.

"So how did things go with Stavros earlier?" Helen asks.

We've had incredible afternoon sex and have sufficiently enjoyed a quiet period of reflective afterglow. Do I mean that ironically? Hmm…tough to tell. Now her head's on my shoulder and she's even remembering to ask about Stavros, which is so sweet, given that she's never met him.

I explain about how the week before, for the first time I noticed that there were lapses in his memory.

"And if anything," I go on, "today it seemed even worse to me."

"How so?"

"Well, last week, it'd been a while since I'd been in. But this week? I'd just been there the Saturday before and yet he obviously didn't remember it."

"Sad," she says. "Doesn't he have any family to look out for him?"

"That's the thing. I don't really know. I know he's never been married but that's all really." For some reason, I don't mention the married mistress he boffs regularly. Anyway, it's not like a married mistress is the person a guy turns to when he starts losing his shit. Not that I have any direct knowledge of any of this.

"How bad do you think it is?" she asks. "Is he safe to work? Should he be on his own?"

Stavros not work? And if Stavros didn't live on his own, where would he go? "Oh, I don't think it's as bad as all that," I'm quick to say. "I'm just a little worried, that's all."

"Still," she says, "it's sad."

"Yes," I agree. "It is that."

We spend so much time in bed talking, just enjoying being together, we even make love a second time—are we killing this marriage stuff or what here?—that time just slips away and before we know it…

"What time did you say people were coming?" I ask lazily.

"Seven," Helen says.

We both look at the clock—shit!—and bolt out of bed.

It's a mad dash of showering, throwing on clothes and soon I'm in the kitchen, hastily throwing a salad together while Helen sets the dining room table. I'm working on a creamy avocado dressing that features garlic, honey, basil and lime, when my cell goes off. As I answer it, I look through to the dining room and see Helen setting the table for four.

"Hey, Johnny, it's Mike," the caller says.

Mike is one of a larger group of guys I hung out with in high school. There were actually two Mikes. For years afterward, we all still hung out whenever we were home from college and then even beyond for a bit, but over time, the group atrophied as groups will until it was just Billy and Drew and me as regulars, so I haven't heard from Mike in at least a few years.

"Hey, what's up?" I say.

Now Helen's cell goes off and I see her fish it out of her pocket.

"Listen, I'm getting married in October and I was wondering: Will you be my Best Man?"

It occurs to me that I haven't been anyone's Best Man in six months. Am I slipping here?

"Of course," I say.

"Of course," I hear Helen say in the other room. "I understand. These things happen."

Something occurs to me.

"Wait a second," I say to Mike. "Which Mike is this, Mike I or Mike II?"

"It's Mike II!" He sounds offended. "You know, Mike Freschetti. Don't you recognize my voice?"

Now Helen's putting her cell back in her pocket.

I ignore his question because any answer I give can only cause offense. The Mikes were never big on personality—not by choice, I don't think; they were just very bland—only ever really distinguishable by number, so instead I just say, "But wasn't I your Best Man six or seven years ago?" Come to think of it, I was both Mikes' Best Men.

Helen looks slightly dejected as she begins removing items from the table. Oh no. Is no one coming? But this meant so much to her, having her own people come.

"Well, yeah," Mike II says, sounding sheepish now, "but I got divorced and now I'm getting married again, so I just thought…"

This is just wrong on so many levels and the wrongness of it absorbs all my attention. I can't accept this gig just to add another notch to my Best Man belt.

"I can't be your Best Man," I say.

"You can't?"

"No! That's double-dipping. That's like the worst thing you can do." OK, maybe, relatively speaking, I've only been married for the equivalent of five minutes, but even I know it's got to be bad karma to do a retread on your bridal party when the first marriage didn't work out. "I mean, you wouldn't get married at the same place, would you?"

"Well, actually…"

"Mike!"

"It was a nice place!"

I spend the next five minutes explaining to him the impropriety of his desires, and by the time we're done, we're mostly good.

"So I'll get a change of—what's the word?—venue," Mike II says with a heavy sigh, "but who'm I gonna get for Best Man?"

"Don't you have any brothers or something?"

"Yeah but they're both douches. One never shuts up and the other flaked and never even showed up the one time he was asked to be Best Man."

Ouch.

"So ask—" I'm about to suggest Billy, but then I think about how things have seemed a little tense in his marriage to Alice lately. Is someone whose marriage has turned a little tense really the person you want giving a wedding toast?

"Ask Drew," I settle on.

"*Drew?*"

I can understand his skepticism. Not only has Drew's marriage to Stacy been tense lately but it's always been that way. And that's why he's the perfect person to have. Tension is status quo for him and will probably carry him and Stacy through until fighting death do they part. Hell, for all anyone knows, they're perfectly happy the way they are.

"It'll be fine," I reassure Mike II. "Just don't let him be in charge of getting the beer for the bachelor party. You know —Budweiser."

"OK, Drew it is then. But at the actual wedding...could you still give the toast?"

I don't even dignify that with a response as I wrap up the call, turn to see a dining room table now set for three—wait a second; didn't one of Helen's brothers just call her and cancel dinner?—and that's when the doorbell rings. Helen's nowhere in sight, just Fluffy underfoot, as I go to answer it, wondering who'd be out trying to sell something on a Saturday night, and open the door to see:

"*Carla?*"

"I'm sorry," she says, not really looking sorry at all; really, annoyed is more like it, and rumpled, which is her usual state, "were you not expecting me?"

How do I put this…? Um, *no*. But of course I can't say that. I can't say I was expecting one of Helen's brothers and one of their significant others—and then I wasn't expecting anyone when Helen got that phone call and I saw her start to remove items from the dining room table—so instead I go with:

"Of *course* I was expecting you! Come in, come in! If I seemed shocked, it was simply that I was overcome with how good it is to see you after so long. After all, it's been at least a few weeks since the wedding—you look great!"

Am I laying it on too thick? I'm laying it on too thick, aren't I?

"Here, let me get you a drink," I offer.

"I'm the only one?" Carla sounds surprised as we pass the table with its three place settings. She's surprised? I'm surprised! I'm going to be eating dinner with just Carla? Not exactly my idea of a good Saturday night. The truth is, I'm not a Carla fan. But that's OK, because she's not a Johnny fan either and in fact she started the not liking first. And if that sounds juvenile, well, that's the way life works. When someone doesn't like you from the beginning and for no apparent reason, it's tough to warm up to them.

We're in the kitchen now where there is the fridge and—thank God!—beer.

"What would you like?" I offer, opening the fridge and grabbing a cold one. "Helen! Carla's here!" Is that desperation in my voice?

"What a great color!" Carla enthuses as she turns in a circle, fully taking in the Canary Yellow walls. It figures she would love it. "Did you do this?" she says, for once sounding impressed with me.

*Only because I had to* is what I'm tempted to say, but instead I go with, "We got beer…we got wine…"

"I gave up drinking. Did you not know this?"

Apparently, I did not. "Oh, well, then…"

"Water's fine."

I get a glass and let the water from the tap run until it's cold.

It never occurred to me before to get one of those fancy see-through pitchers some people have to keep water in the fridge, but I sure wish I had one now because as I hand Carla her glass of tap water it just feels so…unimpressive.

"Cheers," she says, tapping her glass against my beer bottle.

"Back atcha."

"So, what are we having for dinner?"

"I got a nice London broil. I'm going to grill it with—"

"Did you not remember that I don't eat red meat?"

Did I not…? How was I supposed to remember, if I ever knew in the first place, when I never even knew she was coming! I guess this means she'll never be impressed with the tarragon Dijon sauce I whipped together with which to baste the meat?

"It must've slipped my mind," I admit.

"Don't worry about it. I can fill up on the sides. You are making sides, aren't you?"

"Oh, yeah. I found these huge baked potatoes and I figured I'd—"

"Too many carbs. I'm back on Atkins."

Seriously? She's on Atkins and she doesn't eat meat? Isn't that the whole diet on Atkins?

Carla snorts. "I suppose you're serving strawberry shortcake for dessert?"

My eyes widen. "How did you know?"

"Classic male dinner: meat, potatoes, strawberry shortcake. Even if I wasn't doing Atkins, I'm allergic to strawberries."

"Well, I did also make a salad…"

"Carla!" Helen throws her arms around Carla as she walks in.

Helen's finally here. Thank *God*.


*Well, this is fun*, I think, cutting another piece of my meat which, I must say, is grilled to tarragon-Dijony perfection. There's nothing like having someone over for dinner who refuses to eat anything you prepared and is not interested in anything you'd ever want to talk about.

Actually, no, I'm not being fair here. Carla is willing to eat one thing I made—the salad—but only after having me give her a colander so she could wash off the creamy avocado dressing from her portion; she didn't trust me to do it for her.

But as for her being uninterested in any topics I might be interested in? Put it like this: She doesn't watch GH; in terms of politics, which I love, she supports That Guy while I support This Guy (and I think almost all of us can agree That Guy is a douche); *and she's a Yankees fan.* Need I say more? Honestly, except for the no-GH thing, it's hard to fathom how Helen and her ever became friends in the first place.

Yet they are friends. And I can see, looking across the table at my wife who is smiling and laughing as the two of them chat up a storm about who-knows-what, that having her friend here is making Helen happy. So what if I'm not really a part of things? I'm content to sit here and eat my meat in silence, except for…

I notice that a piece from the spinach I used in the salad is stuck between my wife's two front teeth and every time she opens her mouth to smile or laugh, I see that flash of green. Doesn't she feel that? Doesn't it bother her?

"Hey, hon?" I say.

Helen looks away from Carla to me.

To demonstrate the problem, I put a fingernail between my own two front teeth. "Spinach," I say.

Carla's expression darkens. "What are you trying to do, embarrass her? Who does something like that?" She squints at me. "And what the hell did you do with your hair?"

Yes, we are having a lot of fun here.

I elect not to serve the strawberry shortcake because while I feel no qualms about eating meat in front of Carla, I'd feel too guilty eating dessert in front of her when she's on a diet. Plus, she says that even looking at the strawberries will cause her to break out in hives. So we retire to the living room with another round of drinks.

Well, this is awkward.

Carla's only been here an hour, but it feels like forever, and yet it's only eight o'clock at night. The thing is, though, I have to make this last until ten, so it'll be a full three hours.

That's something I learned from Billy. Any social occasions involving one person going to another person's home—unless of course you're talking about drive-bys or condolence calls— must last for a full three hours. Otherwise, it's considered to be rude. Believe me, it's not like Billy's a paragon of etiquette—in fact, most days, he's just one evolutionary step ahead of Drew, as am I—so he certainly didn't come up with that gem on his own. Rather, he got it from Alice. It has, however, served Billy well, because whenever he's compelled to spend time with Alice's family, he simply marks the time on his cell phone when the get-together starts and sets the alarm on it to vibrate three hours hence. Then, as soon as the three-hour mark hits—not a minute before, not a minute after—he either stands to leave or yawns to encourage other people to leave, as the case may be.

I check my watch: now it's been an hour and four minutes, meaning there's still an hour and fifty-six minutes to go. So, much as I'd like to give a monster yawn and wide stretch, signifying an end to the evening, I realize that wouldn't be right. It would be like throwing in the towel and admitting that having Helen's people—or Helen's *person*—over was a complete failure. I can't do that to Helen. Still. What to do…what to do…

"How about a game of pool?" I suggest. After all, who doesn't like to shoot pool?

"I don't like to shoot pool," Carla says.

Oh.

"We could play something else," Helen offers hopefully.

There's something to play, other than pool or poker?

"I've got a whole box of games around here somewhere," Helen says, "from my old place. Let me go see what I can find."

I jump out of my seat. "I could help you look!"

"Don't be silly." Helen laughs, waving me back down. "You won't know where to look. I'm not sure even *I'll* know where to look."

She leaves, I sit, and once again I'm left alone with Carla.

"Beautiful night out, isn't it?" I try.

"I wouldn't know," Carla says. "I'm in here."

"That's a nice outfit you have on."

"It's old."

"Seen any good movies lately?"

"I don't believe in movies."

Screw this.

"Excuse me for a moment," I say. Then I go in the kitchen, get out the shortcake and whipped cream, and eat my dessert, minus the strawberries. Despite my screw-this attitude, I can't bring myself to eat it with strawberries because I'm worried hives might make Carla irritable.

"I found something!" I hear Helen call.

Backhanding the whipped cream from the corner of my mouth, I head back to the living room to see my wife holding a beat-up old box.

"Scrabble!" I say. I *love* Scrabble! "I didn't know you play!"

This is yet another wonderful thing I did not know about my wife.

"Are you kidding me?" she says. "The Troys take their Scrabble playing very seriously. This is the board my parents used to use. They got it when they were first married. They gave it to me because I loved it so much. Look at this."

She opens the lid to reveal an old board, folded in half, the edges worn. There's a felt bag inside and inside that are these beautiful old blond-wood tiles—not a hint of modern tacky plastic in sight.

"This looks like an antique," I say, fingering a smooth tile. It even feels better than any Scrabble tiles I've ever played with before. "Very cool."

"Want to play?" Helen looks at Carla, expectantly, hopeful.

Carla opens her mouth and from the shape of it, I'm sure she's going to say no, perhaps adding that she doesn't believe in Scrabble. But then she must see what I see—how happy and excited Helen looks—and the shape of Carla's mouth changes until what comes out of it is: "Why not? I know a few words."

And in that moment, I almost like Carla, because while we

have almost nothing in common, clearly we do share one goal: we both want to see Helen happy.

"Is the cat going to stay there the whole time?" Carla wants to know.

We're back in our places around the dining room table, which Fluffy has just jumped on, stretching in a very catlike way before he settles down on the vacant space between me and Helen.

What's Carla's problem? There's no food on the table. Fluffy's not bothering anything. This is where the action is, so who can blame him? He just wants to feel like part of the group. And despite the fact that I want to make Helen happy—which, on this evening, entails making Carla happy—I'm disinclined to give Fluffy the hook, what with the way he's been acting out lately.

"He's not bothering anything," I say.

"What if he knocks the tiles all over the place?"

"He won't knock the—" I grab the fourth wooden tile-holder from the box, set it down in front of Fluffy. "There. He'll feel just like us now, minus the tiles, so there will be no need for any knocking."

Fluffy touches a front paw to the tile-holder, perhaps noting that we have tiles in ours while he does not. I'm half tempted to give him seven tiles, just to see what letters he might randomly point to—would they spell a word?—but I'm sensing this is not the group for that.

"Tell you what," I say to Carla in the hopes of mollifying her with my magnanimous gesture. "We won't even draw tiles to see who goes first. Since you're the guest, why don't you go first and cash in on the automatic double-word score…"

Things go along nicely for a good half hour until I make *qwerty*.

"That's not a word!" Carla says.

"Of course it's a word!" I counter.

"What does it mean?"

"It's the modern-day layout for keyboards. It dates back to 1878. The name derives from the letters on the first six keys on the left of the top letter row. Q-W-E-R-T-Y: *qwerty*."

"You're making that up!"

I snort. "Is that a *challenge*? Because we can access the dictionary from my computer—you know, the computer with the *qwerty* keyboard?"

"Never mind," Carla says, grumpily.

She's even more grumpy when I add up my points. My *qwerty* ran down the far left side of the board, the *t* landing beautifully on the red triple-word score, adding on to a word Carly had made previously: *on*. The combined points of my *qwerty* and my *ton* when tripled comes to 72.

I swear, there is absolutely no gloat in my voice when I say that number for Helen, who is scorekeeper, to put down.

The game proceeds in silence for a few rounds with people just making your basic words but then my turn comes again and I'm stuck with an almost complete consonant stew. I've got just one vowel, an *i*, and so, making the most of it that I can, I add it to the right of the *q* at the top of *qwerty* to make *qi*.

"What is that?" Carla objects. "That's not a word."

"*Qi*," I inform her, "is the acceptable variant spelling of *chi*—you know, the vital energy that is held to animate the body internally. It's of central importance in some Eastern systems of medical treatment, like acupuncture, and exercise or self-defense, like tai chi. It is not, however, to be confused with chi as in the twenty-second letter of the Greek alphabet; that chi has no qi spelling variant."

Carla just stares at me for a long moment. "Who knows crap like that?"

I'm about to attempt an answer and it's a good thing Helen chimes in because I got nothing. How do I know what kind of person knows the things I know?

"Johnny graduated Magna Cum Laude," Helen informs Carla. Is that pride I see on her face? Certainly, no one here is gloating! "He's extremely smart."

"You know," Carla says, eyes narrowed as she wags a suspicious finger at me, "I think I recall hearing that about you. Maybe back when you and Helen were first dating? Helen might have even mentioned it more than once." She shrugs. "But for some reason, that knowledge of you has never stuck. I wonder why that is."

"I don't know." Now it's my turn to shrug. I'm tempted to say, *Maybe it's because you've never seemed inclined to see anything good in me?* But, not wanting to be rude to Helen's friend, instead I go with, "Maybe it's because I'm so good at impersonating stupid."

"That must be it," Carla says.

Another few rounds go by and now it's Carla's turn to stare at her tiles like she's stumped.

"Do you by any chance have an *a*?" I ask, thinking to be helpful.

"What? Have you been peeking at my letters?"

"No, but counting the number of *a*'s that are on the board, I figure there are still two outstanding. I know I don't have any, but I figured you might."

"And if I do?"

"You could attach it to the bottom of the *z* at the beginning of *zoo*."

"And that would make…*za*? What the hell is *za*?"

"It's slang for *pizza*."

"*Za*, for *pizza*? I've never heard anyone say that in my life—and, believe me, I've eaten a lot of pizza!"

I'm assuming she means before she went all Atkinsy, but anyway…

"It's in Webster's Eleventh! Look it up if you don't believe me!"

"*Qi, za*," she mutters, although I do notice she adds her *a* to the *z* for a nice eleven-point *za*. "The *qwerty* thing, maybe I can understand—I suppose that might be part of common knowledge, *somewhere*—but who knows *qi* and *za*? That's just plain weird."

"One night," I say, "I didn't have a whole lot going on, so I sat down with the dictionary and memorized all the *q* words that don't have a *u* following the *q* as well as every unusual two-letter word there is. You'd be surprised how helpful an encyclopedic knowledge of two-letter words can be when you reach the endgame in Scrabble. You almost never get stuck with any letters that way. Well, unless you've got a *v*."

"I can't even begin to tell you how odd that strikes me," Carla says, "and yet somehow, you make it sound so reasonable."

I've always been your basic level of competitive when it comes to anything, well, competitive, but glancing at the score on Helen's piece of paper and seeing how sour Carla looks, when I'm up a few turns later, even though I have the final *a* in my possession, I neglect to go for the obvious with *flautist*—triple-word score plus 50 points bonus since it's seven letters or greater; I mean, there's no point in spiking the ball in the end zone. Instead, I do something completely uncharacteristic. I take a dive with a simple *to*. Truthfully, it gives me a bad feeling inside. I mean, historically speaking, guys have forfeited entire professional basketball careers by point-shaving—and now here I am point-shaving at Scrabble, of all things.

But really, it doesn't matter how many dives I take. When the game is over, I still beat my closest competitor, Helen, by a hundred points.

And still there is no gloating here.


"Well, that was fun," Carla says, pushing away from the table. She stretches, rises, yawns. "I should probably get going."

"No!" Helen says, looking disappointed. "Stay! You've only just got here."

I give my watch a surreptitious glance. It's nine o'clock. Seriously? She's only been here two hours? Still, remembering Alice's wisdom on etiquette as received by me through Billy, I add my voice to the objections with, "Stay. Stay at least one more hour."

To make an even three, we just need one more hour—that'll cover us.

"What'll we do then?" Carla says, settling back down.

As tempting as it is to suggest another round of Scrabble, I refrain. Hey, I talked Carla into staying—I did my part. Let the women figure out what we should do next.

As they're figuring, I think about the slight injustice of the situation. For the last two Fridays, Helen has not only beaten my friends at poker, she's positively fleeced them, yet no one is a poor sport about it. They stay, they play, they lose, they lose some more. But here, I beat Carla at one measly game of Scrabble—there's no money on the line and I don't even play my best game—and yet she still gets all pouty face about it. Is that fair?

"…or we could go out," Helen suggests.

Wait? Did someone just say *out*? You mean we can get away from the hell this evening has become—three of us eternally locked around my dining room table, like some suburban social version of Sartre's *No Exit*? We can get away from this table, break the cycle and go *out*?

"But what would we do?" Carla says.

"I don't know," Helen says. "What do you want to do?"

Who cares what we do? We're going out! Let's go out! We could do anything—

"When I was driving over," Carla says, "I saw a bar on that really busy street—you know the one I'm talking about?"

"Main Street?" Helen provides.

"Right. That's the one."

Who cares what street it's on? Anything other than this would qualify as amazing.

"There was a sign out front," Carla says. "It says every Saturday night they have—"

Anything! I'll do anything—

"—open-mic karaoke."

—except that.

"That's fantastic!" Helen says.

No, it's not.

I thought we were past this karaoke stuff. I mean, I was hoping.

"Johnny?" Helen says, expectantly, hopefully.

Oh, geez. I hate to wipe that smile off her face. I know how much she loves karaoke—believe me, I know—and maybe if it was just going to be her and me going, I could maybe just barely make it through one more night of it. But adding Carla into the mix? Karaoke *and* Carla? I just can't bring myself to do it.

"You know," I say, "fantastic as it sounds, I just don't think I'm up to karaoke tonight. I think I may be"—cough, cough—"coming down with a little tickle in my throat."

Carla raises an eyebrow at me. Something I said? The way I said something I said?

I ignore her.

"I know how you hate it," I tell Helen, "when I'm at karaoke with you but won't sing." OK, that was like one time on the cruise ship, but still.

"Well, I don't know if I'd use the word *hate*…" She looks so disappointed. "But if you're not feeling well, I guess we could all just stay—"

"You know what?" I say. "There's no point in letting me ruin the good times. Why don't you and Carla go?"

"Without you?"

"Sure, I'll be fine here."

"Well, if you don't mind…"

A minute later, they're giggling their way out the front door.

"Hey," I call after them. "If you stop for a snack afterward, maybe you could bring me back a slice of za?"

Yes! Yes! Carla's gone, and I didn't even have to make it through a whole three hours! Ye –

But Carla being gone, in this instance, means that Helen's gone too. I'm not used to that. Oh, crap. What am I going to do with myself?

*It'll be fine*, I tell myself. *It's* fine.

I tell myself that while I wash the dishes, after first having another piece of strawberry shortcake *with* strawberries this time.

I tell myself that after calling up Sam to see what she's doing, only to have her say, "I'm watching a repeat of the Stanley Cup Championship." She's watching hockey? Who watches hockey, especially in repeats?

I tell myself that as I sit on the sofa, Fluffy in my lap, as I flick through all the stations on the TV. Wow, it's true what they say—all those stations and sometimes there really is nothing on.

"Geez," I tell the cat, "when's the last time I've had a free Saturday night to myself?" I think back over the year plus since I first started dating Helen; if there was a solo Saturday night in there, I'm not remembering it.

"I'm not used to being home alone without Helen on Saturday night," I continue to the cat. "Hell, I'm not used to being home alone without her on any night. This sucks. I miss her. Don't you miss her?"

Is it just me, or did the cat just shrug?

Fluffy looks at me and yawns, bored. I look back at the cat, bored too.

Then I get an idea.

"Hey," I ask the cat, "you feel like getting out of the house for a bit?"

"Should you drive or should I?" I ask the cat once we're outside.

Fluffy, at the end of his leash, stares back at me.

"It was a joke," I say. "Let's walk."

It's a nice night, the constellations up above twinkling over my small city, and the place I want to go to really isn't that far. We walk and talk and before you know it, we're standing outside of Chalk Is Cheap, a dive bar Sam and me used to frequent on those occasions when we wanted to be out shooting pool with people instead of in my basement, in other words before Helen came along.

"This," I inform Fluffy, as I hold the door open and let him precede me, "is about to be the culmination of a lifelong dream."

It's still relatively early for a Saturday night at Chalk Is Cheap, meaning there are hardly throngs there yet for us to wade through as we make our way to the bar and find two empty stools side by side. I pick Fluffy up, plop him on a stool, and then settle on the one next to him.

The bartender—long blond hair that looks like she irons it, it's so straight; midriff-bearing top with a diamond stud sticking out of her navel—ambles over. As she places both hands wide on the bar, hip cocked, I grow a little concerned. After all, just because I've dreamed of doing this, as with so much else in life there's no guarantee of dream aligning with reality. What if she kicks us out? I mean, it's not like Fluffy's a medical necessity, like a seeing-eye cat or something.

"What'll it be?" she asks.

"A Sierra Nevada Pale Ale for me and a saucer of milk for me furry little friend here?" I ask tentatively. After all, if she's going to kick us out, now would probably be the time.

Bartender eyes cat. Cat eyes bartender.

Then: "Cool," she says—the bartender, not the cat—as she pushes away from the bar to fill our order.

Apparently, Fluffy is not considered to be a health-code violation. Or perhaps, maybe in a bar that prides itself on still having a few patches of threadbare carpet left that patrons have not puked on, 'health code' is a relative term.

A moment later, there's a bottle of beer in front of me and an Old Fashioned glass with milk in front of the cat.

"Is that OK?" the bartender asks, nodding at the Old Fashioned glass. "We don't really have a whole lot of call for saucers around here."

"It's fine," I say.

"Does he want ice? Because I wasn't sure how he takes it."

"It's fine," I say again. "He's not particular."

The thing is, as I take a long pull on my beer, it's more than fine. Except for the part where I was tentative in placing our order, this moment is everything I've ever dreamed it would be. In fact, as I say "Cheers," following which, I clink my bottle against Fluffy's glass, and take another pull on my beer while he laps up some of his milk, I think that it is better than my dreams. This moment is awesome.

• • •

Apparently, I'm not the only one who finds this awesome.

"I never would have thought to bring my cat here."

Who said that?

I swivel on my stool and see…breasts. Not wanting to be staring straight at someone's breasts—I mean, they're only like two inches in front of my eyes—I stare down. But down that way are short shorts, tight in the crotch, and incredibly long legs. That doesn't feel right either, so I immediately swing my gaze upward, blinking as I pass the breasts so I won't be directly eyeballing them again, and settle on the speaker's head: pretty-enough features, spiky blond hair; definitely safer than breasts, crotch and legs.

"Can I buy you and your friend another round?" she offers, eyeing my wedding ring as my hand rests on the bar.

"Thanks," I say, "but we're good for now."

Another woman's voice comes at me from the other side of Fluffy: "Mind if I sit here?" Not waiting for an answer, from me or the cat, she sits down on the stool next to Fluffy. This one's very skinny, not so much in a "I've dieted myself down to almost nothing" skinny, but rather, in a "I was born this way" skinny.

"Some guy over by the pool table was bothering me," Skinny Chick informs me. "I could use a safe haven for a few minutes."

"Be my guest," I say magnanimously, raising my beer bottle.

I see Skinny Chick stare at the hand that's raising the beer bottle, my left hand, more specifically at my wedding ring.

"Do you shoot pool?" Long Legs asks me. "I've got quarters if you want to play."

"I do play," I say. "But, you know, the cat."

"I'll watch him," Skinny Chick offers. "Then, when you're done playing her, you could play me and she could watch him. It could be like a pool-shooting, cat-watching threesome, only you'd never have to watch the cat or sit out."

Tempting as that sounds…

"Another time, perhaps," I say. "I think I'd really better stick with the cat. He's been feeling very neglected lately."

Long Legs and Skinny Chick (hands over hearts): "Awwww…"

And yet a third female voice: "Want to dance?" The person attached to this voice actually touches my hand, the one with the wedding ring, after she asks this. This one's short and a little on the rounded side. I guess we'll go with calling her Pleasingly Plump—but not as a pejorative. She just happens to be both plump and pleasing, like a really great pillow.

"The cat," I explain ruefully. Really, I would never dance with her—I'm married to Helen and happily so—but it seems more polite to blame it on the cat.

"Know any good jokes?" Seriously? A *fourth* female voice? This one's…oh, forget it. This one, we'll just call This One, who continues with, "After the day I've had, I could use a good laugh."

Do I know any good jokes?

It's like all my life I've been waiting for someone to ask me this question. Oh, do I know some good jokes.

I start out small, with the kinds of jokes that almost any reasonable person would find funny—because it's tough to know the humor tolerance level of people you don't know—but as Long Legs, Skinny Chick, Pleasingly Plump and This One laugh appreciatively, and a couple more women wander over to see what the fuss is, I get more bold: nothing completely tasteless, you know, but maybe not completely tasteful either. I even venture into politics, always dangerous territory and especially so in an election year, but it turns out that like me, they're all supportive of This Guy, as opposed to That Guy.

"This is exactly what I needed," This One says during a break in the hilarity.

The break is not long enough to qualify for an awkward silence but it is just barely long enough for me to reflect: Just what is going on here? How did I wind up with—one, two, three, four, five, six—a six-pack of women hanging on my every word? It's safe to say that, me being me, nothing like this has ever happened to me before in my life.

But there's no time for me to analyze events, because now there's a *seventh* woman, only this one's like a compilation of the ones who've come before and as she bends over, cleavage practically in my face as she asks, "Can I pet your pussy?"—she did not just say that to me, did she?—it is finally too much for me. My response has absolutely nothing to do with my love for my wife, which is immeasurable and unending. It's simply Pavlovian. Cleavage + 'pussy' reference = instant hard-on. This means that I am out of here.

On the walk home with the cat, there is time to analyze the evening.

"Does it make any sense to you?" I ask the cat. "Women asking me to shoot stick; to dance; thrusting various…body parts in my direction. When has *that* ever happened before? Usually it's more like there's an invisible cone around me that serves to tell the world: *Men only; women, keep out.*"

The cat looks up at me like, *Dude, what are you obsessing about? It was just a few women. Anyway, it was me they wanted to pet.*

"Yeah, I know, but—" I stop. "Hey, wait a second." I look down at the cat. "Maybe it was you? Maybe you're some kind of, I don't know, chick magnet?"

The cat blinks back.

"I don't know." I start walking again. "I mean, they all saw the wedding ring and still they kept hanging out, some in an extremely friendly fashion. Could that be it—they're all into married men? But no, that would be too sick, at least on what would appear to be a near-universal level." More musing. "It is a puzzle."

The cat doesn't have any answers but that's OK because the ensuing silence affords me just enough time to think and now what I'm thinking is:

It's not just tonight. It's been encounters with women, including Willow's mother, the past several weeks, that have indicated a certain warming on the part of women toward me, a warming that's never been there before, a warming that's even extended—to a certain extent—to Alice. But how can that be? And then I think:

All my life, maybe I've only ever seen myself in the world through Alice-colored glasses before? Maybe, because of the model of womanhood Alice set, I only ever went after the kind of females who would only rebuff me? But maybe there were women out there who liked me, who would have wanted to be with me if I hadn't always been barking up the wrong tree— until I met Helen, that is—or expecting to fail simply because I'd always failed with Alice?

Hmm…

As I turn the corner from the sidewalk to the path leading to our front door, I glance at my watch: *Midnight?* Shit, was I at the bar for that long? I must have really been enjoying my own jokes.

The whole house is lit up—did I leave all those lights on? how environmentally unconscious of me—and as I reach my key toward the lock, the door swings open and I practically fall in.

"Johnny!" Helen says, then she throws her arms around me.

"Helen!" I hug her back, careful not to let go of Fluffy's leash.

"When I got home and you weren't here, I was so worried about you. I should have realized you were just out walking the cat, but when you didn't come back…"

"That's because where we walked was to the bar. We went to—"

"Wait a second." The hug stops and she leans back in my arms, away from me. "You were feeling so unwell"—cough, cough—"you couldn't go to karaoke with Carla and me…*but you were well enough to go out drinking with the cat?*"

Oh. Was I not supposed to do that?

# Weekend Worriers:
## Sunday

You could say that Fluffy and I are in the doghouse.

Apparently, that thing where I went to the bar with the cat instead of to karaoke with Helen and Carla? Yeah, I was not supposed to do that.

"Where's Helen?" Big John, seated in his wheelchair at the front door to his house, cranes his head to the left and the right of me, peering at the path behind me as I stand on the stoop. Maybe he thinks I'm hiding her back there?

"What?" I hear Aunt Alfresca's voice from the kitchen. Her voice gets louder as she nears with: "Is Helen not here?" And now Aunt Alfresca's in the doorway too, laptop tucked under her arm as she starts in with the neck-craning thing. Unsatisfied with the results of this futile exercise, her eyes narrow on me. "What happened? Did you two get in a fight?"

Flash backward to last night, right after I got home:

Apparently, I was not supposed to do that, the *that* in question being me going out drinking with the cat after telling Helen and Carla that I couldn't go to karaoke with them. I can tell that that *that* was the wrong thing to do, simply by seeing the look on Helen's face: sadness, disappointment—and is that a flash of anger there?

But just as quickly as the flash goes on, it switches off. Maybe I was seeing things?

Naturally, I apologize. I say, "I'm sorry. I guess once you left, I missed you and then I didn't know what to do with myself, so I just went out." In truth, I don't really know *why* I'm apologizing. I mean, what's the big deal? Still, it feels like an apology is required, like it's the sort of thing you do in these situations.

"You missed me," Helen says, in an unfamiliar tone of voice. Then she pats me on the cheek, as she adds, "That's sweet."

She turns and heads for the staircase.

"So, we're good?" I call after her as I bend to let Fluffy off his leash.

"We're good," she says, back still turned.

By the time I top off the cat's food bowl, put the house to sleep, wash up in the bathroom—I wish the ticking on that off-centered clock weren't so loud—and crawl into bed beside Helen, she's fast asleep.

Fast forward to this morning, which is still backward from now:

I wake in a good mood, which is not unusual for me and is in fact pretty much well the norm. What can I say? I'm a happy guy.

Helen, when she gets up a short time after me, appears to be in a good mood too as she wraps herself in a white silk shortie robe—I love that robe.

After retrieving the *New York Times* from outside and getting the coffee going, I make us a breakfast of chocolate chip pancakes and bacon. It comes out really well. Salty, sweet—we got all the food groups represented here.

Helen and I breakfast together very well. We eat, read the paper—since she starts and finishes with the front section while I'm cooking, and then leaves it near my plate, there's never any awkward competition for sections; when I'm ready to receive Sports, it's perfect timing because she's already done with it. Eating and reading in companionable married silence—there's even time in between for a little conversation.

"I know you never asked," Helen says, eyes on the Metropolitan section, "but Carla and I had a great time last night."

I'm a little puzzled by this; dually puzzled, really: 1) I didn't ask last night? that doesn't sound like me; and 2) was I supposed to ask, like some kind of requirement? And really, if she wants to tell me something or share something with me, does she need to wait for me to ask? Can't she just go ahead and tell or share, just say whatever she wants to say?

"I'm sorry," I say. "I can't believe I didn't ask and obviously I should have." There, that should cover it. "So, tell me now: How great of a time did you have last night?"

She sets down the paper and her smile is genuine when she says, "Really great! You would not believe what an amazing singer Carla is."

This is true. I would not believe that of Carla or anything else that might constitute a positive attribute. The only thing I'd believe is what a bitch she is.

Helen must see some of that on my face because "I'm serious," she objects. "And it's not just me saying so. You should have seen the crowd. People gave her standing O's, they kept asking her to sing again. Honestly, sometimes people will clap for a singer at karaoke just to be polite, particularly if the singer is attractive—"

!!!

"—but people don't beg for more unless the singer is extraordinarily good. I mean, that's never even happened to me."

!!!

There are so many things I don't think it's safe for me to comment about in there, so I just don't. Instead I ask, "What did Carla sing that was so good?"

I'm expecting the choices to come from Helen's awful playlist: ABBA, Bee Gees—really anything that seems to be alphabet-oriented. But instead Helen comes out with, "Pat Benatar."

Huh. Pat Benatar's not bad. And I can definitely picture Carla doing angry-chick rock.

"It's not just the singing, though," Helen continues. "Carla's just a lot of fun to be around."

I'm finding that hard to believe. The last word I'd ever use to describe Carla would be "fun."

"Really," Helen says, taking in my expression. "You just don't know her."

"Oh?" I fold my arms across my chest. "Enlighten me then."

In truth, I am curious. Come to think of it, a part of me has always been curious about what Helen sees in Carla. I mean, I fell in love with Helen. Carla, being Helen's BFF, naturally becomes part of the package, but I've never understood what Helen sees in her. My BFF is Sam and despite her shortcomings—her co-opting of my beer when we were neighbors, the fact that she can ride my ass like nobody's business—I don't see how anyone can look at her and not want a BFF like her. But Carla? Is it possible that there's a side of her I don't know? Could she actually even have more than one side?

"I realize that in the past few years," Helen says, "Carla's gotten a bit…buttoned-down."

Buttoned-down? Oh, is that the term for what she is? I thought it was colossally bitchy.

"But that's just appearances," Helen continues. "She takes her job seriously and thinks it's important to look the part. But before that? When we were in law school together? Carla drove a Harley."

Carla was a biker chick? Apparently, she's a real tough cookie with a long history.

"She was the life of the party. People loved being around her—still do. You know, she's got that dry wit. On top of that, she's an extremely supportive friend."

I guess she is a good friend to Helen. I mean, she was in our wedding party, she came to our house last night even though it meant spending time with me, something she clearly does not enjoy doing.

"I guess I just never saw that side of her," I say.

"I know, right?"

I give an internal wince when she says that—I still haven't found a way to tell her that one's out of play.

Helen looks puzzled as she continues. "I'm not blind. I do see that there's a certain…*tension* between you and Carla, always has been. But she's not like that with anyone else."

Oh, great. So she's the 'life of the party' with everyone else, but with me she's…whatever the hell she is with me? And I suppose this is somehow my fault?

Helen shakes her head at the mystery of it all. "I don't know why that is."

We go back to our papers and before long it's time for *The Chris Matthews Show*. We cuddle on the couch to watch. I love how enthusiastic Chris is about everything, even when he's wrong—it's important to have passion for your work—and I love it that Helen and I are in synch when it comes to politics. But as tempting as it is to segue right into *Meet the Press* afterward, we don't really have time.

"We should get showering and stuff," I say, "if we want to make it to Big John's by noon."

"Oh. Yeah. I think I'm going to pass on that today."

She's going to pass?

"What do you mean, you're going to pass?" Is she still upset about last night? But I thought she said we were good.

"I'm just not feeling all that well today."

But she looked fine a second ago. Come to think of it, she looks fine right now.

I point this out.

"I may look fine," she says, "but I don't feel fine. You know, I did have a lot to drink last night."

Actually, I don't know, since I wasn't with them at karaoke, although Helen seemed perfectly sober to me when I got home. But maybe that was just because I was pretty buzzed myself?

Wait a second, though.

"Is this, I don't know," I say, "because I didn't go with you guys last night? Like, I didn't go to your thing so you won't go to my thing?"

"Your thing, my thing—what are we, little kids?" Helen looks at me, shocked, offended. "Are you accusing me of immaturely tit-for-tatting you?"

Immediately, I back down.

"No, of course not. You would never do that."

"Of course I wouldn't."

. . .

And now I'm back in real time, faced by Big John and Aunt Alfresca wondering why Helen's not with me, the latter demanding to know if we had a fight.

"No, we didn't have *a fight*." I feel myself feeling unreasonably exasperated, so I tone it down when I add, "She's just feeling a little under the weather today. Helen and I don't fight."

And I realize as I say this that it is absolutely true. Helen may have been a little…*chilly* when I got home last night, she may be chilly in general from time to time about things that make no sense to me—and I, in turn, am occasionally…*mildly bugged* by this or that little thing—but we've never, in all the time we've known each other, had an actual fight.

Still, as I go through the day—eating, drinking, watching the Mets, trying to convince Aunt Alfresca not to tweet about my life—I do wonder:

Really, is the reason Helen's not with me right now because somehow she's getting even with me?

# Alice May Not
# Live Here Anymore

On Monday, contrary to normal patterns of behavior, I don't tell Sam about what I did with the rest of my weekend after I saw her on Friday. The evening with Carla, going to the bar with Fluffy, Helen not coming to Big John's and Aunt Alfresca's with me—for some reason, I don't feel like discussing any of it. So, instead, I simply mostly listen to her tell me what she did as we work through the day, finishing in time to go back to my place so we can watch GH.

It's an OK enough episode—the baby-switch storyline is heating up, although why anyone would ever depend on a DNA test at General Hospital, I'll never know; their reliability rate is something like zero. But soon the show is over, and there's a promo about how, starting on September 10, GH will begin airing one hour earlier, at two P.M., to make room for the new Katie Couric gabfest.

"I'm going to hate that," I say.

"Me too," Sam says. "I hate change."

Her and me both. But I guess everything changes at some point, whether you want it to or not.

"Not to mention," I point out, "we'll have to knock off painting even earlier to watch, which hardly seems conducive to a strong work ethic."

"We could always DVR it."

True. But somehow that doesn't seem the same.

"Hey," Sam says. "Wasn't something missing today?"

I think about it. "Well, there was no Todd Manning, which qualifies as a minus, but no matter how fun he is to watch, they can't have him on *every* day."

"Not that. I mean, obviously the lack of Todd is a minus. No, I meant Alice. How come she's not here watching with us?"

Huh. I guess maybe, underneath my GH-watching exterior, I've still been obsessed with events of the weekend, so I hadn't noticed the absence of Alice. Given that she came every day last week, it is odd her not being here today.

I shrug. "Maybe she had something else to do?"

But the next day, when the show comes and goes and still no Alice, I actually find myself growing a little concerned. Someone sets a pattern, you get used to that pattern and suddenly they break it—it's a little worrisome.

"Maybe I should just give her a call," I say, locating the number she gave me on my cell phone.

"Hello?" she answers.

"Hey, it's Johnny."

"I know. I saw that on Caller ID."

"Oh. Right. Listen, Sam and me were just wondering: Where've you been the last two days? Did you give up on GH or something?"

"No, I'm still watching. The show could've used more Todd yesterday, but otherwise it's been good."

"Then where've you been?" I repeat. "Are you not feeling well? Are you sick? Do you need me to bring you something?"

"That is…" There's a long pause and then: "very sweet." Another long pause. "But I'm fine, really, not sick at all."

"So you'll be back tomorrow?"

"Actually, no."

No?

"No," she says again. "Don't get me wrong. Last week was a lot of fun—I can't remember when I ever had as much fun watching as I did with you and Sam—but I think we should just leave it at that."

What? It feels like she's TV-watching breaking up with me.

"I just don't feel right coming there by myself anymore," she says. "I don't think Helen really appreciates it, and I can't say that I blame her."

Oh. Oh!

"But thanks," Alice says. "Thanks for letting me hang out with you guys last week. It really was, you know, a blast."

And that, as they say, is that.

# Sunday in the
# Park with Stavros

The previous weekend's pattern repeats itself with mild variation. On Friday we play poker in the basement with my friends and Big John. On Saturday, we have more of Helen's people over—this time her oldest brother Frankie and his wife Mary Agnes—and the evening is much more pleasant than the previous Saturday; the evening being much more pleasant is the mild variation. I do not, at any point, blow off doing something with Helen or go out by myself with the cat to the bar. And yet still, on Sunday, she doesn't come to Big John's and Aunt Alfresca's with me.

In a way, this is good, I tell myself. When she didn't come last Sunday, even though she denied it, I still got the sense it was a payback for the stuff with Carla, the bar and the cat. But I've done absolutely nothing in the last week to—for want of a better way to put it—make her want to get even with me; hell, she doesn't even find Alice here anymore when she comes home from work. But still, when Sunday morning comes, Chris Matthews ends and it's time to get ready to go, she claims to not feel well again. And yet she looks fine. So, not a get-even but not an ideal situation either. I can't make her go, though, and I can't accuse her of lying about how she feels—if she says she's not physically up to it, I have to respect that. But I did make a commitment to Big John, to come every Sunday, so off I go: alone.

• • •

213

The Mets win, which is good, and rare these days. Big John looks tired, and he's a lot quieter than usual, which is bad. Aunt Alfresca tweets about all of it, plus the fact that her "step-DIL is MIA", adding something she calls a twitpic of my haircut, followed by speculation that the hair is some kind of explanation for the absence of the step-DIL. This is all definitely not good, although it's not bad along the lines of world hunger, so let's just call it supremely annoying.

Driving back home, I'm wondering if this is the wave of the future—me going alone to my dad's every Sunday—so my mind is a little distracted as I pass *Stavros of Greece* meaning I don't notice anything strange at first. But there's a stoplight just beyond the shop that turns red right before I can squeak through and when I stop, I glance to the side and that's when I see all the lights in the shop blazing, Stavros standing in the window wearing his barber jacket, staring out at the street. When the light changes, instead of going forward and on to home, I pull over to the side and get out.

A bell jingles overhead as I yank open the door.

"Stavros," I say, "what're you doing here?"

"Johnny!" Apparently excited to see me, Stavros ignores my question. "It's so good to see you! Come on, come sit in the chair."

He turns his back on me, goes to the chair and picks up a towel draped over the back of it.

"I'm not here for a haircut," I say and he stops. "It's Sunday," I say. "You're not open on Sundays."

"Of course it's not Sunday!"

Oh no. He doesn't know what day of the week it is?

"No," I say gently, "really, it is."

"It is?" He sets the towel back down. "Huh. I was wondering why there were no customers. Was it something I said? Something I did?"

"It's not you. It's just, you know, the wrong day of the week, that's all." I pause. "Just how long were you standing in front of the window, looking for customers?"

He shrugs. "Since regular opening time?"

He normally opens at nine, it's now four, so if he's remembering the day accurately, he's been standing at that window for seven hours waiting for customers who were never going to come.

"You must be hungry," I say.

He shrugs again. "I could eat."

"Here, let me buy you a hot dog."


Stavros locks up the shop and I drive him over to Roger's Park, buy us each hot dogs from one of the food trucks lining the street there. Sure, I just ate a short time ago, and I'll be eating dinner soon enough with Helen, but a guy can always eat a hot dog. Well, unless he's already had five. Of course, even after he's had five, he can still eat more if he's in one of those stupid lots-of-food eating contests, but that's an exception.

"Good dog," Stavros says, saluting me with a hot dog that has one bite missing.

We stand and eat, watching the game for a while. On the field there's an adult-league men's softball game going on.

"I wish it were football," Stavros says. "I only like football."

"Yeah, I know."

"And who plays softball anyway?"

"I don't know. Old, out-of-shape guys who don't want to get hurt?"

"This would be more fun if it was football."

I can't do anything about that, but I remember something Helen said.

"Hey, Stavros. You got any family?"

"*Family*?" He says the word like it's something bad-tasting you spit out of your mouth. "You mean like a *wife*? You know I never got married, Johnny, don't have any kids, least not as far as I know."

"How about, I don't know, siblings that live nearby?"

"No, there's only me. Why you asking these questions?"

"I don't know. I was just wondering."

"You're worried about me." It's a statement, not a question.

"Maybe," I admit.

Stavros sighs. "Yeah, maybe I'm worried about me too, Johnny."

The guy at the plate crushes the ball to left field, or at least as much as you can crush a softball.

"That was pretty good," Stavros concedes. "But it'd be better if it was a football."


When it's time to take Stavros home, I ask him where he lives.

"All these years, you don't know, Johnny?"

Well, it's not like it ever came up in conversation before.

"I live right over the shop," he says.

Geez, that sounds depressing.

When we get back there, he invites me up for a beer, I say yes because I want to see where he lives, and it is depressing.

It's a one-room apartment, the bedroom connected to the living room. Everything's neat enough, but it's so spartanly furnished, like he just moved in, even though he informs me he's been there for decades. When he opens the fridge to get us two beers, I can see from behind him that there's not a whole lot else in there.

"I eat out most meals," he says. "Lately, it's gotten too depressing to eat here by myself."

He catches me looking around.

"I could've had a house," he says. "I've done very well for myself, cutting hair. But I never saw the point in spending the money on just me and it was always so convenient, living over the shop."

Convenience is one thing, but this all seems so…lonely. I can't imagine reaching the end of my days, being alone, living like this.

"I know what you're thinking," Stavros says shrewdly.

He does?

"You're thinking I shouldn't be on my own anymore."

Geez, the guy's a step ahead of me.

"You're thinking I should go into one of those…*places*."

Two steps!

Stavros shudders. "I don't know if I'm ready for that, though. I don't even know how to go about getting into one of those places. And anyway, I think I've still got a little time left of, you know"—he taps himself on the side of the head—"being good."

I don't blame the guy. He doesn't want to give up on the life he has in the world, such as it is, not yet. But he knows things are slipping away on him.

"Maybe," I say, thinking, "there's another way." I look around. "You got, I don't know, a little suitcase or something?"

Driving home, I'm wishing the drive were longer because I could sure use more time to think things through; because, you know, apparently I did not think things through before making this offer.

What's Helen going to say? I mean, I didn't even like it when she brought home a new clock for the upstairs bathroom without consulting me first—although I've never told her how I feel about that—so how's she going to feel about me bringing home an old guy who's starting to lose his stuff?

When I open the front door, Fluffy's waiting on the other side to greet us.

"Hey!" Stavros says. "A cat!"

He bends to scratch Fluffy under the chin and both of them look like they're in heaven. Then Fluffy turns and heads toward the living room, where the sound of television is coming from, and Stavros follows, gym bag in hand. There, Fluffy settles down on the couch to watch ESPN and Stavros drops his bag, settles down next to the cat. I settle down too, wondering where Helen is, what she's going to say.

A few minutes later, she comes downstairs, all smiles when she sees me but then stops smiling when she sees I'm not alone. Her eyebrows shoot up, questioning. Stavros doesn't notice her, he's too busy petting the cat while staring at ESPN, so I get up, gesture with my head toward the kitchen. Once there:

"Who's the old guy on my couch?" Helen wants to know.

I explain about finding Stavros staring out the window of the shop, him not knowing what day it is. I explain how concerned I am for him, how Stavros doesn't have any family, doesn't have anywhere else to go. All the while that I'm explaining, Helen just stares at me, an inscrutable expression on her face, so I continue explaining.

"I just kept thinking: What if it was Big John? What if something happened to me and Aunt Alfresca, he started losing his stuff and there was no one there to care for him? The idea of that just kills me, Big John being all alone. So I just couldn't leave Stavros there, but he's not ready to go into one of those assisted-living places, so I figured I'd bring him back here, just for a short time maybe, just until I can figure out another solution, maybe research some places…"

She's still staring at me.

"But of course, that's crazy. I see that now. It's too much to ask of you, too much to ask of anyone, that you should let some stranger guy stay in your home for an indefinite amount of time. I don't know what I was thinking. I'll just—"

"Shh." She reaches a finger out, stops my lips. Then she goes on tiptoe, replaces her finger with her lips and kisses me, hard. When she pulls away, there are tears sparkling like diamonds in her eyes. "You," she says, "are the most amazing man I've ever known in my life. Only you would do something like this. Of course your friend can stay, as long as he needs to. Somehow, we'll make it work."

I take her hand, squeeze it tightly as we head back to the living room.

"Hey!" Stavros says as we enter. "Who's the pretty lady?"

I look at Helen, who's smiling at him.

"Helen," I say, "I'd like you to meet my friend, Stavros."

She holds out her hand, which he enthusiastically shakes.

"Stavros," I say, "this is Helen, my wife."

"Your *wife*?" Stavros says. "Johnny, when did you get married?"

# The Wife

Last night, the evening we spent with Stavros was mostly very peaceful. We watched a lot of TV, and Helen and Stavros got on well together, although he did keep forgetting who she was. At one point, when she left the room to go to the bathroom, he turned to me and whispered, "She's very pretty, for a housekeeper, but she doesn't really do a whole lot of work around here, does she? Seven o'clock already and I don't see any dinner on the table. Do you see any dinner on the table?"

I reminded him that Helen's my wife, not the hired help. Then, figuring maybe it was all a hint to let me know he was hungry, I headed off to the kitchen to see what I could scrounge up. Stavros followed me and when we looked in the fridge, it turned out there wasn't much to scrounge.

"Wow," Stavros said, "this is almost as bad as my fridge. Still." He grabbed the carton of eggs, and the remains of the salad I'd made the night before. He sniffed the salad. "Dressing's already on, I see, but this could be interesting. You got a fry pan?"

I *did* have a fry pan.

Stavros set the burner to medium and dropped some butter on the pan, waited for it to sizzle.

"Hey," he said, "did I see a little bit of bacon left in the fridge? Why don't you get that going and then we'll crumble it right into the omelet—makes a nice contrasting crunch."

Apparently, Stavros knew what he was talking about, because the omelets we ate a short time later while watching ESPN were not only the fluffiest I'd ever had, but the added crunch was both contrasting and satisfying.

"I thought you said you don't know how to cook," I said.

"No, I'm pretty sure I said I mostly eat out. But I know

219

how to make do with what's lying around, if cooking needs to be done and the hired help is too lazy to do it." He cast a meaningful look at Helen, who failed to notice; she was too busy enjoying her spinach salad and bacon omelet. "But if someone would take me shopping, I could do better than this."

"Really? You want to take over the cooking?"

"Why not?" Stavros shrugged. "I got nothing better to do now."

It surprised me a bit—OK, a lot—how quickly Stavros was willing to give up on his previous life, his home, the barbershop. But my sense was that he'd known for a while that things were sliding downhill and was relieved to have someone—me—make the decision for him of what the next phase of his life would entail and he was also relieved that wouldn't be an immediate nursing home.

Stavros cast another look at Helen. "And the cooking does need to get done."

"Great. I'll take you when I get home from work tomorrow. Well," I amended, "after GH after work."

"What's GH?"

"A TV show. You'll love it."

"Or not," Helen put in.

"Does it have football?" Stavros wanted to know.

"Not exactly."

Since Stavros did the cooking, Helen and I cleaned up. This meant that for the first time, I got a chance to ask her what she did all day while I was at Big John's and Aunt Alfresca's.

"Watched the Mets game." She shrugged.

Really? She could have watched the Mets game with us.

"So you're feeling OK?" I said.

"Yeah, I'm fine. Why?"

"You didn't go because you said you weren't feeling well."

"Well, I'm fine now."

I neglected to point out how this was all making me feel a little…annoyed. I also neglected to direct her attention to what Aunt Alfresca's been saying about us on Twitter. After all, Helen was nice enough—amazing enough!—to take Stavros in, so how could I complain about petty crap like her not going to my dad's and how she spent her day?

Speaking of Stavros…

"Is anybody ever coming back out here?" he called from the living room. "The cat disappeared behind the TV and the TV reception disappeared too."

I went out to the living room, fixed the TVs, found the cat, and soon we were all back to watching stuff. Things went on nicely until time for bed, which was when the trouble started.

"Come on," I said, carrying Stavros's bag as I led him up the stairs. "Let me show you to the room that'll be yours while you're staying with us."

At the top of the staircase, the bathroom lay straight ahead, and I turned right down the short hall and switched on the light in the guest bedroom, gestured for him to enter.

I was figuring Stavros would be impressed with it. The bedrooms in this house are a decent size and even the guest room is bigger than Stavros's old living/bedroom/dining area put together. Plus, when Helen and I first moved in and discovered that the moving people had shoved all our stuff in the master bedroom, we moved the second set of furniture—mine—across the hall to this spare bedroom. If I do say so myself, my old bed and dresser and stuff looked homey in that room, even if the walls were still white because we hadn't gotten around to painting in there yet. Come to think of it, that white was a lot more peaceful than the pink-and-black monstrosity my bedroom had become.

"What do you think?" I asked, setting Stavros's bag just inside the room.

He turned in a slow circle, taking it all in. Then he sat on the edge of the bed, bounced a little, testing it, smiling at the nice level of bounce. A moment later, he sprang up, went to the door and poked his head out, turning his head first left and then right. He came back in, sat down again, bounced some more, only this time the bouncing was less enthusiastic and he was no longer smiling. A wistful expression had replaced the joy on his face and that's when I noticed the tears in his eyes.

"I gotta go back home, Johnny," he said. "It was nice of you to offer, and I'd like to stay here, but I just can't."

"What?" I was confused. "No. You don't understand. It's fine with Helen. She doesn't have a problem with you staying. She already said it's fine with her."

"I'm not worried about the housekeeper." He waved a dismissive hand.

"Then what is it? Why can't you stay?"

"It's..." He looked embarrassed, but finally, after a long pause he came out with it. "It's the bathroom."

"The *bathroom*? But I haven't even showed that to you yet. It's a very nice bathroom. Well, except for the clock."

"I don't care about any stupid clock." Another dismissive wave; really, it was more of a disgusted wave. "The bathroom," Stavros informed me, "is on the wrong side of the hall."

"What?" Now I was really confused.

"At my place, the bathroom is to the left of my bedroom. Here, it's on the right. I can't have that."

"So it's on the opposite side. You'll get used to it."

Stavros continued like he hadn't heard me. "I'll get up in the middle of the night to go, like I always do, then I'll turn left, after which I'll either fall down the stairs or pee on them. You can't have that, Johnny, neither of us can."

"What? No, that won't happen. You'll get used to it," I said again.

"I don't think so," Stavros said sadly. "Sometimes the mistress and me like to spice things up by going to a hotel—you know, play a few games, like Wealthy Widow And Cabana Boy. A few weeks back, we went to our usual hotel but our usual room was taken so they gave us a different one with the bathroom on the wrong side. I fell asleep for a bit and, pfft, it did not end well."

I pictured the scene. It was not pretty.

"I get confused too much," Stavros said. "Some things, I just have to keep exactly the same."

"Hey." Helen's voice, then she was in the doorway beside me. "How are you boys making out?"

"Stavros says he wants to leave."

"What?" Helen had the same reaction I did. "No. Why?"

I led her out into the hall and whispered an explanation, about the bathroom and the confusion and the peeing.

"But that's ridiculous," Helen said sternly, heading back into the guest bedroom.

I tried to stop her. Helen can be a bit brusque at times—that whole no-nonsense-D.A. thing—and I didn't want her telling Stavros he was ridiculous in his fears. How would that help the guy any? What might seem ridiculous to us was clearly very real to him. But as it turned out, I needn't have worried.

"You're not going anywhere," Helen told Stavros firmly. "So the bathroom's on the wrong side of the hall from here? Then you'll take our bedroom and it'll be on the right side. Or at least it'll be on the left side, which is the right side for you." She grabbed hold of one of his large hands with both of her feminine ones. "Come on, I'll show you."

Was she serious? I thought, following behind. Was she going to turn over our bedroom, the bedroom she painted those hideous colors, to my barber? And what was he going to think of all that pink and black?

"Oh," Stavros said, awed, doing that slow-turning-in-a-circle thing again. "This is…*amazing*."

"Isn't it great?" Helen agreed.

"Oh, yes. It reminds me exactly of a bordello I visited one time down in Florida."

I expected Helen to get offended at that last part, but she just smiled.

"We all set then?" she asked. "You'll stay?"

"Oh, yes. I think I could be very happy here."

"Great," Helen said, crossing to the bureau. "Let me just get my things for tonight and for the morning." Next, she hit the closet, picking out a suit and some heels. "Tomorrow after work, Johnny and I can move the rest of our stuff out. Goodnight, Stavros." She gave him a kiss on the cheek. "Sweet dreams."

Stavros and I watched her go.

"She's got a helluva nice walk on her," Stavros pointed out

appreciatively.

"That she does," I said.

It's a decisive walk, with just the right amount of sex and attitude in it. In the Friday *New York Times*, there'd been a review of a new Richard Gere movie in which the reviewer mentioned that Gere had one of Hollywood's great movie walks. At the time, I realized how true this was; as soon as it was said, I could immediately picture Gere walking across the screen in dozens of movies, owning his movement in a distinctive way. Helen's like that, only now I was rolling her walk in my mind with that of Richard Gere's, which was not the image I wanted, so I stopped.

"She's also an incredibly nice lady," Stavros added, indicating the bedroom, now his, at least for the time being, "to do something like this."

"That she is," I agreed.

Then I grabbed my own things from the bureau, my cat-behavior book from the night table, and got out of there.

A short time later, Helen and I lay in bed, the door to our new bedroom closed. A part of me couldn't believe my good fortune. True, the guest room was smaller than the master, but—yes!—I was out of that pink-and-black monstrosity. Still. I took her in my arms.

"I can't believe you did that," I said, "giving Stavros ourbedroom."

"Why? It's no big deal. And if it makes him feel more comfortable and secure here…"

"Yeah, but you *loved* that bedroom. You had it painted *exactly* as you wanted it."

"It's no big deal," she said again. She looked around, a relieved expression on her face, then sighed contentedly as she shut her eyes. "Actually, I kind of like the white in here."

Then why did she insist on painting…

Huh.


And now it's a new day.

I wake earlier than usual, because someone is singing. The

shower is running, but Helen's still beside me, and I realize that the person singing happily is Stavros. The song is in Greek, so perhaps that's an added clue. Helen manages to sleep through it, but much as I try to return to sleep, I'm unable to, so I get up, head downstairs and start the coffee.

A few minutes later, Stavros joins me, all crisply dressed for the day. Beside him struts Fluffy, who is soaking wet.

"What happened to the cat?" I ask, groggily, from where I'm sitting at the kitchen table.

"He jumped in the shower with me!" Stavros is practically giddy with glee as he takes a seat. "And last night, he slept with me!"

The cat jumps up on the table and then settles down, tucking his paws beneath his chest and blinking at us.

"I think he looks like a proud lion," Stavros says. "Do you think he looks like a proud lion?"

"Most definitely."

Turns out we finished the last of the eggs for dinner last night.

"It's still early," Stavros says.

He's telling me? If there were still milkmen in the world, they wouldn't even be up yet.

"Maybe," Stavros suggests, "you could take me grocery shopping now?"

So I get dressed and we do that. I take him to Super Stop & Shop, but I'm still half asleep, so I just push the cart and don't really pay attention as he throws stuff into it. I do notice that not much of what he grabs looks terribly familiar, but hey, if he's willing to cook...

He's also willing to pay.

"I'm not a freeloader, Johnny," he tells me. "I got plenty of cash."

Back home, Helen's up and she sits at the table with me as Stavros makes us breakfast, which turns out to be oranges drizzled with honey and feta-filled croissants.

"Tomorrow, I'll make *tiganites*," Stavros says, "Greek pancakes. You can put syrup on them but I prefer preserves.

You got any brandy in the house?"

Helen smiles, content, as she pops a final orange slice into her mouth. "I could get used to this," she says.

Before Helen and I leave for the day, Stavros asks if there's anything special he should do while we're gone.

I can't think of anything, so I show him where I keep Fluffy's leash. "Maybe walk the cat?"

Driving to work with Sam, I am once again reluctant for some reason to tell her about Helen's failing to come to Big John's with me. But I do tell her about Stavros.

"And Helen's OK with this?" she asks.

"Well, yeah. She even insisted on giving him our bedroom when he got upset about the bathroom being on the wrong side of the hall."

This is enough to make her put down the giant sticky thing she's been eating.

"Do you realize how extraordinary this is?" Sam asks.

"What?"

"Helen agreeing to take in your barber."

"Well," I say, feeling unaccountably stung, "I took him in too. I even took him in first."

"Yeah, but he's *your* barber. Besides, you're crazy like that— you do that sort of thing. But Helen?" I glance away from traffic long enough to see her shake her head. "Look, don't get pissed, but there are times I'm not too thrilled with some of the shit you tell me she does. And don't get me wrong, I like her well enough, but I never could have pictured her doing something like this."

"Yes, it's a nice thing for her to do."

"*Nice?*" Sam says. "*Nice* is I hold the door open for the person behind me."

"Actually, that's just good manners."

"Whatever. But this? *This* is extraordinary."

I guess, I don't know, maybe.

"*I* wouldn't do it for your barber, Johnny," Sam continues. "I'm not sure I'd do it for *you*. And I'd never expect anyone to do it for me. When the time comes that I start losing my shit, just put me on an ice floe and send me out to sea."

"I am *not* going to put you on an ice floe."

The conversation degenerates into squabbling about what we would/wouldn't do with each other when we get old and a debate about global warming in general, but Sam has set me thinking.

And what I'm thinking is how truly extraordinary my wife is.

When we arrive home in time for GH, the whole place smells like lemons. True, Helen gave the place a good cleaning prior to Carla's visit on Saturday, but in the way of two people who don't generally like to spend their free time housekeeping, we'd let it deteriorate to its usual messy state on Sunday. But now the hardwood areas are shined to a high polish, the carpeting has vacuum tracks in it, and when Sam and I enter the living room, we find Stavros folding laundry. To be specific, he's got a pair of Helen's underpants in his hands.

"What're you doing?" I ask, after introducing him to Sam.

"I've got to make myself useful, don't I?"

"Not really."

"OK, then. I *want* to make myself useful. Besides, after taking the cat for three walks, I needed something else to do with my time, didn't I?"

As we settle down to watch GH, at first Stavros isn't too into it. He has trouble keeping all the characters straight but that's hardly a sign of dementia; soaps can be confusing. But then I remember what Billy once told me about watching soaps before I was into it, about how if you treat it like another sport and lay bets on things, it can seem like more of a sport. So we lay short-term bets on whether any real progress will be made on the baby-snatching storyline by episode's end or if it'll just be a retread of old information; medium-term bets on how many episodes the characters wear the same clothes, because a day can last a really long time in Port Charles; and long-term bets on who the next woman will be that Sonny gets pregnant. I bet on Elizabeth because I'm pretty sure she's the only female, not a relative, that he still hasn't slept with.

And so the time passes.

At one point, Stavros goes into the kitchen to get us all another beer and freshen the snacks.

"You know," Sam says, "even though Alice was only with us a week, I kind of got used to her. I even missed her a bit when she stopped coming. But this could work."

So Sam's happy.

And when Helen comes home from work to warm gyros in soft pita bread with yogurt sauce, she's happy too.

As the week goes on, everybody's happy, although Helen and I are both disturbed one early morning to hear sounds coming from Stavros's room, only to realize he's got a guest in there, his mistress Magda—red beehive hairdo, harlequin glasses, on the slightly less pleasing side of plump. At first, we're nonplussed but then we realize the guy's not dead yet—he's got a right to conjugal visits, although it might be nice to have a little warning.

But then Friday comes and I arrive home from work with Sam to realize that, no, not everybody is happy.

Stavros isn't happy.

"Um," I tactfully ask Stavros, who's looking a little sheepish, as I circle Fluffy, "what happened to the cat?"

"I gave him a little trim."

"A little trim? He's bald!"

"No, Johnny," Stavros is quick to reassure as he fluffs what remains of the cat's hair. "It's a crew cut—in this summer heat, he'll love it!"

If the cat looked ridiculously hairy before, this is even worse, and I suppose I don't do a good job of hiding my dismay.

"I'm sorry, Johnny." Stavros is crestfallen. "Sometimes I don't know what to do with myself. The cooking, the cleaning—I like taking care of you and the lazy housekeeper, but it's not enough. I like watching the catsom—etimes, he watches the giant praying mantis outside the window, so I watch the cat and then I wonder: does the praying mantis watch me? Is this what you call a vicious circle? Even philosophical considerations like that are not enough." He sighs, an incredibly sad sigh. "I miss cutting hair, Johnny. I know I can't run the shop anymore, I no longer have the head for managing a business, but I don't know who I am without cutting hair."

This, I can understand. For a long time now I've been known to say: Paint—it's who I am.

"We'll work something out," I tell Stavros, although I don't know what that might be. "In the meantime, I think I could use a trim."

"Are you sure? I mean, your show…"

"I'm sure. Why don't you get your stuff and we'll do it in the kitchen? Sam can call out the good parts from the living room."

A few minutes later, Stavros is snipping away when a thought occurs to me.

"Hey, how'd you get the cat to sit still for you to cut his hair like that? I have enough trouble when all I want to do is clip his nails."

"It was easy. I just gave him a treat occasionally."

"A treat? What kind of treat?"

Stavros stops what he's doing long enough to open the fridge and pull out the canister of Indoor Adventures, the chicken-flavored treats Fluffy loves.

"Have you seen these things?" He waves the canister at me. "It's like an indoor adventure!"

At the sound of the rattling treats, Fluffy comes running like he always does; really, for a cat, he's very Pavlovian.

"Here, you give it to him." Stavros hands me the canister. "I'm kind of busy cutting hair here."

When I take off the lid, I realize there are only a few left and I could swear it was nearly full last time I checked.

"Stavros," I say in an even voice, "how many of these did you give him?"

"I didn't count." *Snip, snip.* "At least one between every snip." *Snip, snip.* "How else're you going to get a cat to sit still for so long?"

He gave him a whole can practically? The cat's bald, he's going to get fat, next stop stupid and he can hit for the trifecta.

"You're not supposed to—" I start to inform Stavros but then I stop.

Stavros is whistling, he's happy again, at least for the time being—I can't bring myself to spoil that.

A few hours later, Stavros is ecstatic. We're all playing poker in the basement. No, Stavros isn't playing with us ("too much to remember with all those cards, Johnny") and he does have trouble remembering everybody's names, even though Big John was the one who first started taking me to see him when I was just a little guy. What Stavros is ecstatic about is having a lot to do: keeping the cat entertained and off the table, making sure everybody's got enough beer, replenishing the snack supplies. And those snack supplies! They go beyond my classic, Chips In A Bowl.

Stuffed grape leaves; *saganaki*, which is a fried Greek cheese; batter-fried zucchini strips.

Really, the food is so good, there's hardly any point in paying attention to the card game.

The others are a little puzzled by Stavros, this non-playing presence at the weekly game. So while he's out of the room, I explain.

I expect Big John to be, I don't know, maybe a little competitive with Stavros; we Smiths have been known to be small-minded that way. But he's fine with it, looks proud even.

"How's it going?" Billy asks, casting a glance at Helen. "I don't think Alice would be too pleased about something like this."

"It's fine," Helen says. "Look at the place: we don't have to do a thing for ourselves anymore."

I agree with her that it's working out fine, for us, but I do mention Stavros being upset earlier about not cutting hair anymore.

"Aw," she says. "You didn't tell me that."

"You got home kind of late." I shrug. "I didn't have time. I take it you haven't seen the cat?"

"No, why?"

"Trust me. When you see the cat, you'll know we've got a problem on our hands."

"That's got to be hard on a man," Big John says, "not being able to do the things he defines himself by anymore."

There are a lot of things Big John can't do anymore that he used to define himself by and that's too sad to think about, so we go back to our cards. But when Stavros comes in a few minutes later to check if anyone needs more beer, Drew says, "Hey, um, Stavros. I hear you can cut hair?"

"Oh," Stavros says, "the heads of hair I have cut in my day, you should've seen them. But that's in the past now."

"No kidding?" Drew says; then, not waiting for an answer, he adds, "That can't be true." He runs his hand down the back of his head. "I'm getting a bit long here. You think you could do something about this for me?"

"When?"

Drew shrugs. "Now's good. We could do it right here."

"Really?" Stavros doesn't wait for an answer, instead heading upstairs to get his gear.

We all stare at Drew.

"What?" he says.

"That was so…nice," Sam says.

"I can't be nice?"

Well, no, I don't think anyone would go that far. But Drew's the guy who always brings Budweiser—unironically, I might add—so it's not like he's exactly known as the soul of generosity.

"Besides," Drew says, throwing his cards on the table, "my hand sucks."

When Stavros returns, in addition to his hair-cutting tools, he's also got some newspaper to put on the floor to catch the clippings.

"I don't want to make a mess." He looks at me meaningfully. "You know, just in case 'the housekeeper' doesn't come this week."

Soon, not to be outdone by skinflint Drew, Billy's asking Stavros for a trim, Steve Miller too.

I look at my friends like: I can't believe you guys are doing this.

"Ah, it's no big deal," Steve tells me. "And it kind of beats being fleeced by your wife," he adds in an undertone, but there's no malice in it.

Big John's hair has been mostly gone for a long time now, meaning he hasn't needed a professional cut in years. But, not to be outdone, he finds a single strand and extends it in Stavros's direction. "Hey, Stavros, when you finish with those guys, can you do something about this here? It's just the one, but it's been bugging the crap out of me."

Stavros, needless to say, is over the moon at all this.

My family. My friends. Are they doing it for Stavros, who they don't really know, or are they doing it for me? Who really cares?

"I guess that's everybody," Stavros says with a sigh, once he's dispensed with Big John's lone troubling hair. The look on Stavros's face is like Fluffy when I've been petting him and then I stop, like he was hoping it could go on forever.

"What about Helen?" Sam suggests.

"*Me*?" Helen actually points at her own chest. Then she turns that pointer right at Sam. "What about *you*?"

"Hey." Sam holds her palms up. "Your house, your barber."

Helen looks reluctant, but Stavros seems so hopeful again, standing there with his scissors, she relents.

"OK," she says, assuming the chair, "but just one of those minor trim things, like you gave the other guys."

Stavros studies her head from all angles but, unlike with the men, he doesn't get right down to work.

"Maybe," Stavros suggests, "you got one of those ladies' magazines hanging around here somewhere with a picture of how you'd like it to be?"

"Really, I just want—"

"I'll find something," Sam offers, tearing up the stairs.

We wait.

Sam returns with a magazine I didn't even know we had and then she's flipping through the pages, making faces at a lot of what she's seeing. "Nah...Nah...Nah." Then: "This!" She stabs the page with her finger.

"Let me see," Helen says, but Sam hands the open page to Stavros, pointing.

"Oh, yeah!" Stavros says. "I better get started."

He sprays the back of Helen's head to get it wet, runs a comb through it.

"You know," Stavros says, "I never cut a woman's hair before."

"You never—" Helen tries to rise but Stavros puts a staying hand on her shoulder.

"Don't worry," he tells her. Then to Sam, "Hey, girlie, can you hold that magazine steady in front of me?"

It takes Stavros more time to cut Helen's hair than it did everyone else's put together. When he's done, we all stare at Helen, who gives us a trepid look.

"So?" She smiles stiffly. "How is it?"

Billy: "Amazing."

Steve Miller: "Very unbuttoned-down."

Big John: "Lovely."

Drew: "Yowza."

"You guys are kidding, right?" Helen says, clearly convinced they're lying. She turns to Sam for help. "Do you have a mirror on you?"

"Do I *look* like the kind of woman who carries a mirror?"

And that, my friends, is what is called a rhetorical question.

"But," Sam adds, "everything they're saying is true."

Obviously not trusting anyone, it's Helen's turn to go tearing up the stairs and soon we hear a shriek from the main-floor bathroom, followed by, "I look fucking beautiful!"

And she does, or at least she did when she was still in the room. Helen has never been anything less than gorgeous. But now? The cut is angular, geometric, I don't know the right words for it. All I know is it makes all the various shades in her auburn hair—from honey gold to wine red—stand out in relief and it is all just so, so beautiful.

Now Helen's back, she's giving Stavros a loud smack on the cheek with her lips, and then her arms are around me and she's kissing me too; only, you know, it's hot.

"We," she says between kisses, "have the best wife in the world."

# Tick

Time goes on as time will do, no matter how much we humans may do to try to change it.

The months fly by—July, August, September, the first half of an October that does not include the Mets making it into the World Series, not even close – and we settle into married life together.

The joint poker games on Friday night continue, with Stavros, who is still living with us, providing snacks and haircuts.

Saturdays, we have Helen's people over. I almost never know in advance who I'm going to find at my dining room table, but that's OK, since mostly it's her parents or one of her brothers and a spouse or Carla. Some might think it odd, me never knowing who I'm going to find on the other side of the door, but I enjoy the mystery of it all; you know, unless it's Carla. That is the least enjoyable, for me at least, but it's also the only times Stavros joins us for these dinners. When it's Helen's family, he says he doesn't feel right about it—"I don't want to be a fifth wheel," he says, adding that he thinks Helen and me should be able to have a social life that doesn't include him; plus, he likes spending quality time, just him and Fluffy. But with Carla, he says that he's a fourth wheel so that's OK, and, wonder of wonders, he and Carla get along well. Part of that could be that he gave her a killer haircut that she attributes to being the single thing that's scored her more dates in the last three months than she's had in the last three years. So that's our Saturdays taken care of.

As for Sundays, I still go to Big John's and Aunt Alfresca's every week. Now that Stavros lives with us, he likes to go too and Helen rarely bows out.

So you could say we have an established pattern of activity, which I refer to as our routine. Sam calls it a rut.

Really, almost everything Helen and I do is joint, except occasionally shopping, which means that Helen keeps showing up with new things for our home. I'm not sure who is bothered by this more, Sam or me.

Here's Sam on the first time it happened back in June with that clock:

"That's kind of a big deal," Sam said at the time. "She's making changes to your environment without consulting you first?"

"What?" I said. "She has to ask me about every little thing?"

This, in fact, was pretty much what Helen said to me the morning after I discovered the clock and I raised the issue again.

At the time, my reply was, "No, but—"

I never got any further, because it occurred to me that she had a point. It was her house too. Why shouldn't she bring home whatever she wanted?

"But would you ever do that?" Sam asked when I told her that. "C'mon, you'd never bring home something like a clock without seeing if it was a clock she liked too or even if she wanted one at all first."

"It's just a clock."

"A clock is never *just* a clock, Johnny."

"Hey, didn't Freud say that?"

"It's not funny. She should care what you think about these things."

"Aw, what does any of it even matter? So long as she's happy—"

"What about you being happy? Isn't it your environment too?"

Over time, I simply stop telling Sam about it when Helen brings home surprise items that are not exactly to my taste. What's the point in having Sam get all worked up? Especially after Sam coins the phrase "hostile purchases" to refer to them. Why have Sam get upset? After all, it really doesn't bother me. It's fine. It's *fine*. So long as Helen's happy, I keep telling myself, isn't that the important thing?

And I go on telling myself that until one day Helen brings home something that's a little too big to ignore, the first of two things that will jar us out of our routine—or rut, depending on who's describing my life. That's the day in October when Helen says she has a surprise for me, disappears for a few hours, and comes home with…

# Woof

...a dog.

And not just any dog. It's a really big dog. According to Helen, his name is Bowser. Me, I'm thinking Cerberus would be a more accurate name as the beast from hell strains against the leash Helen's barely holding on to, drool dropping from his mouth onto the hardwood floor. The coat of the animal is a dark fawn color with black on the muzzle, ears and nose, and around the eyes.

"What is that thing?" I say, tempted to back away. "It's huge."

"Huge?" Her voice strangles a bit on the laugh that follows as she adds a second hand to what looks like it may be a futile leash-holding operation. "He's still just a puppy."

"A puppy? How big is that thing going to get to be?"

"It's not a thing. It's a *he*." Then: "I don't know." She shrugs. "A hundred and fifty? Two-hundred fifty pounds?"

"Two...What is it, I mean *he*, an elephant?"

"Oh, no," she says, quite serious. "Elephants grow much bigger." She removes a hand from the leash just long enough to scratch under the dog's chin. "Bowser's an English Mastiff."

"A Eng—" OK, I know I'm starting to sound like Little Sir Echo here, but honestly, I may not exactly be speechless over this, yet, but it's definitely causing me to be speech-impaired. "But aren't those, like, the biggest breed of dog in the world?"

"Not *like*." More petting. "*Are*. They *are* the biggest dog breed in the world. The largest one ever weighed three hundred and forty-three pounds—I looked it up—but after 2000, Guinness stopped recording largest and heaviest pets, so who knows? The breed could be growing bigger all the time." She looks at the dog, addressing him as she scratches under his chin.

"You going to be a champion-sized dog? Who's a good dog, Bowser? Yes, you are. Yes, you are."

God, that's annoying.

"But don't you think," I say, careful not to let that annoyance show, "that Fluffy might be, oh, I don't know, traumatized by the size of this thing?"

Needless to say, there's a lot of barking going on, because that dog wants off that leash, like, yesterday. Helen struggles to hold him. Despite her own slenderness, I've always thought of her as tough, strong, but that *puppy* must weigh at least sixty pounds. And what, by the end of the year, he'll grow to be two and a half to four times that size? The mind reels.

At my own mention of Fluffy, I turn around. When Helen came through the door, Stavros and Fluffy and me had just been hanging in the living room, but now I see that Fluffy's gone, Stavros too. Yup, the cat must be traumatized already, probably hiding out under a bed upstairs; again, probably Stavros too.

"I'm sure the cat's fine," Helen says. "Anyway, I got him for you."

When did I ever ask for a dog?

"What," she says, before I can point this out, "was I supposed to ask your permission first before getting myself a dog?"

Wait a second. Didn't she just two seconds ago say the dog was for me? Now it's her dog?

"So," she says, bending down, "I'm going to let him off his leash now…"

"Excuse me for a minute," I say, backing up, then I turn and head for the stairs.

"Where are you going?" she asks when I'm already heading up.

Below me, the dog's already tearing around the living room.

"Bathroom," I say.

"What's wrong with the one down here?"

I give myself a hit on the side of the head to indicate, *What was I thinking of?* and say, "Well, I'm already halfway up," and then continue the rest of the way. Once on the second floor, before proceeding to my ultimate destination, I check the bedrooms. Sure enough, the cat's under the bed in Stavros's room. Even though the spread goes to the ground, I know the cat's under there because Stavros is down on all fours, his butt facing me as he tries to talk some calmness into the cat.

"He's really upset, Johnny," Stavros says.

Who can blame him? All that barking—it probably acts on him like that stupid ticking clock acts on me.

"I'm doing what I can," I tell him.

"Don't worry about it," Stavros says. "We'll be fine."

I go to the bathroom, shut the door and call Sam. When she answers, I fill her in on what's happened.

"That's a hostile act," are the first words out of her mouth when I'm finished.

"What? *No*. It's not a—"

"Then how else would you describe it? This isn't like her bringing home a *clock* without asking you first or picking out whorehouse colors for your bedroom without consulting your opinion. She brought home a *dog*, a big fucking dog. If that's not a hostile act..."

"So, what," I say, recalling something Helen said just a few minutes ago, "was she supposed to ask my *permission* first?"

"*Yes*. OK, maybe not that, but she at least should have discussed it with you before bringing home something that could wind up weighing two hundred and fifty pounds."

"Wait a minute. How did you know they can weight that much? I never said anything about that part."

"What do you think? I've been googling. Holy crap, I hope your dog doesn't end up like Zorba."

"Zorba? Who the hell is Zorba?"

"Three hundred and forty-three pounds, heaviest dog on record, at least according to Guinness, who stopped—"

"Yeah, I know all about Guinness and that guy," I cut her off. "I just didn't have a name for him before. Christ. *Zorba*."

"It says here that due to their massive size and need for space, the dogs are best suited to country or suburban life. Where does Helen think you guys live? You got a lot of space there, *Squire*?"

"Well," I say, starting to feel offended on Helen's behalf, "maybe it's not the country, but Danbury is a suburb."

"Try it's more like a small city. You got some landed estate you're hiding over there, *Squire*—"

"Stop calling me that."

"—because last time I was there, it looked more like a patch of grass."

"Yes. Well."

"No two ways about it, it's a hostile act."

"And stop saying *that*."

"It's true, though. What else would you call it? *Everyone* knows you love that cat of yours. So what could Helen have been thinking? Did she somehow think that you and the cat and your barber would all be *happy* about this?"

I don't know. I don't know what Helen was thinking. I'm only sure of one thing: It's not this 'hostile act' Sam keeps referring to, a thought I distance myself from as I realize this isn't helping the situation any.

"I gotta go," I say.

"Prior to today, did Helen ever *profess* some great desire to have a dog?"

Did she pro—

"I gotta go," I say again.

"Oh, wait! Here's some good news."

"What?"

"According to the American Kennel Club, English Mastiffs have 'a combination of grandeur and good nature as well as courage and docility.' Who would've thought a monster that size would be docile? Think about it. If you can just get through the puppy stage, he might wind up a perfect companion for Fluffy."

"If Fluffy doesn't have a heart attack from fear or commit suicide first."

"He's not going to—Oh, more good news."

"I can't wait."

"The breed is susceptible to a lot of health issues—hip dysplasia, allergies, hypothyroidism, etcetera—but you got a boy instead of a girl, so at least you don't have to worry about vaginal hyperplasia."

Yes, at least there is that.

As I exit the bathroom, I hear my wife calling from downstairs:

"Johnny? We got a situation here!"

When I hit the top of the stairs, there's an odor and it gets stronger the lower I descend. At the bottom of the staircase, I look around and spot the source of the stench. It's a pretty big source.

"Ah," I say. "Not toilet-trained yet, huh?"

"He's just a puppy," Helen says defensively.

Never mind puppy. He's huge and what comes out of him is proportionally so.

Well, this is new and different, I think, searching for something to clean it up with. I also think that even once the dog is trained, I'm going to need to get a shovel and a Hefty bag to follow him around the neighborhood with.

As predicted, by me, the cat is traumatized.

For hours, Fluffy won't eat, won't use the litter box at all, won't even come out from under Stavros's bed, let alone go downstairs. I look through my cat-psychology book, but honestly, there are no chapters on how to help a lone little cat adjust to having a huge dog in the house.

This can't go on, I think. The little guy's gotta be able to drink water and eat, plus, it's not good for him to hold stuff inside for hours on end. So, eventually, I drag his furry little body out from under the bed and carry him in my arms downstairs like a baby. Helen's watching pre-season basketball on TV and the dog's sleeping on the area rug in the living room, which is a good thing, so I carry the cat to his litter box on the landing to the basement, set him down in it so he can do his business.

"It's OK," I tell him when he looks up at me with fear and a question in his eyes. "I'll stay right here. I got your back."

Once that's done, the results neatly buried—cat's are so much easier than dogs—I go up and grab his food and water bowls from the kitchen, bring them down. I encourage him to eat and drink, staying right beside him all the while. He seems better now, calmer and almost happy again, but when we leave the landing, the cat in my arms again, and enter the main floor, the barking starts.

Fluffy freaks out, struggling to get out of my arms, I'm guessing to run upstairs again. But here's the thing: Yes, the dog is barking, but while he's doing so, he's backing up, all the while staring at Fluffy like the cat's some kind of monster.

"Oh, geez," I groan. "Not you too."

Helen gets on the floor to reassure the dog, but he keeps backing up until he's all the way in the corner with nowhere else to go.

I suppose now I'm going to have to get a book on dog psychology too?

"I will not have this," I announce looking from the cat to the dog and back again. "I refuse to live in a house divided."

Fluffy's still squirming but I refuse to let him go as we approach the dog and I tell Helen to hold onto Bowser.

Then I thrust the cat practically in the dog's face.

"We're not going anywhere, pal," I inform Bowser, who tries to shrink back. "This is Fluffy."

Then I take Bowser's head, move it closer to Fluffy's.

"This is Bowser," I tell Fluffy. "Yeah, I know, but you two are going to need to work this out because I don't think either of you are going anywhere."

Basically, I spend the next hour making the cat deal with the dog and making the dog deal with the cat. It's hell on the knees, but seriously, I will not live in a house divided.

"You really think this is going to work?" Helen asks at one point.

"I figure it has to. Left to their own devices, they'll just hide from each other forever. But if we just keep forcing the issue, they're going to have to find a way to deal."

Before too much more than an hour goes by, they get tired

of resisting. First one yawns, then the other yawns, and before I know it, the beast is sacked out on the floor, the cat cradled in the crook of his arm like a toy.

"Nice work," Helen says.

"Timely too. I didn't think it worth waiting for Bowser to get docile, like he will be when he gets older, to try to work things out between him and the cat."

"He's going to get docile?"

I nod.

"How'd you know that?"

I wave the question away like *Doesn't everyone know the behavior patterns and temperament of English Mastiffs?* In reality, it's just not a question I particularly care to field at the moment.

Now that it's finally quiet, Stavros makes his way downstairs.

He looks touched at the scene as he pets Bowser tentatively for the first time.

"Who's going to train him?" he asks.

"I guess we'll all pitch in," I say.

"Yeah," Stavros says, "but you guys work during the week. That's a long time for a dog like this to be cooped up inside."

He's got a point there.

"So?" Stavros shrugs. "I'll train him, take him for walks."

Coming from anyone else, this would seem insanely generous, too much to accept, but since Stavros has been with us, he's gone out of the way to pick up the slack on anything that Helen or I need doing.

"I don't know." I'm feeling skeptical. "That is one huge dog."

"So?" Stavros shrugs again. "You forget, I'm Stavros...of Greece! Growing up, we had goats. How different can this be?"

# The E-Cigarette Who Came to Dinner

The second thing to jar Helen and me out of our routine—or rut—occurs on Saturday night, at precisely seven P.M. It happens with the ringing of the doorbell.

Helen's still upstairs, so I go to answer it, only to find:

Daniel Rathbone, leaning against the doorjamb.

He's wearing a skinny suit and tie, the kind of thing you'd expect to see on Rod Stewart. In one hand, an e-cigarette is poised.

Somehow, I'd managed to forget about this guy.

"John-O!" he says, straightening, the hand without an e-cigarette in it thrust out for a shake.

"Dan," I say, accepting the shake, resisting the sudden urge to give him a bone-crusher.

"Actually," he says, "I prefer Daniel."

"And I'll take Johnny, thanks. Come in."

I shut the door and glance at the dining room table, hoping to see it fully set for eight or ten—maybe Helen decided to throw a party and forgot to tell me?—because if there are lots more people coming, maybe, *maybe* I can take this guy for a whole night; or at least the three-hour minimum dictated by etiquette. But all I see are three place settings. Crap. Not even Carla? I never thought the day would come when I'd say this, but I'd kill to see Carla right now.

"Nice place," Daniel says, looking around, "and that is one big dog over there."

"Thanks," I say, "but Helen picked out the dog. He kind o goes with the kitchen."

"How's that?" Daniel looks puzzled. Then, seeing Fluffy, his pretty face gets a look like he's got a lemon in his mouth. "Oh. A cat."

He's not bothered by Cerberus but he's got an issue with the cat?

"Is that a problem?" I ask.

"Just a touch allergic."

"Perhaps you shouldn't be here, then?"

"Don't be ridiculous. I can always take a pill. Besides, I see his hair is extremely short."

Indeed it is. Stavros's work.

"It should be OK then," Daniel says. "It's really the dander I'm allergic to."

Fucking Stavros.

"So," Daniel says brightly, "how's the painting business treating you these days? Paint any interesting rooms lately?"

"Actually…"

I'm about to tell him that I *have* been painting some interesting rooms lately. In Connecticut, there are more Hollywood stars than anywhere outside of California and sometimes those stars call me as happened just this past week. It can be more challenging than usual, working those jobs, because it's tougher talking people with film-sized egos out of picking the wrong colors than it is your average doctor or lawyer. Plus, it can be fun dancing with their Oscars when they're not around.

But I don't get to say any of this because just then, Helen comes practically flying into the foyer, wearing an outfit I've never seen before: peach-colored skinny jeans, tight; a sleeveless maroon smock shirt; high-heeled strappy sandals, all sparkly with rhinestones and stuff. It must be tough to fly in those sandals.

"Daniel!" she cries as she throws her arms around him, like she didn't see him at work just yesterday. "I'm so glad you finally made it."

*Finally?* What, this guy was supposed to come here sometime before?

"Me too," he says, hugging back, a hug in which his e-cigarette hand floats a little too far down toward her jeans-encased butt for my taste. But it stops just shy of being totally offensive and I tell myself that they work together every day. Maybe this is how colleagues greet one another? I can't say Sam and I have ever done this, but it's not like Sam and I are big huggers, generally speaking.

"Johnny," Helen says after they finally break apart, "did you offer Daniel a drink?"

"Oh, right." Where are my manners? "What can I get you? A beer—"

"A glass of wine?" Helen interjects. "I picked up a nice Pouilly-Fuisse earlier today."

She did? When did that happen?

"That sounds heavenly," Daniel tells her. "But you know what?" He turns to me, practically poking me in the chest with that e-cigarette. "I think I'd rather have that beer."

"Great," I say, forcing an enthusiasm I don't feel into my voice, "I'll get us all some drinks. Helen?"

"Oh?" She seems distracted. Then: "Oh, right. I'll take a beer too. Daniel, would you like to come into the living room?"

While they do that, I grab three Sierra Nevada Pale Ales from the fridge—two in one hand, one in the other—and go to join them.

Daniel's already seated on the sofa, close to one side, with Helen perched on the armrest right beside him. I'm not quite sure of the etiquette here: Helen's the only woman in the room but he's the guest, so do I give her a beer first or him? All I know is, I'm not supposed to serve myself first, so I simply offer out the two I'm holding in the same hand. Then, I immediately twist the cap off of mine and toss it on the table.

Perhaps it makes me a small-minded petty person, but at least I'm honest enough with myself to admit that it gives me great pleasure to see that Daniel, having tucked his e-cigarette into the corner of his mouth, is struggling to open his.

Yeah, Sierra Nevada can be a little tricky to open. Some people just use an opener.

"Here," I offer, "do you need me to—"

"Thanks," Daniel says, through gritted teeth as he finally

succeeds in opening his own beer, "but I think I've got it."

"Would you like a glass?" Helen offers.

"No, thanks." Daniel holds the bottle up and peers at it like he's trying to study the contents inside, like he would a fine wine. "This is perfect the way it is. It's *so*...proletarian." Then, with a look toward me to indicate that what follows is for my benefit, he adds, "Proletarian, as in a member of the proletariat, as in a member of the working class, as in the class of industrial workers who lack their own means of production and hence sell their labor to live."

Geez. Merriam-Webster much?

Helen looks at me, expectantly; expectant of what, I'm not sure.

All I know is that I, who have never hit first, am tempted to deck this guy. Who does he think he is? But I can't do that... can I? I mean, he's a guest in our home, he's Helen's guest, she works with him...

So, instead:

"Thank you," I say, feigning sincerity so well, I almost believe myself. "I appreciate you taking the time to define that term for me."

Now Helen looks, I don't know, disappointed? But in what? Was I not polite enough to this total asshat? Geez. I'd better cover my dislike for him harder.

Daniel takes a sip of his beer, then: "Ah. That's not half bad. You know, I don't think I've had one of these since college." He studies the label. "Huh, though. I was half-expecting Budweiser."

Budweiser? Who does he think I am, Drew?

"Oh, look," Daniel says, as if just noticing, when really, it's the first thing new visitors always comment on when seeing our living room. "Two televisions! You know," he confides, "Karl Marx said religion was the opiate of the masses but these days, I think it's TV. And look at you with two of them!"

Actually, what Marx said was that 'Religion is the opium of the people,' but who am I to quibble with my scholar-guest *Dan*? And besides, what do I know? After all, I'm just a member of the proletariat.

"Yes," I say, "I am fortunate to have double the usual prescription for keeping my mind occupied with silly fluff so I don't attempt to rise above my station."

Daniel's eyes narrow a bit, then he points his e-cigarette at me. "You know, that's very astute, Johnny. You surprise me."

I wonder what surprises him. And I wonder where Helen is in all of this. At the very least, couldn't she point out the fact that she likes a little celluloid opium too?

"Why don't I put on some music?" Helen claps her hands against her thighs, rising. This is not exactly the kind of spousal support I was hoping for—Helen putting on some of her music before I can head her off by putting on something decent—but I take the opportunity to check on my hors d'oeuvres.

For tonight's dinner, I recreated the meal I made the first time we had dinner guests—the *amuse bouches*, the homemade pizza and salad—so I toss four stuffed mushrooms and the other little things onto a tray, toss some napkins on, and head back out, only to be greeted by the opening notes of the soundtrack from *Saturday Night Fever*.

"I *love* this music!" Daniel says. "You know, it's been so long since I've heard it, but whenever I do, I think: What man *wouldn't* want to be a woman's man with no time to talk?"

Actually, I'm more of a man's man, and I always have time to talk, at least with people I like, but I neglect to point this out.

"Ah!" Daniel eyes my tray. "*Amuse bouche*—how amusing!" He grabs a stuffed mushroom, pops it into his mouth and before he's swallowed says, "Helen, these are absolutely divine."

"Actually," she says, "Johnny made them."

"*Johnny*?" He eyes me, then: "Well, I suppose when a person doesn't have a real job, there's time in the day to do all sorts of things."

Oh, how I would love to use some of that extra time in my day to do something to this guy.

But I swallow my feelings and extend the tray again. "Perhaps you'd like to try one of my mini quiches?"

• • •

It would be nice to say that once we get to the table and sit down to dinner proper, that things improve, but I'm just an honest member of the proletariat and I can't say that they do.

After bringing out the pizza, I grab us all another round of beers.

"All this beer," Daniel says, accepting his, "it really does remind me of college days. I keep half-expecting you to trot out a keg."

"Yeah." I slug back about half my bottle. "I guess we did all drink a lot of beer back then."

"Oh?" Daniel cocks one single eyebrow. "You went to college? Norwalk Community, I suppose?"

Actually, I went to a good four-year university and graduated Magna Cum Laude.

"Actually—" Helen starts, but I cut her off.

"Yeah," I say, giving the guest what he wants, "it was something like that."

We begin to eat and it's like Old Home Week between the other two. They discuss cases they've worked on together and everything is all "Remember the case when…" and "Remember the time we…"

I just listen, soaking it all in, particularly the moment when, in the middle of an anecdote about a tort, Daniel reaches out and covers Helen's hand with one of his. I grind my teeth and force a smile as I tell myself this is just the sort of things colleagues might do, even when Helen squeezes back.

"I must apologize, Johnny," Daniel says, withdrawing his hand.

Yes, I think, you really must.

"All this talk about legal cases Helen and I have worked on together—it must be frightfully boring for you."

Once again, I'm about to give the guest what he wants— feigning my own ignorance—but this time it's Helen who cuts *me* off.

"Actually," she says, "Johnny's always been very interested in the law."

"Really." Daniel regards me with critical interest but then

a smile breaks across his face. "Of *course*! I understand people like you enjoy all those legal-eagle TV shows, *Law and Order* and all that."

I could say that, actually, I was a Poli-Sci major and, Magna Cum Laude from a good university in pocket, once flirted with the idea of law school, but I do not say that, nor do I give Helen the chance to.

Pointing the neck of my bottle toward him, I make a gun-cocking click sound as I wink and say, "Got it in one."

I notice Helen's starting to look a bit disgusted. *Finally*. And who can blame her? This guy is such a dick.

When I bring out the dessert and the coffee, Daniel pulls out his e-cigarette.

"You really like that thing, don't you," I observe.

"This?" He waves the e-cigarette. "Why? Does it bother you?"

"No, not at all," I say, and it's true. Oh, sure, Daniel *Rath*bone gets on my nerves waving that thing around constantly, but everything Daniel *Rath*bone does gets on my nerves. But e-cigarettes in general? Nah, give me something real to get exercised about.

"You could say I like to push the envelope with these." He examines the tip. "I take them out everywhere. Recently, I pulled it out on a plane and got thrown off for it. I'm trying to put together a lawsuit, but so far, it's a bit slow-going. New ground and all that, so the law's a bit murky."

"Maybe Johnny can help with that," Helen suggests.

"Johnny?" Daniel says.

I wouldn't go so far as to say the guy snorts but it's definitely implied.

"Sure," Helen says. "Johnny's great with legal loopholes."

"Really," Daniel says.

In truth, I love finding loopholes in things. And, oh, there's so much to play with here. First, of course it would be helpful if he could establish that e-cigarettes pose no threat whatsoever to those in the vicinity of the e-smoker. But after that? He could argue that the device is ill-named, creating a built-in prejudice against it, when in reality it's not a cigarette at all, since it doesn't behave like one; rather, it's a nicotine inhaler, no different or more harmful than a nicotine patch. Does the law want to outlaw those? Hardly. They're good at reducing the effects of smoking and smoking in general. He could argue that to ban something that is harmless to others simply because it visually resembles something that's harmful is akin to outlawing water pistols. Or what if someone could locate those candy cigarettes that used to be popular—would they be told they can't eat chocolate on the plane because it's a certain sinister shape and wrapped in paper? Not to mention, from what I've read, there is no consistency in terms of enforcement, like with real cigarettes; no rule that covers all airlines or even consistency within a single airline.

Frankly, I'm a bit shocked. Why hasn't *Dan* the brilliant lawyer thought of all this, when it seems so obvious to me that he's got a strong case for damages against the airline for kicking him off the plane without just cause.

Yeah, I could say all that on the subject, and more, but I don't feel like it. Instead, I say:

"Let's see." I run the items off on my fingers. "Ice holes, sinkholes, peepholes, blowholes—I know a little bit about each of those. But loopholes?" I shrug. "I got nothing."

Daniel gives me a smug look as if to say, *Just as I expected.*

"Yeah," I respond to his unvoiced thoughts, "you could say I'm a real asshole like that."

"Yes. Well." He looks at his watch: a Rolex. "Oh, look at the time! Can you believe I've been here three hours already?"

No, because it feels like thirty.

"Must run," he says. "But let's do this again real soon, shall we?" He regards me. "It was interesting getting to spend some time with Helen's Boy Toy." Then he gives my wife one of those uncomfortable-for-me, nearly-touching-her-butt extended hugs, and he's gone.

Helen and me work side by side in the kitchen, in silence, tidying things up and putting things away.

"Some night," I finally say, trying to force a hearty tone into my voice. "I hope you had a good time with your friend."

Helen turns to me sharply and there's something in her eyes. It mirrors something that's been growing in me for a long time now, something I haven't permitted myself to voice, not even to myself.

"I don't believe you, Johnny," she says. "What is *wrong* with you?"

And now, at long last, I am neither miffed, nor peeved, nor annoyed, nor perturbed.

I'm mad.

# Tock

"What's wrong with *me*?" I don't even try to modulate my voice.

The cat's been hanging out in the kitchen, no doubt hoping to scrounge some leftovers from dinner, but at the sound of rising voices he runs for cover. A part of me wishes I could go with him, but whatever's about to happen here, I know I can't run or hide from it.

"Daniel insulted you all evening," Helen says.

"Yes, I'm well aware of that fact. So? He was your guest."

"You let him get away with it. You just sat there smiling, accepting everything he said."

"He was your guest."

"Why didn't you stand up for yourself? Why didn't you fight back?"

"Perhaps you didn't hear me the first two times? *He. Was. Your. Guest.*" I hit those last four words so hard, the dog starts whimpering. "And what did you expect me to say?"

"I don't know. How about pointing out that you graduated with honors? Or telling him you were on track to be a lawyer but then changed direction to please your father?"

"I'm not going to get into a pissing contest with that guy. I'm not going to defend what I do for a living. So, what? Am I supposed to become a lawyer now? Would the world be a better place if everyone who possibly *could* become lawyers *did* become lawyers? And what would we have then—basically everyone just suing one another? Oh, right. That's what we have now."

"So now you're saying *my* profession's stupid?"

"No, of course not. But why'd you invite that guy over anyway? I can't stand that guy."

"Since when?"

"Since forever."

"Oh, so now you hate all my friends?"

"*No.*" I can't keep the mocking tone out of my voice. "I don't 'hate' all your friends." Well, there is Carla too, but maybe I should hold that one in reserve. "Just that guy."

"Hey, it was your idea to have him over."

Now, hold on here. I'm pretty sure that if it was my idea, I would remember that insane fact.

"*No,*" I say scornfully.

"Uh-huh," Helen says, sounding like she's about six years old and we're in the middle of a playground fight. "Back on the cruise ship—"

"That was four months ago!"

"I don't care how long ago it was. There is no statue of limitations on what you say to me. *You* said we should have him over sometime for dinner when we got back."

"Oh, yeah? Well, if we're going all the way back to the cruise ship…*how could you leave me alone when I was so sick?*"

"What? You told me to go."

"I was being magnanimous!"

"How was I supposed to know that?"

"I gave you the only magic make-this-stomach-hell-stop pill that we had."

"Who asked you to?"

"Are you saying I shouldn't have? Are you saying you wouldn't have done the same for me?"

"No and no, but—"

"And if it had been the other way around, if you'd saved me instead of yourself, I damn well would have stayed by your side until you were better instead of traipsing off with a dozen German volleyball players."

"There were only nine."

"Whatever."

"So if it bothered you so much, why didn't you just come out and say so at the time?"

"Oh, I don't know. Maybe because I was too busy puking my guts up to have the energy left over to give you etiquette lessons?"

Bowser starts to whimper more loudly.

"And *that*," I say, pointing toward the living room.

"What *that* are we talking about now?"

"That giant dog you brought home."

"You don't like him?"

"I'm starting to, but that's not the point. Who brings home a massive dog like that without notice? Do you not *see* what a hostile act that was?"

"He was a present for you!"

"No." I wave my finger back and forth. "Whatever that was all about, whatever you were trying to do, it was *not* about giving me a present. I had a cat already, a cat who was very traumatized by the advent of that dog."

"But it turned out fine."

"But it might not have."

"Yeah, about that cat. Don't you think he's, I don't know, a bit of a pussy? 'Who's a proud lion? Who's a proud lion?'"

If I weren't so mad, it'd be easier to admit that that's a hell of an imitation of me.

"I'm not sure of a whole lot in this world anymore, Johnny, but there's one thing I do know. That cat is *not*"—and here she stabs the air between us with her finger—"a proud lion."

"Oh, yeah? Well…it'd be a lot easier to conduct a reasonable discussion with you…*if we weren't standing in this ridiculous kitchen*."

"What's wrong with this kitchen?"

"Canary Yellow? Please. That's the one color I will fight my customers to the death over to prevent them from making a tragic mistake."

"Then why didn't you say so before?"

Actually, I'm fairly certain I did, although perhaps not that strenuously.

"Because you wanted it," I say.

"So? You can't just tell me it's not what you want? I suppose you didn't like the pink and black for the bedroom either."

I mutter something.

"What was that?" Helen says.

"I *said*, it's fine if you live in a bordello, which worked out fine in the end, come to think of it, because Stavros loves it."

"Oh yeah. Stavros."

"What about Stavros?"

"*You* criticize *me* for bringing home a dog? *You brought home a whole person!*"

And now the dog is no longer whimpering. He's howling.

"What?" I demand. "Now you're telling me you don't like Stavros?"

"No." She immediately backs away from that, for the first time looking contrite. "I don't just like Stavros, I *love* Stavros. Even though it's not how I pictured my first year of married life—"

She didn't picture things being like this? Well, I didn't either. I sure never pictured this fight.

"—I can't imagine what it would be like without him. As far as I'm concerned, *he* can stay forever."

I'm not sure how crazy I am about the emphasis she put on that *he*.

"*But*," she adds, "you could have asked me if it was OK to move him in *before* not *after* the fact."

"Oh, right. And you would have just said yes right away without even meeting him?"

"Of course not. I'd have thought you were out of your fucking mind. But it would've been nice to be asked first. And, you know, once I'd had the chance to think about it, I'd have asked to meet him, and it all would have worked out the same in the end."

"I'll try to remember that the next time."

"Please do. And Sam? Does she really need to be here every day for GH? You know, it's really not that great of a show."

Where the hell did that come from?

"She's my friend," I say.

"And imagine how thrilling it was for me that week that Alice was here every day, how wonderful to see you and your old girlfriend cuddling on my couch."

"Alice was never my girlfriend. She's just a friend."

"Right. Your friends. Your family. Do you think I really want to go to your father's every Sunday for the rest of my life?"

Now hold on. "You don't like my dad?"

Again, she backs away from this, softens. "No, that's not it. I love your dad. Who in their right mind doesn't love Big John? But *every Sunday, Johnny*? Especially when it means I have to put up with Aunt Alfresca too?"

"So she's a little hard to take at times."

"A little hard to take?" The laugh Helen gives out here is just a touch maniacal. "The woman hates Switzerland, Johnny! What kind of person hates Switzerland?"

"Hey," I say, "after my mother died, that woman made sure I was fed. She gave up her own life to take care of us."

"She also kept telling you that you killed your mother."

"So? That's just her way." It feels so odd to be defending Aunt Alfresca and yet even as the words leave my mouth, I recognize their simple truth: "I don't care how batshit crazy she is, I love that woman."

"When she thought my shorts were too short, she tweeted 'I see London, I see France, I see D.A. Helen Troy's underpants.'"

"She's just obsessed with social media right now. She'll get over it soon. I'm almost sure of it."

"And then she critiqued my underpants…on Twitter!"

"Well, you have to admit, you were wearing that nasty pair you reserve for when you have your period."

"I don't want the world to know that!"

"And who can blame you? But you can't give Aunt Alfresca ammunition like that. It's like, I don't know, an open invitation."

"Are you *defending* what she did?"

"Not even close but—"

"There should be no *but* in that sentence. *But* has no place in this, unless you want to talk about what a *butt* you're being about everything."

"Hey now!"

In addition to the hiding cat and the howling dog, we now have an upset Stavros I see as he knocks on the wall outside the kitchen.

"Is it OK if I…" He indicates the fridge. "I just wanted maybe a little milk…"

"Now look what you did," I say to Helen as I reach for a glass for Stavros.

"What'd I do?"

"You upset Stavros." I get out the milk. "Look at him." I pour.

"You're crazy," she says as I put the milk back in the fridge. "I'm not the one shouting 'hey now!' at the top of my lungs. If anyone's upsetting him, it's you."

"Oh, please." I hand the glass to Stavros. "I'm not the one who—"

"It's all fine." Stavros drains the glass, backhands a milk mustache away and sets the glass in the sink. "I'm going to go watch some TV. Just let me know who gets custody of me when you're through here."

And he's gone.

But wait a second. He thinks we're going to split up over this?

"So where were we?" Helen asks, like she was on a roll and can't wait to get back to it.

But you know what? Never mind what she feels like attacking me about. I've still got a few of my own complaints to register here.

"That clock," I say.

"*What?*" she says. "We weren't talking about a clock. What clock?"

"The one in the bathroom upstairs, the one you bought without consulting me first, the one that incessantly goes *tickticktickticktickticktick-tick*. You know." I pause before delivering the *coup de grace*. "*The one that isn't even centered properly.*"

"It isn't...What are you even talking about?" She shakes her head. "You know what? Never mind what you're talking about, Johnny. I've had enough."

"Oh, you have, have you? And what are you going to do about it?"

"I'm going out."

"Where?"

She folds her arms across her chest defiantly. "Karaoke."

I'm a hairbreadth away from saying fine and that her singing sucks, but some still-sane part of me knocks the words back down my throat, saving me from saying something hurtful that I would never be able to take back, and all I'm left with is the juvenile: "Karaoke is stupid."

"Oh, yeah? Well, you're stupid."

"Oh, yeah? Well, maybe before you go out singing in public, you should try looking in the mirror first."

"What's that supposed to mean?"

"Spinach, Helen." I make a face like a beaver and indicate the space between my front teeth.

I can't believe I used to find that charming or cute. How is it possible she never notices that there? It is so annoying.

Reflexively, her hand flies to her mouth.

"How long has it been like that?" she asks from behind her hand.

I shrug. "A few hours, maybe?"

Now the eyes above the hand look horrified. Is it because of me seeing her like that, I wonder, or because of Daniel?

She straightens proudly, not like a lion exactly, but still. Then, talking through a tight mouth so I can no longer see the spinach between her teeth, she says with dignity, "I'm going out now."

Purposefully, she strides to the front door, slams it behind her. As soon as she's gone, a thought occurs to me, so when she comes back in a minute later, I'm standing by the doorway, waiting.

"Did you forget these?" I hand over her bag and keys. "You have a nice night now. Who knows? Maybe I'll go out too."

It's not until she's gone for the second time that the smug satisfaction and haze of anger lifts just enough for me to wonder if Stavros was right:

Did Helen and I just break up?

# Long Night's
# Journey Into Day

I look at my watch and see it's just after eleven. Well, if Helen's just going to stomp off, I'm not going to stick around here all night like a dog waiting for her to decide to come home again. So after talking with Stavros and making sure he feels OK with being left alone for a while so late at night—"What am I, a little kid, Johnny? I may have lost a few steps in the old memory department, but I'm not ready to burn the house down yet!"—I head over to Chalk Is Cheap for a beer or two.

In a way, it's much similar to my last visit a few months ago. I'm arriving a little later than I did on that occasion, so the place is hopping a bit more, but a lot of female attention is directed my way and that's even with me being without a cat this time. I can't say it's not flattering—what guy doesn't want to feel attractive to the opposite sex? unless, you know, he's gay— and yet. I don't care how steamed I am at Helen, I don't want to dance with some other woman. I don't even want to play pool with another woman, although I am asked. Still, it's nice to know that, should this really be the end for Helen and me, I may never recover from that but at least I'm no longer whatever the opposite of catnip is to women.

Right now, though, there's really just one woman I want to see:

Sam.

As I pull into a guest spot right outside of my old condo, I'm relieved to see Sam's place all lit up. I didn't think she'd really be asleep this early on a Saturday night—not Sam—but there was always the possibility she'd be out somewhere; not to mention, although it's sometimes hard to believe, people do change. Still, when I hit the buzzer and then try knocking—and knock and knock and knock—there's no answer. So finally, I have to admit that sometimes all the lights are on and there really is nobody home.

I'm just turning away from Sam's door when the one for the condo to the left of Sam's—my old door—opens, and out pops Sam's head.

"Johnny!" she says, beer in hand, looking very happy to see me. "I *thought* I heard someone at my door. Lily had some kind of work thing so I'm hanging out here tonight. Come on in."

This is so typical Sam. She's inviting me in like the place belongs to her, like she used to offer me beer from my own fridge, but this place isn't hers. Of course it doesn't belong to me either. It's the new guy's. Who, I must admit, I'm curious about.

"Thanks," I say, entering.

The first thing I see is the guy sitting on the couch. And then it hits me: I *know* this guy.

"Bailey?" I say.

"Johnny!" Bailey says.

"You two know each other?" Sam asks.

"Of course," I say. "Bailey's the guy who bought the coffee shop after Leo died."

Sam shoots him a surprised look. "I didn't know that."

"I guess you wouldn't," I say, "since you always have me go inside in the morning to get you your sugar bombs. But come on. How long have you been hanging out with this guy?"

Sam and Bailey look at each other, shrug.

"Off and on?" Sam considers. "About three months, maybe?"

Bailey nods agreement. "When I first bought the coffee shop, I lived in the apartment over it, but that was too close to work so I started renting this from the owner."

That accent. Huh. I never noticed what a strong Massachusetts accent he has before tonight.

"And in all that time," I say to Sam, "you never thought to ask him what kind of work he does?"

Another shrug from Sam. "Why would I?" Then she lifts a bare foot a few feet off the ground and waves her toes at me. "But look: he did my nails for me."

"Very nice," I say, but really, I'm feeling unreasonably hurt. That used to be my job. How easy it is to be replaced. Maybe Helen will think so too?

"You want a beer?" Sam offers, just like she used to when I owned the place.

I consider. "Yeah. I could drink."

I follow her to the kitchen and that's when I see a hula-girl chandelier hanging over the dining room table. Huh. I used to have one just like it. What are the odds…

"Isn't that my…"

"Yes."

"But I threw that thing out."

"And I salvaged it from the Dumpster and stored it in my basement. I don't know why. It just seemed too cruel to the world to have it disappear forever. I knew it would come in handy someday."

She hands me a beer: Sierra Nevada Pale Ale.

"Nice beer," I compliment Bailey when Sam and I are back in the living room.

"Thanks," he says, looking inordinately proud, when I think we all know who's responsible for what kind of beer he stocks his fridge with.

"Hey." I gesture back toward the hula-girl lamp. "Doesn't your wife object to that thing?"

"What wife?"

"Didn't you buy the coffee shop with your wife?"

"No. I don't know where you got that idea. I bought it myself."

Huh. Where did I get that idea? I don't even remember. Great. So now, on top of everything else, I can't completely rely on what I'm sure I know because apparently some of what I think I know is wrong. What a world.

"So what're you guys up to?" I ask, feeling awkward as I take a seat in my old living room. But before they can answer, I can see what they're up to. I don't know how it escaped my notice before, but what they're watching on TV is hockey. Or "hawkey," as Bailey informs me, so apparently Sam hasn't bred that out of him. Yet.

"Hey," Sam says defensively, "baseball season's over, there's no football on Saturday night, and I can't take watching the pre-season Knicks. It's too nerve-wracking. What are they up to now? An injury per game?" She shudders. "Besides, hockey's a legitimate sport."

"Go, hawkey." Bailey raises his beer glass.

It strikes me that Bailey's a funny guy in a goofy kind of way.

"Actually, Johnny," he says, "it's a good thing you came by. Perhaps you can settle a dispute for us."

A dispute? I love disputes. Maybe this will take my mind off my own troubles.

"Sure thing," I say. "Shoot."

"Do you think Mr. Peanut's a snob?"

"What?"

"You know, the guy on the Planter's Peanuts products."

"Yeah, I know who Mr. Peanut is."

"Well, do you? Think he's a snob, I mean. Sam says no but I'm going with yes."

"He's offering the world peanuts," Sam says. "You can get peanuts at any ballpark. How can a peanut-vendor be a snob?"

"But he's wearing like a top hat," Bailey says. "No vendors dress like that at the ballpark."

"Yeah," Sam says, "but if he were a snob, Mr. Peanut would be selling wasabi nuts, not just garden-variety peanuts."

"Actually," I interject, "you can probably get wasabi nuts at any ballpark these days too."

"No shit?" Bailey says.

I nod.

"See?" He points his beer at me. "*That's* why I don't go in for any of that baseball/football crap."

I ignore this aspersion to two out of my three favorite

sports. And anyway…

"I'm afraid I've got to side with Bailey on this one," I say.

"*What?*" Sam is outraged.

"Come on," I say. "Mr. Peanut? Dude wears a monocle. How can he *not* be a snob?"

"*Thank* you," Bailey says, with a vehemently appreciative head nod.

"You're welcome." I head-nod him back.

"Geez," Sam says, "look at the two of you. You're so proud of yourselves, you might as well be wearing monocles."

We watch the hockey game in silence for a few minutes, but really, hockey?

I shoot a look at Sam who's sitting curled up in a corner of the couch, catch her eyes, raise my brows. She rolls her eyes like, *I know, right?* If she still said that. *Hockey?* But she's smiling good-naturedly as she does so, like, *Hey, tonight it's the only game in town.*

"So," she says at last, "just what are you doing here tonight? Did Helen kick you out?"

"Actually, she walked out on me."

Hearing my response to her joke, Sam's no longer smiling. Instead she's moved to the edge of her seat, concerned.

"What? No. Why?"

"We had a fight." I can't believe I've finally said the words out loud. It sounds so awful.

"Wait a minute. You had *a* fight?"

I nod glumly.

"And now everything's over?" she says. "What are you, a Kardashian?"

"I don't know what you're talking about," I say.

"You know? They get married, spend ten million dollars on the wedding, then get divorced before the year's up?"

"Sorry, that doesn't compute. I don't keep up with those people."

"But you know who they are, right?"

"I think I've seen a few. Or maybe it's always the same one but with different hairstyles and, I don't know, she keeps losing and gaining weight quickly?"

"There's more than one. You don't think they're hot?"

"God, no. You?"

"God, no. I'm more of an Emily Blunt girl."

"Oh, yeah. I know who she is. I'd totally do her. Well, I would have when I was single. If she'd have had me. Which of course she wouldn't."

Sam waves this all off like I've loosed a stream of annoying hornets around her head.

"Getting back to the matter at hand," she says, "what makes you think everything is over just because you had *a* fight?"

"Because we've never fought before," I say.

"So? Everyone fights."

"I don't think that's true." In fact, I'm almost sure of it.

"Name one couple that doesn't fight."

"OK, what about Leo and The Little Lady?"

"HA!"

"Did you just 'HA!' at me?"

"I most definitely did. How can you say they never fought? They were married for how many years?"

"Over seventy, if I remember correctly."

"Right. Longer than a lot of people will ever be alive. And you don't think in all that time they ever fought?"

"Not that I saw."

"Yeah, well, most people don't go to their place of business and get in huge public fights. I mean, you and I bickering a lot— that's different. And maybe when they got older, when they finally got used to each other's ways, Leo and The Little Lady didn't fight. But it can't have been like that forever. I'm sure, in the beginning, they must have had issues with lots of things. Everyone does." She pauses. "What were you thinking, that after you and Helen got married, life together was going to be perfect forever and ever?"

When she puts it like that, it makes me sound like a naive schmo.

"Well, no, but—"

"So you had *a* fight."

"You keep saying that, but it was more. It was like, I don't know, the kitchen sink of all fights."

"What do you mean?"

"We threw *everything* at each other: my not standing up for myself to her stupid friend, *Daniel*; the amount of time we spend with my friends and family, the pets, the annoying clock, even stuff that happened on the cruise ship."

"That is a lot of stuff. Maybe it would've been, I don't know, more useful to address these issues in a calm manner as they actually arose?"

"You make that sound so...*reasonable*."

"Oh, come on, you know me. Even on my best days, I'm about as far from reasonable as a person can get. But since I found Lily, I'm starting to learn. She's worth it."

"Hey, how's that working?"

"It takes time. But I think we're getting there."

"I don't know." I run a hand through my hair. "Some of the things we said...I even told her I don't like karaoke."

"Crap." Sam's so far on the edge of her seat now, another inch and she'll fall off. "You didn't tell her she sings like shit, did you?"

"God, no. What do you think I am, a complete idiot? I mean, the words were right there in my mouth, but I managed to force them back down again."

"*Thank* you." Sam collapses back in relief. "Just so long as you didn't say that, everything can still be worked out. You just have to figure out how best to do that."

Yes, that is the thing I need to do. Sam makes it sound so easy. But if it's so easy, why do I still feel like this could be the end of my world?

There's only so much *hawkey* a guy can take, or this guy, so after about fifteen minutes of trying to follow the puck, I make my excuses and depart. It's only about twelve-thirty in the morning now, though, and I'm still not ready to go home. What if Helen's not back yet? A part of me may want to fix things, a part of me may be sorry that any of this ever happened, but another part of me is reluctant to be the guy waiting home for her whenever she decides to just stroll in. And what if she never decides to stroll in? That notion is just too depressing.

So I decide to head over to Billy's place. Billy's always been a night owl. He's sure to be up.

Sure enough, when I pull up in front of his raised ranch, I can see lights on through the living room curtains. Still, after trudging up the front steps, I tap lightly, just in case Alice is asleep.

But it's Alice who answers the door. She's wearing a green tank, gray sweat pants and pink fuzzy slippers, and she looks dejected standing there with a half-filled wineglass in her hand, tilted at a hard enough angle I worry some might slosh out onto the hardwood floor of the entryway.

"Johnny!" She visibly brightens upon seeing me, which, I must say, is gratifying. What man doesn't want women to be happy to see him? And really, when has Alice ever looked so happy to see me? It does feel good.

"Hey, Alice," I say. "Is Billy around?"

"I'm sure he must be around somewhere," she says, "but he's not around here." She opens the door wider. "Come on in."

"That's OK. If Billy's not here, I don't want to distur—"

"Come on." She hooks her free hand through my elbow, gives a little yank, and I'm in. Also, that yanking shakes her own body enough that some of her white wine does slosh out on the floor. "Oops." She giggles.

I follow her into the living room where it looks like she's been having a party for one. There's an empty wine bottle on the coffee table and a second that looks like it's missing about a glass. The crumbs all over the table and a lone potato chip suggest that at one point, there was food involved.

I'm about to park myself in a side chair, when Alice grabs my elbows—not so easy to do with the hand that still has the wineglass—and pushes me toward the couch and down onto it. "Here, sit, sit. Would you like some wine?"

"That's OK. I—"

"I'll go get you a glass."

There's some noises from the kitchen and a minute later she's back, sits down on the couch a few feet away from me, sets the glasses down on the table. When she goes to reach for the wine bottle, her hand misses.

"I got it," I say, lifting the bottle. I pour myself a half glass but don't top hers up, even though it's empty. It's not like I want to hog it all for myself, but rather, Alice looks like she might be done for the night, even if she doesn't know it yet. Really, I've never seen Alice look so…*un*-Alice before, and it's kind of disturbing, so I study the label on the wine bottle instead.

"Huh," I say, reading the label, "Diet Girl. I don't think I've ever heard of that vintner before. Why would you buy something like this? It seems, I don't know, demeaning to women. Besides, you don't need to drink diet."

"I know," Alice says, "but look at the cartoon girl on the label. She looks like she's having such a good time."

"You think? I don't get that at all." I study the label more closely. "To me, she looks kind of bitchy, like maybe she'd be happier if she ate a cookie now and then or something."

"That's what I've always liked about you, Johnny." She winks one eye as she sights along her extended index finger and cocked thumb, like it's a gun pointed at me. "You've always been different."

When has Alice ever had something she always liked about me? This Alice is not only un-Alice; this Alice is downright unsettling.

"Where'd you say Billy is?" I say. "Maybe I should go."

But apparently Alice doesn't want to talk about Billy.

"Do you think it's too bright in here?" She pops off the couch, starts turning off lights. "I think it's too bright in here."

Mission accomplished, she returns to sit beside me, only now she's not a few feet away, she's right next to me. It's a good thing the moon's low on this side of the house, there are street lamps on outside and the drapes are sheer, because otherwise I'd be completely in the dark here.

"There, that's better," Alice says, inching closer still so that now…Hey, is that her thigh pressing against mine?

269

"What are you doing, Alice?" I say, doing a little hop move away from her to make our thighs stop touching.

But she answers my retreat with another advance and, yup, that thigh is back again.

"Alice," I try again, hop-moving at the same time, "what are you doing?"

"Something I've been wanting to do for a really long time now," she says, and despite the darkness, I see her head making incremental advances toward mine. Wait. Are her lips heading for my lips?

There were so many times, countless times, growing up and even well into adulthood, that I fantasized about such a moment: Alice—beautiful and unattainable and always untouchable Alice, the one and only girl of my childhood dreams—making the moves on me. But I never once, in all my fantasizing, was delusional enough to actually believe such a thing would ever happen. I mean, how would such a thing ever occur? Alice never could stand me, or at least, for the longest time she couldn't. No way would Alice ever want to kiss me, let alone initiate it. Against all odds, though, it would seem that a moment I dreamed of so many times is finally here.

And yet now that the moment is here, with her lips just a single breath from mine...

I place my hands on her shoulders. As gently as possible, I push her away.

"You don't want to kiss me?" Her voice when she speaks is puzzled, wounded, small.

"It's not a question of want, Alice." I think about how best to say this, knowing I only have the one chance to get it exactly right. "I know I've never said it to your face before, and yet I'm certain you've always known: growing up, as far as the opposite sex was concerned, you were everything to me. I knew I'd never have you, but it didn't stop me from dreaming, and there were times I would have given almost anything to make dream become reality. But you're Billy's wife—you're *my best friend's* wife—and I'm married to Helen, who I love and would never cheat on. So while I'm flattered—you will never know how flattered I am that you would think of me that way, even for a second—the answer has to be no. I will always treasure this moment, but it can't be anything. And while I don't think you've ever thanked me for anything, believe me, when you get up tomorrow morning, you will thank me for this."

And just like that, Alice's face crumbles and she starts to cry. I don't know what I was expecting with my speech—that she'd get angry in typical Alice fashion, or be hurt which would manifest itself as anger in typical Alice fashion—but I never expected this. If Alice trying, *wanting* to kiss me was surprising, it pales in comparison to this. In over a quarter of a century knowing her, I have *never* seen Alice cry before. Even when we were nine, playing in a game of neighborhood baseball with Alice pitching, and Drew hit the ball straight back at her, a bullet that nailed her right in the left boob. Instinctively, her gloved hand went right to her chest but when people crowded around to see if she was OK, she just gritted her teeth and angrily waved everyone away. I could see tears in her eyes, but she just willfully blinked them back, because no matter how much pain she might be in, Alice could not, *would* not let anyone see her cry.

So to see her like this now is—no other word for it —shocking.

I don't know what to do so, tentatively, I reach a hand out, give her a few pats on the shoulder. I even murmur "there, there" a few times, which, let me tell you, is not all that effective. Finally, I just open my arms and she falls into them, resting her head against my shoulder as she cries.

"Oh God." She sobs. "Billy."

"Billy? What's wrong with Billy? He's not sick, is he?"

"No, he's not sick," she says, pushing away from me and wiping at her wet nose with the back of her hand in a move that is so un-Alice, I feel like we've entered another dimension. "But during the week, we're mostly never here at the same time. And when we are, all we seem to ever do is fight."

"Is that why he's not here right now?"

"He just stormed off. He does that. I don't know where he goes. Maybe he's cheating on me?"

"No, you can't think like that."

"What else should I think? It's, what, nearly two in the morning?"

"Well, I'm not at home, it's nearly two in the morning, and I'm not cheating, so I don't think you can draw a direct relationship between a person's absence from home and marital infidelity."

"Wait a second. Why are you here at two in the morning?"

"Because Helen and I had a fight," I say, the awfulness of it all rushing back at me.

"I don't believe it," Alice says, rising abruptly. Then: "Give me a minute."

The minute is more like five, during which I hear a lot of clattering from the kitchen and the sound of running water more than once. When she finally returns, she's carrying a tray with cups and saucers, her hair's been pulled back in a ponytail, and there are still some drops of water on her face—I'm thinking she threw water at herself.

She sets the tray down on the coffee table and hands me a cup. "Here's your tea," she says, then she turns the lights back on before resuming her seat beside me, taking the other cup in her hands. "I'm ready to sympathize now. What's going on?"

So I tell her.

I tell her, not only about the fight we had tonight, but also about all the months leading up to it, all the little things that kept getting on my nerves, sometimes without me even realizing that was what was happening, without saying anything about it.

"I think that could be your biggest problem right there," she interjects at one point, "letting things just build up like that, keeping too much inside."

"Well, forgive me for saying so, but it seems to me that you and Billy have been letting things out too much."

I expect her to get mad at this because, you know, she's Alice, but she just gives me a rueful smile. "Maybe so," she concedes, taking a sip of tea. "Go on."

So I do.

As I talk—and talk and talk and talk—it turns out that Alice is a fantastic listener. Why didn't I ever know this about her? But not only that, she's good at giving practical advice too.

Alice says that Helen and I, what with the regular routine we've lapsed into, have been spending way too much time with other people—family and friends—when we really need to make a point of still going on dates together, just us; that we need more quality alone time as a couple.

Alice says that going for so long without saying what's on our minds is a big problem and we're going to need to learn how to express our thoughts as things occur.

Alice says that, even though it's important to express our thoughts, we need to pick our actual battles, as in: "Is this thing that's bothering me now going to still matter in five minutes? Five days? Five years?" And Alice says that we should only ever fight about the specific matter at hand, meaning we shouldn't use it as an occasion to dredge up every last little thing that's ever gotten on our nerves.

"Geez, this is some good shit you got here," I say. "Maybe I should take notes? You know, make a list?"

I half expect her to laugh in my face at this, but she disappears into the kitchen again, returning with two legal pads and two pens.

"Why two?" I ask.

She shrugs. "Maybe it's time I started taking my own excellent advice."

I write down what I can remember of what she told me, which, since I didn't indulge in any of the Diet Girl, turns out to be quite a bit.

"Oh, oh!" Alice gets excited. "Also, you should make a list of all the things you like about Helen, you know, all the positive things that made you fall in love with her in the first place. It's hard to stay mad at someone when you're busy thinking about how wonderful they are."

"Hey." I point my pen at her. "That is *good*."

This is such an easy list to make: *smart, funny, sharp, talented, loves sports, took in Stavros* and—I study the list, know something's missing then realize what it is—*beautiful*. And then, of course, there are specific instances of her being all those things, which I start to list too, sometimes laughing appreciatively as I do so.

Soon, the page is completely full, with extra notes crowding the margins. I look over at Alice's sheet, which is much less crowded, substantially so. Still, there are a few lines filled, so maybe there's some hope.

"I'll have to keep working on it," Alice says pensively.

I fold my own sheet in half several times and hold it in the air—"Thanks for this," I tell her—before putting it in my pocket.

"Anytime." She doesn't even bother to stifle her yawn.

"Hey." I look at my watch. "Look at the time." It's nearly four in the morning. "I should let you get some sleep."

"That's OK," she says, walking me to the door. "I'm going to wait up until Billy comes home."

"OK," I say, "but, you know, when he comes in, maybe don't yell at him right away?"

"Would I do that?" She laughs, but there's a peculiar-for-Alice self-awareness to that laugh that gives me hope for her and Billy. "We'll see. Oh, I almost forgot!"

"What's that?"

"Another piece of advice. It's good to talk in a relationship. But it's possible to talk *too* much. Like, you know how people say, 'I want to know everything about you?' Believe me, *no one* wants that."

"I'll try to keep that in mind."

"And hey, while you've been making a list of all the reasons you love Helen, I hope she's been making a list of all the wonderful things she sees in you."

"That," I say with a rueful laugh, "would have to be an extraordinarily short list."

"Are you kidding me?" I guess that must have been a rhetorical question because without waiting for an answer, Alice bulldozes ahead. "You're a good, kind man. You're a faithful friend. And look at the way you are with your dad."

"Aw, everyone loves Big John."

"I know that. I love him too. But you *carry* him, Johnny."

"So? He carried me when I was young."

"I don't mean just physically. You carry him, Johnny. In your own weird way, you carry everybody."

"I'm glad you added the word 'weird.'" I laugh nervously. "For a minute there, I thought we were having a moment there."

"We are," she says. "Since it's true confession time tonight, let me just say that I've always known you were great."

"Even when you thought I was a total dick?"

"Yes, even then. Oh, I'm not saying you didn't get on my nerves—growing up, you hopped on every last nerve I had—but I always knew, deep down, what an innately good person you are. It just shines off of you. Sure, you get things wrong, but you mean well—sometimes, I think you mean well more than anyone I've ever known."

I feel a sensation that's odd in that I've never experienced it around Alice before so it takes me a moment to identify it. When I do, I realize that what I'm feeling is contentment. For the first time in our lives together, I feel that Alice and me are friends.

"Well, thanks for this." I pat the pocket that has the folded-up sheet of paper in it. "And thanks for everything else too."

"Hey," she says, "just because I often think you're a jerk, it doesn't mean it's escaped my notice how good you are."

When I key the ignition a few minutes later, I'm feeling better than I did when I arrived a few hours ago, but I'm still not quite there. Who else can I go see tonight? Who would be up at four in the morning?

Big John, I think.

Big John's always complaining about how he has so much trouble sleeping, sometimes he just gives up and starts the day early.

I think, I decide, I'll go see Big John.


"You're up early," Big John says when he answers the door, leaning on just one cane, so it must be a good day. "Who are you, the fucking milkman?"

He laughs at his own joke and I laugh too, even though what he said really isn't that funny. I've been up so long, maybe

275

I've moved from tired to punchy?

"Christ, shh." Big John puts his finger to his lips then whispers, "Don't wake your aunt or there'll be shit to pay. Here, let me just leave her a note, then we can go for a drive."

Once we're buckled in, Big John turns to me. "So, you and Helen finally got in a fight, huh?"

"How'd you know?"

"It was bound to happen sometime. Drive."

"OK, but where am I driving?"

"The cemetery. Let's go see your mother."

In late October, a Connecticut cemetery can be a cold place to be in the early hours of the morning and the air is crisp as a green apple, the sun barely breaking on the horizon as I pull into the drive. It's been a long time since I was last here, so Big John has to direct me to the plot where my mother is. After helping Big John out of the car and walking over with him, I see an addition has been made. Previously, there was just my mom's grave with a marker to the right of it with Big John's name and date of birth on it. Now, to the right of that is a marker for Aunt Alfresca.

"You did what," I ask, "purchase an add-on after you and Aunt Alfresca got married?"

"No, I purchased that years ago. I always figured that whether we got married or not, we'd all be together through eternity. You may not know this, but your aunt doesn't like to be alone."

It's difficult to picture Aunt Alfresca being vulnerable about anything. Huh. People can surprise you.

"Why do you think she was always hanging around after your mother died?" Big John says. "I just didn't want her to have to worry about getting lonely in the afterlife."

That, I think, is incredibly sweet.

"Of course," he adds, "your aunt hating being alone also means that we're going to have to speed this little shindig up. Because if I'm not home before she rises, there'll be hell to pay."

Now that sounds more like the Aunt Alfresca I know.

I look at my mother's tombstone, the dates on it. She was so young when she died. I've already lived far longer than she ever got the chance to.

The grass over her is extremely tidy and there's even a little vase attached to the left of the tombstone with a single rose in it that's starting to wilt.

"They take good care of the dead in this place," I observe.

"They do OK," Big John says. Then, as difficult as it is for him to do so, he bends over to pluck at a stray weed that's growing at the base of the granite. "But I do better. I've got to remember to bring a new flower next time I come. That one's starting to look like shit."

"You come here a lot?"

"Once, twice a week." He shrugs. "Who else is going to take care of her if I don't? You know, some days, I can barely remember my life with her, it's been so long, but being here always makes me feel peaceful, helps me think—and believe me, I need all the help I can get. I get all my best thinking done here. I like to talk to her when I have something I need to figure out. She wasn't always the best listener when she was alive. But now? She's great at it."

"Wait a second. You come here every week? How did I not know this?"

He shrugs again. "Well, it's not exactly the kind of thing you advertise. 'Hey, poker buddies, for the last thirty-four years I've been consulting a dead woman for help with my problems. OK, who's in? And can I get another beer here?' Nah, better to keep it to myself."

"Does Aunt Alfresca know?"

"Christ, no, and don't you tell her. I don't think she'd be jealous, much, it's more that she hates graveyards. You know your aunt is terrified of death?"

I shake my head. Another thing I didn't have a clue about.

"Why do you think she always gave you a hard time growing up about your mother dying?"

"I don't know. Because she blamed me?"

"No. Because she blamed the universe. She couldn't understand how someone she loved could just come to the end suddenly like that, with no real reason. It scared her so much, still does, but she couldn't let that show, so instead she just turned it into anger."

I let that digest and we just stand there in silence for a time, staring at the stone and the two markers: the one who has gone and the two yet to come.

"The thing is," Big John says, launching into my…*issue* without preamble, "you have to figure out how to fight with each other. Specifically, you need to figure out what kind of fighter Helen is so you know what you're up against. Like, is she a stewer or a screamer?"

"Um, Dad, what are you talking about?"

"What I just said!" His voice booms across the empty graveyard, signifying his aggravation. "Is your wife a stewer or a screamer? Because which she is will determine the best way for you to respond."

I still have no clue as to what he's talking about, but I also don't feel like hearing his voice boom like that again, so I try to work this out on my own. Unfortunately, I do that out loud.

"So, let me see if I have this straight. A screamer is one who screams. So a stewer would be…one who stews?"

"Yes. Christ, what have I been saying here? Do I need to spell everything out for you?"

For a guy who says he finds the graveyard peaceful, he sure gets irritated easy here.

"A stewer," he says, still irritated, "one who stews. Stew, stew, stew, stew, stew. Like on the old *Carol Burnett Show*. Harvey Korman would be playing her husband, asking her what's wrong, and Carol would clench her jaw, smile tightly and say, one eye twitching, 'Nothing. *Nothing.*' There's your classic example of one who stews."

OK, I think I'm getting this now. TV anecdotes can be so useful in explaining real life to a person.

"Now, your mother," he goes on a little more calmly, fondly even, "*that* woman was a screamer."

Wait a second. "What? That can't be true. You and Aunt Alfresca are always going on about what a saint my mother was."

"Oh, a saint, sure, but a screamer too. When your mother got going, people could hear her all the way over in the next block. A screamer can be tough." He reflects. "The thing about screamers is, you get caught up with the screaming with them, and that's when you have to be doubly careful, which is tough to do when you're both screaming. The thing you *don't* want to do is say every cleverly nasty thing that comes into your head. Just because you can think it, it doesn't mean you should ever say it. That way lies madness...and divorce. One time, we were arguing real fierce and a line came into my head that was so excellent, I started smiling. Your mother asked me what was so funny, but I couldn't tell her, so she got mad about that too. But that was OK. At least I had the satisfaction of thinking 'When you're mad, you walk like a duck' *without* hurting her feelings."

Huh.

"So," I say, "I guess if my mother was a screamer, Aunt Alfresca must be an even bigger screamer, right?"

"Oh, no. You're aunt is a classic stewer."

"You gotta be kidding me. Aunt Alfresca screams, like, all the time."

"That." He waves off my objection. "That's just her speaking voice. But when she's mad? That woman has stewing down to an art. Never met a more frustrating woman in my life."

"Oh, yeah? What does she do?"

"Changes the station from whatever I'm watching, for one thing."

I vaguely remember him saying something like this at one of our poker games but I guess at the time, I didn't believe it. "Like with no warning?"

"Exactly. One minute I'm watching the Knicks pre-season and then—*click*—there's some basketball player in the European league and his wife trying to find a house for a year in Spain on HGTV. Sure, both shows have basketball players involved, but it's hardly the same thing."

I think about it. "That'd piss me off."

"I know, right?"

I think about correcting him but it occurs to me that with the exceptions of Sam not saying it and Helen not knowing we're not saying it, I have no clue what anyone's saying anymore.

"But don't worry." He nudges my elbow with his. "I know how to get even."

"Oh?"

"Yeah. Whenever she does finally decide to start talking to me about what's on her mind?" Dramatic pause. "I *whistle.*"

"When she's trying to talk to you, you *whistle*? You mean like—" I try to demonstrate but my lips are so cold, I can hardly muster a decent tweet.

"Yeah," he says, "only much better than that. Pisses her right off."

"I gotta say, that'd piss me off too. If it's all the same with you, I don't think I'll try that on Helen."

"To each his own." He shrugs. "So tell me, which one is Helen, a stewer or a screamer?"

I think about how she was screaming at me last night but how she kept everything in for months before that.

"Both," I finally say. "I think we both might be both."

"Oh, Christ, I don't know how to help you with that."

"You mean I'm screwed?"

"No. It's just that, we can gather all the advice out there, but then it's up to each of us to figure out how to make a marriage work."

"Ah."

"We better get going. If I'm not there when your aunt gets up, she'll be mad and I can't have that."

"Knicks's are playing this afternoon?"

"You got it."

"If it's OK, even though it's Sunday, I don't think I'll be coming by later."

"That's fine. You need some time alone with your wife. Besides, I got to see you now. I hope I helped, at least a little."

"You always do, even when you don't really. I love you, Dad."

"And that's why I'll always be the luckiest man alive. Let's hit it."

We turn away from the grave but then Big John stops. "I almost forgot," he says, going back.

I watch as he takes something small and red and crinkly-looking from his pocket, puts it on top of the gravestone, touches his fingers to his lips and then presses his fingers to the granite.

"What was that?" I ask when he rejoins me.

"In addition to keeping things tidy and the vase filled," he informs me, "I always like to bring your mother a little something when there's a holiday."

"What holiday?"

"Don't you know? Halloween's right around the corner. So I brought her a fun-sized $100,000 Bar. They were her favorite." His smile is wistful. "She used to love those things. She used to say, 'Can you imagine if this really *was* a hundred thousand dollars?'"

"You were a good husband," I say. "You *are* a good husband."

"Yeah, well." Now he's embarrassed.

A few minutes later, when we're back in the car, rubbing our hands together waiting for the heat to kick in, he has once last piece of advice. "Oh, and don't forget to pick up flowers on the way home."

"Flowers? Why flowers?"

"Because women love that shit."

Great. Where am I going to get flowers? It's not like there'll be any florists open at six-thirty on a Sunday morning. And I can't just steal flowers from somebody's lawn—that would hardly be in the spirit of the thing. Besides which, it's nearly the end of October and we had that big storm last week, so the pickings from other people's lawns would be slim.

And then it hits me. There is one place, open 24/7 as they say, that should have flowers.

Super Stop & Shop this early on a Sunday morning is a shockingly empty place. Who knew? Usually, I come after work or in the middle of a weekend afternoon, when the place is jamming, the lines long. But now? There're just workers stocking the produce section and the aisles, a handful of stray shoppers scattered about. Maybe I should get the week's shopping done? I could zoom through this place in record time, not even having to wait to check out.

But no, I realize, of course I can't do that. What was I thinking? If I show up at home with bags of groceries, it'll just look like I went shopping for my own convenience, the bouquet of flowers coming across as some kind of afterthought—hardly the impression I want to project. So, despite the tempting allure of a restocking the larder at home, I make my way to the in-store florist, pick out an impressively lovely display, if I do say so myself—there are so many different colors in this bouquet, what woman wouldn't be impressed?—and head toward the first available checker, which is, like, every checker.

I must be really punchy from lack of sleep because I actually stand there for a moment debating—do I go to the 12-items-and-under checker or one of the regular ones—when I hear a voice call: "Mr. Smith? Mr. Smith, is that you?"

Turning, I see my half-pint little friend standing there, Willow.

"Willow! What are you doing here?"

"Walk with me, Mr. Smith?"

Walk with me? What little kid talks like that?

I'm about to explain to her that I don't really have time to walk and talk right now, but then I see the look on her face. Willow looks, no other word for it, woebegone. What could make this staunch little kid look like that?

"Yeah, sure," I say. "I could spare a few minutes. Where do you want to walk?"

She sweeps her hand out, gesturing toward the whole of Super Stop & Shop. This should be some walk, I think as we set off.

"So, you never answered my question," I say as we proceed down the coffee and cereal aisle. "What are you doing here?"

"Why else would anyone be here? I'm shopping."

"Yeah, but where's your mom?"

She gestures vaguely as we turn a corner, start up another aisle. "She's around here…somewhere."

"Isn't it a little early for grocery shopping?"

"You're here," she says pointedly.

"But you don't even live in Danbury."

Now we're passing the spaghetti sauce. Man, there sure are a lot of different brands of spaghetti sauce.

"My mom lost her job, so we've been staying with relatives."

"Oh, geez, Willow, I'm sorry to hear that. Is there anything I can do?"

"Not unless you're hiring. Does your painting company need a systems analyst?"

Embarrassed, I give a rueful shake of my head.

"That's what I figured," she says. "Anyway, my mom keeps getting up earlier and earlier. Today she decided to do the grocery shopping for the house before everyone else was up and she woke me to come with her. She gets manic like this sometimes."

We're in the pet supplies section. I'm tempted to get Fluffy a new toy—he would love that plush mouse with the bell in it—or maybe a rubber bone for Bowser, but then I remember that coming home with something in addition to the flowers will dilute the floral effect.

"But that's just an exaggeration, right?" I say. "I mean, your mom isn't like, I don't know, manic-depressive, is she?"

"Actually, she is, and it's mildly distressing." Willow heaves a heavy sigh. "OK, it's really distressing."

I don't know what to say. This poor kid.

"Is there anything I can do?" I offer again.

"You could just keep walking with me for a bit," she says hopefully.

"You got it."

So that's what we do.

We keep walking up and down aisles, not even talking anymore, but it's an OK silence, the silence of friends.

"My favorite aisle," Willow says with a sigh that's happy this time.

283

We're standing in the middle of the seasonal aisle, the one that changes depending on what holiday is at hand. All the bags of candy that surround us and the small display of costumes reminds me that Halloween is right around the corner.

"I still haven't decided what I want to be this year," she says, eyeing the costumes.

"Do any in particular look good to you?"

"Mm…I can't really decide. The fairy costume *is* tempting. But maybe I'm ready to be a vampire?"

"I don't know," I say. "I'm not sure it's such a good idea to rush these things. Maybe you should try one on?" I shift the flowers from my right hand to my left before reaching for a hanging costume.

"Hey," Willow says, "you're buying flowers."

If she's only noticing this huge bouquet for the first time now, what's going on with her mom must really be distressing. Well, who can blame her?

"Is it Mrs. Smith's birthday?" she asks.

I shake my head.

"Your anniversary?"

Another shake.

"Oh no." She looks disappointed now, so disappointed. "You had a fight, didn't you?"

Before my head can respond, Willow continues.

"Well, I suppose that was to be expected. I mean, who didn't see *that* coming? Still—"

I cut her off. "I suppose you're going to tell me I need to learn to fight right too?" I feel bad about cutting her off, but at this point, if I hear that advice one more time…

"Of course I wasn't going to say that." Willow looks offended. "Why would I say such a thing? No, what *I* was going to say is that I'm a little shocked that in such a situation, you would resort to such a clichéd thing as buying flowers."

Stung, I gaze down at my bouquet. "What's wrong with flowers?"

"Nothing, in and of itself. But everyone does that." Once again, Willow looks disappointed, only this time it's at the clichéd atrocity that is apparently me. "What you need is something *in addition to*."

Something in addition to—what's she talking about? What else could I get at Super Stop & Shop, the cat toy and the rubber bone? But those were for the pets.

As if reading my thoughts, Willow shakes her head in disgust. You need something that will show Mrs. Smith how you really feel." Dramatic pause. "You need to make...*a grand gesture*."

*A grand...*

I'm thinking the words she's spoken, in my head, over and over again. And as I'm thinking, I'm looking all around me, when suddenly, over her shoulder I catch sight of something and in that moment, I am forced to admit how perfectly Aristotelian life can be, because what I see, the solution to my problems, is both surprising and inevitable.

"Willow," I say, grabbing a hanger and something off the shelf above to go with it, "you're a genius!"

"Not really, Mr. Smith." She gives a rueful smile. "I only measure 139 on the Stanford Binet, but I'm working hard to make up for that missing point."

"Well, you're close enough for me." I slap the thing I took from the shelf on my head. "How do I look?"

She tilts her head to one side. "I think," she says, "you are perfectly achieving the effect you want to achieve."

"Excellent!" I look at my watch. I can't believe how late it is. I mean, it's still early, but yeah. "I hate to say it, but I really gotta go, Willow. Are you going to be OK here?"

"Of course. My mom's probably in the produce section even as we speak."

Not wanting to take a chance, though—what if her mother deserted her here?—I insist we make our way to that section of the store just to make certain.

Sure enough, when we poke our heads around the corner, Willow's mom is there, fingering some fruit.

"See? I told you," Willow says. "In an uncertain world, my mother finds fresh produce *very* reassuring."

"Well, thanks for everything," I say, indicating the things

I'm holding that are *not* flowers, but *in addition to*.

"Anytime." She pauses. "Hey, if I give you my number, could you maybe call me later and, you know, give me a report on how it goes?"

"Sure thing, kid." I hand her my phone, watch as she turns it on and programs her number in, which gives me an idea. "Hey, why don't you put my number in your phone too?" I suggest. "You know, just to have in case of…whatever." I don't want to say in case her mother gets more manic or more depressive but it's in the air.

"Thanks, Mr. Smith." She looks relieved as she follows my suggestion. Then she looks up at me, head on an angle. "It helps to have friends, doesn't it?"

Finally back in the car, I put on the things I've bought.

Great, I've got my flowers, my grand gesture, my plan.

But what if it's not enough?

# Be a Clown

If these were normal circumstances, I might register the importance of the vehicle parked at the curb in front of my house. The fact that I've been up for twenty-four hours straight, however, coupled with my determination to see Helen, means that as I approach the door wearing my grand gesture and bearing my bouquet of flowers, the black-and-white car means nothing to me.

But it sure registers, it sure means something when a uniformed police officer comes to the door.

Holy everything that is holy, did something happen to Helen?

I don't even get a chance to ask, though, because there's Helen, coming up behind the police officer and pushing him out of the way. She's wearing the same clothes she had on Saturday night and tear tracks stain her face.

"I don't know what you're trying to sell," she says angrily, "you crazy...*clown*, but whatever it is, we're a little bit busy here right now."

I can't believe she doesn't recognize me. Maybe the red wig, which has come loose and is dipping down over my eyes, is a bit much in conjunction with my clown costume?

Helen moves to close the door in my face, but I stop it with my bouquet hand.

"Helen!" I say. "It's me!"

She squints at me. Then: "*Johnny?*"

"Of course," I say. I wave the flowers, my piece offering. "Who else would bring you these?"

Helen gestures at me, a flat palm outstretched as she turns to the cop. "And *this* is the missing person I was telling you about. Meet my husband, the clown."

Well, when she puts it like that…

"Wait," I say. "You reported me *missing*?"

"What else did you think I was going to do? I came back an hour after I left—"

She's been here all that time?

"—but you weren't here, so I waited and waited, and kept trying your cell—"

Huh. I must've had it turned off, which obviously I did, since Willow had to turn it on to program her number.

"—and when you never answered, I got worried, so I called the cops."

She was worried about me? But: "I always thought they wouldn't come out for a missing person until twenty-four hours or something."

"Your wife's an important person," the police officer interjects to inform me.

Like I don't know that.

"She's a D.A.," he expands.

"But not in this town," I say.

"Still, you never know when she might come in handy." He turns to Helen. "Everything OK now, Ms. Troy?"

"As well as can be expected. You can leave me here with"— another open-hand gesture—"my clown."

The officer tips his hat to her and he's gone, leaving the door open behind him and us standing in the doorway.

"What is the *matter* with you?" She hits me, but not too hard at least, in the shoulder.

"What?" I mean, obviously, there's a lot the matter with me. I'm just curious which particular aspect she's focusing on right now.

"How could you leave here like that?"

"You left first!" Well, she did.

"But you left second! And then, you stayed out all night."

"I figured you were out all night too, you were so mad when you left. I don't know. I never expected you to come right back in an hour."

She ignores that.

"And then," she says, "when you finally do come back, you're dressed like *that*? What did you do while you were gone? Did you join the circus?"

"No," I say, and in that instant it hits me, how ridiculous what I've attempted is. "I was trying to make a grand gesture."

And something about me saying that—or maybe it's the sad way I say it?—causes realization to dawn in her eyes and her hand goes to her mouth.

"You're dressed as a clown," she says, stunned.

I thought we'd already established this fact but apparently I need to say the word out loud: "Yes."

"But you *hate* clowns." Now all the anger is finally out of her voice and what remains is just fear and confusion. "You're scared of them. Everyone knows that about you. One of our first dates, when you took me to that crazy carnival/circus, when a clown passed by unexpectedly, you shrieked, 'Eek! A clown!'"

Not my bravest moment, I'll grant you.

"I know," I concede the point.

"So why would you…" And again with the hand gesture.

"Because I wanted to do something big, something that scares me, to prove how much you mean to me."

Her hand goes to her chest and her eyes are shiny as she says, a tiny break in her voice, "I still…mean a lot to you?"

I nod. How can she doubt this?

"Some guys," she says, "if they wanted to do something big, might just settle for the flowers. Or, if they wanted to go really big, I don't know, might jump out of a plane."

"Yeah, well…" I scuff my oversized shoes.

"I thought we were over," she says.

"How could you…?" But then I realize that I thought that too, and I reassure her, "Of *course* we're not over. Because of one fight? We could never be over. We just need to learn to, I don't know, fight better or something."

"I don't know, Johnny." Now she looks more than just a little fearful. She looks frightened. "When you find out what I've done, you may not feel so sure about our future anymore."

Wait. What? She said she was only gone for an hour last night. Did she manage to find someone to cheat on me with in just one hour? Oh no. Maybe she hooked up with Daniel—much better a total stranger than *Daniel*; I'm not sure I could take that. But even if that's the case, wouldn't I forgive her? Wouldn't I somehow find a way to forgive her, because aren't we in this thing together til death us do part? Still, I have to know and she's just standing there, waiting for my response.

"What did you do?" I ask hesitantly, not sure I really want to know.

"I guess I put that wrong." She twists her fingers. I've never seen her this nervous. She can't do that thing with her hands in front of a jury, can she? "I shouldn't have said 'what I've done.' I should have said 'what I've *been* doing.'"

But wait. That grammar usage—"*been* doing"—indicates an ongoing thing, not an isolated event. So she's been…cheating on me for a while now?

I can't take this not knowing anymore. The suspense is killing me.

"Just tell me, Helen," I say, trying to keep my voice reasonable and not sounding at all how scarily desperate I feel, like our whole future depends on whatever this thing is. "Whatever it is, we'll work it out."

"I've been…I've been…"

Oh, the temptation to just say, "Please, just spit it out!" But instead, I reach out with my bouquet-free hand and grab onto her twisting fingers, stilling them. "Really, I tell her. It's OK."

"OK," she says. Deep breath. "I've been…testing you."

Wait. *What?* That's not what my brain was expecting, not even remotely.

"You were *testing* me? What are you talking about?"

"The dog, the off-centered clock in the bathroom, having Daniel over, the yellow kitchen, the pink and black bedroom—it was all a test."

I just stare at her.

"I couldn't stand that bedroom after I painted it," she says. "I mean, who would like it? OK, so maybe Stavros does.

But pink and black? They're fine separately. But together? In a bedroom?" She shudders.

I'm speechless. OK, maybe not. "Why would you do that?" I say. "Why would you feel the need to...*test* me like that?"

"I don't know!"

But she must know, so I wait for it to come, as patiently as I can.

"It took me a long time to realize that I was even doing it," she finally says. "It wasn't like I planned to do it. There was no *intent*. I just...I think a part of me still couldn't believe it, still couldn't believe *you*, still couldn't believe *us*. All my life, I wanted love but never had it, not really. I think I just finally gave up. Then you came along and even after we got married, I think I still didn't believe in it. I'd think, 'How can anyone possibly love me like this? How can *he* love me?' So I guess I started testing you, maybe even trying to push you away in a sense, because I couldn't trust that it was all real."

"You *have* to trust that it's real, Helen. How can this ever work if you don't trust in it?"

"I know, Johnny, I know." She wipes at her face with the back of her hand before returning that hand to my grasp. "Are you mad at me? Because of the testing?"

"Well, I have to admit, it's not great."

Still, I suppose it's a lot better than if she'd cheated on me with Daniel *Rath*bone.

"I thought being married was going to be easy," I confess, "but it's not. It's hard."

"Too hard?" she asks, and I can see from the jut of her chin that her defenses are up now. She's preparing for the worst.

"No," I say softly but with determination, "it's never going to be too hard."

And suddenly I'm thinking of Leo and The Little Lady, and I'm seeing for the first time what their life together was like, all seventy-plus years of it.

"It's not going to be perfect," I say. "There will be fights. There will be conflict. But if we just show up every day, and I mean *really* show up, if we keep choosing one another not just once but over and over again, if we fall in love with each other again repeatedly, like I'm falling in love with you again *right now*, I think we're going to be OK. You have to trust that."

"I do," she says. "I trust *you*."

And then she's kissing me and we've both got morning breath—do we have morning breath!—but who cares about that right now? Because Helen, *my wife Helen*, is kissing me.

When at last we separate, she looks at me, her smile mischievous.

"You said it won't be perfect, right?" she says.

I nod.

"I'll be a bitch sometimes!" she declares.

"Yeah, I got that," I agree with a rueful grin. "And occasionally, I'll be an idiot!"

We declare more things to each other in shouting voices, all the things we foresee ourselves as doing wrong and it's like we're pledging our vows all over again, only this time, we're getting it right.

We are flawed human beings, and we will spend the rest of our lives being flawed together.

From the doorway behind us, we hear voices—"Hello! Hello!"—and we turn to see a couple standing there, about our age, the wife part of the couple bearing a covered dish in her hands.

"Hey, neighbors," the man says.

"We just wanted to welcome you to the neighborhood," the wife says.

"We've been here four months," I say, laughing. I don't say "What took you so long?" but I'm thinking it's implied.

"Sometimes," Helen says, laughing too, "things just take a little time."

And then Fluffy's there, no doubt looking for a top-up on his kibble bowl; Bowser's there, no doubt hoping for a walk; and Stavros is there in his jammies, scratching his belly.

"Who are these people?" He looks at the neighbors, then shrugs. "Anyone feel like breakfast?"

"It's going to be a crazy life together, isn't it?" Helen says.

"It is," I agree.

I'm not daunted at all by that prospect and from the look on her face, neither is she.

"Now take that wig off, please, so I can kiss you again," she says. "You look ridiculous."

I smile and do as she asks, lowering my lips to meet her waiting ones, but before our lips touch, I have one last thing to say:

"I know, right?"

MORE FROM LAUREN BARATZ-LOGSTED

LAUREN BARATZ-LOGSTED is the author of over 25 books for adults, teens and children, which have been published in 15 countries. She lives in Danbury, CT, with her husband, daughter and cat. You can read more about her life and work at **www.laurenbaratzlogsted.com** or follow her on Twitter **@LaurenBaratzL**.

## THE BRO-MAGNET:
## A JOHNNY SMITH NOVEL

Poor Johnny Smith.

At age 33, the house painter has been a best man a whopping eight times, when all he's ever really wanted is to be a groom. But despite being everyone's favorite dude, Johnny has yet to find The One. Or even anyone. So when he meets high-powered District Attorney Helen Troy, and falls for her hard, he follows the advice of family and friends. Since Helen seems to hate sports, Johnny pretends he does too. No more Jets. No more Mets. At least not in public. He redecorates his condo. He gets a cat. He takes up watching soap operas. Anything he thinks will earn him Helen, Johnny is willing to do. There's just one hitch: If he does finally win her heart, who will he be?

## THE THIN PINK LINE:
## A JANE TAYLOR NOVEL

Jane Taylor is a slightly sociopathic Londoner who wants marriage and a baby in the worst way, and she's willing to go to over-the-top lengths to achieve her dream. When Jane thinks she's pregnant she tells everyone. When it turns out to be a false alarm, she assumes she'll just get pregnant, no one the wiser. But when that doesn't happen, well, of course she does what no one in her right mind would do: Jane decides to fake an entire pregnancy!

## CROSSING THE LINE:
## A JANE TAYLOR NOVEL

In the madcap sequel to the international hit comedy *The Thin Pink Line*, London editor Jane Taylor is at it again, only this time, there's a baby involved. Having—SPOILER ALERT!—found a baby on a church doorstep at the end of the previous book, Jane is forced to come clean with all the people in her world when it turns out that the baby is a different skin color than everyone had expected Jane's baby to be. As Jane fights to keep the baby, battling Social Services and taking on anyone who seeks to get in her path, what kind of mother will Jane prove to be?

Only one thing's for certain: no matter how much kinder and gentler she is now, she is still and will always be crazy Jane.

9 781626 817616